The Letter of Marque

'Badly described, the books sound very little different from standard adventure yarns. They do work very well indeed on that level – each has its share of high courage and desperate situations – but there is far more to them. Filled with poetry, humour, rue and human folly, they provide a complex and beautifully detailed portrait of an era. The chief characters perfectly encapsulate the burgeoning nineteenth century: Maturin its mind, Aubrey its muscle. And O'Brian has so thoroughly steeped himself in every aspect of the age, and writes with such wit, deftness and authority, that his books might well have been the product of one of Jane Austen's sea-going brothers, had they, as well as she, been writers.' Richard Snow, *American Heritage*

'Even the addict of historical fiction must admit that, depending on whether the emphasis is on the history or the fiction, the usual options are waxworks or the antics of a pantomime horse. Patrick O'Brian's Jack Aubrey novels are proof that a living fusion between the two elements is not impossible. Thoroughly steeped in the Nelsonian period, they were originally hailed as Hornblower's natural successor and in certain important respects – humour, characterisation – have succeeded in stealing the wind from that paragon's sails.' Stephen Vaughan, *Observer*

PATRICK O'BRIAN

The Letter of Marque

Fontana

An Imprint of HarperCollins*Publishers*

Fontana
An Imprint of HarperCollins*Publishers*
77–85 Fulham Palace Road,
Hammersmith, London W6 8JB

Published by Fontana 1989
3 5 7 9 8 6 4

First published in Great Britain by
Collins 1988

ISBN 0 00 617704 2

Set in Imprint

Printed in Great Britain by
HarperCollinsManufacturing Glasgow

MARIAE DUODECIES SACRUM

CHAPTER ONE

Ever since Jack Aubrey had been dismissed from the service, ever since his name, with its now meaningless seniority, had been struck off the list of post-captains, it had seemed to him that he was living in a radically different world; everything was perfectly familiar, from the smell of seawater and tarred rigging to the gentle heave of the deck under his feet, but the essence was gone and he was a stranger.

Other broken sea-officers, condemned by court-martial, might be worse off: indeed, two had come aboard without so much as a sea-chest between them, and compared with them he was uncommonly fortunate, which should perhaps have been a comfort to his mind – it was none to his heart. Nor was the fact that he was innocent of the crime for which he had been sentenced.

Yet there was no denying that materially he was well off. His old but beautiful frigate the *Surprise* had been sold out of the service, and Stephen Maturin had bought her as a private ship of war, a letter of marque, to cruise upon the enemy; and Jack Aubrey was in command.

She was now lying at single anchor in Shelmerston, an out-of-the-way port with an awkward bar and a dangerous tide-race, avoided by the Navy and by merchantmen but much frequented by smugglers and privateers, many of whose fast, rakish, predatory vessels could be seen along the quay. Turning in his mechanical walk on the starboard side of the quarterdeck, Jack glanced at the village and once again he tried to make out what it was that made Shelmerston so like the remaining pirate and buccaneer settlements he had seen long ago in the remoter West Indies and Madagascar when he was a youngster in this same *Surprise*. Shelmerston had no waving coconut-palms, no brilliant coral strand; and yet there was this likeness; perhaps it lay in the large and flashy public houses, the general air of slovenliness and easy money, the large number of whores, and the feeling that only a singularly determined and well-armed press-gang would ever make an attempt upon it. He also noticed that two boats had put off for the *Surprise* and that each was stretching out to reach her first: neither however contained Dr Maturin, the ship's surgeon (few people knew that he was also her owner), who was to come aboard today. One of these boats was coxed by an extraordinarily pretty girl with dark red hair, newly come upon the town and enjoying every minute of it; she was a great favourite with the privateers-men and they responded to her shrill cries so heroically that one broke his oar. Although Jack Aubrey could never fairly have been described as much of a whoremonger, he was no celibate and from his earliest youth until the present he had taken the liveliest pleasure in beauty, and this spiri-ted girl, half standing and all alive with excitement, was absurdly beautiful; but now he only observed the fact, and in a genuinely indifferent tone he said to Tom Pullings, 'Do not let that woman come aboard: take only three of the very best.'

He resumed his pensive walk while Pullings, the bosun, the gunner and Bonden, his own coxswain, put the men through their paces. They had to lay aloft, timed by a log-glass, loose and furl a topgallant sail, then traverse and point a great gun, fire a musket at a bottle hanging from the foreyardarm, and tie a crowned double wall-knot before the eyes of a crowd of thorough-going seamen. Ordinarily, manning a ship, a King's ship, was an anxious business, with the impress-service doing what it could, with humble prayers for a draft of sometimes criminal nondescripts from the receiving-ship, and with the boats cruising in the Channel to take hands out of homeward-bound merchantmen or to raid towns along the coast, often with so little success that one had to put to sea a hundred short of complement. Here in Shelmerston on the other hand the

Surprise might have been fitting out in Paradise. Not only were all marine stores delivered the same tide by the willing and competitive chandlers whose well-furnished warehouses lined the quay, but the hands needed no pressing at all, no solicitation at the rendezvous, no beating of the drum. Jack Aubrey had long been known among seamen as a successful frigate-captain, a fighting captain who had been exceptionally fortunate in the article of prize-money, so fortunate that his nickname was Lucky Jack Aubrey; and the news that his own frigate, a remarkable sailer when skilfully handled, was to be converted into a letter of marque with himself in command brought privateersmen flocking to offer their services. He could pick and choose, which never happened aboard King's ships in wartime; and now he lacked only three of the number he had set as the proper complement. Many of the foremast jacks and petty officers were old Surprises who had been set free when the frigate was paid off and who had presumably avoided the press since then, though he had a strong suspicion that several had deserted from other King's ships, in some cases with the connivance of particular friends of his – Heneage Dundas, for example – who commanded them: and there were of course the personal followers such as his steward and coxswain and a few others who had never left him. Some of the men he did not know were from merchant ships, but most were smugglers and privateersmen, prime seamen, tough, independent, not much accustomed to discipline, still less to its outward, more ceremonial forms (though nearly all had been pressed at one time or another), yet eager and willing to serve under a captain they respected. And at this point Jack Aubrey was, in a privateersman's eye, an even more respectable commander than he himself might have supposed: he was leaner than he had been but he was still uncommonly tall and broadshouldered; his open, florid, cheerful face had grown older, less full; it was now lined and habitually sombre, with a touch of latent wickedness, and anyone used to the abrupt ways of the sea could instantly tell that this was not a face to be trifled with: if such a man were put out the blow would come without a moment's warning and be damned to the consequences – dangerous because past caring.

The *Surprise* now probably had a more efficient, more professional ship's company than any vessel of her size afloat, which might well have filled her captain's heart with joy: and indeed when he reflected upon the fact it did bring a certain amount of conscientious pleasure and what joy the heart could hold; this was not very much. It might have been said that Jack Aubrey's heart had been sealed off, so that he could accept his misfortune without its breaking; and that the sealing-off had turned him into a eunuch as far as emotion was concerned. The explanation would have been on the simple side, yet whereas in former times Captain Aubrey, like his hero Nelson and so many of his contemporaries, had been somewhat given to tears – he had wept with joy at the masthead of his first command; tears had sometimes wetted the lower part of his fiddle when he played particularly moving passages; and cruel sobs had racked him at many a shipmate's funeral by land or sea – he was now as hard and dry-eyed as a man could well be. He had parted from Sophie and the children at Ashgrove Cottage with no more than a constriction in his throat which made his farewells sound painfully harsh and unfeeling. And for that matter his fiddle lay there still in its wax-clothed case, untouched since he came aboard.

'These are the three best hands, sir, if you please,' said Mr Pullings, taking off his hat. 'Harvey, Fisher and Whitaker.'

They touched their foreheads, three cousins with much the same long-nosed, weather-beaten, knowing faces, all smugglers and excellent seamen – none others could have passed the short but exceedingly severe examination – and looking at them with a certain mitigated satisfaction Aubrey said 'Harvey, Fisher and Whitaker, I am glad to see you aboard. But you understand it is only on liking and on passing the surgeon?' He glanced again at the shore, but no surgeon's boat did he see. 'And you understand the terms of pay, shares, discipline and punishment?'

'We do indeed, sir. Which the coxswain read them out to us.'

'Very well. You may bring your chests aboard.' He resumed

his steady to and fro, repeating Harvey, Fisher, Whitaker: it was a captain's duty to know his men's names and something of their circumstances and hitherto he had found little difficulty even in a ship of the line with six or seven hundred aboard. He still knew every one of his Surprises of course, shipmates not only in the last far Pacific voyage but sometimes for many years before; but the new men escaped his memory most shamefully and even his officers called for an effort. Not Tom Pullings, naturally, once one of Aubrey's midshipmen and now a half-pay commander in the Royal Navy, perfectly unblemished but with no hope of a ship, who, on indeterminate leave from the service, was acting as his first mate; nor the second and third mates, both of them former King's officers with whom he had been more or less acquainted and whose courts-martial were clear in his mind – West for duelling and Davidge for an unhappy complex affair in which he had signed a dishonest purser's books without looking at them – but he could remember his bosun only by the association of his massive body with his name, Bulkeley; fortunately no carpenter ever objected to being called Chips nor any gunner Master Gunner; and no doubt the unfamiliar petty officers would come in time.

To and fro, to and fro, looking towards the shore at each turn, until at last the seaweed high on his cable and the run of the water told him that if he did not get under way precious soon he would miss his tide. 'Mr Pullings,' he said, 'let us move outside the bar.'

'Aye aye, sir,' said Pullings, and he cried 'Mr Bulkeley, all hands to weigh anchor.'

The quick cutting notes of the bosun's call and the rush of feet followed instantly, a fair proof that the Shelmerston men were well acquainted both with the frigate's draught and their own uneasy bar. The messenger was brought to, the capstan-bars were shipped, pinned and swifted as briskly as though regular Surprises alone were at it; but as the capstan began to turn and the ship to glide across the harbour towards her anchor, some of the hands struck up the shanty

Walk her round and round she goes
Way oh, way oh

which had never happened in her life as a King's ship, working songs not being countenanced in the Royal Navy. Pullings looked sharply at Jack, who shook his head and murmured 'Let them sing.'

So far there had been no bad blood between the old Surprises and the new hands and he would give almost anything to prevent it arising. He and Pullings had already done their best by mixing the gun-crews and the watches, but he had no doubt that by far the most important factor in this strangely peaceful relation between two dissimilar groups was the unparalleled situation: all those concerned, particularly the Surprises, seemed amazed by it, uncertain what to say or what to think, there being no formula to hand; and if only this could last until some three- or four-day blow in the chops of the Channel or better still until a successful action began to weld them into a single body, there were fair prospects of a happy ship.

'Up and down, sir,' called West from the forecastle.

'Foretopmen,' said Jack, raising his voice. 'D'ye hear me, there?' They would have been mere blocks if they had not, for the 'there' came back loud and clear from the housefronts at the bottom of the bay. 'Away aloft.' The foreshrouds were dark with racing men. 'Let fall: let fall.'

The topsail flashed out; the larboard watch sheeted it home and without a word they ran to the halliards. The yard rose smoothly; the foretopsail filled; the *Surprise* had just enough way on her to trip her anchor, and in a pure, leisurely curve she stood for the bar, already a nasty colour in the green-grey sea, with white about its edges.

'The very middle of the channel, Gillow,' said Jack to the man at the wheel.

'The very middle it is, sir,' said Gillow, a Shelmerstonian, glancing left and right and easing her a spoke or so.

In the open sea the *Surprise* folded her wings again, dropped the anchor from her cathead, veered away a reasonable scope and rode easy. It had been a simple operation, one that Jack had seen many thousand times, but it had run perfectly smoothly, without the slightest fuss or fault, and it pleased him. This was just as well, since for some considerable time a feeling of indignation at Maturin's lateness had been growing in him: his huge misfortune he could, if not accept, then at least endure without railing or complaint, but small things were capable of irritating him as much as ever they did – indeed a great deal more – and he had prepared a curt note for Stephen, to be left on shore, appointing another rendezvous in a fortnight's time.

'Mr Davidge,' he said, 'I am going below. If the Admiral should come round the headland, pray let me know directly.' Admiral Russell, who lived at Allacombe, the next cove south but one, had sent word to say that wind and weather permitting he would give himself the pleasure of waiting on Mr Aubrey in the course of the afternoon and that he hoped Mr Aubrey would spend the evening at Allacombe with him: he sent his compliments to Dr Maturin, and if he was aboard, would be delighted to see him too.

'Directly, sir,' said Davidge, and then more hesitantly, 'Just how should we receive him, sir?'

'Like any other private ship,' said Jack. 'Man-ropes, of course, but nothing more.' He had a horror of 'coming it the Royal Navy'; he had always disliked the close imitation of naval ways by the East India Company and some other large concerns and by the bigger, more ambitious privateers; and at present he was dressed in a frieze pilot-jacket and tweed pantaloons. On the other hand he was perfectly determined that the *Surprise*, though shorn of pennant, gold lace, Royal Marines and many other things should still be run man-of-war fashion in all essentials and he was fairly confident that the two were not irreconcilable.

He would have given an eye-tooth to avoid this meeting with Russell. But he had served under the Admiral as a midshipman; he had a great respect for him and a lively sense of gratitude, since it was to Russell's influence that he owed his lieutenant's commission. The unfortunate invitation had been as kindly phrased and as kindly meant as possible; it could not in decency be refused; but Jack most heartily wished that Stephen had been there to help him through the evening. At present he had no small social gaiety to draw upon and he dreaded the presence of other guests, particularly naval guests – the sympathy of any but his most intimate friends, the supercilious, distant civility of those who did not like him.

In the great cabin he called 'Killick. Killick, there.'

'What now?' answered Killick in an ill-tempered whine from where Jack's cot was slung; and for form's sake he added 'Sir.'

'Rouse out my bottle-green coat and a decent pair of breeches.'

'Which I've got it here, ain't I? And you can't have it these ten minutes, the buttons all being to be reseated.'

Neither Killick nor Bonden had ever expressed the slightest concern about Captain Aubrey's trial and condemnation. They had the great delicacy of feeling in important matters that Jack, after many, many years experience and very close contact, had come to expect of the lower deck; there was no overt sympathy whatsoever apart from their attentive presence, and Killick was if anything more cross-grained than he had been all these years, by way of showing that there was no difference.

He could be heard muttering in the sleeping-cabin – God-damned blunt needle – if he had a shilling for every button that fat-arsed slut at Ashgrove had put on loose, he would be a rich man – no notion of seating a shank man-of-war fashion – and the twist was the wrong shade of green.

In time however Captain Aubrey was dressed in newly-brushed, newly-pressed clothes and he resumed his habitual solitary pacing on the quarterdeck, looking now at the land, now at the cape to the southward.

Ever since Stephen Maturin had become rich he was troubled from time to time by fits of narrowness. Most of his life he had been poor and sometimes exceedingly poor, but except when poverty prevented him from satisfying his very simple needs he had taken little notice of money. Yet now that he had inherited from his god-father (his own father's particular friend, his mother's third cousin once removed, and the last of his wealthy race), and now that the heavy little iron-bound cases holding don Ramón's gold were so crowding his banker's strong-room that the door could scarcely be closed, a concern with pence and shillings came over him.

At present he was walking over a vast bare slightly undulating plain, going fast over the short turf in the direction of the newly-risen sun: brilliant cock-wheatears in their best plumage flew on either side; countless larks far overhead, of course; a jewel of a day. He had come down from London in the slow coach, getting out at Clotworthy so that he could cut across country to Polton Episcopi, where his friend the Reverend Nathaniel Martin would be waiting for him; and there they would both take the carrier's cart to Shelmerston, from which the *Surprise* was to sail on the evening tide. According to Stephen's calculation this would save a good eleven shillings and fourpence. The calculation was wrong, for although he was quite able in some fields, such as medicine, surgery and entomology, arithmetic was not one of them, and he needed a guardian angel with an abacus to multiply by twelve; the error was of no real importance however since this was not a matter of true grasping avarice but rather of conscience; as he saw it there was an indecency in wealth, an indecency that could be slightly diminished by gestures of this kind and by an outwardly unaltered modest train of life.

Only slightly, as he freely admitted to himself, for these fits were spasmodic and at other times he was far from consistent: for example, he had recently indulged himself in a wonderfully supple pair of half-boots made by an eminent hand in St James's Street, and in the sinful luxury of cashmere stockings. Ordinarily he wore heavy square-toed shoes made heavier still by sheet-lead soles, the principle being that without the lead he would be light-footed; and indeed for the first three miles he had fairly sped over the grass, taking conscious pleasure in the easy motion and the green smell of spring that filled the air. Yet now, perhaps a furlong ahead, there was a man, strangely upright and dark in this pale horizontal landscape inhabited only by remote amorphous bands of sheep and by high white clouds moving gently from the west-south-west: he too was walking along the broad drift, marked by the passage of flocks and the ruts of an occasional shepherd's hut on wheels, but he was walking more slowly by far, and not only that, but every now and then he stopped entirely to gesticulate with greater vehemence, while at other times he would give a leap or bound. Ever since Maturin had come within earshot he had perceived that the man was talking, sometimes earnestly, sometimes with extreme passion, and sometimes in the shrill tones of an elegant female: a man of the middling kind, to judge by his blue breeches and claret-coloured coat, and of some education, for at one point he cried out 'Oh that the false dogs might be choked with their own dung!' in rapid, unhesitating Greek; but a man who quite certainly thought himself alone in the green morning and who would be horribly mortified at being overtaken by one who must have heard his ejaculations for the last half hour.

Yet there was no help for it; the halts were becoming more frequent, and if Blue Breeches did not turn off the path very soon Stephen must either catch him up or loiter at this wretched pace, perhaps being late for his appointment.

He tried coughing and even a hoarse burst of song; but nothing answered and he would have had to sneak past with what countenance he could had not Blue Breeches stopped, spun about, and gazed at him.

'Have you a message for me?' he called, when Stephen was within a hundred yards.

'I have not,' said Stephen.

'I ask your pardon, sir,' said Blue Breeches, with Stephen now close at hand, 'but as I was expecting a message from London, and as I told them at home that I should be visiting my dell, I thought . . . but sir,' he went on, reddening with confusion, 'I fear I must have made a sad exhibition of myself, declaiming as I walked.'

'Never in life, sir,' cried Stephen. 'Many a parliament-man, many a lawyer have I known harangue the empty air and thought nothing of it at all, at all. And did not Demosthenes address the waves? Sure, it is in the natural course of many a man's calling.'

'The fact of the matter is, that I am an author,' said Blue Breeches, when they had walked on a little way; and in answer to Stephen's civil enquiries he said that he worked mostly on tales of former times and Gothic manners. 'But as for the number that you so politely ask after,' he added with a doleful look, 'I am afraid it is so small that I am ashamed to mention it: I doubt I have published more than a score. Not, mark you,' he said with a skip, 'that I have not conceived, worked out and entirely composed at least ten times as many, and on this very sward too, excellent tales, capital tales that have made me (a partial judge, I confess) laugh aloud with pleasure. But you must understand, sir, that each man has his particular way of writing, and mine is by saying my pieces over as I walk – I find the physical motion dispel the gross humours and encourage the flow of ideas. Yet that is where the danger lies: if it encourage them too vigorously, if my piece is formed to my full satisfaction, as just now I conceived the chapter in which Sophonisba confines Roderigo in the Iron Maiden on pretence of wanton play and begins to turn the screw, why then it is done, finished; and my mind, my imagination will have nothing more to do with it – declines even to write it down, or, on compulsion, records a mere frigid catalogue of unlikely statements. The only way for me to succeed is by attaining a near-success, a *coitus interruptus* with my Muse, if you will forgive me the expression, and then running home to my pen for the full consummation. And this I cannot induce my bookseller to understand: I tell him that the work of the mind is essentially different from manual labour; I tell him that in the second case mere industry and application will hew a forest of wood and carry an ocean of water, whereas in the first . . . and he sends word that the press is at a stand, that he must have the promised twenty sheets by return.' Blue Breeches repeated his Greek remark, and added, 'But here, sir, our ways must part; unless perhaps I can tempt you to view my dell.'

'Is it perhaps a druidical dell, sir?' asked Stephen, smiling as he shook his head.

'Druidical? Oh no, not at all. Though something might be made of druids: *The Druid's Curse*, or *The Spectre of the Henge*. No, my dell is only a place where I sit and contemplate my bustards.'

'Your bustards, sir?' cried Stephen, his pale eyes searching the man's face. '*Otis tarda?*'

'The same.'

'I have never seen one in England,' said Stephen.

'Indeed, they are grown very rare: when I was a little boy you might see small droves of them, looking remarkably like sheep. But they still exist; they are creatures of habit, and I have followed them since I was very young, as my father and grandfather did before me. From my dell I can certainly undertake to show you a sitting hen; and there is a fair chance of two or three cock-birds.'

'Would it be far, at all?'

'Oh, not above an hour, if we step out; and I have, after all, finished my chapter.'

Stephen gazed at his watch. Martin, an authority on the thick-kneed curlew, would forgive him for being late in such a cause; but Jack Aubrey had a naval regard for time – he was absurdly particular about punctuality to the very minute, and the idea of facing a Jack Aubrey seven feet tall and full of barely-contained wrath at having been kept waiting two whole hours, a hundred and twenty minutes, made Stephen hesitate; but not for very long. 'I shall hire a post-chaise at Polton Episcopi,' he said inwardly, 'a chaise and four, and thus make up the time.'

The Marquess of Granby, Polton's only inn, had a bench along its outer wall, facing the afternoon sun; and on this bench, framed by a climbing rose on the one hand and a honeysuckle on the other, dozed Nathaniel Martin. Swallows, whose half-built nests were taking form in the eaves above, dropped little balls of mud on him from time to time, and he had been there so long that his left shoulder had a liberal coating. He was just aware of the tiny impact, of the sound of wings and the tumbling, hurried swallow-song, as well as the remoter thorough-bass of a field full of cows beyond the Marquess's horsepond; but he did not fully wake to the world until he heard the cry 'Shipmate, ahoy!'

'Oh my dear Maturin,' he exclaimed, 'how happy I am to see you! But' – looking again – 'I trust no accident has occurred?' For Maturin's face, ordinarily an unwholesome yellow, was now entirely suffused with an unwholesome pink; it was also covered with dust, in which the sweat, as it ran down, had made distinct tracks or runnels.

'Never in life, soul. I am so concerned, indeed so truly distressed, that you should have had to wait: pray forgive me.' He sat down, breathing fast. 'But will I tell what it is that kept me?'

'Pray do,' said Martin, and directing his voice in at the window, 'Landlord, a can of ale for the gentleman, if you please: a pint of the coolest ale that ever you can draw.'

'You will scarcely believe me, but peering through the long grass at the edge of a dell and we in the dell looking outwards you understand, I have seen a bustard sitting on her eggs not a hundred yards away. With the gentleman's perspective-glass I could see her eye, which is a bright yellowish brown. And then when we had been there a while she stood up, walked off to join two monstrous tall cocks and a bird of the year and vanished over the slope, so that we could go and look at her nest without fear. And, Martin, I absolutely heard the chicks in those beautiful great eggs calling peep-peep peep-peep, like a distant bosun, upon my word and honour.'

Martin clasped his hands, but before he could utter more than an inarticulate cry of wonder and admiration the ale arrived and Stephen went on, 'Landlord, pray have a post-chaise put to, to carry us to Shelmerston as soon as I have drunk up this capital ale: for I suppose the carrier is gone long since.'

'Bless you, sir,' said the landlord, laughing at such simplicity, 'there ain't no shay in Polton Episcopi, nor never has been. Oh dear me, no. And Joe Carrier, he will be at Wakeley's by now.'

'Well then, a couple of horses, or a man with a gig, or a tax-cart.'

'Sir, you are forgetting it is market-day over to Plashett. There is not a mortal gig nor tax-cart in the village. Nor I doubt no horse; though Waites's mule might carry two, and the farrier dosed him last night. I will ask my wife, Anthony Waites being her cousin, as you might say.'

A pause, in which a woman's voice could be heard calling down the stairs 'What do they want to go to Shelmerston for?' and the landlord came back with the satisfied expression of one whose worst fears have been realized. 'No, gentlemen,' he said. 'Not the least hope of a horse; and Waites's mule is dead.'

They walked in silence for a while, and then Stephen said, 'Still and all, it is only a matter of a few hours.'

'There is also the question of the tide,' observed Martin.

'Lord, Lord, I was forgetting the tide,' said Stephen. 'And sailors do make such a point of it.' A quarter of a mile later he said, 'I am afraid my recent notes may not have given you quite all the information you might have wished.' This was eminently true. Stephen Maturin had been so long and so intimately concerned with intelligence, naval and political, and his life had so long depended on secrecy that he was most unwilling to commit anything to writing; and in any event he was a most indifferent correspondent. Martin said 'Not at all,' and Stephen went on 'If I had had any good news for you, believe me, I should have brought it out with great joy directly; but I am obliged to tell you that your pamphlet, your very able pamphlet, enveighing against whoredom and flogging in the service, makes it virtually impossible that you should ever be offered a naval chaplaincy again. This I heard in Whitehall itself, I grieve to say.'

'So Admiral Caley told my wife a few days ago,' said Martin

with a sigh. 'He said he wondered at my temerity. Yet I did think it my duty to make some kind of a protest.'

'Sure, it was a courageous thing to do,' said Stephen. 'Now I will turn to Mr Aubrey. You followed his trial and condemnation, I believe?'

'Yes, I did; and with the utmost indignation. I wrote to him twice, but destroyed both the letters, fearing to intrude and hurt with untimely sympathy. It was a very gross miscarriage of justice. Mr Aubrey could no more have conceived a fraud on the Stock Exchange than I : rather less so, indeed, he having so very little knowledge of the world of commerce, let alone finance.'

'And you know he was dismissed from the service?'

'It cannot be true!' cried Martin, standing there motionless. A cart plodded by, the driver staring at them open-mouthed and eventually turning bodily round so that he might stare longer.

'His name was removed from the post-captains' list the Friday after.'

'It must have gone near killing him,' said Martin, looking aside to conceal his emotion. 'The service meant everything to Mr Aubrey. So brave and honourable, and to be turned away . . .'

'Indeed it killed his joy in living,' said Stephen. They moved on slowly, and he said 'But he has great fortitude; and he has an admirable wife –'

'Oh, what a present comfort a wife is to a man!' exclaimed Martin, a smile breaking through the unaffected gravity of his expression.

Stephen's wife, Diana, was not a present comfort to him but a pain at his heart, sometimes dull, sometimes almost insupportably acute, never wholly absent; he said composedly, 'There is much to be said for marriage. And they have these children, too. I have hopes for him, particularly as when he was removed from the service so also was his ship. His friends have bought the *Surprise*; she has been fitted out as a private man-of-war, and he commands her.'

'Good Heavens, Maturin, the *Surprise* a privateer? Of course

I knew she was to be sold out of the service, but I had no notion of . . . I had supposed that privateers were little disreputable half-piratical affairs of ten or twelve guns at the most, luggers and brigs and the like.'

'To be sure the most part of those that ply their trade in the Channel are of that description, but there are foreign-going private men-of-war of much greater consequence. In the nineties there was a Frenchman of fifty guns, that wrought terrible havoc on the eastern trade; and you can scarcely have forgotten the prodigious fast-sailing ship that we chased day after day and so very nearly caught when we were coming back from Barbados – she carried thirty-two guns.'

'Of course, of course: the *Spartan*. But she was from America, was she not?'

'What then?'

'The country is so vast that one has an indistinct notion of everything being on a larger scale, even the privateers.'

'Listen, Martin,' said Stephen, after a slight pause. 'Will I tell you something?'

'If you please.'

'The word privateer has unpleasant echoes for the seaman, and it might be thought injurious, applied to the dear *Surprise*. In any case she is no ordinary privateer, at all. In an ordinary privateer the hands go aboard on the understanding of no prey, no pay; they are fed but no more and any money must come from their prizes. This makes them unruly and contumelious; it is their custom to plunder without the least mercy and strip their unfortunate victims; and in the case of the most wicked and brutal it is said that those prisoners who cannot ransom themselves are thrown overboard, while rape and ill-usage are commonplace. In the *Surprise* on the other hand everything is to be run on naval lines; the people are to be paid; Captain Aubrey means to accept only able seamen of what he considers good character; and those who will not undertake to submit to naval discipline are turned away. He sails with his present crew directly, on liking, for a short cruise or two – one to the westward and another to the north, probably the Baltic – and those that are found not to answer will be put on shore before the main voyage. So bearing all this in mind, perhaps you would be well advised to refer to her as a private man-of-war, or if you find that disagreeable, as a letter of marque.'

'I am grateful for your warning, and shall try not to offend; yet surely there will be very little occasion for my calling her anything, since however far removed she may be from an ordinary – from the objectionable class of ship – even the best-ordered private man-of-war can hardly require a chaplain? Or do I mistake?' The urgency of his desire to be told that he *did* mistake was so evident in his lean, unbeneficed, anxious face that it grieved Stephen to have to say, 'Alas, there is, as you know, a very absurd superstitious prejudice among seamen: they believe that carrying a parson brings bad luck. And in an enterprise of this kind luck is everything. That is why they seek to ship with Lucky Jack Aubrey in such numbers. But I did not mean to trifle with you when I asked you to meet me at Polton: my intention was to learn whether your projects, plans or desires had changed since last we met, or whether you would be willing to let me ask Mr Aubrey if he would appoint you surgeon's assistant. After these preliminary cruises the *Surprise* is bound for South America, and on such a long voyage there have of course to be two medical men. Your physical knowledge already exceeds that of most surgeon's mates; and I should infinitely prefer to have a second who is also a civilized companion, and a naturalist into the bargain. Do pray turn it over in your mind. If you could let me have your answer in a fortnight's time, at the end of the first cruise, you would oblige me.'

'Does the nomination depend on Mr Aubrey alone?' asked Martin, his face fairly glowing.

'It does.'

'Then may we not perhaps run a little? As you see, the road is downhill as far as the eye can reach.'

'On deck, there,' called the lookout at the masthead of the *Surprise*. 'Three sail of ships – four – five sail of ships fine on the starboard bow.' They were hidden from the deck by the high land to the north ending in Penlea Head, but the lookout, a local man, had a fine view of them, and presently he added in a conversational tone, 'Men-of-war; part of the Brest squadron, I fancy. But there's nothing to worry about. There ain't no sloops nor frigates, and they are going to wear.' The implication was that if they had been accompanied by sloops or frigates, one might have been detached to see what could be snapped up in the way of men pressed out of the ship lying there off Shelmerston.

Soon after this they appeared from behind Penlea: two seventy-fours, then a three-decker, probably the *Caledonia*, wearing the flag of a vice-admiral of the red at the fore, then two more seventy-fours, the last quite certainly the *Pompée*. They wore in succession and stood away into the offing with the topgallant breeze two points free, making a line as exact as if it had been traced with a ruler, each ship two cable's lengths from its leader; in their casual, thrown-away beauty they must have moved any seaman's heart, though most bitterly wounding one excluded from that world. Yet it had to happen sooner or later, and Jack was glad that the first shock had been no worse.

This particular misery had many aspects, not the least being his sharp, immediate, practical realization that he was the potential prey of his own service; but he was not much given to analysing his feelings and once the squadron had disappeared he resumed his dogged walk fore and aft until as he turned he caught sight of a lugger hoisting her sail in the harbour. A small figure was waving something white in the bows, and borrowing Davidge's telescope he saw that the waver was Stephen Maturin. The lugger went about to cross the bar on the starboard tack and Stephen was made to get out of the way – to sit upon a lobster-pot amidships; but even so he continued his thin harsh screeching and the waving of his handkerchief; and to Jack's surprise he saw that he was accompanied by Parson Martin, come to pay a visit, no doubt.

'Bonden,' he said, 'the Doctor will be with us very soon, together with Mr Martin. Let Padeen know, in case his master's cabin needs a wipe, and stand by to get them both aboard dry-foot, if possible.'

The two gentlemen, though long accustomed to the sea, both had some mental disability, some unhappy want of development, that kept them from any knowledge of its ways; they were perpetual landlubbers, and Dr Maturin in particular had, in his attempts at coming up the side, fallen between more ships and the boat that was carrying him than could well be numbered. This time however they were ready for him, and powerful arms heaved him gasping aboard, and Jack Aubrey cried 'Why, there you are, Doctor. How happy I am to see you. My dear Mr Martin' – shaking his hand – 'welcome aboard once more. I trust I see you well?' He certainly saw him cold, for Martin was exhausted and the sea-damp breeze had pierced his thin coat through and through during the passage from the shore; and although he smiled and said everything proper, he could not keep his teeth from chattering. 'Come below,' said Jack, leading the way. 'Let me offer you something hot. Killick, a pot of coffee, and bear a hand.'

'Jack,' said Stephen, 'I do most humbly beg your pardon for being late; it was my own fault entirely, so it was – a gross self-indulgence in bustards; and I am most infinitely obliged to you for waiting for us.'

'Not at all,' said Jack. 'I am engaged to Admiral Russell this evening and shall not sail until the beginning of the ebb. Killick, Killick, there: my compliments to Captain Pullings, who is in the hold, and there are some friends of his come aboard.'

'Before dear Tom appears,' said Stephen, 'there is one point that I should like to settle. The *Surprise* needs a surgeon's mate, especially as I may have to be absent some part of the time, early on. You are acquainted with Mr Martin's competence in the matter. Subject to your consent, he has agreed to accompany me as my assistant.'

'As assistant-surgeon, not as chaplain?'

'Just so.'

'I should indeed be happy to have Mr Martin with us again,

above all in the physical line. For I must tell you, sir' – turning to Martin – 'that even in a King's ship the hands do not take kindly to the idea of having a parson aboard, and in a letter of marque – why, they are even more given to pagan superstition, and I fear it would upset them sadly. Though I have no doubt that in case of accident they would like to be buried in style. So that as long as you are on the ship's books as assistant-surgeon, they will have the best of both worlds.'

Pullings hurried in, with the friendliest welcome; Padeen tried to find out in his primitive English whether the Doctor would like his flannel waistcoat; and Davidge sent word that the Admiral's cutter would be alongside in five minutes.

The Admiral's cutter came to the larboard side to avoid all ceremony, and with an equal lack of pomp Stephen was handed down the side like a sack of potatoes. 'It is very kind of you to invite me too, sir,' he said, 'but I am ashamed to appear in such garments: never a moment did I have to shift since I arrived.'

'You are very well as you are, Doctor, very well indeed. It is only myself and my ward Polly, whom you know, and Admiral Schank, whom you know even better. I had hoped for Admiral Henry, who is very much in the medical way, now that he is at leisure; but he was bespoke. Left his best compliments, however, and I have his latest work for you, a very pretty book.'

The pretty book was called *An Account of the Means by which Admiral Henry has Cured the Rheumatism, a Tendency to Gout, the Tic Douloureux, the Cramp, and other Disorders; and by which a Cataract in the Eye was removed*, and Stephen was looking at the pictures while Polly, an enchanting young person whose black hair and blue eyes brought Diana even more strongly to mind, played some variations on a theme by Pergolesi, when Admiral Schank woke up and said 'Bless me, I believe I must have dropped off. What were we saying, Doctor?'

'We were speaking of balloons, sir, and you were trying to recollect the details of a device you had thought of for doing away with the inconvenience, the mortal inconvenience, of rising too high.'

'Yes, yes. I will draw it for you.' The Admiral, known throughout the service as Old Purchase because of his ingenious cot that could be inclined, raised, lowered, and moved from point to point by the man who lay in it, even a feeble invalid, with the help of double and triple pulleys, and many other inventions, drew a balloon with a network of lines round the envelope and explained that by means of a system of blocks it was designed to diminish the volume of gas and thus its lifting-power. 'But, however, it did not answer,' he said. 'The only way of not going too high, like poor Senhouse, who was never seen again, or Charlton, who was froze, is to let out some of the gas; and then if the day cools you are likely to come down with shocking force and be dashed to pieces, like poor Crowle and his dog and cat. Was you ever in a balloon, Maturin?'

'I was in one, sure, in the sense that the car contained me; but the balloon was sullen and would not rise, so I was obliged to get out and my companion was wafted off alone, landing three fields away, just inside the County Roscommon. Though now they are grown so fashionable again, I hope to make another attempt, and to observe the soaring flight of vultures close at hand.'

'Was yours a fire-balloon or one filled with gas?'

'It was meant to be a fire-balloon, but the turf was not as dry as it should have been and that day there was a small drizzle wafting across the whole country, so though we blew like Boreas we could never make it really buoyant.'

'Just as well. If you had gone up, and if the envelope had taken fire, as they so often do, you would have spent your last few seconds regretting your temerity. They are nasty, dangerous things, Maturin; and although I do not deny that a properly anchored gas-balloon let up to say three or four thousand feet might make a useful observation-post for a general, I do believe that only condemned criminals should be sent up in them.'

A pause, and Admiral Schank said, 'What has happened to Aubrey?'

'Admiral Russell has taken him into the library to show a model of the *Santissima Trinidad*.'

'Then I wish he would bring him back again. It is several minutes past supper-time – Evans has already looked in twice – and if I am not fed when I am used to being fed, your vultures ain't in it: I tear my companions and roar, like the lions in the Tower. I do hate unpunctuality, don't you, Maturin? Polly, my dear, do you think your guardian is took poorly? The clock struck a great while ago.'

In the library they stood gazing at the model, and Admiral Russell said, 'Everyone I have spoken to agrees that the Ministry's action against you, or rather against your father and his associates, was the ugliest thing the service has seen since poor Byng was judicially murdered. You may be sure that my friends and I shall do everything we can to have you reinstated.' Jack bowed, and in spite of his certain knowledge that this was the worst thing that could possibly be done, far worse than useless, since the Admiral and his friends belonged to the Opposition, he would have made a proper acknowledgment if the Admiral had not held up his hand, saying 'Not a word. What I really wanted to say to you was this: do not mope; do not keep away from your friends, Aubrey. By people who do not know you well, it might be interpreted as a sense of guilt; and in any case it makes for brooding and melancholy and the blue devils. Do not keep away from your friends. I know several who have been hurt by your refusal, and I have heard of more.'

'It was very handsome of them to invite me,' said Jack, 'but my going must have compromised them; and there is such competition for ships and promotion nowadays that I would not have my friends in any way handicapped at the Admiralty. It is different with you, sir: I know you do not want a command, and an Admiral of the White who has already refused a title has nothing to fear from anyone, Admiralty or not. But I will follow your advice as far as –'

'Oh sir,' said Polly in the doorway, 'the kitchen is all in an uproar. Supper was half on the table as the great clock struck and now it is half off again, while Evans and Mrs Payne wrangle in the corridor.'

'God's my life,' cried the Admiral, glancing at the library timepiece, a silent regulator. 'Aubrey, we must run like hares.'

Supper wound its pleasant course, and although the soufflé had seen better times the claret, a Latour, was as near perfection as man could desire. At the next stroke of the clock Polly said good night; and once again the particular grace of her curtsey, the bend of her head, gave Stephen a vivid image of Diana, in whom grace stood in lieu of virtue, though indeed she was usually honourable according to her own standards, which were surprisingly rigorous in some respects. It was pretty to see how Polly blushed when Stephen opened the door for her, she being still so young that it was a great rarity in her experience; and when the men sat down again Admiral Russell took a letter out of his pocket and said 'Aubrey, I know how you value Nelson's memory, so I mean to give you this; and I hope it will bring you good fortune in your voyage. He sent it to me in the year three, when I was with Lord Keith in the Sound and he was in the Mediterranean. I will read it to you first, not so much out of vainglory, as because he wrote it with his left hand, of course, and you might not be able to make it out. After the usual beginning it runs "Here I am, waiting the pleasure of these fellows at Toulon, and we only long to get fairly alongside of them. I dare say, there would be some spare *hats*, by the time we had done. You are a pleasant fellow at all times; and, as Commodore Johnstone said of General Meadows, *I have no doubt but your company would be delightful on the day of battle to your friends, but damned bad for your enemies*. I desire, my dear Russell, you will always consider me as one of the sincerest of the former."' He passed it, still open, across the table.

'Oh what a very handsome letter!' cried Jack gazing at it with a look of unfeigned delight. 'I do not suppose a handsomer letter was ever wrote. And may I really have it, sir? I am most exceedingly grateful, and shall treasure it – I cannot tell you how I shall treasure it. Thank you, sir, again and again' – shaking the Admiral's hand with an iron grasp.

'They may say what they like about Nelson,' observed Old Purchase, 'these fellows so ready with their first stones. But even they will admit that he put things very well. My nephew Cunningham was one of his youngsters in *Agamemnon* and Nelson said to him, "There are three things, young gentleman, which you are constantly to bear in mind. First, you must always implicitly obey orders, without attempting to form any opinion of your own respecting their propriety. Secondly, you must consider every man your enemy who speaks ill of your King: and thirdly, you must hate a Frenchman as you do the Devil."'

'Admirably well put,' said Jack.

'But surely,' said Stephen, who loved un-Napoleonic France, 'he cannot have meant *all* Frenchmen?'

'I think he did,' said Schank.

'It was perhaps a little sweeping,' said Russell. 'But then so were his victories. And really, upon the whole, you know, there is very little good in the French: it is said that you can learn a great deal about a nation from its proverbial expressions, and when the French wish to describe anything mighty foul they say, "sale comme un peigne", which gives you a pretty idea of their personal cleanliness. When they have other things to occupy their mind they say they have other cats to whip: a most inhuman thing to do. And when they are going to put a ship about, the order is "à-Dieu-va", or "we must chance it and trust in God", which gives you some notion of their seamanship. I cannot conceive anything more criminal.'

Jack was telling Admiral Schank how Nelson had once asked him to pass the salt in the civillest way imaginable, and how on another occasion he had said 'never mind about manoeuvres; always go straight at 'em', and Stephen was about to suggest that there might be some good Frenchmen, instancing those who had made this sublime claret, when Admiral Russell, returning from a brief reverie, said, 'No, no. There may be exceptions, but upon the whole I have no use for them, high or low. It was a French commander, of excellent family as these things go with them, that played me the dirtiest trick I ever heard of in war, a trick as loathsome as a French comb.'

'Pray tell us, sir,' said Jack, privately fondling his letter.

'I will only give you the briefest summary, because if you are to sail on the turn of the tide I must not keep you. It was when I had the *Hussar* – the old *Hussar* – at the end of the last American war, in eighty-three, a neat weatherly little frigate, very like your *Surprise*, though not quite so fast on a bowline: Nelson had the *Albemarle* on the same station, and we got along admirably well together. I was cruising rather north of Cape Hatteras, in soundings – fresh gale in the north-north-west and hazy February weather – and I chased a sail standing to the westward with the starboard tacks on board. I gained on her and when we were quite near – damned murky it was – I saw she was under jury-masts, uncommon well set-up, and that she had some shot-holes in her quarter. So when she showed an English ensign reversed in her main shrouds and English colours over French at the ensign-staff it was clear that she was a prize to one of our ships, that she had been battered in the taking, and that her prize-crew needed help – that she was in distress.'

'It could mean nothing else,' said Jack.

'Oh yes it could, my dear fellow,' said the Admiral. 'It could mean that she was commanded by a scrub, a dishonourable scrub. I stood under her lee to hail and ask what they needed, and jumping up on to the hammock-netting with my speaking-trumpet to make them hear over the wind I saw her decks were alive with men – not a prize-crew at all but two or three hundred men – and at the same moment she ran out her guns, putting up her helm to lay me athwart hawse, carry away my bowsprit, rake me and board me – there were the boarders by the score in her waist all on tiptoe, all a-grinning. Still with my speaking-trumpet up I roared out "Hard a-weather" and my people had the sense to shiver the after-sails even before I had time to give the order. The *Hussar* obeyed directly, and

31

so we missed most of the raking fire, though it did wound my foremast and carry away most of its starboard shrouds. We were both by the lee forward, almost aboard one another, and my people hurled cold round-shot down at their boarders – with prodigious effect – while the Marines blazed away as quick as they could load. Then I called out "Boarders away," and hearing this the scrub put up his helm, wore round and made sail before the wind. We pelted away after him. After an hour's brisk engagement his fire slackened and he clapped his helm a-starboard, running to windward on the larboard tack. I followed him round to jam him up against the wind, but alas there was my foremast on the point of coming by the board – bowsprit too – and we could not keep our luff until they were secured. However, we accomplished it at last, and we were gaining on the Frenchman when the weather cleared and there to windward we saw a large ship – we soon found she was the *Centurion* – and to leeward a sloop we knew was the *Terrier*; so we cracked on regardless and in a couple of hours we were abreast of him – gave him a broadside. He returned two guns and struck his colours. The ship proved to be *La Sybille*, thirty-eight – though he threw a dozen overboard in the chase – with a crew of three hundred and fifty men as well as some American supernumeraries, and the scrub in command was the comte de Kergariou – Kergariou de Socmaria, as I recall.'

'What did you do to him, sir?' asked Jack.

'Hush,' said the Admiral, cocking an eye at Schank. 'Old Purchase is fast asleep. Let us creep away, and I will run you back to your ship; the breeze serves, and you will not lose a minute of your tide.'

CHAPTER TWO

Dawn found the *Surprise* far out in the grey, lonely waste that was her natural home; a fine topgallant breeze was blowing from the south-west, with low cloud and occasional wafts of rain but promise of a better day to come; and she had topgallantsails abroad although it was so early, for Jack wished to be out of the ordinary path of ships on their way to or from the various naval stations. He had no wish to see any of his men pressed – and no King's officer could resist the temptation of such a numerous, hand-picked crew of able seamen – nor had he any wish to be called aboard a King's ship to show his papers, give an account of himself, and perhaps be treated in an off-hand manner, even with familiarity or disrespect. The service was not made up solely of men with a great deal of natural or acquired delicacy and he had already had to put up with some slights; he would get used to them in time, no doubt, but for the present he was as it were flayed.

'Get under way, Joe,' said the quartermaster, turning the watch-glass, and a muffled form padded forward to strike three bells in the morning watch. The master's mate heaved the log and reported six knots, two fathoms, a rate few ships could equal in these conditions and perhaps none surpass.

'Mr West,' said Jack to the officer of the watch, 'I am going below for a while. I doubt the breeze will hold, but it looks as though we may have a pleasant day of it.'

'It does indeed, sir,' replied West, ducking his head against a sudden shower of spray, for the *Surprise* was sailing close-hauled south-south-east with choppy seas smacking against her starboard bow and streaming aft, mixed with the rain. 'How delightful it is to be at sea once more.'

At this early stage Jack Aubrey was three persons in one. He was the ship's captain, of course; and since no candidate he could approve had appeared among the many who came forward, he was also her master, responsible for the navigation among other things; and he was her purser as well. Officers commanding vessels sent on exploration were usually their pursers too, but this role had never fallen to Jack, and although as captain he had always been supposed to supervise his pursers and required to sign their books, he was astonished at the volume and complexity of the necessary accounts now that he came to deal with them in detail.

There was already light enough to work at the stern window of the great cabin – a curving series of panes the whole width of the ship that gave him a certain pleasure even at the worst of his unhappiness, as indeed did the cabin itself, a singularly beautiful room with scarcely a right-angle in it – curved deck, curved deck-head, inclined sides – and with its twenty-four feet of breadth and fourteen of length it provided him with more space than all the other officers together; and this was not everything, since out of the great cabin there opened two smaller ones, one for dining, the other for sleeping. The dining cabin, however, had now been made over to Stephen Maturin, and when breakfast arrived, Jack, having dealt with almost a third of the invoices, advice-notes and bills of lading, nodded towards its door and asked 'Is the Doctor stirring?'

'Never a sound, sir,' said Killick. 'Which he was mortal tired last night, like a foundered horse. But maybe the smell will wake him; it often does.'

The smell, a combination of coffee, bacon, sausages and toasted soft-tack, had woken him in many latitudes, for like most sailors Jack Aubrey was intensely conservative in the matter of food and even on very long voyages he generally contrived, by carrying hens, pigs, a hardy goat and sacks of green coffee, to have much the same breakfast (apart from the toast) on the equator or beyond the polar circles. It was a meal that Maturin looked upon as England's chief claim to civilization; yet this time even the coffee did not rouse him. Nor did the cleaning of the quarterdeck immediately over his head, nor the piping-up of hammocks at seven bells nor that of all hands to breakfast at eight, with the roaring, rushing and bellowing that this always entailed. He slept on and on, through the gradual dropping of the wind and through the wearing of the ship to the larboard tack, with all the hauling, bracing round and coiling down that accompanied the manoeuvre; and it was not until well on in the forenoon watch that he emerged, gaping and stretching, with his breeches undone at the knee and his wig in his hand.

'God and Mary with you, gentleman,' said Padeen, who had been waiting for him.

'God and Mary and Patrick with you, Padeen,' said Stephen.

'Will I bring a clean shirt and hot water for shaving, now?'

Stephen considered, rasping his chin. 'You might bring the water,' he said. 'The weather is calm, I find, the motion slight, the danger inconsiderable. As for the shirt,' he went on, raising his voice to overcome the cheerful conversation of a working-party eleven inches above him, 'as for the shirt, I have one on already, and do not mean to take it off. But you may desire Preserved Killick to favour me with a pot of coffee.' The last was said still louder, and in English, since there was a strong likelihood that Killick, always intensely curious, would hear it.

Some time later, shaved and refreshed, Dr Maturin came on deck: that is to say he walked out of his cabin by the forward door, along the passage to the waist of the ship and so up the ladder to the quarterdeck, upon which the captain, the first mate, the bosun and the gunner were in consultation. Stephen made his way to the taffrail and leaned there in the sun, looking forward the whole length of the ship, some forty yards, to the point where the rising bowsprit carried it farther still; the day had indeed turned out to be pleasant, but the breeze was on the wane and in spite of a noble spread of canvas the *Surprise* was making no more than two or three knots, with barely a tilt on her deck.

Everything looked superficially the same – the familiar sun-filled white curves above, the taut rigging and its severe shadows – and he had to search for some while before he could tell where the essential difference lay. It was not in the lack of naval uniforms, for except in flagships and some others, commanded by very 'quarterdeck' captains, it was now quite usual for officers to wear nondescript working clothes unless they were invited to dine in the cabin or were engaged upon some official duty; and as for the hands, they had always dressed as they pleased. Nor was it the absence of a man-of-war's pennant streaming from her masthead, which he would never have noticed. No: part of it lay in the absence of the Marines' scarlet coats, always a striking patch of colour against the pale deck and the unemphatic variations of the sea, and in that of boys of any kind, ship's boys or young gentlemen on the quarterdeck. They were not much use; they took up valuable room; it was difficult to make them quietly attentive to their duty; but they did add a certain shrill cheerfulness. Cheerfulness was still present; in fact it was considerably more audible – hands laughing in the tops, along the gangway and on the forecastle – than it would have been in the Royal Navy under an equally taut captain; but it was of a different nature. Stephen was pondering upon this further difference when Bonden came aft to attend to the ensign, a red one, which had become entangled, and they had a word. 'The hands are most uncommon pleased about Lord Nelson's letter, sir,' said Bonden, after they had discussed the breeze and the possibility of taking codlings with hook and line. 'They look upon it as what you might call a sign.' At this point the bosun's pipe called Bonden and all hands to get the blue cutter over the side and Jack walked aft. 'Good morning to you, sir,' said Stephen, 'I am sorry not to have seen you at breakfast, but I slept as the person in Plutarch that ran from Marathon to Athens without a pause would have slept if he had not fallen dead, the creature. Poor Martin is sleeping yet, blisters and all. Lord, how we skipped along, so pitifully anxious not to miss the boat. Sometimes, on very steep hills, he led me by the hand.'

'Good morning to you, Doctor; and a pretty one it is,' said Jack. 'Mr Martin is aboard, then? I had imagined he was gone home to make his arrangements and that he would rejoin when we put in to Shelmerston again.'

'Sure, I had no time to speak to you about him or anything else yesterday afternoon, and at night I was asleep before ever you came below. And even now, although this is not the Admiral's supper-table,' he said quietly, looking at the wheel, which in the *Surprise* was just forward of the mizenmast, ten feet away, with its helmsman and the quartermaster at the con, to say nothing of the officer of the watch by the capstan and a party of seamen running up the shrouds to arm the mizentop, 'it is scarcely a place that I should choose for confidential talk.'

'Let us go below,' said Jack.

'And even here,' said Stephen in the cabin, 'even in what seems the true penetralia of the frigate, little is said that does not become known, in a more or less distorted form, throughout the ship by nightfall. I do not allege any malignance, any wicked evil intent in any soul aboard, yet it is a fact that the people are already aware of Lord Nelson's letter. They know – that is to say they believe they know – that the *Surprise* was bought by a syndicate of which I was the mouthpiece, while its members almost certainly include my former patient Prince William. And they know that Martin has put off his clerical character for that of a surgeon, he having been unfrocked for rogering – do you know the expression *rogering*, Jack?'

'I believe I have heard it.'

'His bishop's wife; unfrocked and therefore incapable of bringing us bad luck. As for his presence, I did suggest that he should go home with an advance on his pay, as you were so very kind as to give me long, long ago, and come aboard with his sea-chest when we next put in; but he preferred to send his wife the advance and to stay aboard. His affairs are in a desperate way, I am afraid: no hope of a living, none of a naval chaplaincy since his unfortunate pamphlet, and an inimical father-in-law; and he is in danger of an arrest for debt if he returns. Besides, although we are to be out only a fortnight, he is happy to put up with the inconvenience of no spare shirt and shoes worn through on the off-chance of our taking a prize. I explained our system of shares, which he had not understood; and fourpence would make him happy. There are other things, however, that I have been most impatient to tell you. Suppose we climb into the top, when those men have finished what they are at?'

'They will be some time yet,' said Jack, who had climbed into the top with Stephen before this. 'Perhaps a better plan would be to pull round the ship in your skiff after the great-gun practice. In any case I wish to look at her trim.'

'Would you be intending to exercise the great guns directly?'

'Why, yes. Did not you see the blue cutter going over the side with the targets? Now that we are in an out-of-the-way corner of the sea I should like to find how the new hands shape with live ammunition. We mean to fire half a dozen rounds, starbowlins against larbowlins, before dinner. We shall have to look precious sharp.'

'Targets away, sir,' said Pullings at the cabin door; and he did in fact look sharp, as keen as a terrier shown a rat, in striking contrast to Jack Aubrey.

Stephen had the impression that his friend would not greatly care if the targets quietly sank of their own accord, and this impression was strengthened during the first part of the exercise. The stimulus of Nelson's letter and the Admiral's kindness had long since died away; sombreness had returned. This sombreness was not accompanied by any lack of conduct; Aubrey had far too strong a sense of duty to his ship to be anything but exact and punctilious. Yet Stephen observed that even the smell of the slow-match, the splitting crash of a gun, the screech and twang of its recoil, and the powder-smoke eddying along the deck did not really move him now. He also observed that Pullings, who loved Jack Aubrey, was watching him with anxiety.

What Stephen did not observe was that the great-gun and

musketry exercise was exceedingly poor, for these activities had usually taken place in the evening, when all hands were piped to quarters, to their action-stations, and as surgeon his was far below, where the casualties were to be received. He had little experience and almost no appreciation of the frigate's outstanding gunnery in former times. Jack Aubrey, from his earliest dawn of naval reason, and even more certainly from his very first command, had been convinced that accurate, rapid gunfire had more to do with victory than polished brass: he had worked on this principle in all his successive ships and he had brought the *Surprise*, which he had commanded longest, to a high pitch of excellence. In good conditions HMS *Surprise* had fired three accurate broadsides in three minutes eight seconds, which in his opinion no other ship in the Navy could equal, far less surpass.

The present *Surprise*, though shorn of her HMS, nevertheless carried all her old guns, *Wilful Murder*, *Jumping Billy*, *Belcher*, *Sudden Death*, *Tom Cribb* and the rest, together with many of her old gun-crews; but in order to produce a united ship's company, or rather to prevent more animosity and division than was inevitable, Jack and Pullings had mixed old men and new; the result was pitifully slow, blundering, and inaccurate. Most of the privateersmen were much more accustomed to boarding their opponents than to battering them from a distance (apart from anything else, battering was sure to spoil the victim's merchandise), and few were qualified to point a gun with anything like precision. Many a nervous look did the old Surprises throw at the captain, for in general he was a most unsparing critic; but they saw no reaction of any kind, nothing but an unmoved gravity. Only once did he call out, and that was to a new hand who was too close to his gun. 'The boarder at number six: James. Stand free or you will lose your foot on the recoil.'

The last shot was fired, the gun sponged, reloaded, wadded, rammed and run out. 'Well, sir . . .' said Davidge, uneasily.

'Let us see what they can do with the larboard guns, Mr Davidge,' said Jack.

39

'House your guns,' called Davidge; and then, 'All hands about ship.'

The newcomers might be weak on gunnery, but they were thorough-going seamen, and they ran as fast as the Surprises to their appointed sheets, tacks, bowlines, braces and back-stays, and the familiar cries followed: 'The helm's a-lee', 'Off tacks and sheets', but the full-voiced 'Mainsail haul' was im-mediately followed by a shrieking hail from the masthead: 'On deck, there. Sail one point on the larboard bow.'

The sail could be seen even from the deck, bringing up the breeze at a fine pace. The look-out had obviously been watching the exercise rather than the horizon. The *Surprise* paid off; Jack laid her foretopsail aback, and slinging his telescope he made his way to the top. From there she was hull-up and even without the glass he could tell what she was: a big cutter, one of those fast, nimble, weatherly two or three hundred ton vessels used by smugglers or those who pursued smugglers. She was very trim for a smuggler; too trim; and presently the telescope showed him the man-of-war's pennant clear against the mainsail. She had the weather-gage, but the *Surprise* could almost certainly outsail her going large; yet this would mean running right out into the regular track of shipping, and the likelihood of being brought-to by some rated man-of-war that would rob him of many more men than a cutter. And escape by beating to windward was out of the question; no square-rigged ship could lie as close as a cutter.

He returned to the deck and said to the officer of the watch, 'Mr Davidge, we shall lie to until she comes up, and continue the exercise afterwards. Stand by to dip topsails and ensign.' There was a murmur, more than a murmur, of strong disap-proval from the new hands at the quarterdeck carronades, most unwilling to be pressed, and one said 'She's only the *Viper*, sir, nothing like as swift as us before the wind.'

'Silence, there,' cried Davidge, striking at the man's head with his speaking-trumpet.

Jack went below and after a moment he sent for Davidge. 'Oh, Mr Davidge,' he said, 'I have told West and Mr Bulkeley, but I do not think I have mentioned it to you: there will be no starting in this ship, no damning of eyes or souls. There is no room for hard-horse officers in a private man-of-war.'

Davidge would have replied, but a look at Jack's face checked his words: if ever there was a hard-horse officer, ready with a frightful blow regardless of persons it was Jack Aubrey at this moment.

Killick silently brought in a respectable coat, blue, but with no naval marks or lace or buttons; Jack put it on and began to gather the papers that he should have to present if he were called aboard. He looked up as Stephen came in and said with a forced smile, 'You have a paper too, I see.'

'Listen, brother,' said Stephen, drawing him to the stern window, 'it is not without some inward wrestling that I produce this, because there was a tacit assumption that it was designed to cover our South American voyage alone. Yet the carpenter tells me that this *Viper* is commanded by a peculiarly busy coxcomb, a newly-appointed lieutenant who is habitually rude and tyrannical, and it appears to me that if the puppy were to be as provoking as I fear he may be, you might commit yourself and there would be no voyage to South America, no voyage at all.'

'By God, Stephen,' said Jack, reading the document, which was the Admiralty's letter of exemption from impressment for the entire ship's company, 'I admire your judgment. I have looked at the Navy List, and *Viper* is commanded by the son of that scrub in Port Mahon, Dixon. It might have been hard to avoid kicking him, if he gave himself airs. By God, I shall be easy in my mind now.'

Even so, Jack Aubrey required all his self-command – more indeed than he thought he possessed – to avoid kicking the young man; for the loss of almost all pleasurable emotion left susceptibility, irritation, anger and rage intact or in fact strengthened, except during his long periods of apathy; and this was not one of them. When the *Viper* was within hailing-distance she ordered the *Surprise* to come under her lee, to send her master aboard with his papers, and to look hellfire quick about it, the order being emphasized with a gun across her bows.

Jack was pulled across in the target-towing boat and on going aboard the *Viper* – a mere two steps up the side, these vessels being so low in the water – he saluted the quarterdeck: the youth who had the watch, a master's mate, made a sketchy motion towards his hat and told him that the captain was busy: he would see Mr Aubrey later. With this he returned to his conversation with the captain's clerk, walking up and down and talking with an affectation of easiness. Cutters' midshipmen were notorious in the service for ill-breeding and the *Viper*'s ran true to form, leaning against the rail with their hands in their pockets, staring, whispering, sniggering, and staring again. Farther forward the cutter's warrant-officers had gathered in a body, watching with silent disapproval; and a middle-aged seaman who had sailed with Jack many years before stood motionless at the bitts with a coil of rope in his hands and a look of positive horror on his face.

At length the captain of the *Viper* received him in the low booth that passed for a cabin. Dixon was sitting at a table: he did not offer Aubrey a chair. He had hated him from those remote days in Minorca and ever since the *Surprise* had heaved in sight he had been preparing sarcastic remarks of a particularly cutting nature. But the sight of Jack's bulk towering there, filling the meagre space and all the more massive since he had to crouch under the low deckhead, his grim face and the natural authority that emanated from him, overcame young Dixon's resolution; he said nothing when Jack pushed some objects from a locker and sat down. It was only when he had leafed through the papers that he said 'I see you have a very full ship's company, Mr Aubrey. I shall have to relieve you of a score or so.'

'They are protected,' said Jack.

'Nonsense. They cannot be protected. Privateersmen are not protected.'

'Read that,' said Jack, gathering up the other papers and standing over him.

Dixon read it, read it again and held the paper against the light to see the watermark: while he did so Jack gazed out of the scuttle at his boat's crew's tarpaulin-covered hats, rising and falling on the gentle swell. 'Well,' said Dixon at last, 'I suppose there is nothing more to be said. You may go.'

'What did you say?' said Jack, turning short upon him.

'I said there is nothing more to say.'

'Good day to you, sir.'

'Good day to you, sir.'

His boat's crew greeted him with radiant smiles, and as they neared the *Surprise* one of the Shelmerston men called out to his friends peering over the hammocks, 'Mates, we'm protected!'

'Silence in the boat,' cried the coxswain in a shocked voice.

'Silence fore and aft,' called the officer of the watch as the cheering spread.

Jack's mind was still too full of Stephen's paper and its possible implications to take much notice of the din, and he hurried below. But scarcely was his file in its proper place before a far greater hullaballoo broke out: as the *Viper* filled and gathered way all the men from Shelmerston and all those Surprises who were deserters raced up into the weather shrouds, facing the cutter. The yeoman of the sheets called out 'One, two, three,' and they all bellowed 'Hoo, hoo, hoo' and slapped their backsides in unison, laughing like maniacs.

'Belay there,' roared Jack in a Cape Horn voice. 'God-damned pack of mooncalves – is this a bawdy-house? The next man to slap his arse will have it flogged off him. Mr Pullings, the Doctor's skiff over the side directly, if you please, and let three more targets be prepared.'

'Stephen,' he said, resting on his oars some two hundred yards from the frigate, 'I cannot tell you how grateful I am for that exemption. If any of our old shipmates who are deserters had been taken – and I am sure that poor mean-spirited young hound would not have spared them – they would have run the risk of hanging: of several hundred lashes, in any case. And

43

we should have been perpetually playing hide-and-seek with King's ships; for although a little common sense will generally keep you out of the way of any squadron, you cannot be nearly so sure of cruisers. I believe I must not ask you how you came by it.'

'I shall tell you, however,' said Stephen, 'for I know you are as silent as the tomb where discretion is required. On this South American journey I shall hope to make some contacts that may be of interest to government. In a hemi-demi-semi official way the Admiralty is aware of this; it is also aware that I cannot reach South America in a ship stripped of its hands. That is why this protection was given. I should have told you before. Indeed there are many things that I should have told you, had we not been so far apart, or had they been fit subjects for correspondence.' Stephen paused, staring at a distant kitti-wake; then he said, 'Listen, now, Jack, till I gather my wits and try to tell you the present position. It is difficult, because I am not master of what I can say, so much of what I know having been told me in confidence. And then again I cannot remember how much I told you during that horrible time: the details are clouded in my memory. However, *grosso modo* and including what you obviously know, this is how things stand. The case for your innocence was that Palmer was under great obligation to you, and by way of return he told you that a peace-treaty was being signed, that prices would rise on the Stock Exchange, and that you would be well advised to buy certain stocks in anticipation of that rise. The case for your guilt was that there was no Palmer at all and that you yourself spread the rumour: in short that you rigged the market. At the time we could not produce Palmer, and in front of such a judge our case was hopeless. Later, however – and now I come to a part of which I believe you know little or nothing – some of my associates and I, helped by a most intelligent thief-taker, found Palmer's body.'

'Why, then –'

'Jack, I beg you will not require me to be more explicit or break my train of thought. As I have said, I am not a free agent, and I have to steer very carefully along my line.' Another pause while he considered and the boat rode smoothly on the swell. 'Palmer's principals, the men who had put him up to deceiving you, had him knocked on the head; as a cadaver, and a mutilated, legally useless cadaver at that, he could not compromise them. His principals were French agents, Englishmen highly placed in the English administration; but in this case their chief motive was to make money. They wished the market to be rigged, but to be rigged or apparently rigged by some other person. One of these men was Wray – do not, do *not* interrupt, Jack, I beg – and since he was perfectly aware of your movements and of your presence aboard the cartel he was able to arrange the sequence of events with striking success. Yet although this was obvious enough after the event, we might never have found out that Wray and his friend were the prime movers if an ill-used French agent, in this case a Frenchman, had not given them away.' Stephen contemplated for a while; then, feeling in his pocket, he brought out a great blue diamond that half-filled his hollowed palm; he rolled it gently so that it flashed blazing in the sun, and went on, 'I will tell you this, Jack: the Frenchman was that Duhamel with whom we had so much to do in Paris. Diana had tried to ransom us with this pretty thing and part of the agreement when we left was that it should eventually be restored: Duhamel brought it. And then in exchange for a service I was able to do him he not only gave me the name of Wray and his colleague Ledward, Edward Ledward, but set them as elegant a trap as Wray set for you. They were both members of Button's, and while I watched from the window of Black's he met them in St James's Street, just outside their club, gave them a packet of bank-notes and received a report on English military and naval movements and English relations with the Swedish court. My associates and I crossed the street within a very short time, but I grieve, I most bitterly grieve to say that we bungled it. When we asked for Wray and his friend they were denied – wished to receive no visitors. Most unhappily one of my companions tried to force his way in: this made a noise, and by the time we had the proper warrant they had bolted, not through the kitchen or the stable doors, for we had men on each, but through a little small skylight in the roof and so along the parapets to Mother Abbott's, where one of the girls let them in, thinking it was a frolic. They went to ground and so far those in charge of the matter have not been able to tell where. Ledward must have had some suspicion that he was in danger: his papers told my friends nothing at all and they fear he may long since have arranged for an intelligent way of escape. Wray was less cautious however and from what was found at his house it is clear that he was implicated in the Stock Exchange business and that he profited largely from it. In any case the report they handed to Duhamel was utterly damning, particularly as some of the information can only have come from inside the Admiralty. There. I think I have told you all I can. It is hardly worth adding that my colleagues, who never thought you could have been anything more than indiscreet with those vile stocks and shares, are now wholly convinced of your innocence.'

For the last few minutes Jack's heart had been beating with steadily greater strength and speed and now it seemed to fill his chest. Breathing deeply and controlling the pitch of his voice with some success he said 'Does that mean I may be reinstated?'

'If there were any justice in the world, I am sure it would, my dear,' said Stephen. 'But you must not look for it with any kind of certainty – never with any kind of strong hope at all. Ledward and Wray have not been taken: they cannot be brought to trial. It is not impossible that someone more highly-placed than either is protecting them: certainly there is a strange reluctance to move . . . In any event the Ministry has no wish to offer the opposition a blazing and most discreditable scandal; and *raison d'état* may very easily outweigh wrongs inflicted upon an individual, particularly an individual with no political interest: or even indeed with the reverse, for in that respect you will allow me to say that General Aubrey is a sad handicap. Then again all authority implies an extreme reluctance to admit past error. On the other hand I believe a friend would advise you not to despair; above all not to give way to melancholy – be not idle, be not alone, as dear Burton says. For activity, naval activity is the solution, if solution there be.'

'I am sorry if I seemed so hipped this morning,' said Jack. 'The fact of the matter is – I do not mean to complain, Stephen, but the fact of the matter is, I had just had a dream so real and true that even now I can touch it. The dream was that the whole affair, the trial and everything that followed, was itself a dream; and my huge relief, my joy at realizing this, my immense happiness I think it was that woke me. But even then I was still partly in the dream and for a moment I looked confidently for my old uniform coat.' He dipped his oars and completed his circle round the ship, looking attentively at her trim: his reason acquiesced in everything Stephen had said, but in his irrational part a very small glow was dissipating the most extreme unhappiness.

As he pulled towards the frigate he said, 'I am glad you saw Duhamel again. I liked him.'

'He was a good man,' said Stephen. 'And restoring this diamond when he was cutting all ties with his own country – going to Canada – was as striking an example of liberal behaviour as I can recall. I regret him much.'

'He is not dead, poor fellow?'

'I should not have mentioned his name if he had been living. No. Heneage Dundas, on my guarantee, was to carry him to America, where he meant to settle by the bank of a trout-stream in the province of Quebec. He had changed all his not inconsiderable fortune into gold, which he carried in a belt about his waist; he went aboard at Spithead in a turbulent sea, and as I have sometimes done he slipped between the boat and the side: his fortune sunk him without the least hope of recovery.'

'I am heartily sorry for it,' said Jack, and rowed a little harder. He wondered whether he might speak of Diana and her diamond – it seemed inhuman not to do so – but he decided that the matter was altogether too delicate. He might easily be laid by the lee; he might easily give pain; and silence was better until Stephen should mention her again.

When they were aboard the ship once more he sent the other targets out. The larboard watch had their turn with the guns – a slightly more creditable performance, accompanied by a running fire of criticism, advice and even praise from the quarterdeck – and then the *Surprise* was indulged in two broadsides at much closer range. They were rippling broadsides, the guns firing in succession from forward aft, because her timbers were too old for the simultaneous crash except in great emergency; but private ships of war had to find themselves in powder, that costly substance, so in most of them broadsides, rippling or otherwise, were extremely rare; and all hands perceived these as a celebration of their triumph over the *Viper*. The celebration ended with the captain and the gunner firing the bow-chasers, two very finely-bored long brass nines, strikingly accurate far-carrying guns, Jack Aubrey's private property. They fired at the floating remains of the target shattered by the broadsides, and although neither did spectacularly well, they raised a fervent cheer. As Jack came aft, wiping the powder-marks off his face, Martin said to Stephen, 'Surely the Captain is looking more himself, do not you think? Yesterday evening I was extremely shocked.'

The extreme edge of unhappiness might have gone, but there was still room for a very great deal of worry and anxiety. Quite apart from his strongly intrusive necessary reflections upon domestic and legal complications (and he was not the resilient, sanguine being of even a year ago), Jack had not realized the difficulty, the near impossibility, of recruiting a ship's company of much the same quality throughout. He had not realized how very far years of team-work and constant practice on the same gun with the same partners had raised the old Surprises beyond the common level. The privateersmen were strong and willing; in dumb-show – the ordinary form of exercise, powder being so dear – they could rattle the guns in and out with great force and spirit; but it was clear that months or even years would be needed to give them that perfect timing, coordination and economy of effort that made the regular Surprises so dangerous to their enemies. In the meantime he could either restore the guns to their former crews or he could change his strategy, and instead of weakening his opponent from a distance, perhaps even knocking a topmast away, before manoeuvring to cross his bow or stern for a raking broadside and then if necessary boarding, he could follow Nelson's advice about 'going straight at 'em'. But that advice was given early in the last war, when French and Spanish gunnery, French and Spanish seamanship were so markedly inferior; at present a ship bearing down with a light breeze over a smooth sea would be exposed, head-on and unable to reply, to the enemy's full broadside for twenty or thirty minutes, and she might well be so mangled by the time she came alongside that she would herself be taken – the biter bit. Then again he had worked out his practice when he was commanding a King's ship, always happy of course to take an enemy merchantman or privateer but primarily intended to take, burn, sink or destroy the enemy's national ships of war. Now the case was altered: now his chief prey was to be merchantmen or privateers, undamaged if possible; and that called for a different approach. Of course, of course, three times of course he would delight in an engagement with an opponent of equal strength belonging to the French or American navy, a hard-hitting battle with no notion of financial gain: for a discarded privateer to take an enemy frigate would be glory indeed. But unhappily the *Surprise*, though fast and weatherly, belonged to a former age as far as glory was concerned. There were only five twenty-eight-gun frigates left in the Royal Navy and of these five, four were laid up in ordinary, unused. Most frigates now displaced well over a thousand tons and carried thirty-eight eighteen-pounders as well as carronades, and the *Surprise* could no more have tackled one of them than she could have faced a ship of the line. She gauged less than six hundred tons; she carried twelve-pounders (and if her knees had not been specially strengthened to bear them she would have been happier with nines); and even with her full extravagant Royal Navy complement she had fewer than two hundred men as opposed to the more than four hundred in one of the big Americans. Yet she was still a frigate, and for her there would be no glory in capturing anything of nominally inferior rank, such as the heavier post-ship and any of the sloops, ship-rigged or otherwise.

'Perhaps it would be better to go back to carronades,' he reflected. At one time the *Surprise*, apart from her chasers, had been armed entirely with carronades, those stumpy little objects, more like a mortar than a gun, which were light (a carronade throwing a thirty-two pound ball weighed only seventeen hundredweight as opposed to the twelve-pounder long gun's thirty-four) and easily managed. That gave the ship a broadside weight of metal of 456 pounds. To be sure, the 456 pounds could not be thrown very accurately, nor very far; these were short-range weapons. Yet a carronade did not require great skill in the handling; and although its massive balls had a terrible smashing effect, liable to ruin or even sink a prize, the same weapon loaded with case-shot cut up the enemy's rigging and cleared his open decks most efficiently, above all if they were crowded with men intending to board. Counting four hundred shot to a canister, with a broadside of fourteen carronades, that came to more than four thousand; and four thousand iron balls screaming across the deck at 1674 feet a second had a discouraging effect, even if they were fired by inexpert hands . . . perhaps that was the right solution, although of course it did away with all the finer points of a single-ship action, the high seamanship of manoeuvring for position, the deliberate firing of the most accurate guns separately at very long range, the rate of fire increasing as the range shortened until they were hammering it out yardarm to yardarm in the paroxysm of battle – an incessant roaring in deep clouds of smoke. 'But that belongs to an almost entirely different world,' he reflected, 'and I can hardly hope to be so fortunate as to know it again. Yet I believe I shall open my mind to Stephen.'

As the captain of a King's ship, Jack Aubrey had never

opened his mind on such matters to anyone. He had always been a silent captain in the matter of strategy, tactics and the right course of action, and this was not from any theory but because it seemed to him evident that a commander was there to command rather than to ask advice or preside over a committee. He had known captains and admirals call a council of war, and the result had nearly always been a prudent retreat or at any rate an absence of decisive action. But now the case was altered: he was no longer commanding a King's ship but a ship belonging to Dr Maturin. He might find it impossible to believe with anything but the very top of his mind that Stephen could conceivably own the *Surprise*, yet the fact was there, and although from the start they had agreed that the command of the frigate should be carried on in the former manner, with the captain having sole authority, he felt that some degree of consultation was the owner's due.

'Little do I know of naval battles,' said Stephen, having listened attentively to the arguments for and against carronades. 'For although I have been present at the Dear knows how many, I have nearly always been present at a remove, under the water-line, waiting for the wounded or dealing with them, poor souls; and my views are scarcely worth the uttering. Still and all, in this case why may not you endeavour to have your cake and eat it too? Why may you not train the new teams with much longer bouts of firing the great guns, and then if that do not answer, changing to the carronades? For if I understand you right, you are determined not to have some crews made up of old Surprises and others of new?'

'Exactly. That would be the best way of dividing the ship's company into two and a most disagreeable division at that – the right gunners on the one hand and the boobies on the other. There is bound to be a certain amount of jealousy – I wonder that it has scarcely shown itself yet – and I should do anything not to increase it: a happy ship is your only efficient fighting ship. But as for blazing away without regard, to see whether the boobies can be turned into right gunners, it would be far too expensive.'

'Listen, my dear,' said Stephen, 'I honour your desire to save our joint venture every penny you can, but I deplore it too, for there are savings that defeat their own ends so there are, and at times it seems to me that you pinch and scrape beyond what is right – beyond what is indeed useful to the cause. I am not to teach you your own profession, sure, but if a dozen barrels of powder a day will help make up your mind one way or another on a matter of such consequence, pray indulge me by using them. You often used to treat the ship to powder out of your own pocket when you were in funds from prize-money; and at present an impartial accountant would not value the expense at three skips of a louse. And in any event, as far as guns and gunnery are concerned you are to consider the immense saving brought about by Tom Pullings' knowledge of the world. The carronades did not have to be purchased.'

Tom Pullings' knowledge of the world by land was about the same as his captain's, and he too had been cruelly deceived before this; but he was intimately well acquainted with what might be called the limicole world, that of the minor and middling officials who lived with one foot upon the shore and the other on the sea – master-attendants and their seconds, people from the ordnance and navy boards, and the like – and though in all ordinary matters he was as honest as the rising sun he, like so many of his friends, looked upon government property as a world apart. He had gone down with Stephen when the *Surprise* was sold out of the service; he had feasted with many of his associates in the port; and the moment he learnt for sure of the frigate's new destination he spoke privately to those whose province it was, pointing out that her guns were hopelessly old-fashioned – they could never be re-issued now – the second reinforce and the muzzle astragal were in every case different from the present regulation piece, and it would not surprise him at all to learn that after so much wear they were in a sad state, honeycombed and only fit for scrap-metal. His friends understood him perfectly well, and although the *Surprise* was not actually paid for carrying her own guns away to Shelmerston, she was, by way of gratification allowed an equally defective set of carronades, which now made a small part of her 160 tons of ballast, stowed rather high to keep her stiff, in breaks fore and aft of her ground tier.

'No, indeed,' said Jack, smiling; and after a moment he went on, 'The service's notion of morality is an odd one and I should be puzzled to define it, in some cases. Yet I think almost every sailor knows just about where to draw the line between culpable capabarre and traditional friendly accommodation; and after all Tom did part with enough to leave no one out of pocket, at least on a scrap-metal basis – nothing very criminal in that, I believe. Which reminds me of another thing: punishment in a private man-of-war. You know what I think about flogging. I hate ordering it, and it had occurred to me to follow the quite usual practice in such ships of letting the hands decide the sentence.'

'They would scarcely be very hard on their shipmates, I imagine,' said Stephen.

'And yet they are, you know. During the great mutinies of ninety-seven the men kept the ships in strict order, and if anyone misbehaved – I mean misbehaved according to their notions – the grating was rigged. Sentences of two, three and even four dozen were by no means uncommon.'

'You decided against it, I collect.'

'Yes, I did. I reflected that if there should be bad blood between the new and the old hands – and you know how very difficult it is for a mixed ship's company to settle down together at first – then if an old Surprise were brought up for sentence, they might give him a really heavy dose; and I am damned if I will have any of my men flogged like that.'

'Let us hope that the constant firing of the great guns will bring them better friends. I have often observed that extremely violent noise and activity go with good-fellowship and heightened spirits.'

In the matter of extremely violent noise and activity, the *Surprise*'s surgeon and his mate were well served in the following days; Jack took Stephen at his word, and not only was the latter part of the forenoon watch given over to real gunfire, but in the evening quarters invariably saw the ship stripped for action, roaring away, sometimes even firing both sides at once, jetting flame in the midst of a dark pall of smoke, a self-contained volcano.

Martin was a quiet, humane being, and so, essentially was Maturin; they both disliked the enormous din – not merely the great crash of the repeated explosions, but the roaring of the carriages as they rushed in and out and the general thunder of feet racing to and from the magazines and shot-lockers – they both disliked the murdering-pieces themselves, and they particularly resented the way quarters would stretch out well into the last dogwatch, at a time when the ship was reaching some particularly interesting waters from the naturalist's point of view. Not only did the *Surprise* keep up such an infernal bellowing that no bird, no mobile jellyfish or pelagic crab would stay between the same horizons with her, but they were confined to the orlop, their station in time of battle and indeed of practice, for many an unfortunate was brought or even carried below with bruises, burns, crushed toes or fingers, and even once a broken leg.

Occasionally Stephen would make his way up the ladders to the main hatchway and peer fore and aft along the busy deck, and it did his heart good to see Jack Aubrey hurrying from gun to gun in the smoke, sometimes violently lit by the great stabs of flame, sometimes a tall wraith, advising the crews in a steady, wholly competent roar, shoving the awkward hands into the right position, sometimes clapping on to a side-tackle to run the gun up, sometimes heaving on a crow to point it, always with the same eager, intense concentration and a look of grave satisfaction when the shot went home and the gun-crew cheered.

It was tense work, a very fair imitation of a real engagement, for the guns were fired so fast they soon heated and grew skittish, leaping high and recoiling with frightful force. Once Jumping Billy broke both breeching and after side-tackle and since there was a heavy swell from the south-west the whole lethal mass of gun and carriage would have run amok on the deck if Padeen, who was enormously strong, had not wedged it with a handspike until his mates could make all fast. They worked as quick as ever they could, but all this time Padeen had to stand there with his excoriated hand pressed hard against the hot gun, so hot that his blood hissed as it ran down the metal.

Bonden, the captain of the team, brought him below, openly weeping with the pain, and as they came he could be heard comforting him in the loud and distinct voice used for invalids, foreigners and those who were not quite exactly (and Padeen for the moment had all these qualifications): 'Never mind, mate, the Doctor will soon put you right – what a rare plucked 'un you are, to be sure – you smell like a grilled beefsteak, mate – he may save your poor bloody hand too, I dare say – anyway he will take away the pain.' And reaching up, for Padeen was far taller, he gently wiped the tears from his cheeks.

The Doctor dealt with the pain, the very severe pain, by an heroic dose of laudanum, the alcoholic tincture of opium, one of his most valued medicines. 'Here,' he said in Latin to his mate, holding up a bottle of the amber liquid, 'you have the nearest approach to a panacea that has ever been found out. I occasionally use it myself, and find it answers admirably in cases of insomnia, morbid anxiety, the pain of wounds, tooth-ache, and head-ache, even hemicrania.' He might well have added heart-ache too, but he went on, 'I have, as you perceive, matched the dose to the weight of the sufferer and the intensity of the suffering. Presently, with the blessing, you will see Padeen's face return to its usual benevolent mansuetude; and a few minutes later you will see him glide insensibly to the verge of an opiate coma. It is the most valuable member of the whole pharmacopoeia.'

'I am sure it is,' said Martin. 'Yet are there not objections to opium-eating? Is not it likely to become habitual?'

'The objections come only from a few unhappy beings, Jansenists for the most part, who also condemn wine, agreeable food, music, and the company of women: they even call out against coffee, for all love! Their objections are valid solely in the case of a few poor souls with feeble will-power, who would just as easily become the victims of intoxicating liquors, and who are practically moral imbeciles, often addicted to other forms of depravity; otherwise it is no more injurious than smoking tobacco.' He corked his valuable flask, observed that he had a couple of carboys of it in the store from which it must be refilled, and went on 'It is now some time since they stopped their hellish banging, so perhaps we might go and take a cigar on the quarterdeck. They can hardly object to a little more smoke up there, I believe. Padeen, now, how do you come along?'

Padeen, his mind soothed by the Latin and his pain by the drug, smiled but said nothing. Stephen, having repeated his question in Irish with no better result, desired Bonden to see him lashed carefully into a hammock so that his poor arm could not wave about, and led the way to the quarterdeck.

Its emptiness startled him until he saw Mr West poised in the mizen shrouds and looking fixedly at the maintop, where the captain and Pullings could be seen with their parallel telescopes trained to the windward.

'Perhaps they have seen a Caspian tern,' said Martin. 'Mr Pullings noticed the plate in your Buffon – I had it open in the gunroom – and he said he believed he had seen them quite often in these latitudes.'

'Let us run up the rigging and surprise them,' said Stephen, feeling a sudden unusual gaiety – it was indeed the sweetest evening, balmy, a golden sky in the west and a royal-blue swell, white along the frigate's side and in her wake.

Several old Surprises, Stephen's patients these many years, came hurrying aft along the gangway, calling 'Don't look down, sir – Don't clap on to them ratlines – Hold the shrouds, the thick uns, with both hands – Easy does it, sir – Don't let go on the roll, whatever you do.' Presently anxious hands were placing their feet from below, up and up, a great way up, since the *Surprise* had a 36-gun ship's mainmast, and presently two delighted faces gazed into the top through the lubber's hole.

'Do nothing rash,' cried Aubrey. 'You have not come by your sea-legs yet. This is no time for skylarking. Give me your hand.' He heaved Stephen and then Martin up on to the platform, and once again Stephen wondered at his strength: Stephen's bare nine stone was perhaps natural enough, but Martin was far more stoutly built. For all that he was swung up with a lift as effortless as though he had been a moderate dog, held by the nape – swung right up through the hole and set down on his feet.

It was no Caspian tern that they were looking at, but a sail, and a sail no very great way off. 'What airs these eighteen-gun sloops do give themselves, to be sure,' said Pullings in a discontented voice. 'Look how she is cracking on! It will be moonrakers next. I will lay half a crown she carries away that foretopgallant studdingsail in the next five minutes.'

'Should you like to have a look at her, sir?' asked Jack, passing Martin his glass.

Martin clapped his one eye to it, silently recorded a stormy petrel, and after a pause exclaimed 'It has fired a gun! I see the smoke! Surely it will never have the temerity to attack us?'

'No, no. She is one of ours.' The boom reached them. 'That is a signal for us to lie to.'

'Would it not be possible to feign deafness, and to sail off in the opposite direction?' asked Stephen, who dreaded another encounter.

'Most private men-of-war avoid their public brethren if they can possibly outsail them,' said Jack, 'and the notion did occur to me when first she was sighted. But she altered course so quick – hauled her wind five points – that I am sure she recognized us; and if we were not to lie to after a gun, and this is the second, and if she were to report us, we might very well lose our letter of marque. *Surprise* is so damned recognizable: it is this most uncommon mainmast – you can smoke it ten miles away, like a bear with a sore thumb. Tom, I believe we must use the spare stump topgallant for ordinary cruising:

57

we can always sway this one up for a determined chase.'

Pullings did not answer: he crouched lower and lower over his telescope, poised on the top-rail, focussing more exactly, and all at once he cried, 'Sir, sir, she's the *Tartarus*!'

Jack caught up his glass, and after a moment and in what for him was a happy voice he said 'So she is. I can make out that absurd bright-blue bumpkin.' Another gun, and he said 'She has made her number. She will be signalling presently: William was always a great hand with the bunting.' Directing his voice downwards he called 'Mr West, we will close the sloop under all plain sail, if you please; and let the signal yeoman stand by. Yes,' he went on to those in the top as a distant line of flags appeared, 'there he is – such a hoist. Tom, I dare say you can read it without the book?'

Pullings had been Jack's signal lieutenant, and he still had much of the list by heart. 'I'll have a try, sir,' he said, and slowly read out '*Welcome* . . . repeat *welcome* . . . *happy see* . . . *beg captain sup* . . . *have message* . . . *hope* . . . now he is telegraphing: P H I Z . . . the signal-mid can't spell . . .'

On the quarterdeck the yeoman of the signal's mate, a Shelmerstonian, asked 'What does the brig mean with her P H I Z?'

'She means our doctor; which he is not a common twopence-a-go barber-surgeon but a genuine certificated physician with a bob-wig and a gold-headed cane.'

'I didn't know,' said the Shelmerstonian, staring hard at the maintop.

'You don't know much, mate,' said the yeoman, but not unkindly.

'The approaching vessel is under the command of Mr Babbington,' said Stephen to Martin. 'You remember Mr Babbington at the cricket-match?'

'Oh yes,' replied Martin. 'He made several late cuts, most beautifully timed; and you told me he had played for Hambledon. I should be happy to see him again.'

A little later he did see him again. The ships were lying to with their topsails backed, not very close, because of the growing sea: the *Tartarus*, with great politeness, had run under the frigate's lee, and her captain, his face bright red with the pleasure and exertion, was urging Jack not to get his boats off the booms – *Tartarus* had quarter-davits – *Tartarus* would lower her cutter down in a split second.

'Should be very happy, William,' called Jack in a conversational voice that carried easily over the hundred yards of sea. 'But it can only be a short visit: I have a great deal of southing to make up, and it is likely to turn dirty.'

The cutter splashed down; the guests were pulled across, and Jack, forgetting for a moment that he was in no position to give orders, said to the midshipman in charge, 'Larboard side, if you please,' for this meant no ceremony. Yet he recollected himself when the boat hooked on and he made Pullings and Stephen, both King's officers, take precedence. The momentary awkwardness was drowned by Dr Maturin's shrill indignation at the bosun's chair that had been rigged to bring him aboard dry, without anxiety: 'Why this injurious distinction?' he cried. 'Am not I an old salt, a hardened sea-dog?' But his voice changed entirely as he was set down on deck and found his old shipmate James Mowett standing there to receive him. 'Why, James Mowett, joy, how happy I am to see you. But what are you doing here? I thought you were to be first of the *Illustrious*.'

'So I am, sir. William Babbington is just giving me a lift to Gibraltar.'

'Of course, of course. Tell, how does your book come along?'

Mowett's exceptionally cheerful face clouded slightly: 'Well, sir, publishers are most hellish –' he began. But Babbington interrupted to welcome the Doctor aboard; and eventually, laughing and talking, he shepherded them all into the cabin, where they found Mrs Wray, a rather short-legged, swarthy young lady, but now downright pretty in her blushing confusion, her mixture of distress at being seen and her delight at seeing. Nobody was particularly surprised: all the men present had known one another at very close quarters for a very long time – the younger three had been in the midshipmen's berth of Jack Aubrey's first command – and they all knew that Babbington had been more attached to Fanny Harte, as she was before her marriage to Wray, than to any other of his innumerable flames. They might think it was coming it a little high to sail about the main with the wife of the acting second secretary of the Admiralty board, but they all knew that Babbington was rich by land, with enough parliamentary votes in his family to protect him from anything but serious professional misconduct, and they all had at least some notion of Wray's reputation. The only person really surprised, concerned, upset, was Fanny herself; she was particularly terrified of Mr Aubrey and sat as far from him as possible, wedged behind Stephen in a corner. Through the steady roar of voices he heard her whispering '. . . looks so very odd, don't it, almost compromising, so far from land – feel quite uncomfortable – am come for my health – Dr Gordon positively insisted upon a short sea-voyage – of course I have my own maid with me. Dear me: oh yes – So very glad to see poor Captain Aubrey tolerably well though dear me what the poor man must have been through and indeed he does look somewhat ancient now and who can be surprised; and rather severe – Shall I have to sit next to him at supper? But William has a letter from his wife and perhaps that will mollify him.'

'My dear Fanny,' said Stephen, 'he needs no mollifying. He has always liked you; and if there were any stones to throw he would never at any time reach for one. But tell me – last time we were talking about Captain Babbington you referred to him as Charles, which puzzled me; though no doubt he has several names to choose from, and prefers this to the others.'

'No, no,' said Fanny, blushing again. 'I was all confused that day – my mind if you can call it one was all of a fluster. We had been to Mrs Graham's masked ball a little while before, me as a Highland sheep and William as the Young Pretender – how we laughed, oh Lord! So I went on calling him Charles for days afterwards – he was so beautiful in his filibeg. You will think me a pitifully simple ninny, I am afraid. But, however, I am amazingly glad to hear what you tell about the

Captain's liking me. I shall sit next to him quite happy now. Lord, how I hope the suet pudding ain't raw: William made such a point of it for him. He swears it can be done in a trice in a Papin's digester; but puddings always took hours and hours when I was a girl.'

Supper was a cheerful meal, with a great deal of talk and laughter; and merely from the animal point of view it was most uncommonly welcome after the *Surprise*'s Spartan fare. At this point the frigate had no captain's cook and no gunroom cook; Jack had laid in no private stores, out of economy, Stephen out of absent-mindedness, the gunroom out of stark poverty; they all lived on ship's provisions and, since the ship was still in home waters, they drank not grog but small beer or swipes, smaller day by day. The cabin's only luxury was breakfast, which Killick had provided for on his own authority. During the course of the meal Babbington told them how the *Tartarus* had chased an amazingly swift-sailing American schooner for two days and a night, a certain blockade-runner trying to get into Brest or Lorient. 'I sent up light hawsers and cablets just as you used to do, sir,' he said, 'and I really believe we should have had her, if both main and fore topsails had not blown out of their boltropes at the same moment. Yet at least we set her three or four hundred miles south of her course, and she will have to run the whole gauntlet again before she sees the coast of France.'

'Mr Mowett,' called Stephen in the pause while the table was clearing to make room for the pudding, and pudding-wine – in this case Frontignan and Canary – was handing about, 'you were telling me about your publishers.'

'Yes, sir: I was about to say that they were the most hellish procrastinators –'

'Oh how dreadful,' cried Fanny. 'Do they go to – to special houses, or do they . . .'

'He means they delay,' said Babbington.

'Oh.'

'Yes. The book was supposed to come out on the Glorious First of June; then it was put off to Trafalgar Day; and now they say nothing but the anniversary of Camperdown will really suit the public mind. Yet at least it has this advantage – I can polish what is already down and I can add a new piece I have written.'

'Tip us the new piece, Mowett,' said Pullings.

'Yes, do,' said both Babbington and Fanny.

'Well,' said Mowett with mixed pleasure and modesty, 'it is rather long. So if I may, ma'am,' – bowing to Fanny – 'I will just say the end verses: it is about a battle, and these lines are meant to show the carnage at its height:

'Swift o'er the deep with winged speed they flew
And nearer now the frowning squadrons drew.
"Quick, clear the decks," the shrill-voiced boatswain
  cries
"Quick, clear the decks," each hollow ship replies.
Pale grows each cheek, with strange unwonted fear:
All stand a moment, lost in fixed amaze,
In awful silence, and unconscious gaze.'

A crash somewhere forward, not unlike the firing of a twelve-pounder, interrupted him, but only for a moment.

'Death strides from ship to ship with sweeping scythe;
On every poop damned fiends of murder writhe,
Demons of carnage ride th'empurpled flood,
Champ their fell jaws, and quaff the streaming
  blood . . .'

'Oh sir, if you please,' cried a tall, pale, frightened midshipman at the cabin door, 'Mr Cornwallis's duty, but the digesting machine has burst.'

'Is anyone hurt?' asked Babbington, rising.

'No one actually dead, sir, I believe, but . . .'

'Forgive me,' said Babbington to his guests. 'I must go and see.'

'How I hate foreign inventions,' said Fanny in the anxious pause.

'Nobody dead,' said Babbington, returning, 'and the surgeon says their scalds are of no consequence – will heal in a month or so – but I am very much concerned to have to tell you, sir, that the pudding is spread just about equally over the cook and his mates and the deck-head. They thought it might cook quicker if they put a smoothing-iron on the safety-valve.'

'It was a pity about the pudding,' said Jack, when they were back in the cabin of the *Surprise*, 'but upon the whole, I have rarely enjoyed a supper more. And although Fanny Harte may be neither Scylla nor Charybdis, they are very, very fond of one another, and when all is said and done, that is what really signifies. On his way down to Pompey William looked in at Ashgrove Cottage to ask Sophie how she did, and she gave him a note for me in case we should meet: all is well at home, and my mother-in-law is less of a trial than you might suppose. She declares I am cruelly ill-used and that Sophie and I deserve all her sympathy: it is not that she supposed for a moment that I am innocent, but that she thoroughly approves of what she thinks I did – if she had the least opportunity, she would certainly do the same, and so would any other woman who had a proper sense of duty towards her capital . . . Surely that is not the Marseillaise you are picking out?'

Stephen had his 'cello between his knees and for some time now he had been very quietly stroking two or three phrases with variations upon them – a half-conscious playing that interrupted neither his talk nor his listening. 'It is not,' he said. 'It is, or rather it is meant to be, the Mozart piece that was no doubt lurking somewhere in the Frenchman's mind when he wrote it. Yet something eludes me . . .'

'Stephen,' cried Jack. 'Not another note, I beg. I have it exactly, if only it don't fly away.' He whipped the cloth off his violin-case, tuned roughly, and swept straight into the true line. After a while Stephen joined him, and when they were thoroughly satisfied they stopped, tuned very exactly, passed the rosin to and fro and so returned to the direct statement, to variations upon it, inversions, embroideries, first one setting out in a flight of improvisation while the other filled in and then the other doing the same, playing on and on until a lee-lurch half-flung Stephen from his seat, so that his 'cello gave a dismal screech.

He recovered, bow and strings unharmed, but their free-flowing rhythm was destroyed, and they played no more. 'It is just as well, however,' said Jack, 'I should very soon have been most damnably out of tune. During the great-gun exercise I ran up and down without a pause, doing what half a dozen midshipmen usually do, each for his own set of guns – I never knew the little brutes were so useful before – and now I am quite fagged out. Hold hard, Stephen,' he cried, catching Stephen as he fell again, this time from a standing position. 'Where are your sea-legs?'

'It is not a question of sea-legs at all,' said Stephen. 'The ship is moving about in a very wild, unbridled manner. A crocodile would fall, in such circumstances, without it had wings.'

'I said it was going to be a dirty night,' said Jack, walking over to the barometer. 'But perhaps it is going to be dirtier than I thought. We had better snug down here as well. Killick, Killick, there.'

'Sir?' said Killick, appearing instantly, with a padded cloth under his arm.

'Strike the Doctor's 'cello and my fiddle down into the bread-room, together with the *article*.'

'Aye aye, sir. The Doctor's 'cello and your fiddle down into the bread-room it is, together with the *object*.'

Early in their marriage Diana had given Stephen a singularly splendid but nameless example of the cabinet-maker's art and ingenuity: it could be, and generally was, a music-stand, but various levers and flaps turned it into a wash-basin, a small but quite adequate desk, a medicine-chest and a book-case, and it had seven secret drawers or compartments; it also contained an astrolabe, a sundial, a perpetual calendar and a quantity of cut-glass bottles and ivory brushes and combs; but what really pleased Killick was the fact that its hinges, keyhole-scutcheons, door-straps, finger-plates, bottle-stoppers and all other fittings were massive gold. He took idolatrous care of it – the padded cloth was only the innermost of its three rough-weather cases – and he thought his captain's name for it improper, disrespectful and out of place. *Object* was the appropriate word – a word that had not the remotest connection with chamber-pot but on the contrary with holiness: holy object – and steadily, for years, Killick had tried to impose it.

Jack stood there for some moments, swaying easily with the twisting roll and pitch: his mouth was poised for whistling, yet in fact it was not music at all that ran through his mind but a set of calculations of position, currents, wind-force and the changing barometric pressure, all set against the immediate past and a background of a great many similar patterns in this part of the Atlantic. He put on a pilot-jacket, made his way to the quarterdeck and considered again, this time more instinctively, taking the feel of the wind at the sea directly. The topgallantmasts had already been struck, the hatches battened down, deadlights shipped and the boats on the booms double-griped. He said to Davidge, 'When the larboard watch is called, let the topsails be close-reefed. Call me if there is any change in the wind. Captain Pullings relieves you, I believe?'

'Yes, sir.'

'Then let him know what I have said. Good night to you, Mr Davidge.'

'Good night, sir.'

Back in the cabin he observed, 'This may be the blow I was talking about, when I said that an action or a storm pulled a mixed crew together wonderfully. I wish I may not have spoken like a fool. I wish it may not have been thought I desired a really violent blow.'

'My godfather's great-great-grandmother lived at Avila, in a house that I shall show you and Sophie when the war is done; she knew Saint Theresa, and the saint told her that more tears were shed over prayers that were granted than ever were shed over prayers that were refused.'

CHAPTER THREE

It was indeed the prayed-for blow, with the wind backing and strengthening until on the third day it reached the east-north-east, where it blew a hard gale for two watches on end without varying a single point; but then, with the *Surprise* under a close-reefed foresail and mizen storm-staysail, it began to veer and haul in a most confusing manner, and with even greater force.

At this point, well on in the graveyard watch, past three in the morning and with rain sweeping in almost solid sheets across the deck, Tom Pullings left his cot, put on his oilskins and crept up the ladder to see how Davidge was weathering it. Most of the watch were in the waist, sheltering from the worst of the spray, rain and flying water under the break of the forecastle, but the four men at the wheel and the officer standing behind them with one arm round the mizenmast, had the full choking sweep, and they kept their heads down to be able to breathe. Davidge was an experienced, capable seaman and he had known some monstrous seas in his time, yet even so he answered Pulling's enquiry, roared with cupped hands into his ear, with 'Pretty well, sir, I thank you. But I was thinking of calling the captain. Every time she comes up a trifle the helm gives a kind of judder, as though the tiller-ropes were either slipping on the barrel or growing frayed.'

Pullings shoved in among the men at the wheel – all of them Shelmerstonians as it happened – gripped the spokes, waited for her to come up after a heavy sea had knocked her head to leeward, felt the familiar hesitation, smiled, and called out 'It is only one of her little tricks in this sort of weather. She has always done it. We can let him lie in peace.'

Here a singularly prolonged and vivid series of lightning flashes lit up the low black clouds and the streaming ship; an enormous thunder-clap roared out almost within hand's reach; and the wind turned without the slightest warning, filling her staysail crack-full and bringing the *Surprise* four points up, heading straight into a very high sea with far greater speed. Her first plunge sent her entire forecastle deep under green water. The whole ship pitched at such an angle and with such force that Jack, dead asleep in his hanging cot after thirty-six hours on deck, was dashed violently against the beams overhead.

'I doubt she will ever rise again,' said Pullings to himself: and the glow of the binnacle lights showed the same grave expectation of the end on the faces of the men at the wheel. Everything seemed to be happening very slowly: the bowsprit and part of the forecastle heaved up as dark as a whale in the white turmoil: the enormous body of water filling the waist surged aft, flooding the quarterdeck and bursting the cabin bulkhead inwards. In the almost continual lightning the men of the watch could be made out clinging in bunches to the life-lines that had long since been stretched fore and aft between the guns; and before the water had poured from the quarterdeck scuppers Jack Aubrey was seen swarming up the ladder in his nightshirt.

'Does she steer?' he cried, and without waiting for the answer he took the wheel. The subtle current of vibrations between the thrust of successive waves on the rudder told him that all was well – his ship was answering as she had always answered. But as he peered down at the compass his blood dripping over the glass turned the binnacle light red.

'You are hurt, sir,' said Pullings.

'Damn that,' said Jack, heaving on the wheel to spill the wind. 'Haul up the foresail. Forward, there, look alive. Man the fore clew-garnets.'

This was in fact the last of the storm's more outrageous freaks. At the change of the watch the wind, returning to the east-north-east, whipped the clouds off the moon, showing a tolerably dismal sight – jib-boom, spritsail yard and bumpkins carried away, bowsprit and foreyard sprung, and spanker-boom broken, together with a great deal of cordage – dismal, but by no means desperate: no hands had been lost, little water had got in below, and although the cabin was bare, damp, austere and, with the loss of its bulkhead, stripped of all privacy, by breakfast-time the ship was making a creditable five knots under topsails alone in a moderate, slackening gale, the galley fires were in full action, and Killick had recovered his coffee-mill from the bilges, where some irrational blast had hurled it when the carpenter's mate went below to attend to the well.

Jack Aubrey had a bloody bandage round his head, obscuring one eye; he usually wore his long yellow hair neatly plaited and clubbed with a broad ribbon behind his neck, but so far he had not had time to wash the pints of clotted blood out of it and the stiffened locks stood out in all direction, giving him a most inhuman look; yet he was pleased with the way the ship's company had behaved – no moaning over short commons, though biscuit and cheese and small beer had been their fare for three days, no hanging back when they were required to go aloft, no skulking below, no wry looks – and his remaining eye had a benevolent expression. 'It is a remarkable fact,' he observed at breakfast, 'that in the course of many years at sea, I have never yet come across an incompetent carpenter. Bosuns, yes: because they often top it the tyrant and turn the hands awkward. Even gunners, who cannot always be brought to accept the slightest change. But not carpenters: they seem to have their trade born in them. Our Mr Bentley has almost finished the larboard bumpkin, and the bowsprit is already fished; we can – what the devil are they hallooing about in the waist?' Bending and looking forward under the long overhang of the quarterdeck, he saw the men who had been set to repair the gripes all standing up and shouting to the lookout at the masthead.

'I beg pardon for not knocking, sir,' said Pullings, running in, 'but there is nothing to knock on. A sail, sir, hull-down to leeward.'

'Hull-down? Then in that case we have time to finish our coffee,' said Jack. 'Sit down, Tom, and let me pour you a cup. It tastes a little odd, but at least it is hot and wet.'

'Hot and wet it is, sir,' said Pullings, and to Maturin, 'I am afraid you must have had quite a tiresome night of it, Doctor. Your cabin is a rare old shambles, if I may use the expression.'

'At one time I was deeply uneasy, I will admit,' said Stephen. 'It appeared to me through my dreams that some criminal hand had left the door open, and that I should be exposed to the falling damps. But then I perceived that there was no door, at all, and composed my mind to sleep.'

Immediately after breakfast the *Surprise* sent up her top-gallantmasts. It had soon become apparent that the chase was of no great consequence, but even so Jack began methodically spreading his canvas until she threw a fine bow-wave and the water sang down her side in a long curve, drawing a wake as straight and urgent as though she had been in pursuit of the Manilla galleon. She had the wind on her starboard quarter and now she could just bear weather studdingsails alow. This was the first time Jack had really driven her since they left Shelmerston; the first time the new hands had seen what she was capable of. The speed pleased every man aboard, and not only the speed, but the ship's gallantry – the way she took the seas under her bow and tossed them aside. Although the wind was more moderate, it now blew across the current and the remaining swell, cutting it up in an ugly fashion; yet she ran through the short, uneven seas as sweetly as ever a ship could run, and when the log was heaved at four bells in the forenoon watch, taking ten knots clean off the reel, there was a universal cheer.

There was very little likelihood of trouble, but even so Jack had the hands piped early to dinner, watch by watch; and most of them soon returned eating what they could carry, in order to miss nothing. The chase had early been seen to be a crippled fore-and-aft vessel, and the probability of her being Babbington's schooner grew stronger the nearer she came. Her foremast was sound and she had foresail, foretopsail and a fine array of jibs, while her people were working extremely hard on a jury-mainmast. But it was no use: even if they did manage to set a mainsail on it, they must be overhauled quite soon. Uninjured and beating into the wind she had outsailed the *Tartarus*; but crippled and above all sailing large she was no sort of match for the *Surprise*.

'So that is a schooner,' said Martin, as they watched her from the forecastle. 'How can you tell?'

'It has two masts. The second is now being attempted to be erected.'

'But brigs, ketches, bilanders, galliots and doggers also have two masts. What is the difference?'

'Curlews and whimbrels have a general similarity, and both have two wings; yet to any but the most superficial observer there is an evident difference.'

'There is the difference of size, eye-stripe and voice.'

'Bating the voice, much the same applies to these two-masted vessels. The accustomed eye,' said Stephen, not without a certain complacency, 'at once distinguishes the equivalent of eye-stripes, wing-bars and semi-palmated feet.'

'Perhaps I shall come to it in time,' said Martin. 'But there are also luggers, bean-cods and herring-busses.' And having considered this for a while he went on 'Yet surely it is very curious that apart from some pilchard-boats off the Lizard and the two men-of-war this should be the first vessel we have seen in such a length of days? I remember the chops of the Channel as being crowded with shipping – vast convoys, sometimes stretching over miles, and separate ships or small groups on their own.'

'I believe,' said Maturin, 'that to the mariner paths are stretched across the ocean according to wind and weather: these he follows with as little thought or concern as a Christian might walk down Sackville Street, cross Carlisle Bridge, pass Trinity College and so come to Stephen's Green, that haunt of dryads, each more elegant than the last. Captain Aubrey, on the other hand, has taken care to avoid these paths; as do, indeed, the smugglers whom that disagreeable cutter was looking for. I have little doubt that the vessel over there, the schooner, is one of them.'

In this Dr Maturin was mistaken: certainly the schooner was built for speed, and she might very well have carried contraband; but an even more discerning eye would have seen that while even now her small crew was furiously labouring with backstays and a maintopsail yard, another body of men and three women were clustered at the taffrail, waving and calling out – the very picture of a retaken prize, or rather a prize about to be retaken.

The *Surprise* swept closer and ranged alongside, taking the wind out of the schooner's sails: she fired a gun to windward and the schooner struck her colours.

'Shipmates,' said Jack Aubrey in a strong voice. 'You all know the terms of our agreement: if any man should so far forget himself as to rob any prisoner or ill-use him, or pillage the schooner, he will be turned out of the ship. Lower down the blue cutter.'

Yet the schooner, the *Merlin*, proved not to be a retaken prize at all; nor, whatever her captain – a French-speaking American from Louisiana – might say, was she an independent privateer: from the enormously prolix yet concordant testimony of the released prisoners it became apparent that she was the consort of a much more formidable ship, the *Spartan*, fitted out by a Franco-American consortium to prey on the West Indian trade of the Allies.

Jack knew the *Spartan* very well indeed, having chased her for two days and two nights through fair weather and foul, very foul. He had the highest opinion of her captain as a seaman, yet even so he was astonished to learn that he had taken no less than five prizes this voyage – two Port Royal sugar ships whose slowness had separated them from their convoy in the night, and three other West Indiamen with even more valuable cargoes of indigo, coffee, logwood, ebony, old fustic and hides that, being fast sailers, had chanced it on their own – and still more astonished to learn that they had all five been moored in the harbour of Horta, on Fayal, while their captains, the wives of those that sailed in married comfort, and the merchants of their factors had been packed off to France in the schooner, there to make what arrangements they could to ransom themselves, their ships and their cargoes.

'Why in Heaven's name did he not make for home as fast as ever he could pelt, with such a prodigious haul?' asked Jack. 'I have never heard of a private ship doing so amazing well in one short cruise: nor in a long one, neither.'

The answer was obvious enough, but nobody found it out until that evening. The schooner's captain gave nothing away, and his small crew was incapable of doing so, being totally ignorant of the general design; while Jack's and Pullings' minds were too much occupied with the former prisoners, the present prisoners and the refitting of the prize.

The American captain, the merchants and their wives had come aboard at once, and ordinarily, out of common decency, Jack would have invited them to dinner – the officers' hour was fast approaching. But at present he had no cabin in which to feed them; nor had he anything that he could put on the table if a cabin had existed.

'Mr Dupont, sir,' he said to the American captain, who was brought aft in reasonable privacy to show the *Merlin*'s papers, 'you could oblige me extremely, were you so inclined.'

'I should be happy to do anything in my power, sir,' replied Dupont, looking doubtfully at the figure before him: privateer captains had a solid reputation for brutal rapacity, and Jack Aubrey, tall, gaunt, unwashed, with yellow bristles glinting on his unshaved face, his bloody bandage bloodier still from recent activity and his blood-stiffened hair still hanging about him like a horribly dyed female wig – a figure from which the merchants' wives had recoiled with silent horror, though accustomed to the sea. 'Anything within my trifling means.'

'The fact of the matter is, we are short of provisions. For the ship's sake and for my own I should be distressed if I were obliged to offer you and these ladies a dinner consisting of salt beef, dried peas, and beer so small as to be scarcely drinkable.'

'Command me, sir, I beg,' cried Dupont, who had foreseen

something more disagreeable by far. 'My stores are not inconsiderable, though the tea is almost gone; and though my cook is black he is not without skill – I bought him from a man who fairly worshipped his belly.'

This was an erroneous form of worship, sure, but after such a blow and after so many days with little more than ship's bread, the captain and the officers of the *Surprise* felt that there might be something in it. Even their guests were agreeably surprised, for although the black man had always done them well, he now burst out with an extraordinary profusion: his *vol-au-vent* made the ladies stretch their eyes, and his apple tart was worthy of Fladong's.

The Surprises attributed this to his happiness and gratitude, for as soon as he came across, Killick, who as captain's steward was naturally in charge of these things, took him by the arm and called out slowly into his perhaps uncomprehending ear, 'You Free Man Now. Huzzay,' making the gesture of one released from his manacles, and thus signifying that the moment the black set foot on a British ship he was no longer a slave. 'You' – touching his breast – 'Free Man.'

'Parm me, sir,' said the black, 'my name is Smith.' But he spoke so gently for fear of giving offence, that, in the midst of the cheerful hullaballoo, his words had no influence whatsoever upon public opinion.

The feast took place in the gunroom, with Jack Aubrey, now smoothed and presentable, at one end of the long table and Pullings at the other; and when it was over at last Stephen and the man who had sat on his right walked on the leeward side of the quarterdeck, smoking little paper cigars in the Spanish manner. They conversed in Spanish too, for his companion, Jaime Guzman, was a Spaniard, originally from Avila in Old Castile, a partner in the Cadiz firm that had bought the greater part of the old fustic in the captured *William and Mary*: he could speak a certain amount of commercial English, but he had not been on speaking-terms with any of his fellow-captives for a great while. He was naturally a communicative man, yet for weeks and weeks he had been deprived of the power of speech, and now he talked with an almost alarming volubility.

'Those women, those odious, odious women,' he said, smoke issuing from his mouth and nose, 'would never allow me this indulgence even on the outward voyage. Voluptuous civets. But quite apart from that I found them all profoundly disagreeable. At one time I thought of helping them to improve; but then I reflected that whoever washes an ass's head loses both his time and soap. None of those people would ever have been received in Avila: your godfather's grandmother would never have consented to receive them.' An account of the Avila of Guzman's youth led to observations on the town of Almadén, where Guzman's brother supervised the business side of the quicksilver mines, and upon Cadiz, where Guzman now had his being, a sadly depraved and abandoned city. 'Like yourself, don Esteban,' he said, 'I am an old and mellow Christian, and I am very fond of ham; but there is as who should say no ham to be had in Cadiz. And why is this? It is because under the pretence of being new Christians the people are all half-Moors or half-Jews. There is no dealing with them, as my poor brother finds. They are shockingly dishonest, two-faced, grasping, and, like most Andalusians, inhumanly eager for the gain.'

'He who wishes to grow rich in a year, will be hanged in six months,' observed Stephen.

'They cannot be hanged too early nor too often,' said Guzman. 'Take the case of my poor brother, now. Quicksilver has to be sent to the New World, of course: they cannot extract gold without it. When England and Spain were at war, it was sent by frigates; but time and again they were taken, through the treachery of the wicked clerks of Cadiz, who told the Jews of Gibraltar the time of sailing and even the number of bags – for you must know, don Esteban, that quicksilver is packed in sheepskin bags of half a hundredweight apiece. Now that the war has changed, no frigates can be spared, still less ships of the line, so having waited for years my poor brother, pressed and harassed on all sides, has chartered the most powerful and trustworthy privateer on the coast, a ship called the *Azul*,

74

much the same size as this, to carry a hundred and fifty tons to Cartagena. A hundred and fifty tons, don Esteban, six thousand bags! Can you imagine six thousand bags of quicksilver?' They took several turns, imagining six thousand bags, and Guzman went on, 'But I am afraid the same wickedness has been at play. The *Spartan* knows very well that the *Azul* was to sail eight days ago and to touch at the Azores. That is why she is waiting. Perhaps she has taken her already. But the great point is this – and I know it because the young officers in the *Spartan* were very far from being as discreet as Mr Dupont – at the end of the month the American frigate *Constitution* and a sloop will pass by the Azores, coming from the south: the *Spartan* and her fleet of prizes will join her and sail back to the States in safety.'

Jack Aubrey had the rare virtue of listening to an account without interrupting, and on this occasion he even waited for the afterword: 'I tell you all this, Jack, as I received it. I have reasons for believing that Guzman's words about the Gibraltar Jews are mistaken – he longs for the return of the Holy Office with all its ardent zeal – but I think it by no means improbable that this Franco-American concern should know about the present shipping of quicksilver. And it seems to me that Guzman's good faith can hardly be questioned. What do you think of his observations about the *Constitution*?'

'If Mr Hull still has her, she is likely to be as near her day as is humanly possible; in their navy he has the reputation of being as regular as Old Time. We could not look at her, of course: she carries forty-four twenty-four-pounders – fires a broadside of 768 pounds – and has scantlings like a ship of the line. They call her Old Ironsides. Nevertheless . . .' His voice trailed away, and his mind's eye beheld a chart of the Atlantic between thirty-five and fifty degrees north, with the Azores in the middle. The *Spartan* would be cruising between St Michael's and St Mary, to windward, in order to have the weather-gage of the *Azul* when she appeared; and at this time of the year windward meant west or something north of west.

The recent blow might well have made the *Azul* lie to, though it might possibly have set her forward; on the other hand it would certainly have held the *Constitution* back, an essential factor in the plan that was taking shape in his mind – the plan of leading the *Spartan* to believe that the *Surprise* was the *Azul* at least long enough for them to come to grips. The dates, the recent weather, the probable speed of an efficient though unhurried *Azul*, and the *Surprise*'s actual position presented themselves in due order; and it appeared to him that if the breeze stayed fair and if the ship could log a hundred and twenty-five miles a day, there was a possibility of getting there in time. Not a very strong possibility, but one at least worth a great deal of effort.

'If the breeze stayed fair.' The barometer had been rising and falling most erratically and there was no forecast to be made: the only thing to do was to carry on without one, and straight away.

Once more Stephen heard the words 'there is not a moment to be lost', and then Jack ran up on deck to tell Pullings to set all hands to work on the refitting of the *Merlin* with the utmost speed. Returning, he said 'Stephen, would you be so kind as to interpret while I ask the gentleman about the *Azul*?'

From his connections and his calling, Guzman knew much more about ships than the ordinary landsman and his statement that the *Azul* had three masts, that she was barque-rigged and that she gauged about five hundred tons was perfectly convincing. So was his description of her as being painted a beautiful blue, with her black port-lids looking quite like those of a man-of-war; but these words made Jack Aubrey very pensive. Rigging the *Surprise* barque-fashion presented no difficulty, since it meant little more than unshipping her crossjack and mizentopsail yards, so that she carried only fore-and-aft sails on that mast; but this had been intended as a trial cruise, no more, and she carried little in the way of stores. Black portlids were very well, since she had them already, never having deviated from the Nelson chequer, but the blue sides – that was another matter.

'Pass the word for Mr Bentley,' he called: and when the carpenter appeared, 'Mr Bentley, what do we possess in the way of blue paint?'

'Blue paint, sir? We have just enough to give the blue cutter a couple of coats, spread thin, precious thin.'

Jack thought for a moment and said to Stephen 'Pray ask whether the blue is light or dark.' And when it appeared that the *Azul* was pale, as pale as the early morning sky, he turned to the carpenter to find how they stood in the matter of plain white. The answer was almost equally discouraging: a small hundredweight, with a shove.

'Well, well,' said Jack. 'We must do what we can. Tell me, Mr Bentley, how does the schooner come along?'

'Oh sir,' said the carpenter, brightening at once, 'our second-best spare foretopmast, with a butt coaked on to the heel and a little trimming at the partners, has made her as pretty a mainmast as you could wish. Bosun is setting up the shrouds this minute, and as soon as they are rattled down we can send up a mighty elegant topmast.'

'You have been uncommon busy, Mr Bentley, you and your crew.'

'Busy, sir? Bees ain't in it.'

Bees were not in it the next day either, for in the course of his nightly pacing of the deck Jack had hit upon a solution to the problem of changing the *Surprise*'s outward appearance. Several coats of blue, laid on thick, would be needed to cover the broad black bands above and below the white belt with the black portlids in it, and all the paint they possessed would not give more than a single coat to half one side: one coat would do on the white; it would be useless on the black. Yet paint would lie on canvas. Paint lay admirably well on white canvas; and on white canvas a willing mind could make a very little light blue go a very long way.

As soon as the idlers were called in the first morning light he had a long conference with the sailmaker, finding out just what was thinnest, whitest and most easily spared in the sailroom. Some good number 8 had to be sacrificed, but most of what they chose was poor thin stuff fit only for repairing topgallants or royals; for the *Surprise* was sold with all her equipment, and these sails had been sun-bleached and worn threadbare in the tropical Pacific during her last commission.

When the decks were dry – for nothing but imminent action could suspend the cleaning of the almost spotless ship – the canvas was spread, measured, remeasured, tried against the topsides, marked with great precision, tried again and eventually cut out and painted. The work was done on the quarterdeck, a very carefully shrouded quarterdeck. With the present sea running and the present speed required there was no question of hanging stages over the side, pinning the cloth and painting it there: the forecastle was too confined, and the waist, with its booms and the boats upon them had too little free run, while the gangways were in perpetual use, for the blessed north-north-easter had backed surprisingly in the course of the night – the weather was most unsettled – and although it was still a fine topgallant gale, it was now only one point free, so that continual attention to brace and bowline was called for, and very careful steering, to get the best out of her.

When Stephen came on deck, therefore, he found the after part of the ship unusually crowded, unusually busy. As it often happened, he had spent much of the night awake thinking about Diana and seeing brilliantly clear mental images of her, particularly one of her setting her horse at a monstrous fence where many men turned back and she flying over with never a pause; then at about two o'clock he had taken his usual draught, sleeping late and waking stupid. Coffee had revived him somewhat, and he would have sat with it longer if a glance at his watch had not told him that presently he must be about his duties, attending at the sick-bay with Martin while Padeen, the acting loblolly boy, beat a brass basin at the mainmast and sang

> Let the sick assemble here,
> For to see their Doctor dear,

78

since although he stammered extremely in ordinary speech he could sing quite well.

First, however, Stephen meant to look at the sky, bid his companions a good morning, and see whether the *Merlin* was in company: yet he had barely climbed the ladder – he had barely received more than a general impression of warmth, brilliant sunlight, brilliant sky and a crowd of blinding white sails reaching up into it – before a cry of universal disapprobation wiped the smile off his face.

'Sir, sir, get off it, sir.'

'Stand back, Doctor, for Heaven's sake stand back.'

'He will fall into the pot.'

The new hands were as vehement as the old Surprises, and much ruder – one called him 'Great ox' – for they had very soon understood what was afoot and nothing could have exceeded their eagerness to engage with the *Spartan* nor their zeal in preparing for the engagement, hypothetical though it might be.

'Hold hard,' said Jack, grasping him by the elbows. 'Do not stir. Padeen. Padeen, there. Bring new shoes for your master, d'ye hear me, now?'

The new shoes came. Stephen stepped into them, gazed at the blue-painted strips stretching away to the taffrail, at the stern but relenting faces turned towards him, said to Jack 'Oh how sorry I am. I should never have looked at the sky,' and then after a moment, 'Padeen, it is the face again, I find.'

The face it was. The poor soul's cheek was swollen so that the skin shone bright, and he answered with no more than a groan.

Five bells struck. Padeen beat his basin and chanted his piece in a strangled voice; yet although the *Surprise* had the usual number of hypochondriacs aboard the activity on deck was so earnest, intense and single-minded that not a single patient reported to the sick-bay except Padeen himself. Stephen and Martin looked at him sadly: for some time they had suspected an impacted wisdom-tooth, but there was nothing that either of them could do and presently Dr Maturin, having taken Padeen's pulse and looked into his mouth and throat again, poured out a generous dose of his usual physic, tied up the face in a rabbit-eared bandage, and excused him duty.

'It is almost your panacea,' observed Martin, referring to the laudanum.

'At least it does something,' said Stephen, drawing up his shoulders and spreading his hands. 'And we are so very helpless . . .' A pause. 'I came across a capital word the other day, quite new to me: psychopannychia, the all-night sleep of the soul. I dare say it has long been familiar to you, from your studies in divinity.'

'I associate it with the name of Gauden,' said Martin. 'I believe he thought it erroneous.'

'I associate it with the thought of comfort,' said Stephen, caressing his bottle. 'Deep, long-lasting comfort; though I admit I have no notion whether the state itself is sound doctrine or not. Shall we walk on to the forecastle? I do not believe they will persecute us there.'

They did not: they were far too busy with their sailcloth and with painting the white band on the ship's windward side, at least aft of the forechains, by leaning perilously out of the gunports. The forecastle deck was tilted eleven or twelve degrees to the sun, and the warmth was wonderfully agreeable after a long and desolate English winter. 'Blue sea, blue sky, white clouds, white sails, a general brilliance: what could be more pleasing?' said Stephen. 'A little sportive foam from the bow-wave does not signify. Indeed, it is refreshing. And the sun penetrates to one's very bones.'

After dinner, a hurried, scrappy meal, eaten with little appetite, the hands returned to their work, the surgeons to their contemplation, this time with the comfort of spare paunch-mats to sit upon. The *Merlin*, which had been sailing dutifully in the frigate's wake since dawn, a cable's length away, now overhauled her, making eight knots for the *Surprise*'s six, being so much faster close to the wind, and coming alongside hailed to say they were taking mackerel as fast as they could haul them in. Yet even this, the hands' favourite amusement – favoured above all in times of short allowance – could not disturb them from their task. Several of the new men could navigate; most of the old Surprises had a very fair notion of where the ship should lie if she was to have a chance of finding the *Spartan* in time; they had all seen the officers taking the sun's altitude at noon, and they had all, with great satisfaction, heard Davidge say 'Twelve o'clock, sir, if you please; and forty-three degrees fifty-five minutes north,' while the Captain replied 'Thank you, Mr Davidge: make it twelve.'

This meant that as far as latitude was concerned they had only about six degrees to run down in three days; there was perhaps still a little westing to be made up, but even so an average speed of five knots should do it handsomely; and hitherto no heave of the log had ever shown less than six. They might be in action, gainful action, on Thursday, and to spoil their chances of closing with the *Spartan* for the sake of a few mackerel, Spanish mackerel at that, would be foolish indeed.

Even so, between two strokes of his paintbrush Bonden ran forward with a basket of hand-lines, and Stephen and Martin, sharing strips of a red handkerchief between them as bait, plucked the fishes from the sea. They had half-filled the basket – they had caught sight of bonitoes pursuing the mackerel and their hopes were on tiptoe when there came the dismal cry 'Man overboard!'

'Come up the sheets,' called Jack, leaping over the painted strips and on to the hammocks in their netting. Men threaded their way with the utmost speed though still with the utmost care to their appointed ropes, and within the minute there was an all-pervading roar of sails flacking and slatting as they spilt the wind – a horrible sound. Jack had his eye fixed on the man, a painter who had leaned out just too far, and saw that he was swimming: he also saw the *Merlin* port her helm and drop the boat from her stern davits and he rebuttoned the coat he had been about to fling off. 'Back the foretopsail,' he said, and the way came off the *Surprise* – an odd dead feeling aboard, after so much urgent rhythmic life.

The *Merlin*'s boat, with the rescued man aboard, caught her up, and warned by vehement cries not to touch her sides, hooked on at the stern. Pullings came up the ladder, then some bags were passed after him, and last came the sodden object of their solicitude, an elderly Surprise by the name of Plaice, Joe Plaice: he was not welcomed aboard, though he had many friends and even relations in the frigate; he was not congratulated on being alive. 'I dare say the lubber dropped his —ing brush as well,' said one of his shipmates as he passed, bowed with shame. 'You had better go and shift yourself, Plaice,' said Jack coldly, 'If your improvident habits have left you any dry clothes,' and raising his voice he gave the series of orders that set the ship progressively back in motion – anything sudden might have endangered the topgallants, though it was true that the breeze already had a most unpleasant declining feel about it.

'How does she handle, Tom?' asked Jack, nodding towards the *Merlin*.

'Oh, as sweet as you could wish, sir,' said Pullings. 'Dry and weatherly, and steers herself. But, sir, the ladies are creating something cruel – insist upon being taken to England directly – will report us – will have the law of us – we shall be transported to Botany Bay.'

'I thought I heard them screeching when you hailed us about the mackerel,' said Jack. 'You can tell them it will soon be over. We cannot stay out any longer than Thursday unless we eat our belts and the soles of our shoes. I shall have to put the people on short allowance tomorrow in any event: four upon two. And even if we did stay out, I do not think there would be any chance at all of finding our man after Thursday. Indeed, Thursday is the very farthest limit; perhaps even beyond it.'

'As for belts and shoes, sir, I have ventured to bring a few comforts over, in those bags. They were voluntary offerings,' he added, seeing Jack's look of reserve and feeling that the word 'pillage' might have entered his mind.

'Thankee, Tom,' said Jack absently. He walked forward,

whistling, and scratched a backstay. 'If the wind hauls northerly again, and strengthens, as I hope and pray it will –'

'Amen, sir,' said Pullings, also scratching the backstay.

'– then we shall probably leave you behind. Do not crack on beyond reason to keep company – nothing beyond your topsails – but rendezvous at 37° 30′ N, 25° 30′ W. And thank you for the comforts.'

'37° 30′ N, 25° 30′ W it is, sir,' said Pullings, stepping over the taffrail.

Yet in spite of the whistling and backstay-scratching – and there was not a seaman aboard who did not follow his captain's example – the wind died sickeningly throughout the day and throughout the night, so that the *Merlin*, far from being left behind, was obliged to take in everything but a double-reefed foresail to keep her station.

'It is a rum go,' said Davidge, in the gunroom, 'but I could have sworn the wind would haul into the north, from the look of the day. So could the captain, although the glass was behaving so strangely. But perhaps drinking a health to Boreas might help.' He ladled punch into the glasses – Pullings' comforts had included a bottle of brandy for each of the officers – and said, 'Gentlemen, to Boreas.'

'To Boreas,' said West. 'But in decent moderation. No close-reefed topsails in the graveyard watch.'

'To Boreas, by all means,' said Stephen. 'Yet should he be absent, just for an hour or so in the morning, Mr Aubrey would have the consolation of swimming, and Mr Martin and I that of gathering specimens in the boat. We passed through a flotilla of nondescript jellyfish this afternoon, none of which could be reached with the hand-net.'

'We are very grateful for your mackerel and the bonitoes,' said West, 'but I do not believe there is a single man in the ship that would give up a mile of southing for all the jellyfishes in the world: no, nor yet a hundred yards, even if you were to throw in a barrel of oysters for every mess.'

Yet Tuesday's sun, rising over an opalescent sea with barely a tremor on its surface except where the boat made its trifling wake, lit up the surgeons as they peered into the translucent depths or took up small organisms and floating weed. Jack Aubrey did not in fact console himself by swimming, though he had a great mind to it after a sleepless night, trying to urge the ship on in the dying breeze by force of will, while at every other glass the log took out less and less of its line, until at last not even a single knot ran off the reel, in spite of all the help the quartermaster could give it.

No swimming. As soon as there was light enough he began to organize stages over the side, and by a little after breakfast-time the ship, though drooping in every sail, was once again a hive of industry.

'This is perfect,' he called over the still water to Pullings in the *Merlin*, a quarter of a mile abeam and turning as she very slowly drifted farther. 'This is just what I have been praying for.'

'May God forgive you,' murmured Killick, a few feet below him in the now re-assembled cabin.

'Now we can finish off the upper black-strake and then deal with the lower: we can get right down to the copper.'

A few of the simpler men from Shelmerston may have been deceived, but those who had long sailed with Captain Aubrey either nodded to one another or smiled privately; they knew very well that there were times when a commanding officer was required to talk just like this, just as a parson was required to preach on Sundays. They did not believe him for a moment; yet this did not affect their purpose; and although the watch after watch of calm had taken away from their first enthusiasm, they worked on doggedly. If there was the slightest chance of getting the barky to the height of the Azores by Thursday, it would not be their fault if she was not ready; and indeed by noon both lower black-strakes were coated with sailcloth pinned tight with close-set copper nails above and below the waterline, the guns having been run across the deck in either case to heel the ship. The very last of the blue paint had been laid on, parsimoniously scraped out to cover the greatest possible extent; the blue did not quite meet the surface, but that did not signify, since it shaded down to a rim of mixed filth and cook's slush, in the usual sea-going way. At all events Guzman reported from Stephen's boat that she and the *Azul* now looked as like one another as two chick-peas from the same pod.

Now all that remained was changing her into a barque and striking down her tall and too-recognizable maintopgallant-mast; but this was an operation that Jack meant to leave to the last, since the rig would reduce her speed, and in the present case speed was everything.

It was everything, to be sure: and at noon the ship lay there motionless, not having run eighty miles since the last observation. Crueller still, crueller by far, was the breeze when at last it came, whispering up from the south right in their teeth and strengthening hour by hour.

The *Surprise* dutifully beat up into it, tack upon tack; but it was with death in their hearts that the men braced round the heavy yards and trimmed the sails to the finest possible degree.

Stephen and Martin came upon deck at the second cry of 'All hands about ship' after a prolonged session with their pelagic crustaceans, some of them certainly undescribed and quite unknown to science. 'What a pleasure it is to be moving again,' cried Stephen. 'How the ship bounds along!'

He caught Jack Aubrey's black look of contained exasperation, his tight-shut mouth; he noticed the grim faces of the waisters and afterguard, the general silence; and at the roar of 'Helm's-a-lee' he murmured 'Let us go downstairs again.'

They sat drawing their specimens by the light of the great stern window, and when Killick came in Stephen said to him, 'Pray, Killick, what is the general situation?'

'Well, sir,' said Killick, 'as far as I can see, we might as well pack up and go home. Here we are, plying to windward as hard as ever we can, toiling and moiling, all hands about ship every other glass; and what do we gain? Not above a mile's southing in the hour. And if the wind gets up, if we have to take our topgallants in, we shall lose ground. The barky is a

85

very weatherly ship, but even she makes some leeway; and if it comes on to blow right chronic, even she must lose some southing.'

'Yet surely,' said Martin, 'If this wind holds us back, it must do the same for the *Azul*?'

'Oh,' cried Killick with a kind of howl, 'but don't you see the *Azul* as she calls herself is sailing west? Not south like we, but west? Sailing from Cadiz to St Michael's? So she has this wind on her beam, on her *beam*' – pointing to the ship's side to make his meaning clear – 'so there are those buggers with their sheets hauled aft, standing there with folded arms, spitting to leeward like the lords of creation, making six or seven knots as easy as kiss my hand, bearing off our lawful prize . . .' Indignation choked him.

Yet it was this same Killick who stood by Stephen's cot the next morning, Wednesday morning, with a shining face, shaking the ropes on which it hung and repeating 'Captain's compliments and should the Doctor like to see a glorious sight? Captain's compliments and should the Doctor like to see . . .'

As Stephen slipped from his cot he observed that the deck was tilted by at least twenty-five degrees: leaning cautiously against the bulkhead he stepped into his breeches, huddled on a disgraceful old greatcoat, and emerged blinking into a brilliant day.

The *Surprise* was lying right over, white water all along her lee-rail and spouting high from her cat-head; the strong breeze was a little too far forward for studding-sails to set, but with Jack Aubrey's old practice of sending up cablets and light hawsers as extra preventer-stays, she nevertheless had topgallants abroad, and she was tearing along at a splendid rate – happy seamen all along the windward gangway, laughter on the forecastle.

'There you are, Doctor,' cried Jack. 'Good morning to you. Ain't it charming? The breeze veered in a black squall soon after you had turned in, and began to blow from west by south in the morning watch; and I believe it may haul north of west. But come with me – mind your step.' He led him still blinking and heavy to the taffrail and said 'There. That's what I woke you up for.'

At first Stephen could not make it out: then he realized that the near sea to leeward was filled, *filled* with whales: an immense school of sperm whales travelling in one direction, passing above, below, round and amongst a school of right whales travelling in the other. Everywhere he looked there were huge dark forms rising, blowing, sometimes lying awash, more often diving again almost at once, often showing their enormous flukes above the surface as they did so. Some were so close he could hear their breath, their strong, almost explosive outward breath and their heaving inspiration.

'Lord, Lord,' he said at last. 'What a splendour of creation.'

'I am so glad you saw them,' said Jack. 'In five minutes time it would have been too late.'

'How I wish I had sent to tell Martin.'

'Oh, he was about already. He is in the mizentop, as you see.'

So he was, the intrepid soul, and they waved their pocket handkerchiefs to one another; and as he put his away Stephen looked covertly at the sun. It was on the left hand, not far above the horizon; the ship was therefore racing down towards the longed-for south, and he could safely say, 'I give you joy of your propitious wind.'

'Many thanks,' said Jack, smiling but shaking his head. 'It is certainly better late than never at all. Let us go and drink our coffee.'

'You have but little hope, I am afraid,' said Stephen in the cabin, balancing his cup as well as he could.

'Not very much, I confess. But if the wind does haul northerly, and if it only holds true, there is just a chance we may run off the distance. If nothing carries away,' he added, touching the table-top.

Nothing had carried away by the midday observation, when it was found that the *Surprise* had made eighty-seven miles of southing, almost all of it since the morning watch. The wind, though slightly less strong, was still veering, and a little after dinner-time the first weather studdingsails appeared. All hands watched how they set with the keenest attention; and shortly afterwards, when the log was heaved, the report 'Ten knots and three fathoms, sir, if you please,' was greeted with a satisfied chuckle all along the weather gangway to the forecastle.

The ship was filled with reviving, ebullient hope: only Padeen did not share it. In the morning Stephen had poulticed him, no more, hoping to deal with a possible impostume by that means; he had fed Padeen soup with a spoon at noon, renewing the poultice; but now in the afternoon watch the pain grew worse, and Padeen, rising from his hammock, went to the medicine-chest, dosed himself with laudanum, and stood considering the bottle, a long, thin dropping-flask with marks on its side. Having pondered between the spasms of pain, he put the bottle under his jacket and walked to Mr Martin's cabin: there was nobody in this part of the ship, but even if there had been he would have passed unnoticed, since he looked after Mr Martin just as he looked after the Doctor. Here he took Martin's bottle of brandy, filled the laudanum to its former mark, topped up the brandy with water, and replaced the bottles in their lockers and himself in his hammock. He was quite alone, not only because most of the hands were taking such pleasure in the frigate's course, but also because the cry 'Sail ho!' from the masthead had brought all those who were busy elsewhere up from the store-rooms, the cable tiers or the manger at the run.

The sail was already visible from the deck, some five miles to leeward, yet with the *Surprise* having so much canvas spread and with the forecastle so regularly swept by green water, it was not easy to get a clear view of her, even from the tops; but perched high on the main jack-crosstrees above the top-gallantsail – a post familiar to him from his youth, when he was a midshipman in this same ship – Jack had the whole ring of the horizon at his command. The stranger, though ship-rigged, was quite certainly not the *Spartan*: apart from anything else she was much too far north. In spite of her Spanish colours she was most probably British, square-sterned and British-built: most probably a West-Indiaman. She had been crowding on sail ever since they caught sight of one another, and now, as he watched, her mizen topmast carried away and she was brought by the lee in a horrible flurry of canvas.

If she chose, the *Surprise* could bear up and be alongside her in half an hour; but even if there had been an equal chance of her being lawful prize, that half-hour was too precious to be spared. He shook his head, swivelled about on the jacks and trained his glass northwards. The *Merlin* had been in sight in the forenoon watch; at present there was not so much as a nick in the horizon.

He returned to the deck, the slender topgallant shrouds bending under his weight, and as he stepped from the hammock-cloth to a carronade and so to the quarterdeck, the ship's company gazed silently at his face. He walked over to the binnacle, looked at the compass, and said 'Very well thus. Dyce and no higher.' The course was not to be altered. There was a certain sigh, a sort of rueful acquiescence – a general sound not unlike the expiration of two or three whales fairly close at hand – but nowhere a hint of disagreement or discontent.

As the afternoon wore on the wind lost rather more of its strength, but it also veered still farther, steadying at north-west by west, almost on her quarter; and as it moderated so the *Surprise* spread more canvas: studdingsails alow and aloft, royals, the rarely-seen but useful spritsail topsail, all the jibs that would set and a cloud of staysails. It was a noble spectacle, filling all hands with pleasure as something excellent in itself, not only as a means to an end. Jack was contemplating skysails when the sun, slanting westwards to a deep cloudbank away to starboard, made it clear that this would never do. Far from it: a great deal must be taken in before the watch was set, so that no sudden force of wind should oblige him to call all hands in the middle of the night; for although the breeze seemed firmly settled in the north-west, it might very well change in strength. A quiet night was of the first importance. All hands had been hard at it ever since last week's thundering blow began, and although in general their spirits were still high this was by no means the same thing as a three-day chase with the enemy in sight, which could keep men going without food or rest; and he saw evident signs of exhaustion. His own coxswain, for example, looked grey and old. The foremast jacks had little enough sleep as it was, without having that little broken during their watch below; and this was more than ever true before an engagement.

The likelihood of an engagement tomorrow had never been anything but small and now it was smaller still; yet only a fool would reduce it even more, reduce it to the vanishing-point, after so much pains and such a glorious run. But then again there was such a thing as being too cautious by half: for the chance to have any existence at all the *Surprise* must be present somewhere to windward between St Michael's and St Mary. 'All these things have to be balanced against one another,' he said inwardly as he paced fore and aft; and the result of his balancing was that the *Surprise* sailed into the night with her topgallants abroad, whereas ordinarily she would have furled them and would have taken a reef in her topsails. She had done remarkably well today, and if she made no more than a steady five knots during the night she would still run off her two hundred miles from noon to noon: by daylight he should have his landfall on the starboard bow, the high rocky eastward tip of St Michael's.

'Jack,' said Stephen, looking up from his ruled paper as the cabin door opened, 'I have just finished transposing a Sammartini duo for violin and 'cello. Should you like to try it after supper? Killick promises us pease pudding from the galley, followed by his own toasted cheese.'

'Is it long?'

'It is not.'

'Then I should be very happy. But I mean to turn in early.

Since Tom is away in the schooner, I shall take the middle watch.'

Like many sailors Jack Aubrey had early acquired the habit of going to sleep almost as he put his head on his pillow; but this night he remained at least in part awake. It was not that his mind was torturing itself again with detailed memories of his disgrace, nor with the long-lasting and potentially ruinous law-suits that hung over him, but rather that, physically and mentally very tired indeed, he skimmed along the surface of the immediate present; he listened to the sound of the water against the ship's side and that composite, omnipresent voice that came from the wind in the taut rigging and from the play of the hull, while at the same time, and more consciously, he traced the pattern of the music they had played, occasionally drifting away but always hearing the bells in due succession and always aware of the state of the wind. It was a strange state, very rare for him, almost as restful as sleep and much nearer quiet happiness than anything he had known since his trial.

He was up and dressed when Bonden came to call him and he went straight up on deck. 'Good morning, Mr West,' he said, looking at the gibbous moon, clear in a small-flecked sky.

'Good morning, sir,' said West. 'All's well, though the breeze slackens a little. You are an uncommon good relief, sir.'

'Turn the glass,' said the quartermaster at the con; and Plaice, recognizable from his wheeze, padded forward and struck eight bells.

While the watches changed Jack studied the log-board. The wind had not varied a single point in direction, though as he knew very well it had decreased and readings of under six knots were more usual than those over.

It was a warm night, though the breeze was north of west, and walking aft to the taffrail he saw with pleasure that the wake was luminous, a long phosphorescent trail, the first he had seen this year.

He heard the usual reports: six inches of water in the well

– very moderate indeed after such a blow; but she had always been a dry ship. And the latest heave of the log: almost seven knots. Perhaps the wind was picking up.

The watch could scarcely have been more peaceful: no call to touch sheet or brace, no movement but the helmsmen, the quartermasters and the lookouts spelling one another, the heaving of the log, the striking of the bell. Now and then a man might go forward to the head, but most remained gathered there in the waist, a few talking in low tones but most choosing a soft plank for a doze.

Jack spent the greater part of it gazing at the hypnotic wake as it spun out mile after mile, or watching the familiar stars in their course. The breeze did freshen from time to time and once he was able to chalk seven knots two fathoms on the board, but it was never enough for any change of sail, nor did it alter this faintly moonlit, starlit, dreamlike sailing over the dark sea except by adding a certain deep satisfaction.

He handed over to Davidge and the starboard watch at four in the morning, gave orders that he was to be called with the idlers, went below and plunged straight into his usual profound sleep.

At first light he was on deck again. The breeze was much as he had left it, though somewhat more westerly, the sky clear, except for cloud and haze to starboard. The idlers had already gathered round the pumps – a frowsty, squalid group, not yet washed or brushed – and well clear of the horizon to larboard the newly-risen Venus in her pale blue heaven looked all the purer by contrast. Having bade the quarterdeck good day, Jack said 'Mr Davidge, let us merely swab the decks this morning, and flog them dry. Then, with the idlers at hand – for pumping will not take them ten minutes – I believe we may start making sail.'

That was one of the advantages of a crew of this kind: with the emphatic exception of the surgeon and his mate all the idlers, the men who did not stand a watch, were very able seamen as well as being highly skilled in their particular line – the sailmaker and his mates, the armourer, the gunner's mates, the carpenter's crew, the cooper and all the rest of the special-ists. Another advantage, reflected Jack Aubrey as he made his way up the weather rigging to the maintop and beyond, climb-ing easily, without hurry, scarcely thinking of his lofty path any more than a man going upstairs to the attic at home – another advantage was the hands' singular eagerness to please, not out of imposed discipline, but to avoid being turned away – something quite unknown in his life at sea. In an hour or so hammocks would be piped up, and they would be stowed in the nettings, properly rolled, in five or six minutes, without driving, oaths or rope's ends: not many King's ships could say as much.

'Good morning, Webster,' he said to the lookout at the topgallant-crosstrees.

'Good morning, sir,' said Webster, moving a few steps down the lee shrouds, leaving the crosstrees free. 'Nothing to westwards that I can make out, but maybe with your glass . . .'

It was a very good glass, a Dolland achromatic; and sitting upon the crosstrees Jack focussed it carefully on the western horizon, sweeping the half-circle. But where St Michael's should have been was cloudbank, dark, sullen, purplish-grey and impenetrable. After a while he pushed the telescope shut, slung it over his shoulder, nodded to the lookout and returned to the deck.

There, while his mind checked and rechecked the figures for the night's run, he began to spread more canvas. Well before hammocks were piped up the *Surprise* was making just over eight knots, and as he went below to work out his calculations once more on paper and transfer them to the chart, with various allowances for leeway and error he said, 'It is absurd to be so anxious. I am become a perfect old woman.'

'On deck, there,' called Webster from the masthead. 'Land three points on the starboard bow.'

His shrill voice pierced the general noise of both watches moving about and talking much more than was usual in a King's ship: it came clear through the open cabin door, and Jack, with the chart in front of him and a tell-tale compass in the beam over his head, saw that Ribeira Point in St Michael's should in fact bear south-west by south, exactly three points on the starboard bow.

A knock on the door-jamb, and West came in. 'Land, sir,' he reported. 'Three points on the starboard bow. I caught sight of it from the deck for a moment – the haze is lifting – and it seemed to me about ten leagues off.'

'Thank you, Mr West,' said Jack. 'I shall come and look at it by and by.'

A moment later the bosun's call piped all hands to breakfast, and as though he had been waiting for the sound Stephen hurried in. 'God love you, Jack,' he said, talking rather loud over the muffled thunder of feet, 'what land is this? Not our old friend Cape Fly-Away, I trust?'

'Unless Cape Fly-Away bears exactly south-west by south about ten leagues, this should be the north-east point of St Michael's,' said Jack, showing the chart, with his parallel rulers along the line of bearing.

'Yet you do not seem elated?'

'I am pleased, certainly. But no, I am not as who should say elated. Feelings are curious: they come and go. And in any case this is only one small step; there is still a great way to go.'

'If you please, gents,' said Killick, 'there is a couple of fresh flying-fish, just come aboard, that should be ate hot.'

'There is a charming unction in a really fresh flying-fish,' said Stephen, setting to his plate. 'May I trouble you for the bread-barge? Tell, Jack, did I understand you to say the north-*east* point of the island?'

'Yes. Ribeira it is called. There is a tall cross on top of the headland, as I hope we shall see in an hour or two.'

'Yet I had supposed that if we were lucky enough to find St Michael's at all, a mere speck in the vast breadth of ocean, that we should run down its western side, so as to reach a point midway between St Michael's and St Mary, though somewhat to windward.'

'That is the point we aim at, to be sure. But we must reach it from the east, as though we were sailing from Cadiz. My idea is to run down to 37° 30' N or a little beyond, and then, avoiding the Formigas, to turn westwards, slowly beating up as though we were going to touch at Horta, in the hope that the *Spartan* will be waiting for us. Or rather for the *Azul*.'

'How do you estimate our chances at present?'

'Almost everything depends on the south wind that headed us on Tuesday. If it was blowing down here, and not so hard as to make *Azul* lie to, then it would have hurried her westward and we shall be too late. If it did not blow here, or if it had a great deal of west in it, coming off the islands, then we may still find the *Spartan* waiting. But whether or no, you will still see St Michael's, and if we skirt the little low islands and reefs of the Formigas, you may find some prodigious curious seaweeds and creatures. Tell me, Stephen,' he began after a pause, and he was going to continue 'do you ever feel that what you are doing is not quite real – that you are playing a part – and that what seems to be the present don't really signify? Is it quite usual? Or is it something unhealthy, the beginning of losing your mind?' But it occurred to him that this might be too nearly related to complaint and he substituted 'How is your Padeen coming along?'

'His face is pitifully swollen still, but he has a power of fortitude.'

'Could you do with another flying-fish, sir?' asked Killick. 'They are coming aboard in coveys.'

Throughout the forenoon watch, when they were not trimming sails or going through the great-gun exercise in dumbshow, the greater part of the ship's company gazed at St Michael's, steadily coming nearer, clearer, and now by noon, right on the beam, the tall cross on the headland stood sharp against the sky.

The breeze had backed into the west; at the same time it had slackened, so that the last heave of the log gave only five knots. But this caused no despondency, because the midday observation – and the report was openly listened to, without the least disguise – showed that they had run 210 miles between noon and noon. Once again the general cheer; and once again

Padeen did not hear it, being right down in the orlop, locking away the laudanum, topped up to an even greater extent than before.

'After dinner we must think of rigging the mizenmast barque-fashion,' said Jack to the officer of the watch. 'Mr Bulkeley has been turning it over in his mind and he has laid the cordage aside, together with the blocks: I do not believe it will take very long.'

There was also the maintopgallantmast to be changed, and as soon as dinner was over the work of rousing out the necessary spars began, a tedious business, since the boats, which were stowed upon them, first had to be got over the side, slung from the main and the fore yards. Stephen and Martin, who had a singular genius for getting in the way during manoeuvres of this kind but who were unwilling to go below on such a day, particularly with so many cliff-nesting birds about, took their mats and fishing-lines into the forecastle. 'How very much slower we are going,' observed Martin.

'I made the same remark to the Captain,' said Stephen, 'but he urged me not to fret – it was only because we were in the lee of the island. In an hour or so we shall be spinning along as merrily as ever.'

By the time the gig, pinnace and jolly-boat were towing astern the *Surprise* had rounded Madrugada Point, and there, running before the wind in a course that would soon cross hers, was a gaily-painted St Michael's tunny-boat.

'Back the foretopsail,' called Jack, and the *Surprise* lost most of her way. The tunny-boat altered course in answer to this obvious invitation. 'Pass the word for the Doctor.' And when he came, 'Doctor, I am sure you can speak the Portuguese.'

'I am moderately fluent,' said Stephen.

'Then be pleased to buy some fish if they have any,' said Jack, 'and then to ask them just what winds they have had here this week: you might ask for news of the *Spartan*, if you think proper. But it is the wind that really matters, above all the wind on Tuesday. Was it southerly? Was it strong?'

The boat came alongside: baskets of fish were handed up –

silvery bonitoes about three feet long – and pieces of money, counted loud and plain so that there should be no mistake, were handed down. Then followed a rambling conversation between Maturin and the boat, while West and Davidge had the launch and both cutters hoisted out and lowered down.

Jack went below, and it was here that Stephen told him the bad news: the wind had blown hard from the south on Tuesday, and the tunny-boat's uncle had seen a barque pass westwards yesterday, as though from Cadiz for Fayal. Though it was true that the old gentleman had neither named nor described the vessel apart from remarking that she wore Spanish colours.

'Well, well,' said Jack. 'It was but a very long shot at the best. Still, let us have a can of small beer to celebrate the fishes: there is nothing better than a steak of bonito, grilled. Killick. Killick, there: let us have two cans of beer and a biscuit to help it down with.'

The cool beer was not unpleasant at this time of day, and as they drank it Jack observed, 'If I were a superstitious man, I should say that I had brought this on my own head by crowing so loud and hearty about yesterday's run – about making my landfall so exactly and in such uncommon good time.'

'I never heard you crowing.'

'No, but fate did. Believe me, Stephen, there is more in these feelings than old wives' tales and not walking under ladders. It seems to me that you have to treat destiny or fortune or whatever is the right word with a proper respect. A man must not bounce or presume, but he must not despair neither, for that is ill-bred; so although you may laugh in your sleeve I mean to go through the motions of changing our rig and cruising between St Michael's and St Mary for the rest of the day. Then tomorrow, having done the thing handsomely, we can go home; and if you choose, we will go by the Formigas and land you there for half a tide.'

The *Surprise*, now a pale-blue-sided barque, worked slowly to windward between the two islands. By the middle of the first dog-watch she was in the position her captain had laid down as ideal; but no *Spartan* did she see. Nor was there any expectation of seeing her, since many of the hands could at least follow some Portuguese; their combined knowledge had led them to an accurate conclusion, and it said a great deal for their respect for Jack Aubrey that the change in the frigate's rig had been carried out with such accuracy and speed, and that there was no slackness or murmuring at the present standing off and on – a wearisome series of turns, slower, much longer, but not altogether unlike those of her captain as he paced out his mile after mile between the taffrail and a certain ringbolt just abaft the gangway, a ringbolt that his turning heel had long since polished to a silvery brightness.

This evening there was no beating to quarters, and in such cases the last dog-watch was usually a time of music and dancing on the forecastle. But today the hands sat about in the warmth of the evening, talking quietly.

The sun set, leaving rosy light behind it for a while; hammocks were piped down, the watch was set, and the ship settled into her routine for the night, moving slowly north and south under reefed topsails, and drawing her boats after her. According to the letter of his private law, Jack Aubrey should have had them hoisted in; but as all the changes of this afternoon were to be reversed tomorrow for the homeward voyage and as the tired, dispirited men would have the heavy, useless labour twice over, he left things as they were.

Sitting at his desk in the great cabin he began a new sheet in the serial letter that he wrote to Sophie, a kind of private journal that she was to share.

'Here we are, my dearest Sophie, south of St Michael's in a sea as warm as milk: how I hope your weather is half as kind as ours. If it is, the yellow rose on the south wall will be blowing finely.

'I hope to see it in a week or so, for we turn back tomorrow. Our voyage has not been quite as fortunate as I had hoped, but as I told you we have one quite handsome little prize in the *Merlin*, and the new hands are shaping uncommonly well.

'Stephen says he has rarely seen a healthier crew – not a man in his list except for poor Padeen, with the face-ache – and this he puts down to their having very little to eat and nothing but small beer to drink. At the moment he and Mr Martin are in the boats towing astern, fishing for luminous insects with little hand-nets and strainers; and I must confess –'

Here his letter broke off, for he heard something so like gunfire that he put down his pen. In another moment it was repeated and he ran up on deck. Davidge and West were leaning their telescopes on the larboard rail. 'Right on the beam, sir,' said West. 'There they go again.' And clear under the darkness of the eastern sky Jack saw the gun-flashes, widely separated.

'They are ten miles away,' said Davidge, when the sound reached them at last.

'And at least half a mile apart,' said West.

A long pause while they studied the eastern horizon with the most extreme intensity, a pause during which the left-hand gun fired twice and that on the right, the southern gun, three times.

'Mr Davidge, put the ship before the wind,' said Jack.

'Shall I hoist in the boats, sir?' asked Davidge.

'Not yet. But pray get the Doctor aboard,' said Jack, hurrying below for his glass.

The ship turned slowly on the gentle breeze, steadying with her head due east, and from the foreyard he commanded a vast expanse of sea. It had been fairly clear before and it was perfectly certain now that what he had in his night-glass was a running fight between two ships, the pursuer about half a mile behind and in the other's wake, and both firing most deliberately with their chasers: two bow-chasers on the one hand and two stern-chasers on the other, perhaps with a third on her quarterdeck. The moon would not be up for some hours, but there was still a fair amount of diffused light from the zenith, and catching the gun-flash with the utmost accuracy of focus he established that the leading ship was a barque. The flash of the quarterdeck gun – and there was indeed a gun mounted on her quarterdeck – lit her spanker and showed the utter absence of a mizen topsail. He checked this twice, and called 'Deck. On deck, there. All hands to make sail.'

These might very well be two national ships, French and British, American and British, French and Spanish, and his intimate conviction that the chase was the *Azul* and the chaser the *Spartan* might be born of nothing but an urgent wish that it should be so: yet the barque rig for a man-of-war was virtually unknown in the Royal Navy and very rare in any of the others; and in any event, if he was wrong, it cost no more than one night's rest.

Below him the bosun's calls howled and wailed and he could hear the cries of Tumble up, tumble up, tumble up, rouse out there, you sleepers.

He came down from the yard and took over the deck: he knew very exactly what the *Surprise* liked in this wind – the only wind in which her present want of a mizen topsail was no disadvantage to her – and presently she was running directly before it with spritsail, foresail with studdingsails on either side, maintopsail and topgallant, both with their studdingsails, and a main royal above all.

'And the boats, sir?' asked Davidge anxiously. 'Do you wish to have them hoisted in?'

'No. With the wind right aft it would lose us more time than it would save. You have the Doctor aboard, however, I see. Doctor, should you like to come into the foretop and see what is afoot? Bonden, give the Doctor a hand, and bring me my come-up glass in its case.'

With the foretopsail furled the foretop gave a perfect view. Jack said 'There! Did you catch it? She has no mizen topsail: that means she is a barque, because with the wind on her beam or just abaft of it, she would certainly spread her mizen topsail if she had one. It stands to reason. Shall I tell you what I think has happened, always supposing my wild guess is right?'

'If you please.'

'I believe the *Azul* did lie to on that Tuesday, that the *Spartan* sailed east to look for her, steering rather more to the north than was quite right, and that they came in sight of one another late this afternoon. The *Azul* bore up and ran for it on what I suppose is her best point of sailing; but the *Spartan* has the legs of her, and came within range a little while ago. Since then they have been firing their chasers pretty steady, in the hope of knocking something away.'

'What is the likely event, do you suppose?'

'If the *Azul* does not manage to knock something away, the *Spartan* will overhaul her and then their broadsides will come into play: then everything will depend on their gunnery. But if the *Spartan* can get close enough without losing any important spar, her forty-two-pounder carronades must knock the stuffing out of the barque. No question about it.'

'We are not to be idle spectators, sure?'

'I hope not, indeed. I doubt we can come up with them before the *Spartan* – for so I call her – overhauls the *Azul*, because we are directly before the wind, a poor point of sailing for any ship, even the *Surprise*. But with any sort of luck we should engage her not long after, for, do you see, as they move south and we follow them, so we bring the breeze more on our quarter, and may spread more canvas. We may engage her, and we may take her.' A pause. 'I am glad we did not change our long guns for carronades, however, as I had once thought of doing: I had much rather pepper her from a distance than come close to her forty-two-pound smashers. If we have to chase, I shall cast off the boats with Bonden and a few good hands in the pinnace. But of course, you know, there are a hundred possibilities. The *Azul* may haul her wind, cross the *Spartan*'s hawse, rake her and board her in the smoke. A hundred things may happen.'

Now they fell silent, as did all the hands crowding the forecastle below them, watching the distant battle as it moved slowly across the western sea in a night all the blacker for the flashes of the guns. Once the pursuer yawed to let fly with a full broadside and the brilliant glare showed that she was ship-rigged. 'The *Spartan* for a hundred pound,' muttered Jack.

'What is a come-up glass?' asked Stephen.

'Oh,' said Jack absently, 'it has a lens half way along divided into two, so that it gives you two images. When they separate the ship is moving from you; when they overlap she is coming nearer.'

An hour, an hour and a half went by, and slowly, slowly the pursuer made up the distance lost by her yaw and then began to gain. Now she was firing her forward guns; and now, from the *Surprise*, they were only half way to the horizon.

The crash and rumbling echo of the gunfire grew almost continuous as the two came more nearly alongside; and the smoke rolled away in a solid cloud just aft of the *Azul*. For *Azul* she was. In the blaze of the *Spartan*'s full broadside, a long and rippling broadside, Jack caught her pale sides full in his glass. The *Spartan* was half a mile to windward and edging closer when all at once the *Azul* seemed to put her helm hard over, turning with extraordinary speed as though to run before the wind and then coming up part of the way on the other tack. The *Spartan* at once raked her exposed stern, but it seemed to Jack that the range was too great for the carronades to do much execution; nor was the *Spartan* handled nearly as well as he had expected from their last encounter. She ran on an unconscionable time before her sails were trimmed to carry her after the *Azul*.

'Perhaps the barque will run clear,' said Jack, half aloud. 'Perhaps the *Spartan* has lost a spar.'

But something was wrong. The *Azul* did not seem to be running at all. He fixed her with his come-up glass: the image was steady: she was motionless. What is more lights were running about her deck, and although the *Spartan* was at last bearing down, the *Azul* was lowering a boat. Two boats.

'By God,' cried Jack, 'she has struck on the Formigas.'

All this time the chase had been drawing southward, and he had altered sail accordingly; now he reduced it to fore and main courses alone, the most inconspicuous the frigate could wear, and altered course half a point.

Standing there, with his hands hard-clenched on the top-rim, he watched the continuing battle, closer now by far. The moon rose, lighting the great swathes of white smoke, and to his astonishment he saw the *Spartan* move right in to grapple and board on the far side of the *Azul*, the starboard side, away from the *Surprise*.

He raced down on deck, ordered the arms-chests to be brought up and the few remaining lights to be dowsed; then he ran forward into the bows. Far over the water the gunfire reached its height: three full thundering broadsides from either ship, the last two almost simultaneous, then one or two guns, some musket and pistol shots; then silence, and Jack could see men jumping from the *Azul*'s lit gun-ports into the boats on her larboard side. He saw them pull clear, apparently hidden from the *Spartan*'s view.

Back on the quarterdeck he raised his voice and called 'All hands aft.' When the men had gathered he said 'Shipmates, the *Azul* has struck on the Formigas. The *Spartan* is grappled fast alongside. We are going to take her and her prize in the boats. Mr West, the armourer will serve out pistols, cutlasses or boarding-axes according to choice. I shall lead the way in the launch, followed by Mr Smith in the blue cutter and Mr Bulkeley in the red, and we board the *Azul* – the *Azul*, mind – at the forechains; Mr Davidge takes the pinnace, Mr Bentley the gig and Mr Kane the jolly-boat, and they board the *Azul* at the mizenchains. The boats keep together with a line stem to stern. We board the *Azul*, we cross her deck – remember Nelson's bridge! – and we tackle the Spartans, taking them from the front and the rear. Not a sound, not a sound as we approach, but sing out as you go aboard: and once aboard the watchword is Surprise. Now,' – raising his voice at the first murmur – 'not a cheer, not a sound until we are there. Mr West, I am grieved to say you must stay in the ship with ten men, and move in when I signal with three lanterns; but no nearer than half a mile. We proceed in five minutes' time.'

He stepped below for his sword and pistols, wrote orders for West in case he should be knocked on the head or the expedition should end in disaster, and so made his way down into the launch. The darkness was filled with whispering and this accentuated the extraordinary feeling of eagerness that he felt all around him; he had known many a cutting-out expedition, but never one with quite such a degree of fierce anticipation. Though fierce was not quite the word. 'Ready?' he called softly to each boat in turn, and each replied 'Ready, aye ready, sir.' 'Give way,' he said.

There was an easy southern swell; the breeze was with them; and the boats pulled fast across the water, with never a sound but the creak of thwarts and thole-pins and the gurgle of oars. Nearer, nearer, and nearer still, the boats keeping close together: in the last hundred yards Jack was almost certain that a blast of grape was going to come from the *Azul*'s well-lit gundeck, where men could be seen walking about. He leaned forward and said in a low voice 'Stretch out, now. Stretch out for Doggett's coat and badge.'

He loosened his sword, and as Bonden brought the launch smoothly under the *Azul*'s forechains he sprang into them, up over the rail, leaping with a tremendous shout on to the forecastle, empty but for three bodies. Instantly he was urged on by the jostling crowd of men pushing after him and at the same time he heard the bellowing cheer of the other division coming aboard and the roar of Surprise! Surprise!

Some horrified faces stared up from the three bright hatchways and instantly bobbed down out of sight.

'Come on, come on, bear a hand there,' cried Jack, racing along the gangway and over the grapplings into the *Spartan*. The attack was wholly, utterly unexpected, but twenty-five or thirty Spartans opposed them on the quarterdeck, a close-packed resolute body with what arms they had had time to snatch up. A musket-shot dashed Jack's sword from his hand: a pike-thrust furrowed the side of his neck and a short thick heavy man butted him under the chin, knocking him back on to a corpse. He writhed sideways, pistolled the thick man, caught up a heavy piece of the shattered rail, six feet long, and flung himself at the group, beating with frightful strength. They fell back, hampering one another, and instantly he struck a great scything blow that brought three of them down. He was about to strike again backhanded when Davidge caught his arm, shouting 'Sir, sir, they have surrendered, sir.'

'Have they?' said Jack, breathing heavily, his face losing its pale almost maniac fury. 'So much the better. Belay. Vast fighting, there,' – this directed to a scuffle on the forecastle. He threw down his weapon – it was like a great oak door-jamb – and said, 'Where is their captain?'

'Dead, sir,' said Davidge. 'Killed by the *Azul*. Here is the only officer left.'

'Do you answer for your men, sir?' said Jack to the white-faced young man before him.

'Yes, sir.'

'Then they must go down into the hold directly, except for the wounded. Where are the *Azul*'s people?'

'They went off in their boats, sir, before we boarded her. There were not many left.'

'Mr Davidge, three lanterns from the gundeck, if you please, to be slung in the shrouds.' The lanterns lit up a scene of great destruction. The *Azul*'s gunnery must have been strikingly accurate, and the *Spartan*'s heavy metal at close range could not but smash whatever it touched. The death-toll must necessarily be very high, above all between decks; but from what he could see as he strode among the bodies, none of his men had been killed, though Webster was bent gasping over a wound in his belly, and his mates were putting the gunner's bloody arm in a sling.

'Sir,' said the young man, 'may I beg you to cast off the barque? She cannot float another five minutes. We were only waiting until we had the last of the quicksilver out of her.'

'I am so sorry you missed it, Tom,' said Jack Aubrey, breakfasting in his cabin with Pullings who, true to his rendezvous, had appeared shortly after the rise of the sun. 'It was the prettiest little surprise you can imagine. And there was no other way of doing it, for I was certainly not going to take the ship in among those shoals at night. Most horrible rocks: the *Azul* went down in ten fathom water very shortly after we had taken her wounded out. How that young fool ever came alongside her unhurt I shall never comprehend.'

'But I am sorry you should have been hurt, sir,' said Pullings. 'I only hope it is not as bad as it looks.'

'No, no. It is a trifle: the Doctor himself says it is a trifle, and I never felt it at the time – a pike-thrust, a glancing pike-thrust. We suffered very little. But God's my life, how they did maul one another, *Spartan* and *Azul*; as bloody a little engagement as ever I saw – the gundecks of both were aswim with blood. Aswim. There were only two boat-loads of Azuls left, capable of walking, and I don't think we took over two score Spartans, apart from the wounded. It is true they had sent a great many men away in their five big prizes, yet even so it was a most shocking butchery.'

'Here is the bosun, sir,' said Killick.

'Sit down, Mr Bulkeley,' said Jack. 'What I wished to ask you was, have we plenty of French colours?'

'Not above three or four, I believe, sir.'

'Then you might consider making a few more. I do not say you *are* to make a few more, Mr Bulkeley, for that might be coming it a trifle too high; I only say that you might bear it in mind.'

'Aye-aye, sir. Bore in mind it is,' said the bosun, taking his leave.

'Now, Tom,' said Jack, 'returning to prizes, there is not a minute to be lost. The Doctor will curse, I know,' nodding through the stern window to an islet upon which Stephen and Martin were creeping on all fours, having left the wounded to their respective surgeons, 'but as soon as the *Spartan* is in a state to make sail – and she is very well found in cordage and stores of every kind – we must bear away for Fayal as fast as ever we can pelt, cracking on to make all sneer again, because the end of the month and the *Constitution* are coming closer every day. We must bear away for Fayal: the *Spartan*'s five prizes are lying there in Horta harbour. The *Spartan* appears in the offing, accompanied by something that looks very like the *Azul*. Of course the *Spartan* don't choose to come down that long bay and lose time clawing out; but the *Merlin*, the *Merlin* they know so well, stands in, gives them a couple of guns and the signal for departure; they slip their cables, and join us well out at sea, where we remove the prize-crews and carry the prizes home, hoisting French colours aboard each one, to fox the *Constitution* if she should heave in sight. Do you take my meaning, Tom?'

CHAPTER FOUR

Dr Maturin and his assistant stood in a druggist's warehouse, checking their purchases for the *Surprise*'s medicine-chest. 'Apart from the portable soup, the double retractors and a couple of spare crowbills for musket-bullets, which we will find at Ramsden's, I believe that is everything,' said Stephen.

'You have not forgotten the laudanum?' asked Martin.

'I have not. There is still a reasonable quantity aboard: but I thank you for putting me in mind of it.' The reasonable quantity was in wicker-covered eleven-gallon carboys, each representing more than fifteen thousand ordinary hospital doses, and Stephen reflected upon them with some complacency. 'The alcoholic tincture of opium, properly exhibited, is one of the most valuable drugs we possess,' he observed, 'and I take particular care not to be without it. Sometimes, indeed, I use it myself, as a gentle sedative. And yet,' he added, having looked through his list again, holding it up to the light, 'and yet, you know, Martin, I find its effects diminish. Mr Cooper, how do you do?'

'And how do *you* do, sir?' replied the druggist, with unusual pleasure in his voice and on his yellow, toothless face. '*Surprisingly* well, I trust, ha, ha, ha! When they told me the surgeon of the *Surprise* was in the shop, I said to Mrs C. "I shall just step down and wish Dr Maturin joy of his *surprising* prosperous voyage." "Oh, Cooper," she says to me, "you will never take the liberty of being witty with the Doctor?" "My dear," says I, "we have known each other this many a year; he will not mind my little joke." So give you joy, sir, give you joy with all my heart.'

'Thank you, Mr Cooper,' said Stephen, shaking his hand.

'I am obliged to you for your amiable congratulations.' And when they were in the street again he went on, 'Its effects diminish remarkably: I cannot account for it. Mr Cooper is reliability in person, so he is, and I have used his tincture voyage after voyage – always the same, always equal to itself, always extracted with decent brandy rather than raw alcohol. The answer must lie elsewhere, but where I cannot tell; so as I am resolved never to exceed a moderate dose, except in case of great emergency, I must resign myself to a sleepless night from time to time.'

'What would you consider a moderate dose, Maturin?' asked Martin, in a spirit of pure enquiry. He knew that the usual amount was twenty-five drops and he had seen Stephen give Padeen sixty to do away with extreme pain; but he also knew that habitual use might lead to a considerable degree of tolerance and he wished to learn how high that degree might be.

'Oh, nothing prodigious at all, for one accustomed to the substance. Not above . . . not above say a thousand drops or so.'

Martin checked his horrified exclamation and to conceal even its appearance he hailed a passing hackney-coach.

'But consider,' said Stephen, 'the rain has stopped, the sky is clear, and we have only a mile, an English mile, to walk: colleague, is not this close to extravagance?'

'My dear Maturin, if you had been so poor, and so poor for so very long a time as I, you too might revel in the pomp of high living, when your fortune was made at last. Come, it is a poor heart that never rejoices.'

'Well,' said Stephen, first putting his parcel into the coach and then climbing in after it, 'I wish you may not be growing proud.'

They stopped at Ramsden's, ordered the remaining supplies and so parted, Martin going to match a piece of watered tabby for his wife, and Stephen going to his club.

The porters at Black's were a discreet set of men, but there was no mistaking their significant smiles and becks or the pleasure with which they wished him good day and gave him a friendly note from Sir Joseph Blaine, once more the true head of naval intelligence, welcoming him to London and confirming an appointment for that evening.

'Half after six,' said Stephen, looking at the tall Tompion in the hall with one eye. 'I shall have time to ask Mrs Broad how she does.' To the hall-porter he said 'Ben, pray keep this parcel until I come back, and do not let me go to see Sir Joseph without it.' And to the hackney-coachman, 'Do you know the Grapes, in the liberties of the Savoy?'

'The public that was burnt down, and is building up again?'

'The very same place.'

Had the day been foggy, as it often was down there by the river, or had the evening been far advanced, the Grapes might indeed have been the very same place, for it had been rebuilt without the smallest change, and Stephen could have walked into his own room blindfold; but the new brick had not yet had time to acquire its coat of London grime, while the unglazed upper windows gave the place a sinister air that it most certainly did not deserve; and it was not until he walked into the snuggery that he felt really at home. Here everything always had been spotlessly clean, and apart from the smell of fresh plaster the newness made no difference. It was an inn that he knew particularly well – he had kept a room there for years – a quiet inn, convenient for the Royal Society, the Entomologists and certain other learned bodies, and one whose landlady he particularly esteemed.

At this moment however his esteem for Mrs Broad was a little shaken by the sound of her voice, some storeys up, raised in a very shrill and passionate harangue. Railing in women always made him uneasy and now he stood there with his hands behind his back, his head bowed, and an unhappy expression on his face; it also had much the same effect on the two glaziers who now came down the stairs, directing submissive words to the torrent behind and above them: 'Yes, ma'am: certainly, ma'am: directly, ma'am, without fail.' In the doorway they squared their paper hats on their heads, exchanged a haggard look, and hurried silently away.

Mrs Broad could be heard grumbling her way down: 'Wicked, idle dogs – radicals – Jacobins – pie-crusts – willains –' and as she came into the snug her voice rose to something near its former pitch: 'No, sir; you can't be served. The house ain't open yet, nor never will be, with those wicious monsters. Oh Lord, it's the Doctor! God love you, sir, pray take a seat.' Her usual good-humoured face beamed out like the sun coming from behind a dark purple cloud, and she held out her short fat arms to an elbow-chair. 'And are you in town, sir? We read about you in the papers, and there were prints and a transparency in Gosling's window – dear me, such goings-on! How I hope nobody was hurt – and the dear Captain? Oh, I could weep for wexation – that vile wretch promised the upstairs windows, the windows for your room too, three weeks ago – *three weeks ago* – and here you are and no windows. And the rain coming in and spoiling the girls' fine-polished floors: it is enough to make a woman cry. But there you are with nothing in your hand. What may I bring you, sir, to drink to the new Grapes's health?'

'To bless the house and the lady of the house, Mrs Broad,' said Stephen, 'I will happily drink a tint of whiskey.'

Mrs Broad came back in a calmer mind with glasses and cake on a tray – black-currant cordial for herself, her throat being a little hoarse – and a tissue-paper parcel under her arm; and as they sat there on either side of the fire, after Dr Maturin's solemn benediction, Mrs Broad asked very gently whether he had any news from the North?

She and Diana had both tried to keep Stephen healthy, properly fed, dressed in clean linen and well-brushed clothes suitable to his station, and in the course of this long-drawn-out and largely unsuccessful campaign they had become friends: indeed, they had liked one another from the beginning. Mrs Broad had a pretty clear notion of how things stood between Dr and Mrs Maturin, but the tacitly admitted fiction was that

Diana had gone into the North for her health while Stephen roamed the seas.

'I have not,' said Stephen. 'Yet it may be that I shall be in those parts quite soon.'

'I heard on Lady-Day past,' said Mrs Broad. 'A gentleman from the legation brought me this' – unwrapping a Swedish doll in a fur pelisse – 'and the note said I was to tell the Doctor that there was a waterproof boat-cloak ordered for him at Swainton's that she had forgot to mention. It had to be wove special, but it would be ready by now. The pelisse is real sable,' she added, smoothing the doll's clothes and bright yellow hair.

'Is that right?' said Stephen, getting up and looking out of the side-window into the street. 'Sable, indeed?' How much wiser he would have been to make a clean break with Diana instead of walking about with her absurd great diamond in his pocket like a talisman and his whole spirit jerking at the sound of her name: he had amputated many a limb in the past, and not only literally. On the far pavement he saw his old friend the butcher's dog sitting in the doorway, scratching its ear with a fine dogged perseverance.

He took a piece of cake and walked out. The dog paused in mid-scratch, peered myopically right and left, twitching its nose, saw him, and came bowing across the street, tail waving. Stephen stroked its head, held up with a hideous grin, observed with regret the film of age over its eyes, thumped its massive brindled flanks, and offered the piece of cake. The dog took it gently by the extreme edge and they parted, the dog walking back to its shop, where, having looked carefully round, it put the untouched cake down behind a heap of filth and lay flat; while Stephen, returning to the Grapes, said to Mrs Broad, 'As for my room, never torment yourself for a minute. It is not for myself that I am come but for Padeen my servant. He is to be operated upon at Guy's tomorrow – a sad great tooth-drawing, alas – and I should not like him to lie in a common ward. You have a room downstairs, I am sure.'

'Teeth to be drawn, oh the poor soul. Of course there is the little room under yours ready this moment; or Deb can move in with Lucy, which might be better, as being more aired.'

'He is a good young man, Mrs Broad, from the County Clare in Ireland; he does not speak much English, and that little he speaks with the terrible great stutter, so it is five minutes before he gets his word out and then it is often the wrong one. But he is as biddable as a lamb and perfectly sober. Now I must leave you, I find, for I have an appointment on the far side of the park.'

His road took him along the crowded Strand to the even more crowded Charing Cross, where at the confluence of three eager streams of traffic a cart-horse had fallen, causing a stagnation of waggons, drays and coaches round which horse-men, sedan-chairs and very light vehicles made their way among the foot passengers, while the carter sat unmoved on the animal's head, waiting until his little boy should succeed in undoing the necessary buckles. It was a good-humoured crowd that Stephen slowly traversed, with those round the boy and the horse full of facetious advice, and it was made up of an extraordinarily wide variety of people, much diversified by uniforms, mostly red: an invigorating tide of life, particularly for one fresh from the sea; yet there was rather much striving and pushing, and not without relief he turned into the park and so by way of Black's for his parcel to Shepherd Market, where Sir Joseph lived in a discreet house with a green door, curious double link-extinguishers and a knocker like burnished gold, in the form of a dolphin.

He raised his hand to the splendid creature's tail, but before he could touch it the door flew open and there was Sir Joseph greeting him, his large pale face showing more pleasurable emotion than most of his colleagues would have believed possible. 'Welcome, welcome home again,' he cried. 'I had been watching for you from the drawing-room window. Come in, my dear Maturin, come in.' He led him upstairs to the library, the pleasantest room in the house, lined with books and slim-drawered insect-cabinets, and placed him an easy chair on one side of the fire while he sat on the other, gazing at him with renewed pleasure until Stephen's first question 'What news of Wray and Ledward?' wiped the expression off his face.

'They have been seen in Paris,' he replied. 'I am ashamed to say they got clean away. You may say that with all our services on the watch we must be a sad lot of boobies to let them out of the country; and I cannot deny that our very first move, at Button's itself, was most horribly mismanaged. But there you are: once it was a question of *all* our services, all sorts of possibilities arose, apart from mere stupidity.'

Stephen looked at Blaine for a moment: he knew his chief well enough to understand that he meant to convey not only his lack of confidence in the discretion and competence of some of the intelligence services active in the kingdom but also his conviction that Ledward and Wray had at least one very highly-placed colleague and protector somewhere in the administration. Taking this as understood between them he only said 'But, however, you are now master in your own house again, I believe?'

'I hope so, indeed,' said Sir Joseph, smiling, 'but the service was half wrecked, as you know very well, and it has to be built up afresh. And then again, although my position in the Admiralty is now stronger than it was, I am far from happy about some of our partners and correspondents and . . . I shall certainly not propose any continental mission for your consideration at present. In any event, your observations on the possibilities in South America would be far more valuable.'

'I ask these indiscreet questions partly because I am closely concerned but also because they bear directly on the reinstatement of Captain Aubrey.'

'Lucky Jack Aubrey,' said Blaine, smiling again with lively pleasure. 'By God, was such a stroke ever seen? How did you leave the dear fellow?'

'In the bosom of his family, and happy as far as his pocket is concerned: but, you know, that hardly weighs with him, in comparison with his restoration to the Navy List.'

'As for the formal processes, of course they cannot be begun until the court has condemned Wray and Ledward and Aubrey is pardoned for what he never did – until the conviction is removed. There are the informal processes as well, and with regard to them he has my full support, naturally; but even where patronage is concerned my support is of little consequence and in a matter of this kind it is of none at all. He has other supporters, some of much greater value, but some, like the Duke and a few of the more whiggish admirals, who may do him more harm than good. And there is a general feeling in the service and in the public mind that he was shockingly ill-used. The rejoicing at his present success is very clear evidence of that. By the way, did you know that the committee would not accept his resignation from the club?'

'I did not. But tell me, will not this present success have an effect – will it not help to bring about a change in the official view? It was striking enough, for all love, as you observed yourself.'

'A change? Oh dear me no. For the official mind successful privateering is of no national, no Royal Naval, consequence. No. There has been a hideous blunder; everyone knows it; and when the present generation of officials has passed away in perhaps twenty years, and of course the present Ministry, it is probable that some gesture may be made. But at present Wray cannot be brought to trial – it would be extremely embarrassing to the Ministry if he could, I may add, with this whole series of scandals ripped up – so the blame cannot be shifted, and the only way official face can be saved is an action of obviously national importance that would justify a royal pardon or revision or restoration. If for example Captain Aubrey were to engage a ship of the French or American navy that could be made to appear of equal or superior force and either take her or contrive to be badly wounded or both, he might conceivably be reinstated in a year or so, rather than let us say at the next coronation but one or two. Not otherwise, for as I said or meant to say, privateering is its own reward. And Lord above, what a reward in this case! Why, Maturin, with quicksilver at its present rate he must be one of the wealthiest sailors afloat: to say nothing of all the rest of the booty. But he that hath, to him shall be given: I hear that the West India merchants are presenting him with a dinner-service of plate, in acknowledgement of his taking the *Spartan*.'

'Sure he never need fear an arrest for debt again,' said Stephen. 'The more so as the minute he came home he learnt that the court of appeal had decided a grievous great case in his favour, with costs of the Dear knows how much. The case that had opposed him to the heirs and assigns of a wicked raparee for a great many years, ever since the . . .'

'Lord, what a stroke it was!' said Sir Joseph again, not attending but staring into the fire. 'It was the talk of the service, it was the talk of the town – Lucky Jack Aubrey going out for a trial cruise in a time of dearth – nothing but little coasting hoys and busses or the odd *chasse-marée* taken for months – and coming back with seven great fat prizes at his tail and the precious cargo of an eighth fairly bursting his sides. Ha, ha, ha! It does my heart good to think of it.' Blaine thought of it for a while, chuckling to himself, and then he said, 'Tell me, Maturin, how did you induce the *Spartan*'s prizes to come out of Horta?'

'I interrogated the French-speaking prisoners in the usual way,' said Stephen, 'and on finding that one of them was the *Spartan*'s yeoman of signals I took him aside and represented to him that if he told me what arrangement of flags had been agreed – for as you know Horta is at the bottom of a deep and troublesome bay and it was certain that the parties would communicate at a great distance – that if he told me, then he should have his freedom and a reward, but that if he did not, he must bear the consequences of his refusal, which I did not specify. He laughed and said he would always be happy to oblige me at such a rate, and to earn so much for so little and with an easy conscience at that, for it was only the old blue Peter with a windward gun, which we should certainly have tried straight away. And so it was: the schooner stood in on an almost contrary wind, waved this flag, fired off a cannon, and out they came as fast as ever they could sail.'

'That must have rejoiced your heart, ha, ha, ha!'

'Rejoicing there was, sure, but it was mighty discreet, for fear of an unlucky word or look or gesture. We were on tiptoe, everything was so revocable and precarious, the ice so extremely thin: each prize had to be secured in turn and a crew of our people sent aboard, which left us with a terrible great crowd of angry, determined prisoners and precious few men to keep them down and sail the ship at the same time. And two of the prizes, the *John Busby* and *Pretty Anne*, were so damnably thick and stupid and slow they had to be towed, and at any moment the *Constitution* might heave in sight. Oh, it was the cruel time, though we had a fair wind most of it; we never drew an easy breath till we crossed Shelmerston bar, when we threw off the tow, fired all the great guns, and sent on shore for a feast.'

'The men must have been pleased with Captain Aubrey.'

'So they were too: they dressed ship and cheered him all the way to the strand; and except for those few he turned away for pillaging or misconduct they fairly worship him in Shelmerston.'

'He would have been cheered in the streets here too, if he had come up,' said Blaine. 'There were prints and broadsheets by the dozen: I kept some for you. He went over to a heap of papers on a low table, and as he sorted through them Stephen noticed that he let fall a coloured handbill with the picture of a balloon on it. Balloons had been in Stephen's mind since he crossed Pall Mall on his way: workmen were repairing the conduits that led the coal-gas to the street-lamps there and he had wondered whether the smelly stuff might not be used in place of the even more dangerous hydrogen. He would have made the remark if Sir Joseph had not quickly covered the print and pushed it under the table: instead he reached for his parcel and said 'Aubrey did not choose to come to town himself, but he desired me to give you this, with his compliments. It is the *Spartan*'s log-book, and I think you will find it yield some quite valuable intelligence about French and American agents: she often carried both. And as it was packing up I included my interrogations of the prisoners, which are not without interest.'

'How very obliging in Mr Aubrey,' said Blaine, taking the parcel eagerly. 'Please thank him most heartily from me: and my respectful compliments, if you should think proper, to his wife, whom I remember from Bath as one of the loveliest young women I ever saw. Forgive me for a moment while I run over this log for July last year, when I believe . . .' Sir Joseph did not say what he believed, but it was evidently something discreditable; and while he turned the pages under the green-shaded lamp Stephen leant back in his chair, watching the firelight play on the brass fender, the turkey carpet, and farther off on the books stretching away, row after row of calf or morocco under the singularly light and elegant plasterwork of the ceiling. In his youth he had known Gothic and even Romanesque ceilings (they could retain the winter damp right through a blazing Catalan summer), and in his brief married life with Diana, not a furlong from here, in Half Moon Street, he had known the elaborate ceilings that went with little gilt chairs and a great deal of entertaining; but most of his life had been spent in odd lodgings, inns, and ships. He had never known the quiet, sober, eminently comfortable settled elegance of a room like this. Even Melbury Lodge, the house he had shared with Jack Aubrey for a while during the peace, had not possessed it, and he was contemplating the necessary conditions for its creation when the housekeeper came in and said that if Sir Joseph pleased supper would be on the table in five minutes.

An eminently comfortable elegant supper, and reasonably sober: Blaine's favourite plain boiled lobster, with a glass of muscadet; sweetbreads and asparagus, with a charming little claret; and a strawberry tart. During the meal Stephen fought the battle over again in the usual naval way, with small pieces of bread on the table-cloth; once again he described the Surprises' ecstasy as, telescopes trained, they saw the prizes slip their cables and sail out of Horta harbour, '"like lambs to the slaughter", as Aubrey observed'; and again Sir Joseph cried 'Lord, what a stroke! The quicksilver alone would have paid for the ship ten times over. And no admiral's share! But a kind of vicarious cupidity and delight in gain makes me gross: forgive me, Maturin. Yet I do hope and trust that this access of fortune will not interfere with the South American scheme?'

'Never in life. Aubrey would not happily live ashore, however rich, unless he were restored to the list. And even if that were not the case, he has very handsomely stated that he is entirely bound to the ship for this voyage – that he wishes to make it in any event – and he begs I will sell her to him after it is over. My assistant, Mr Martin, whom you may remember –'

'The chaplain who wrote the unfortunate pamphlet on naval abuses?'

'Just so, and a very sound ornithologist – expressed the same sense of obligation, of engagement, although he is recently married and although he now possesses what he is pleased to call a fortune, enough to live on in comfort: which I take very kindly indeed, on both their parts.'

'I am sure you do. Dear Maturin, forgive me if I grow coarse again and speak of money. I know very well that it is an improper subject, but it is one that I find curiously interesting and I should particularly like to know what Mr Martin regards as a fortune.'

'The capital sum escapes me, but my banker here in London, whom we consulted, stated that if it were placed in the Funds it would bring in £225 a year, leaving a few hundreds over for equipment and *menus plaisirs*.'

'Well, that is more than the average country parson's living, I believe; certainly much more than a curate could hope for. And all won in a fortnight's privateering! Bless him. At this rate he will soon be an archbishop.'

'I do not believe I quite follow you, Blaine.'

'In the gaiety of my heart I was speaking facetiously, perhaps too facetiously where a sacred office is concerned: but it is a fact that Dr Blackburne, the Archbishop of York in my father's time, had been a buccaneer on the Spanish Main. And after all you and Mr Martin will be in those same latitudes. Shall we go back into the library? I have a bottle of Tokay there that I should like you to try, after our coffee; and Mrs Barlow will bring us some little cakes.'

In their absence Mrs Barlow or the powerful black who was the only other resident servant had made up the fire, and the train of conversation being broken both Stephen and Blaine sat staring at it like a pair of cats for some little while. Then Stephen said, 'I regretted Duhamel's death extremely.'

'So did I,' said Blaine. 'A man of outstanding ability.'

'And rectitude,' said Stephen. 'I did not tell you at the time, but he brought me back the diamond that Diana was obliged to leave in Paris, the stone called the Blue Peter.' He took it out of his pocket.

'I recall that one evening when you were so kind as to invite me to Half Moon Street she wore it as a pendant. And I very clearly remember the circumstances in which it was left in Paris. I never expected to see it again. A wonderful great jewel: but, Maturin, should not it be lying in the strong-room of a bank?'

'Perhaps it should,' said Stephen; and after a pause, 'I have been turning the matter over in my mind, and I have decided, if I may be allowed to prolong the ship's exemption from pressing, to go to Sweden and return the stone before setting out for South America.'

'Certainly,' said Sir Joseph.

'Tell me, Blaine,' said Stephen, looking straight at him with his pale eyes, 'have you any information about the position there?'

'I have made no enquiries about Mrs Maturin from the point of view of intelligence, no enquiries whatsoever in my professional capacity,' said Blaine, not without severity. 'None whatsoever. But in my unofficial capacity, my capacity as an ordinary social being, I have of course heard the ordinary gossip of the town: and sometimes a little more.'

'Gossip states that in consequence of my infidelity in the Mediterranean she ran off to Sweden with Jagiello, does it not?'

'Yes,' said Blaine, looking at him attentively.

'Can you tell me anything about Jagiello, at all?'

'Yes, I can,' said Sir Joseph. 'From the point of view of intelligence, he is perfectly sound: his influence, as you may imagine, is negligible, but what he has is wholly in favour of the alliance with us. What is more to the immediate purpose is that I can tell you something that has nothing to do with common gossip, something that I learnt from a man in the legation: it appears that Jagiello is about to marry a young Swedish lady. I also gathered, though this was not directly expressed and I cannot assert that my assumptions are correct and they may very well be wrong – I also gathered that relations between him and Mrs Maturin were not of the nature – were not what they were ordinarily assumed to be. On the other hand I do not think there is much room for mistake when I say that at present she is far from being rich; though to be sure one might make balloon ascents from a spirit of adventure.' He walked over to his low table, felt under it, and brought out the print he had concealed. The picture showed a blue balloon among billowing clouds, surrounded by large red birds, perhaps eagles; in the balloon basket a woman with yellow hair and red cheeks, mounted on a blue horse, held out stiff British and Swedish flags: and from the exclamatory text below leapt the name Diana Villiers, three times repeated in capital letters, with points of admiration fore and aft. That was the name he had first known her by, and Diana Villiers was what he usually called her in his own mind, for their marriage aboard a man-of-war, with never a priest in sight, had convinced him no more than it had convinced her.

He considered the image for a while, the careful drawing of the cords enveloping the balloon and holding the basket, the wooden figure and its expressionless face, the frozen, theatrical posture; and absurdly enough there was something of Diana there. She was a splendid rider, and although she would never have sat like that, even on a blue cross between an ass and a mule, nor ever have struck a histrionic pose, the wild improbability, the symbol for a horse and the figure's total lack of concern did have a real connection with her.

'Thank you, Blaine,' he said after a while. 'I am deeply obliged to you for this information. Is there anything, however tenuous, that you could add?'

'No. Nothing at all. But you may think the absence of any tattle or rumour in such a place as present-day Sweden tolerably significant.'

Stephen nodded, studying the print once more and making a certain amount of sense of the Swedish. 'I should like to make an ascent in a balloon,' he said.

'When I was in France before the war,' said Blaine, 'I watched Pilâtre de Rozier and a friend go up. They had two balloons, a small Mongolfier just over the basket and a larger one filled with gas above it. They rose at a fine pace, but at three or four thousand feet the whole thing took fire: Icarus could not have been more dashed to pieces.' Sir Joseph regretted the words as soon as they were out, but no explanation, no softening, could do anything but make them worse, so he moved about, bringing the wine from its corner and pouring them each a glass.

They talked about Tokay and wine in general until they were half way through the bottle and then Stephen said, 'You spoke of present-day Sweden as being remarkably full of rumours.'

'It is scarcely surprising that it should be so, when you come to reflect: Bernadotte may have been elected crown-prince and he may have turned against Napoleon, but he is still a Frenchman and the French do not despair of turning him back again. They can offer him Finland, Pomerania – quantities of land – and they have a hold on him: half a dozen natural children in Pau, Marseilles and Paris. And if that don't answer there is always the legitimate royal family, the excluded Vasas, who have plenty of supporters and who may contrive a *coup d'état*. Then again the treaty of Abo is much disliked by the better kind of Swedes. And of course the Russians and the Danes are also closely concerned, as well as the northern German states; so in spite of the present alliances Stockholm is full of agents of one kind or another, attempting to influence Bernadotte, his entourage, his advisers and his various opponents, actual or potential; and their doings or their alleged doings give rise to a wonderful amount of talk. It is not our department, thanks be – I have seen Castlereagh bowing under the pile of reports – but naturally we hear our fair share.'

The little silver bracket-clock struck one and Stephen stood up. 'You will never desert a bottle at half-ebb?' cried Blaine. 'Sit down again, for shame.'

Stephen sat, though as far as he was concerned it might have been cocoa; and when the last glass was poured he said, 'Will I tell you a strange example of the power of money?'

'If you please,' said Blaine.

'My servant, Padeen, whom you know, has an impacted wisdom-tooth, from which he suffers extremely. The operation is beyond my skill, and when I took him to the best tooth-drawer in Plymouth nothing would induce him to open his mouth; he had rather put up with the pain. Yet now that I have brought him to London, to be dealt with by Mr Cullis of Guy's, the case is altered: he opens his mouth cheerfully, he is pierced, lanced and probed without a cry; and this is not because Cullis is Sergeant-Dentist to the Prince Regent, which means nothing at all in the County Clare, but because the operation is to cost seven guineas, with half a guinea to the dresser. The expenditure of such a sum, more than Padeen had ever seen in his life before this stroke with the *Surprise*, not only confers a certain status upon a man, but must necessarily entail an extraordinary degree of well-being.'

'Do you mean he is not waiting for you downstairs?' asked Blaine, who could be disappointing at times. 'Do you mean you are going to walk home by yourself? And with that absurd great diamond in your pocket into the bargain? I can easily imagine the insurance declining responsibility in such a case.'

'What insurance?'

'You will not tell me it is uninsured?'

'I might.'

'Next I shall hear that the ship is not covered either.'

'Ah,' said Stephen, struck by the thought. 'There is maritime insurance too, so there is: I have often heard of it. Perhaps I should make some arrangement.'

Sir Joseph cast up his hands, but he only said, 'Come. I will see you to the corner of Piccadilly. There is always a knot of link-boys there. Two will see you home and two will see me back.' And as they were walking along he said, 'When I spoke of Mr Aubrey's engaging a national ship of roughly equal force just now my words were not quite so much in the air as they may have appeared to be. I am right in supposing that he is particularly well acquainted with the harbour of St Martin's, am I not?'

'He surveyed it twice, and he blockaded it for a great while.'

'There may be some possibility – can you stay in town as long as a week?'

'Certainly I can; and I am always to be found at Black's. But in any case we are to meet again at the Royal Society Club's dinner on Thursday, before my paper. I am bringing Mr Martin.'

'I should be very happy to meet him.'

The meeting was indeed happy on both sides. Stephen placed Martin between himself and Sir Joseph, and the two talked steadily until the toasts began. Martin had not, as he admitted, paid as much attention to the coleoptera as he should have done, but in the nature of things he knew more about the habits, if not the forms, of the South American families, having watched them closely on their native soil; and beetles, especially luminous beetles, together with Blaine's outline of a new classification of them on truly scientific principles, were their sole subject.

At the subsequent meeting of the Society Stephen read his paper on the osteology of diving birds in his usual low mumble:

when it was over, and when those Fellows who could both hear and understand had congratulated him, Blaine accompanied him to the great court, and taking him a little aside asked after Padeen. 'Oh it was a shocking affair entirely,' said Stephen. 'I thanked God I had not attempted it myself. The apparent tooth was obliged to be broken and the pieces of nerve that could be seen pulled out one by one. He bore it better than ever I should have done, but there is still a great deal of pain. I reduce it as much as I can with the alcoholic tincture of opium; and to be sure he displays remarkable fortitude.'

'He has had his seven guineas' worth, poor fellow,' said Blaine; and then in another tone, 'Speaking of sailors, it would do no harm if our friend held himself in readiness to set off for a short voyage at even shorter notice.'

'Will I send him an express, so?'

'If you can make it non-committal enough: this may be no more than a false interpretation – mere flim-flam. But it would be a pity not to be prepared if it were to turn out true.'

Ashgrove Cottage could never have been described as an eligible residence at any time, since it stood low on a cold, damp slope facing north, on poor, spewy soil, with no means of access but a hollow lane, deep in mud much of the year and impassable after heavy rain. Yet from the top of the slope, by the observatory, one could see Portsmouth, Spithead, the Isle of Wight, the Channel beyond and the vast amount of shipping; what is more, during the high tides of his fortune Jack Aubrey had made considerable plantations, and he had more than doubled the size of the house. The meagre scrubland of former days was now for the most part decently clothed with young wood, and although the cottage itself could not rival the noble stable-yard with its double coach-house and rows of loose-boxes, it did have some very comfortable rooms. In one of these, the breakfast-parlour, Jack Aubrey and Sophie sat sharing a companionable extra pot of coffee. Although some years had passed since Sir Joseph first saw her in Bath she could still be described as one of the loveliest young women of his acquaintance, for although living with a somewhat difficult, boisterous and over-sanguine husband with little or no sense of business, a husband who might be away for years on end, doing his utmost to risk life and limb in far remote seas, and although bearing him three children had taken its toll, while his infamous trial and disgrace had withered her bloom, the singular beauty of her form, eyes and hair was unaffected, while the intense mental and spiritual activity of keeping their home together in his absence and of dealing with sometimes unscrupulous men of business had done away with any hint of insipidity or helplessness in her expression. But the recent spring tide of gold, which had brought the house back to life – it was difficult to believe now, but only a short while ago this warm, luminous, cheerful, lived-in room had, like many of the other rooms, been locked up, shuttered and shrouded in dust-sheets – had also done wonders for her skin: her complexion was that of a girl.

Yet Sophia Aubrey was no fool. Although she knew that short of defeat in the everlasting war and the bankruptcy of the state they would be unlikely to have any serious material worries again she also knew that Jack would never be really happy unless his name were restored to the Navy List. He was cheerful enough on the surface, pleased to be with her and the children, and of course this release from anxiety and from the apparently interminable law-suit had had a great effect; but she knew perfectly well that his appetite for living was very, very much less than it had been – for one example out of many, the stables contained only two dull utilitarian horses and he did not mean to hunt – and that as far as many sides of his life were concerned he was as it were flayed. They entertained very little and they hardly dined out at all: this was partly because most of his old shipmates were at sea, but even more because he refused all invitations except from men to whom he was particularly obliged or who had shown their friendship quite unmistakably at his trial.

He was easily wounded, and only a little while ago Sophie

had had a difficult time with the representatives of the committee of West India merchants who had talked to her about their present or rather about the arms and the inscriptions that were to be engraved upon it, for the plate was already there in Storr's workshop. She had begged them to omit 'late of the Royal Navy' and 'formerly His Majesty's ship' and the repeated mentions of the word privateer; but the gentlemen had been so pleased with their own composition and so strongly inclined to think it could not be improved upon that she doubted there would be any change.

A party of seamen padded past the window on their way to deal with the drawing-room in the naval fashion; that is to say, to strip it to the boards, scrub and polish everything in sight and then refurnish it completely, chairs, tables and bookcases all exactly squared. Since in the ordinary course of events they did this daily to their captain's quarters at sea, it seemed to them natural that they should do the same by his house on shore; and since the end of their week's leave of solid debauchery in Shelmerston they had repainted all the woodwork at Ashgrove as well as whitening all the stones bordering the drive and the paths in the garden.

They had hardly gone by before a blackbird began to sing from a tree on the far side of the lawn. He was a great way off, but with all its inconveniencies the cottage did have the merit of being a reasonably quiet place and he could be heard in all his glorious purity. 'How I wish I could sing like that,' murmured Jack, rapt in admiration.

'My dearest love,' said Sophie, pressing his hand, 'you sing far, far better.'

The bird stopped in mid-phrase and a hooting and bawling of children could be heard approaching.

'Oh do come on, George, you fat-arsed little swab. Bear a hand, bear a hand there, can't you?' called Charlotte.

'I'm a-coming, ain't I? And you are to wait for me,' cried George, quite faint in the distance.

'Charlotte, you are not to roar out like that so near the house. It ain't genteel and besides they'll hear you,' said Fanny, also

127

in a close-reefed topsail screech. An outsider might have found their conversation coarse and aggressive as well as horribly loud; but they had been brought up largely by the seamen who replaced ordinary servants at Ashgrove, and they usually talked lower-deck when they were at liberty. Their abuse was almost always entirely conventional and they were in fact much attached to one another, which was obvious when they appeared at the window, each girl having her little brother by the hand and all three leaping up and down with delight.

'It's come, it's come,' they cried, but not quite together: a discordant noise.

'It's come, sir. It's come, ma'am,' cried Killick, flinging the door wide open. He performed what he conceived to be a butler's duties at Ashgrove; and in his view butlers were perfectly entitled to grin and jerk their thumbs over their shoulders. 'Which it's in a covered cart with two coves with blunderbusses as well as the driver in the stable-yard, sir. There was a gent in charge, to make an address, but he got pissed pardon me overtook in liquor at Godalming, so they come on alone. The address is wrote on paper, any gate, so you can read it yourself. They ask do you choose to have the crates carried in, sir?'

'No,' said Jack. 'Take them into the kitchen – but they are to unload their blunderbusses before setting foot in the house – and give them beer and bread and cheese and ham and pork pie. And you and Bonden bring in the crates, with a screw-driver and a small crow.'

The crates came, escorted by children crying 'Oh Papa may we open them now?' from as far as the kitchen passage.

'George,' said his father, surveying the trim sealed and banded chests, with *J. Aubrey, Ashgrove Cottage, Hants, Esquire HANDLE WITH GREAT CARE* painted on the top, 'Jump up to your grandmother's room like a good fellow, and tell her there is something come from London.'

Before Mrs Williams could change into a suitable garment, arrange her hair and negotiate the staircase, the lid of the first chest had come off, and an extraordinary amount of straw and wood-shavings had invaded three quarters of the room; she cried out in horror, her powerful voice filling the breakfast-parlour. But Jack Aubrey had reached the layers of tissue-paper that concealed the heart of the matter and his hands were searching for a joint in the close-packed parcels. Sophie watched him with dread in her heart as he heaved at a bulky object in the middle, gently prised it free, unveiled its brilliant form – a soup tureen – and in a tone that quite drowned Mrs Williams' indignation he said 'Wait a moment, ma'am,' and passed it to his wife. The tureen, an ornate affair in the modern style, was so heavy that she nearly dropped it; but seizing the other handle she checked its downward swoop, and even before she had steadied it she saw that the inscription was as she had wished it to be . . . She read it out: *To the most eminently distinguished naval commander, John Aubrey, esquire, this service is offered by the Association of West India Merchants in gratitude for his unfailing support and protection of the country's Trade (its life's blood) in all latitudes and in both wars, and in particular acknowledgment of his brilliant capture of that most determined and rapacious private man-of-war the Spartan, the largest of its class*. Beneath this piece stood the words *Debellare superbos*, with two lions rampant pointing at them from either side.

'Very well put,' cried Mrs Williams. '"Life's blood" is very well put. I congratulate you, Mr Aubrey.' She shook his hand with real cordiality; and taking the tureen from her daughter, she observed, 'It must weigh a hundred and fifty ounces.'

'Oh sir,' cried Charlotte, standing on tiptoe and peering into the chest, 'I believe there is another just the same. Please, *please* may I bring it out?'

'Do, by all means, my dear,' said Jack.

'It is far too heavy and delicate for a child,' said Mrs Williams, eagerly pushing forward and raising the next tureen. 'But she shall have the cover, which I see lies next.'

'May I have a go too, Papa?' whispered Fanny, pulling his sleeve.

Common justice required that she should, and presently the

unpacking turned into a kind of lucky dip, each fishing in strict turn and calling or even shrieking out the name of the catch – sauce tureen, small ladle, large ladle, side-dish, cover, a monstrous epergne and so down to the scores of plates, big and little – until the tables overflowed and there was nowhere to tread without crushing straw or shavings into the carpet, to say nothing of tissue paper and jeweller's cotton, and the place looked like an idealized bandito's lair; for the West India merchants had done the thing handsomely, very handsomely.

'You will have to take on a mate or two in the polishing line,' said Jack to Killick, who was gazing round with a kind of imbecile rapture at the number of surfaces that he might now attack with powdered chalk and shammy leather: like many seamen he had a passion for making metal shine, and he had already reduced Jack's earliest silver plates to something not far removed from foil.

'Now everything must be washed in hot water and soap, because of the children's dirty hands,' said Mrs Williams, 'and when it is thoroughly dry it must be wrapped in baize and locked up in the strong-room. It is far too good for use.'

'Charlotte,' said Jack. 'Here is a spoon for you, for your own; and here is one for Fanny.'

'Oh thank you, sir,' they cried, courtseying and blushing with pleasure: they were twins, and the perfect unison of their cry, expression, movement and blush was particularly absurd and touching.

'And here's for thee, George. You will need one when you join your first ship.'

Mrs Williams expressed her views on naval education; they were familiar to Jack Aubrey from pretty frequent repetition ever since George was breeched, but he heard them with a mind detached.

'Mama,' said Fanny, staring at the inscription on the first tureen, 'you left out *debellare superbos* at the bottom. What does it mean?'

'It is Latin, my dear,' said Sophie. 'And that is all I know.

You will have to wait for Dr Maturin or Miss O'Mara.' Miss O'Mara, the daughter of an officer killed at the Nile, was the promised governess whose name usually darkened the little girls' days with apprehension whenever it was mentioned; but now Fanny scarcely noticed it. 'I shall ask Papa,' she said.

'The parlour, there,' hailed Dray, whose muddy boot (he had but one, the other leg being made of wood) confined him to the kitchen.

'Ho,' replied Killick, in an equally carrying voice.

'Express for the Captain.'

'There is an express for you, sir,' said Killick.

'An express! Oh what can it be?' cried Mrs Williams, putting her handkerchief to her mouth.

'Jump along to the kitchen and fetch it, will you, George,' said Jack.

'The boy fell off his horse in the lane, and is covered with blood,' said the returning George, with some satisfaction. 'So is the letter.'

Jack walked into the deep bow-window, and in the quietness produced by astonishment (an express was a very rare event at Ashgrove Cottage) he heard his mother-in-law whisper to Sophie 'What a shocking bad omen. How I hope it is not to say Mr Aubrey's bank is broke. Blood on the cover! I am certain it is to say Mr Aubrey's bank is broke. No bank is safe nowadays; they break right and left.'

He stood pondering for a moment. It was true that what little refitting the *Surprise* required was well in hand, and if that good, solid, reliable Tom Pullings had been aboard he could have been sure of finding her ready for sea within a very few hours. But Tom was not to report until Tuesday, and although Davidge and West were capable, experienced officers he did not know them well and he would not rely on their judgment alone where preparation for action was concerned: for Stephen would not have spoken of a short voyage or even shorter notice if there had not been some likelihood of action at the end of it.

As he weighed the possibilities he became aware that his

silence and Mrs Williams' foolish whispers were casting a damp upon the occasion; the children were looking quite solemn. 'Sophie,' he said, putting the note into his pocket, 'I believe I shall run down and look at the ship in the morning, rather than wait until Tuesday. But in the meanwhile, let us carry all these things into the dining-room and spread them out as though we were going to give a banquet.'

With two extra leaves the dining-table could seat fourteen people comfortably, and these fourteen people required a prodigious quantity of plate. Although the service was more bulbous, fussy and convoluted than any Jack or Sophie would have chosen, even half-laid the table looked very grand in a rather ostentatious way, particularly as the curtains had been drawn and the candles lit to give the brilliance greater play, and the children were still hurrying to and fro like ants, filled with delight, when wheels were heard outside, and peering through the curtains they saw a chaise and four.

Stephen stepped from the carriage, bent and cramped with his long journey, and Padeen, carrying a bag: the children rushed off in a body, over-excited and shouting far too loud that 'Dr Maturin was come in a chaise and four, and one of the horses was in a fine lather, and Padeen still had his face done up in a bandage.'

'Stephen!' cried Jack, running down the steps. 'How happy I am to see you. You could not have chosen a better moment; we are just about to have a banquet. Padeen, I hope I see you better? Killick will help you carry the Doctor's bags up to his room.'

The post-chaise rolled off, to wait at the Goat and Compasses until the postillion should have the good word, and Stephen walked in, kissing Sophie and the two little faces stretched expectantly up, and exchanged bows with George. 'I am glad to find you here,' he said to Jack in the hall. 'I was afraid you might have run down to Shelmerston yesterday or even the day before.'

'I only had your express an hour or so ago.'

'Good afternoon to you, ma'am,' said Stephen, bowing to

Mrs Williams in the drawing-room. 'Would you believe such a thing? I sent off an express from London town no less – no remote Ballymahon or Cambridge in the bog – two days ago and it arrives only two hours before me. One pound sixteen shillings and eightpence in pure loss, besides half a crown for the boy.'

'Oh, I believe it only too easily, sir,' cried Mrs Williams. 'It is all part of the Ministry's design to ruin the country. We are governed at present by fiends, sir. Fiends.'

'I have a silver spoon of my own, sir,' said George smiling up at him. 'Should you like to see it?'

'Sophie,' said Jack, 'this is the most wonderful opportunity for christening the new plate. Stephen has not dined. We have not dined. Everything is laid out, or as near as damn it, for an admiral's inspection. Could we not run up a simple dish or two – there is some soused hog's face ready, I know – and dine in glory?'

'Of course we can, my dear,' said Sophie without hesitation. 'Give me an hour and there will be at least something under every cover.'

'In the meanwhile, Stephen, let us go into the smoking-room and drink a glass of madeira; and I dare say you would like a cigar after your journey.' In the smoking-room he said, 'Your Padeen looks as if he had been in the wars. Was the operation very painful?'

'It was. It was extremely painful and prolonged. But he came by those lumps and bruises that you observe in a battle at Black's. In the room where the members' servants take their ease, three men put a mock on his bandage and asked him was his father an ass or a rabbit? He destroyed them entirely. Broke the leg of the one – tibia and fibula: a compound fracture – flung the other bodily into the broad old-fashioned fire they have down there and held him on it for a while, and chased the third till he leapt into the lake at St James's park, where Padeen would not follow because of his fine black clothes. Fortunately some of the members are Middlesex magistrates and I was able to bring him away.'

'It will not do to meddle with him. He is the kind of lamb that lies down with the lion, in wolf's clothing. I saw him board the *Spartan* like a good 'un.'

'So he did, too.' Stephen walked over to the fire, lit his cigar and said 'Listen, Jack: we have the possibility of a truly naval action, by which I mean attacking a frigate of the French navy. I am assured that success or even honourable failure in such an encounter might have a favourable effect upon your eventual restoration to the post-captains' list.'

'By God, I should give my right arm for that,' said Jack.

'Pray do not say such things, my dear,' said Stephen. 'It is tempting fate. My friend holds out no sort of guarantee of course, but it is a fact that to the official mind a battle with a national man-of-war counts, whereas an equally severe battle with a private man-of-war does not. Now very briefly the position is this: among the shipping at St Martin's there is a new frigate called the *Diane*, of thirty guns. She has been particularly designed and fitted out for a voyage to South America, particularly Chile and Peru, not unlike ours, and perhaps to the South Seas to harry our whalers there. Her stores are almost all aboard; so are the more or less official French representatives; and she is to sail at slack water on the night of the thirteenth, the dark of the moon, to clear the Channel before daylight. She and some other vessels in St Martin's have been blockaded there for some time by a small inshore squadron that included the *Nymph*, perfectly capable of coping with her and any of the brigs or gunboats that might come out to help her. Yet the exigencies of the present situation are such that during this critical period neither the *Nymph* nor her frequent companion the *Bacchante* can be spared from a more important operation elsewhere and the squadron is reduced to the *Tartarus* and the decrepit *Dolphin*. This deficiency is endeavoured to be concealed by the presence of the *Camel* store-ship and another vessel, but the enemy are aware of our motions and mean to carry out their plan. It therefore occurred to my friend that if the *Surprise* were to intervene it might be to the benefit of all concerned.'

'By God, Stephen,' said Jack, shaking his hand, 'you could not have brought me happier news. May I tell Sophie?'

'No, sir, you may not; nor anyone else until we are at sea or upon the very point of heaving our weigh – I mean topping our boom. Now listen, Jack, will you? I have taken it upon myself to give your consent –'

'And well you might, ha, ha, ha!'

'– to the operation, to the *attempted* operation, and to the somewhat devious official aspect that it is to assume. We have let or hired the ship to the Crown, and the Admiralty has provided a document that will deal with the situation in the event of any serving officer's proving difficult or legalistic. Since dear William Babbington is now the senior officer present the likelihood of disagreement seems tolerably remote; but it is as well to have the paper and we may well think it the best cover or protection for our South American voyage. It begins *By the Commissioners for executing the office of Lord High Admiral of Great Britain et cetera* and it is addressed *To the Flag Officers, Captains and Commanders of His Majesty's Ships and Vessels to whom this shall be exhibited*. Then the body of it runs: *Whereas we have directed John Aubrey, Esquire, to proceed in His Majesty's hired vessel the Surprise upon a particular service, you are hereby required and directed not to demand of him a sight of the Instructions he has received from us for his proceedings on the said service, nor upon any pretence whatever to detain him, but on the contrary to give him any assistance he may stand in need of, towards enabling him to carry the said instructions into execution*. And it is signed by Melville and two other lords of the Admiralty, and at their command by that black thief Croker. And as you see, it is dated and sealed.'

Jack took the paper as reverentially as he would have taken an infinitely more holy substance: tears came into his eyes, and Stephen, knowing how apt the English were to display embarrassing emotion, said in a harsh voice, 'But I must tell you however that the *Diane* is commanded by an exceptionally capable officer, the brother of that Jean-Jacques Lucas who fought the *Redoutable* so nobly at Trafalgar. He has been allowed to pick his crew, and he has trained them according to his brother's methods: their agility in changing the sails and so on surprises qualified observers, even more so the speed and accuracy of their small-arms and great-gun fire. The ship will most probably have some civilians and their papers aboard and it would be a great stroke if we could seize them intact. Now have you a map, a plan, a *chart* of the place at all, so that we may pore over it?'

'I have my own survey,' said Jack. 'The second one. Shall we walk into what I rather absurdly call the library? Bring your wine with you.'

Jack Aubrey was singularly exact and methodical in matters of this kind and within two minutes he spread out a slightly yellowed sheet on the library table, observing that he had made it with Mr Donaldson, the master of the *Bellerophon*, the best hydrographer in the Navy, during the year ninety-seven: 'the variation of the compass had altered thirty-one seconds eastwards since then and some of the soundings would need revision, but he would undertake to lead in and moor his ship under the batteries without a pilot.'

The chart showed a deep narrow harbour, less than a quarter of a mile wide at its mouth and two miles deep, with a six-gun battery at the bottom of it, the entrance narrowed by a breakwater. Both shores were fairly steep-to, but that on the southern side, which ran out in a bold headland carrying a lighthouse was much higher except at its junction with the mainland, where the low isthmus was guarded by a considerable fortification. The town spread over most of the headland east of the lighthouse and on the other side of the port; the men-of-war lay along a fine stone quay on the south side of the harbour; the merchant-men were generally but not always on the other side, while the smallcraft and fishing-boats kept to the bottom. The town might have four or five thousand people as well as the garrison, and there were three churches. And of course the quite well known ship-building yards and stores.

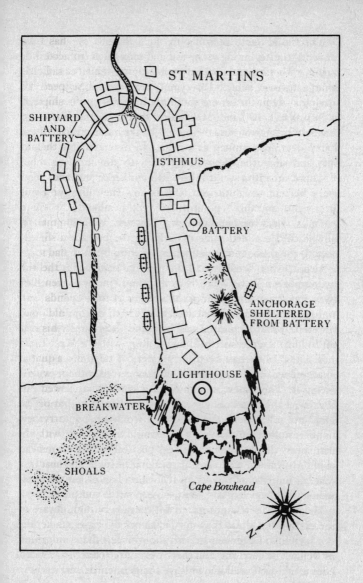

ST MARTIN'S

SHIPYARD
AND
BATTERY

ISTHMUS

BATTERY

ANCHORAGE
SHELTERED
FROM BATTERY

LIGHTHOUSE

BREAKWATER

SHOALS

Cape Bowhead

N

'This,' said Jack, pointing to the isthmus, 'is where we landed at the beginning of the war and took them from behind, burning the yard and a twenty-gun ship on the stocks. Lord, what a famous blaze! Tar, paint, timber and sailcloth all roaring away in the strong southerly breeze – you could read as easy as kiss my hand. It was after that caper they threw up this battery. As you see, these sand-banks made it difficult for a ship drawing as much as a frigate to move straight in and out; and since the *Diane* don't want to run into the main off-shore squadron well to the north and since she must soon shape her course south-west, this is how she must come out on the ebb, and this' – pointing to a bold headland – 'is where we must wait for her, all lights dowsed. We call it Cape Bowhead.' He added some remarks on the breezes to be expected, the tides, and the effect of the wind upon them.

At last, when Stephen had the port, its approaches and the surrounding hills very clearly in his mind, Jack put the chart away and stood gazing out of the window at the slope that ran up to his little astronomical observatory with its copper dome. His credit with his children was, he found, enormously important to him: the pleasure of showing away with the West India merchants' silver had been far greater, of far more essential consequence than ever he could have conceived without experiencing it. They knew something of what had happened, but how exact their knowledge was or what they thought of it he could not tell; yet he did know that from this point of view alone, restoration to the Navy List would be well worth a right arm: even the thought of its real possibility made his head swim. He was on the point of speaking of his reflections in a general, impersonal way when Killick, in his ceremonial coat, opened the door and said 'Wittles is up sir, if you please.'

Mrs Williams was not gifted with any very high degree of perception, but she was as startled as her daughter when they saw Jack follow Stephen in, and she whispered 'If you cannot get Killick to keep the decanters well away from Mr Aubrey, I am afraid we shall have to leave the gentlemen very early in the meal.'

CHAPTER FIVE

Jack Aubrey had always disliked the practice, by no means uncommon in the Navy, of coming aboard without notice and catching his ship's people unawares; but this time, there being neither ship's boat nor coxswain at hand, he had no choice. And he was just as glad, because now as he and Stephen were being taken out in a Shelmerston skiff, he saw that the *Surprise* was a quite unfeigned model of industry. Stages were over the side; the last traces of blue paint had vanished under a fine fresh white; Mr Bulkeley and his mates were creeping about the rigging like huge spiders, renewing fair-leads and clapping red leather jackets on to the larger strops, a very pretty touch; and although her trim was not quite what he could have wished – she was a trifle by the head – it was clear that she had most of her water in. Shelmers-ton water was the best south of the Thames for going far foreign, but it was not easily come-at-able and in his absence the Surprises must have made many a weary voyage in the boats.

As he contemplated the ship he listened with half an ear to the boatman, whose son (like so many others in the little town) was very wishful to ship with Captain Aubrey: he was a right seaman, had made three Canton voyages and one to Botany Bay, rated able from the first, and was a rare hand with the fiddle; sober, too, and not in the least quarrelsome, except on the enemy's deck; Church of England, and (emphatically) always obedient to command.

'Ay,' said Jack, 'I am sure he is a good young man. But we have all the hands we need, you know. Still, when the rest of the prize-money comes in and is properly shared out there may be some vacancies: I believe there are men who mean to set up on their own, or buy public houses.'

'But what about the awkward sods you turned away, your honour?'

'Lord love you, their places were filled up that very evening. No. Let your boy come and see me or Captain Pullings when everything is settled, in about a fortnight's time, and we will have a look at him. What is his name?'

'Abel Hayes, sir, if you please. Abel. Not Seth,' said the boatman with a particularly significant look: its significance was quite lost on Jack, who said, 'Just pull me round the ship, will you, before going alongside.'

The skiff passed the frigate's stern at about a cable's length and moved up her immaculate starboard side: immaculate but for the name Seth painted neat and clear on the white band, amidships, between the black ports of guns twelve and fourteen. Jack made no observation, but his face, which had regained something of its former habitual pink-gilled gaiety during their journey down, tightened, became grey and humourless once more. 'Larboard mainchains,' he said after a pause: and arriving there he ran up the side to the quarterdeck, which he saluted, every quarterdeck having carried a crucifix less than three hundred years before: the salute was returned by Davidge and West and by Martin, who had reported on Saturday, to avoid the Sunday travelling that disturbed neither Jack nor Stephen. All three were much better dressed than when first they joined the ship and evidently far more prosperous; yet they all had anxious, careworn expressions. 'Good evening, gentlemen,' said Jack. 'I am going below, Mr Davidge, and shall be happy to hear your report in five minutes time.'

There were several letters and messages for him in the cabin, most of them requests to be taken aboard, but others brought congratulations and good wishes from old shipmates, some of them as far afield as Greenwich Hospital. He was still reading one of these when Davidge came in and said 'Sir, I am truly concerned to have to report a mutiny aboard.'

'A mutiny, eh? But from the look of the ship I presume it is far from being general.' He had indeed noticed the absence of cheerful talk and laughter as he came aboard and the presence of glum and apprehensive looks; but nothing in the least like ill-will. Man and boy he had known several mutinies quite apart from the great outbreaks at Spithead and the Nore and he had heard of many more – they were surprisingly common in the Navy – but never aboard a prosperous, busy ship, with plenty of shore-leave and all the delights that money could buy just at hand. 'Who are the men concerned?'

'Slade, the Brampton brothers, Mould, Hinckley, Auden and Vaggers, sir.'

'Oh dear me.' These were among the best of the Shelmerstonians, two of them quartermasters, one a gunner's mate, the others thorough-going seamen, quiet, solid fellows: prize hands. 'Sit down, Mr Davidge, and give me a short account of the affair.'

Davidge however was incapable of giving a short account that was also sequential, coherent and inclusive; his mind did not work that way. Although he was a competent officer, who had no hesitation in giving a rapid series of orders to deal with a dangerous situation in foul weather on a lee-shore, he wandered sadly in his narration and Jack was by no means sure that he had the whole at his command when Davidge's repetitions and parentheses came to an embarrassed close. What he did gather was that on Sunday morning the seven men, who were all Sethians – 'What are Sethians, Mr Davidge?' 'Oh, a kind of Ranters or Methodies I believe, sir: I did not go into that' – Sethians from Old Shelmerston, a village a little way inland, had gone to their meeting-house. They had then had dinner on shore and on returning to the ship some or all of them had gone out on the stage that was still hanging over the starboard side and had there painted the offending word.

Davidge had not noticed it at once, because the gunroom was entertaining Mrs Martin to dinner, her first visit to the ship; but on returning from seeing the Martins ashore he had of course seen the word standing out from a great distance, the ship having swung with the turn of the tide, and he had at once ordered it to be removed. Nobody seemed to know who had done it; nobody seemed willing to scrape it off or paint it out – endless excuses: the brushes had been cleaned – Sunday – best clothes – just going to the head – bowels upset by eating crab. Eventually Auden acknowledged having painted the name. He refused to remove it – said he was unable to do so in conscience – and in this he was backed up by the other six. He was not violent or abusive – no foul language – nor was he obviously drunk – but he and the others stated that if any hand attempted to remove the name, his first stroke would be his last. Davidge and West had had no support from the bosun, gunner or carpenter, still less from any of the hands, who, though in no way riotous, were clearly heard to say that they would do nothing to bring bad luck on the ship. For fear of making the position even worse, Davidge had therefore given no further direct, unmistakable orders: nor, having no Marines of course, had he put the seven men in irons. Since the Articles of War did not apply, and since the ship was not at sea, neither he nor West had been certain what to do. He had nevertheless suspended the men from duty pending the captain's arrival and had forbidden them to come on deck. Perhaps he should have sent them ashore directly; if he had done wrong he was heartily sorry for it; but he appealed to Captain Aubrey's candour.

'Did you consult Mr Martin?' asked Jack.

'No, sir. He only returned a few minutes before you.'

'I see. Well, I think you did tolerably well in a difficult situation. Pray ask the doctors if they can spare me a moment.' In the short time he had to wait various possibilities flashed through his mind, but the arguments for and against each were still equally balanced when the cabin door opened. 'Mr Martin,' he said, 'you have no doubt heard about the present trouble. Please tell me all you can about these Sethians. I have never heard of them.'

'Well, sir, they descend from the Valentinian Gnostics, but the descent is so long, remote and obscure that there would be little point in tracing it. In their present form they are small independent communities with I believe no governing body; but it is difficult to be sure of that, since they were in danger of persecution as heretics for so long that they are naturally reserved; and there is still something of the air of a secret society about them. They believe that Cain and Abel were brought into being by angels, whereas Seth, who, as you will recall, was born after Abel's murder, was the Almighty's direct pure creation, and not only the ancestor of Abraham and all men now living, but the prototype of our Lord. They have the utmost veneration for him, and believe he watches over Sethians with particular care. But they have little opinion of angels, holding that by their – how shall I express it? – that by their mutual impurities they brought about Noah's flood. This should have wiped out their descendants, but some crept into the ark; and they, not Seth, are the ancestors of the wicked.'

'It is odd that I should never even have heard of them. Do they often go to sea?'

'I imagine not. Most of the few I have come across or heard of live in small scattered groups in remote inland parts of the West Country. They sometimes carve the name Seth on their houses; and they fall into two schools, mutually hostile, the old school that writes the S backwards and the new that writes it as we do. Apart from that and an unwillingness to pay tithes, they have a reputation for holding together and for being honest, sober and reliable, not unlike the Quakers. Yet unlike the Quakers they have no dislike for warfare.'

'But they are Christians, are they not?'

'As for that,' said Martin, looking at Stephen, 'there are some Gnostics who would puzzle St Peter.'

'The Valentinians were good enough to say that Christians might be saved,' observed Stephen. 'We might perhaps return the compliment.'

'In any event,' said Martin, 'these people have left the gnosis of Valentinus infinitely far behind: it is quite forgotten. Their holy books are ours. I believe we may certainly call them

Christians, though somewhat heterodox on certain points of doctrine.'

'I am glad to hear it; and I am obliged to you, sir, for all you have told me. Maturin, does any observation occur to you?'

'Never a word. I am not to be teaching Martin theology, and he a bachelor of divinity.'

'Then let us take a turn on deck, and after that I will speak to the Sethians.'

He took his turn, and a sweet evening it was; but he had not resolved upon any clear line of approach before he returned to his cabin and sent for the mutineers. In human relations he was no Macchiavel, and it was with perfect sincerity that he now said to them 'Here's a pretty kettle of fish, upon my word. What in the Devil's – what in Heaven's name induced you to paint Seth on the ship's side?'

The seven men stood there toeing a line athwartships in the checkered sailcloth deck-covering; they had the light of the broad stern-window full on them, and Jack, standing with his back to it, saw them with the utmost clarity – grave, steady men, oppressed by the occasion and perhaps somewhat apprehensive, but not sullen, far less malignant. 'Come,' he said. 'Slade, you are the oldest. Tell me how it came about.'

Slade looked right and left at his companions, who all nodded, and began in his rumbling West-Country burr, 'Well, sir, we are what are called Sethians.'

'Yes. Mr Martin has just told me about them: a respectable Christian body.'

'That's right, sir. And Sunday we went to our meeting-house in Old Shelmerston –'

'Just past the smithy,' said the simpler Brampton brother.

'– and there we were put in mind that Seth' – they all jerked their right-hand thumbs up and sideways at the name – 'had been uncommon good to us last voyage.'

'That's right,' said his mates.

'And then when we ate our dinner at the William we considered as how, time out of mind, our people had always put

144

the name on their house, come any particular blessing, by way of what we call a thank-witness. So when we come back, we put it on the ship.'

'I see. But on being told to take it off again, you did not do so.'

'No, sir. For us the name is holy. It must never be touched. There is not one of us could bring his hand to do it.'

'That's right,' said his mates.

'I see your point,' said Jack. 'But tell me, when you were eating your dinner, what did you drink?'

'We weren't drunk, sir,' said Slade.

'So I have been told. But you did not eat dry and it stands to reason that with gold in your pocket you did not drink water or buttermilk: just what did you drink?'

Their account, which had a religious accuracy in this case, came to slightly over a quart of beer or cider for each man except for Slade and Auden, who had shared a bottle of wine.

'That is moderate enough, in all conscience,' said Jack. 'Yet it is amazing how a couple of glasses of wine can affect a man's judgment without his knowing it. If you had not drunk your wine, you would have reflected that the *Surprise* is a private man-of-war and so she must rely on passing unknown and deceiving the enemy. But how can she pass unknown or deceive the enemy with that name painted clear amidships? Then again, every Christian knows he must do as he would be done by. You have a hundred shipmates and more: are they to be done out of the chance of prize-money because of your particular custom? Clearly, it ain't fair or right or just. The name must go. No, no,' he went on, seeing their lowering and dogged look, 'I do not mean it must be scraped out, nor painted out, nor even touched. We will cover it with a piece of fine sailcloth as we did when we were running down to St Michael's: then maybe we will paint the sailcloth over in case of foul weather; but the name will still be there. So the influence will still be there. After all, it was there when we were painted blue.'

He saw most of the men nod privately, and then when Slade looked right and left they all jerked their heads in assent. 'Well, sir,' he said, 'being it is to be like that, we are quite satisfied; and we thank you, sir, for hearing us so fair.'

'I should have been sorry to turn good seamen away,' said Jack. 'Yet there is still one thing left to be done. You spoke very chough to Mr Davidge, and you murmured. You must beg his pardon.'

After some moments of hesitation, with the men looking at one another with doubtful faces, Auden said, 'The rub is he is such a fine gentleman, sir; we are only simple chaps, and should not know what to say.'

'You must go up to him,' said Jack, 'and pull off your hats, as is right, and one of you must say "We ask your pardon, sir, for answering chough, and murmuring."'

'It is a little awkward, not having Killick here until tomorrow,' said Jack Aubrey, helping Stephen to a great piece of the veal and ham pie that Sophie had put up for their supper, 'but I would not have had him here this evening for a hundred pound. He is somewhat given to listening, you know, and although I spoke perfectly sincerely to the Sethians, I could not have carried on about moral duty and the rest with him in earshot.'

'When shall we see the men from Ashgrove?' asked Stephen.

'About four in the afternoon, I believe, if all goes well and the coach don't overset. About the same time as Pullings.'

'Well, that is the black dismal news, upon my soul. I forgot to put up a clean shirt, and I had forgot to change this one last week, and in their swelling pride and glory now that they have two guineas to rub together the gunroom mean to ask us to dinner tomorrow so that you may be introduced to Mrs Martin. I have a great esteem for her, and should not wish to appear a shoneen dragged in from the Liberties.' He looked at the cuff of his shirt, which had been somewhat squalid before their long night in the greasy chaise, and which was now a disgrace to the ship.

'What a fellow you are, Stephen,' said Jack. 'After all these years at sea you still have no notion of life aboard. Give your shirt to any old Surprise you have cured of the pox or the flux, any Surprise you like to name – Warren, Hurst, Farrell, anyone – and he will wash it in fresh water abaft the scuttle-butt, dry it in the galley and give it you in the morning. In the meanwhile you walk about in a dressing-gown. I shall look forward to seeing Mrs Martin at last, particularly as you so rarely praise a woman. What is she like?'

'Oh, she has no pretensions to beauty, at all. She has no pretensions of any kind for that matter, intellectual, artistic or social. She is neither tall nor slim and on occasion she wears spectacles; but she is perfectly well bred and she has so sweet a nature and such a fund of good humour that she is a most valuable companion.'

'I remember your telling me that she nursed Martin quite devotedly after you had opened his belly. I shall be happy to have the meeting at dinner-time, because a few hours later it would be too late, and I should not wish to seem wanting in attention. But as soon as Pullings and Bonden and Killick and the rest are aboard I believe we can put to sea: there may still be a little to fetch in the way of stores and perhaps I may be able to pick up a cook; but this tide or the next will see us out in the Channel.'

'You astonish me, brother: I am amazed. The *Diane* does not sail until the thirteenth. Today, if I do not mistake, is the fourth. In less time than that we could swim to St Martin's or rather to the point in the ocean where you mean to intercept her.'

Jack uncorked another bottle of wine, and after a while he said, 'In the night, as we were coming down, I turned the whole thing over this way and that; and I have thought about it since, bearing in mind what you told me about her commander and his picked crew. And it appears to me that rather than waiting off the cape for him to come to us, with all the chances of thick weather, awkward breeze, weather-gage and so on, the clever thing is for us to go to him. Besides, it is very likely that a corvette or a brig will see him clear of the Channel. When French gunnery is good, it is very good; and although the old *Surprise* could do it, with our present complement we cannot fight both sides of the ship at once as well as I could wish.'

'Will you not engage more men, then, for all love? Are they not calling out after us in the street, begging to be taken on?'

'Believe me, Stephen, it would not answer. You cannot make a gunner in a week, no nor in a great many weeks. And then again, we cannot go into the street and whistle for Marines. You will say they are only soldiers, which is perfectly true, but they are steady, trained, disciplined men, and the thirty-odd we used to have were very valuable in action. You have but to remember their small-arms fire.'

For a moment it occurred to Stephen to ask why the *Surprise* did not have her former complement, with the equivalent of these Marines, by whatever name they came aboard; but the answer was obvious – in this, as in so many other things, Jack was sparing his friend's pocket.

'Dear Lord,' said Jack smiling, 'I told you just now that I was perfectly sincere in talking to the Sethians as I did; and certainly I meant every word I said. But I dare say the fact that I was damnably unwilling to part with seven prime hands made me a little milder than I might have been with a full complement and the Articles of War behind me. Yet on the other hand it is but fair to say that coming down heavy in a case like that is just the kind of thing that upsets a ship's company worse than hard-horse officers, too much flogging, and no shore-leave – far worse.'

'You acted for the best, sure: men will go to the stake for names much less respectable than Seth,' said Stephen. 'So you mean to put to sea, I find?'

'Yes. Because it seems to me that the best thing to do is to cut her out – to try to cut her out – by night. You can cruise for a ship very assiduously indeed quite well in with the shore and still miss her; but if you run into her port before she has sailed you are at least sure of finding her, which is the necessary beginning for any sort of battle.'

'I should never deny it, brother.'

'So, do you see, I mean to weigh tomorrow at the latest, tell the people what we are about, make them understand the shape, nature, soundings and bearings of St Martin's on a thundering great chart I shall draw, showing just where the *Diane* lies and where we shall lie, and then run down to Polcombe or any of those little lonely coves, according to the weather, moor the ship, and practise cutting her out with the boats night after night, till every man knows exactly where he is to be and what he is to do.'

'I applaud your design extremely,' said Stephen. 'And if during these exercises the ship could refrain from any communication with the shore, how very charming that would be: schemes of this kind are so very easily blown upon, particularly on a smuggling coast, with much going to and fro. Perhaps it would be out of place to suggest the hiring of some fine stout desperate fellows just for this operation?'

'I quite take your point about no communication, and I had it in mind myself; but as for your hired ruffians, I am sure William and his companions will provide us with all the volunteers their boats can hold – men accustomed to naval discipline. My only dread is –' he coughed '– that there may be too many, and that they may talk or make a noise.'

Even a little wine, as he had said earlier in the day, could affect a man's judgment, and he had been on the point of saying that he was most horribly afraid Babbington's zeal and friendship (infinitely mistaken friendship in this case) would lead him to join the expedition: for then in the event of success the *Diane* would have been 'cut out by Captain Babbington of HMS *Tartarus*, with the help of boats from the other men-of-war under his command, and from a privateer'. The offer he dreaded could not be refused, since if the *Diane* were captured the action would make William Babbington, now only a commander, a post-captain, the essential step to a flag and high command. Jack had been on the point of telling Stephen this: but it would not do. William must see it for himself or not at all. Jack had not the slightest doubt of William's affectionate loyalty – it had been most amply proved – but an excellent heart did not necessarily argue a brilliant intelligence, capable of instantly assessing the relative value of the near-certainty of promotion on the one hand and the remote possibility of reinstatement on the other. Yet Babbington, well-connected, with strong parliamentary interest, was pretty well sure of promotion soon in any event, whereas such an opportunity as this might never come Jack's way again in a lifetime. He looked across the table at Stephen, who said 'These night exercises of yours are a most capital notion.'

'I hope they may prove so. At least it is better than rushing at a bull in a china-shop without a plan. The *Spartan* was different. There it was simply a question of hammering the enemy hand to hand. Here we must not only hammer the enemy but sail his ship out of the harbour too, under the fire of his batteries and whatever men-of-war may be present. It has to be done neatly or not at all. Tell me, Stephen, would you say that William Babbington had a quick, lively apprehension?'

Stephen almost laughed: wheezing with amusement he said, 'I love William Babbington, but I do not think anyone could call his apprehension, his grasp, his intellection, quick or lively, except perhaps Mrs Wray. In the rough sports of war and in the immediate perils of the ocean, no doubt he is eminently quick; but for a rapid appreciation of more complex issues perhaps it would be better to look elsewhere. For these night-exercises of yours, however, springing from one clearly-defined point to another in the wet and the dark, with an express purpose, he would be most admirably suited. As I said, I think them a capital notion.'

Dr Maturin's views were shared by all hands. They studied the great chart that Jack had chalked out between the mizen-mast and the taffrail with the utmost attention as the ship ran down under easy sail to Polcombe; several of the hands had been in St Martin's during the peace, and they confirmed the unchanging general disposition of the port, the yard, and the navigable channels. And they, together with all the seamen present, took Jack's point that the one anxious part of the approach was the breakwater that guarded the harbour from westerly seas; it ran out from the south side, under the light-house cliff, and sentries patrolled its rampart. The boats necessarily had to pass within hail. But fortunately, the *Surprise* had two Jerseymen, Duchamp and Chevènement, 'And if we are challenged,' said Jack, 'they can sing out something short and quick, like "hands and supplies for *Diane*".'

When they reached Polcombe the breeze failed them, but they towed her in at slack water, so far in that they would certainly have to tow her out again, since the high cliffs cut off every breeze that would allow her to sail, while the ebb set hard against the reefs of Old Scratch, the rocky island that guarded the mouth of the cove – it might almost have been called a little bay – sheltering it from the heavy southern and south-western seas. Here, watched by a thousand sheep peering from the turfy brink so high above and by a moon-struck shepherd, they moored her with springs to her cables and began to lay out buoys limiting the harbour of St Martin's by the distances and angles that Lieutenant Aubrey had measured so exactly so many years before. They were even able to place tolerably accurate marks representing the tip of the cape with the lighthouse on it and the breakwater with the awkward rampart: by this time it was well on in the evening, but the men's spirits were so high that the boats gathered round Jack's launch, and with a liberty arising from the general good humour, the growing darkness and their distance from the ship, the hands urged him to let them pull out to the point where the ship would lie in the offing and then 'let them have a go'.

'Very well,' said he. 'But it must be done thorough-pace: a line from stern to stem; pull easy, and all hands to row soft and row dry, not to wet your mates' priming; not a word, no not a single goddamned whisper; this is not Bartholomew Fair, and the first man to speak may swim home on his own.'

The boats stood out to sea until it appeared to Jack that they were just where he would wish to anchor the ship off Cape Bowhead. Here he gave a clear account, three times repeated without the slightest variation, of where each boat was to board and what each group of men was to do; and he repeated his words about silence with even greater emphasis. The stars were already pricking out in the clear sky, and with Vega and Arcturus as his compass above he guided the line back to the mark for the headland and then after a dog-leg turn at the breakwater, where Duchamp called out 'New hands for the *Diane*', straight for the unsuspecting ship. They pulled smooth, mile after mile, they pulled away – the quiet tide was just making – until at last Jack murmured 'Cast off and stretch out' and the boats, freed from the line that had kept them together, dashed to the points of attack, the beakhead, the forechains, the mainchains, the mizenchains and the stern-ladder, and invaded the ship simultaneously with a horrible roar. A party of the most active young topmen raced aloft to loose the courses and topsails; Padeen and an equally powerful black man flew to the cables and stood over them each with a hypothetical axe; two quartermasters seized the helm; Jack Aubrey darted into the cabin, not so much to go through the motions of seizing the captain, his civilians and their papers as to check the time. 'I think it was an hour and forty-three minutes,' he said. 'But I could not be sure of the start. Next time I shall take a dark lantern. Was our howl unexpected?'

'Entirely,' said Stephen.

'A complete surprise,' said Martin.

'Was you terrified?'

'Perhaps we should have been if there had been less merriment. Old Plaice's hoarse chuckle could be recognized a great way off.'

Martin said 'Might not a sudden silent attack be even more disconcerting? An unprovoked, unheralded violence contradicting all social contract, which calls for at least a cry of challenge or defiance? But even as it was, the assault terrified your new cook, sir. We were talking to him about a pilaff for your supper when the howl broke out: he uttered a cry in what may have been Armenian and ran from the room, crouched inhumanly low.'

'A pilaff? What an admirable notion. I dearly love a good

pilaff. You will give us the pleasure of your company, Mr Martin?'

The next few days were quite remarkably happy. The ordinary routine was cut to a minimum, and apart from attacking the ship twice a night, the hands spent a great deal of earnest, concentrated effort in cutlass or boarding-axe practice and in pistol-fire. The rest of the time – for these were sunny days – they lay about the forecastle or gangways with an easy lack of restraint rarely to be seen in a man-of-war, public or private. It astonished the watchers who had come to join the sheep high above, and the nearby hamlets learnt that a pirate was moored in Polcombe cove, intending to ravish the countryside, carrying off the maidens to Barbary. At this the young women for some miles around hurried to the edge of the precipice, to view their ravishers, and perhaps to implore their mercy; while a revenue cutter, suspecting uncustomed goods, ran in and had to submit to the ultimate humiliation of being heaved off the tail of the Old Scratch reef by two cables, spliced end to end and carried out to the *Surprise*'s capstan.

Jack was physically extremely active, which suited him through and through: during the night attacks he often took Stephen's personal skiff and accompanied the line of boats, paying close attention to the style of pulling in each and timing the various stages of the operation to the second. And after the first assault, which had been carried out mostly for the fun, he organized a kind of resistance. The defenders were allowed nothing more lethal than swabs, but the delay they were able to cause gave him a somewhat better estimate of the probable duration. In common justice the teams were changed and mingled, half-watch by half-watch, and twice a night Jack Aubrey either attacked or defended. All hands expended an immense amount of energy, and their captain, as was but right, expended even more. He was a powerful swimmer and during his naval career scarcely a commission had passed by without his having saved some Marine or seaman from drowning, so that there were at least half a dozen old Surprises now aboard who would have perished but for him; but at present he far outdid the past, for in repelling boarders he and his mates often flung them backwards into the sea and in one night alone he plucked out five – no fuss: simply an ape-like arm reaching down from the chains or a boat's gunwale and heaving them bodily up.

This intense physical activity did him a great deal of good, of course – his powerful great body called for much more than shipboard life could ordinarily give him – but it did even more good to his wounded heart and mind, since there was no time for the misery of retrospection nor for the corresponding phantasms of unrealistic success that so very often struggled for expression.

The combination brought back something of the appetite he had had before his trial: it would have been a shame if it had not done so, for Killick had laid in captain's stores on a scale he thought suitable to their new-found wealth, and the captain's cook, Adi, would have graced Lucullus' flagship. He was a gentle timid little greyish-brown man, round and greasy, easily moved to tears: he was utterly useless as a combatant, since no words, good or bad, could induce him either to attack or defend the ship; but he understood the whole range of naval cookery from Constantinople to Gibraltar; and although his maids of honour brought Rosia Bay to mind rather than Richmond Hill, they went down wonderfully well; while he could also turn out a creditable suet pudding.

From Maturin's point of view also these days were a blessed holiday. He could do nothing about his future plans, being as far out of touch with London as if he were in the Pacific; and although Diana was never far from his mind – he carried her talisman in his breeches pocket – his chief present occupation was to take in as much sun as his meagre form could absorb. He had been starved of it so long during the English winter that in these brilliant days he grudged every moment spent between decks or in the shade.

Fortunately for him and Martin, who formed no part of the boarding or defending teams and who otherwise would have been left to mope, there was Old Scratch, a delight for both the naturalist and the sun-worshipper. At one time sheep and rabbits had been introduced: the sheep had long since vanished but the rabbits were still there, and it was on their close-clipped southern lawns that Stephen basked when he and Martin were not taken up with the many other delights – the tide-pools, the seals that bred in the northern sea-caves, the uncommon plants such as bishop's snodgrass, the puffins nesting in rabbit-burrows, and the stormy petrels, which could be heard churring in their companionable way, far down in their musky holes.

It was on one of those perfect afternoons, with a long south-western swell beating with slow, deep, measured strokes on the seaward face of Old Scratch, that they sat on the grass, watching the series of small waves that followed each impact and that ran into the cove in spreading half-circles, diminishing with perfect regularity until they lapped against the ship, a fan-like pattern of quite unusual beauty.

'That ship,' observed Martin, 'contains a surprising number of beliefs. No doubt others of her size contain as many, but surely not quite so various, for I must confess that although I was prepared for Gnostics, Anabaptists, Sethians, Muggletonians and even those who follow Joanna Southcott, as well as the odd Jew or Mahometan, I was quite taken aback to find we have a Devil-worshipper aboard.'

'A true, literal, open worshipper of the Devil?'

'Yes. He does not like to mention the fiend's name, except in a hand-shaded whisper, but refers to him as the Peacock. They have an image of a peacock in their temples.'

'Would it be indiscreet to ask which of our shipmates holds these eccentric views?'

'Not at all, not at all. He did not speak in confidence. It is Adi, the Captain's cook.'

'I had supposed he was an Armenian, a Gregorian Christian.'

'So had I; but it appears that in fact he is a Dasni, from the country lying between Armenia and Kurdistan.'

'Does he not believe in God at all, the animal?'

'Oh yes. He and his people believe that God made the world; they look upon our Lord as having a divine nature; they acknowledge Mahomet as a prophet and Abraham and the patriarchs; but they say God forgave the fallen Satan and restored him to his place. In their view it is therefore the Devil who rules as far as worldly matters are concerned, so it would be a waste of time to worship anyone else.'

'Yet he seems a mild, amiable little man; and he is certainly the cook of the world.'

'Yes: he was showing me how to prepare the true Turkish delight – Deborah is almost sinfully fond of it – in the kindest way while he told me all this. He also spoke of the desolate mountains of the Dasni country, where the people live in partially subterranean houses, persecuted by the Armenians on the one hand and the Kurds on the other. But the families seem very loving and united, and they are sustained by a strong affection that extends to the remotest kinsman. It is evident that the Dasni do not practise what they preach.'

'Who does, indeed? If Adi had an accurate knowledge of the creed we profess to follow and if he compared it with the way we live, he might look at us with as much surprise as we look at him.' Stephen thought of asking Martin whether he did not perceive a certain analogy between the Dasnis' and the Sethians' opinion of angels, but he was stupid with comfort and the warmth of the sun and he only said 'There is a puffin flying with three fishes in his bill: I cannot make out how he manages to take the second and the third.'

Martin had no useful suggestion to offer and they sat on in silence watching the sun until it sank behind the far headland; then they turned with one accord to gaze at the ship, which was going through one of the strangest manoeuvres known to seafaring man. Getting boats over the side, first hoisting them up from the skid-beams, heaving them outboard, and then lowering them down by tackles on the fore and main yardarms had always been a laborious business, accompanied time out of mind by a great deal of shouting, rumbling and splashing, compounded in this case by the Shelmerstonians' habit of yeo-heave-hoeing loud and clear whenever they clapped on to a fall. On a quiet night, with the air drifting landwards, it was possible that even from far out in the offing this din might wreck the most carefully prepared and otherwise silent raid, and Jack Aubrey was trying to make the operation noiseless; but it went strangely against the grain, against all known habits and customs, and it rendered the hands slow, nervous and awkward – so awkward indeed that the stern of the launch came down with a horrid splash while its bows were still a fathom from the sea, and the captain's enormous roar of 'Forward, there. Let go that goddam fall,' filled the cove until it was drowned by an even greater howl of laughter, at first choking and repressed, then spreading uncontrollably, so that all hands staggered again.

This was almost the last sun Stephen saw in Polcombe cove, and almost the last laughter he heard. Foul weather came up from the south-west, bringing rain, sometimes heavy, sometimes very heavy, almost blinding; heavy seas, too, which grew into solemn great rollers with the making tide, and cut up into a nasty short chopping surface on the ebb. Throughout this period the Surprises and their officers continued to attack or defend their ship twice a night: but boarding in oilskins or tarpaulins, with scarcely a gleam of light, after having pulled out and back over such an uneasy sea, was no small matter; and after several accidents and one near-drowning Jack was obliged to diminish both the outward voyage and the defence.

Yet even so the casualties increased, strains, cruelly barked shins and cracked ribs mostly, from falling back into the boats from the wet and slippery sides, but also some badly broken bones like young Thomas Edwards' femur, a compound fracture that made Stephen and Martin very thoughtful indeed. He was one of the topmen whose duty it was to lay aloft the moment they were aboard, run out on the yard and loose the topsails: but he had not expected the defenders to strap up the foot-ropes and he had pitched backwards, falling headlong until the mizenstay checked him just above the quarterdeck, saving his life but breaking his leg.

Stephen and Martin relayed one another in the sick-berth, and night after night in that damp and fetid atmosphere (for most of the time the hatches were closed) the casualties came down, none so serious as young Edwards, whose leg would have to come off at the first sign of gangrene, but none trivial.

By this time Maturin was heartily sick of the exercises, and he wondered that even Jack, with so very much at stake, should persist in this shocking discomfort, wetness, danger and cold, when every hand had been through all the motions in all their varieties so very often. He wondered still more that the hands, who had only money to gain and probably not very much of that — far less in any event than their late glorious haul — should turn to with such zeal: devoid of merriment now, but apparently unabated.

He made the remark to Martin as they sat each side of Tom Edwards, Stephen's left hand on the wound, feeling for the coldness of gangrene, and his right taking the patient's fine steady hopeful pulse: he made it in Latin, and in the same language or rather his comic English version of it Martin replied 'Perhaps you are so used to your friend that you no longer see what a great man he is to the sailors. If he can leap and bound at night in the pouring rain, defying the elements, they would be ashamed not to do the same, though I have seen some almost weep at the second assault, or when they are desired to go through the cutlass exercise once more. I doubt they would do so much for anyone else. It is a quality some men possess.'

'I dare say you are in the right of it,' said Stephen. 'But if he were to ask me to come out in a rowing-boat on a night like this, even wrapped in waterproof garments and wearing a cork jacket, I should decline.'

'I should never have the moral courage. What do you say to this leg?'

'I have great hopes,' said Stephen. He bent over the wound and smelt it. 'Great hopes indeed.' And in English he said to Edwards, 'You are coming along very well, joy. So far, I am quite satisfied. Mr Martin, I am going to my cabin. If there are any casualties at the second boarding, do not hesitate to call me. I shall not be asleep.'

Dr Maturin might be satisfied with the compound fracture, but he was satisfied with little else. The weather, now not unlike that south of the Horn but with no chance of an albatross, had cut him off from Old Scratch just as an oyster-catcher was about to bring off her eggs; his laudanum was having less and less effect and since he was determined not to increase his usual dose he spent much of the night in musing, not often happily; and he was dissatisfied with Padeen. He did not indeed see a great deal of his servant, who was much taken up with practising his part as boarder and axe-man, but what he did see displeased him. Not long since he had suddenly chanced upon Padeen coming from his sea-chest, which was stored below, with a brandy-bottle under his jacket. As far as his stammer would allow him to be understood he said that 'it was only a bottle', but his maidenly blush proclaimed that it was filled entirely with guilt.

Spirits were not allowed aboard a King's ship except in the form of the official grog: Stephen had no notion of what was the case in a privateer, nor did he care; but he did know what drink could do to his countrymen and since then he had been trying to think of some way of turning the hitherto sober Padeen away from it. Already the young man's behaviour had changed; although he was still perfectly well conducted there was an approach to something like confidence – no very amiable quality in the Irish sense of the word – and sometimes a strange dreamy exhilaration.

In fact Padeen was by now a confirmed opium-eater or rather drinker, a sixty-drops a day man. When he was ashore he had made some attempts at buying a supply of his own, but since he had caught no more of the name than tincture and since he could neither read nor write he had no success. 'There are hundreds of tinctures, sailor,' the chemists had said. 'Which one do you want?' and answer he had none. The alcohol was easier. Very early in his acquaintance with the tincture he had heard Dr Maturin observe that it was compounded with respectable brandy, and at present it was with the very best the grog-shop could produce that Stephen's own dose was steadily diluted: steadily, but so gradually that he never suspected it, any more than he suspected the possibility of the medicine chest's being opened. Yet given far more than common strength nothing was easier. The *Surprise* had begun life as the French *Unité*, and her medicine-chest, which was built into her, had its massive door hung on pintles in the French manner and an exceedingly powerful man could lift it straight off its hinges.

Stephen's dissatisfaction vanished in the morning, however. He was up very early and clear-headed, a rare thing for him, though somewhat less unusual now that his effectual night-draught was so diminished. A rapid tour of the sick-berth showed him that Edwards' leg was almost certainly safe and that no particular urgency attached to any of the other cases, and he went on deck; here he found the air warm and still, the sky pure, with the remains of night over the land and the entire eastern bowl a delicate violet shading down to pale blue on the horizon. Swabs were busy, advancing towards him; they had already reached the hances, and Tom Pullings, the officer of the watch, was sitting on the capstan with his trousers rolled up, out of the coming flood. 'Good morning, Doctor,' he called. 'Come and join me on neutral ground.'

'Good morning to you, Captain Pullings, my dear,' said Stephen. 'But I see that my little boat is attached to those cranes at the back, and I have a month's mind . . .'

The form of the *Surprise* did not allow her to have the quarter-davits that were coming into general use and that equipped all modern ships of her size, but she did have a pair over the stern, and these at present held the Doctor's skiff.

'Avast swabbing and lower down the skiff,' cried Pullings. 'Doctor, step into it amidships and sit quite still. Handsomely, now: handsomely does it.'

They set him gently down on the smooth water and he

rowed off towards Old Scratch – rowed, that is to say, in his odd paddling fashion, facing the direction in which he meant to go and pushing his oars: this he justified by stating that it was far better to look steadily towards the future rather than to gaze back for ever at the past; but in fact it was the only way he could avoid turning in circles.

The island had not disliked the foul weather: far from it. Although no one could have called it dusty or in need of swabbing before, it now gave an impression of extraordinary brilliance and cleanliness: the turf had taken on a far, far more lively green, and now that the sun had climbed high enough to send his beams over the cliff that formed the seaward side, daisies were opening their innocent faces in countless thousands, their first adventure, a delight to the heart. He walked up the slope to the rocky edge, and there spread before him and on either hand was the immeasurably vast calm sea. He was not very high above it, but high enough for the busy puffins, hurrying out to sea or back with their catch, to seem quite small below him as he sat there among the sea-pink with his legs dangling over the void. For some time he contemplated the birds: a few razorbills and guillemots as well as the puffins – remarkably few gulls of any kind – the oyster-catchers' parents (he was confident of the chicks' well-being, having seen the neat shells from which they had hatched) – some rock-doves, and a small band of choughs. Then his eye wandered out over the sea and the lanes that showed upon its prodigious surface, apparently following no pattern and leading nowhere, and he felt rising in his heart that happiness he had quite often known as a boy, and even now at long intervals, particularly at dawn: the nacreous blue of the sea was not the source (though he rejoiced in it) nor the thousand other circumstances he could name, but something wholly gratuitous. A corner of his mind urged him to enquire into the nature of this feeling, but he was most unwilling to do so, partly from a dread of blasphemy (the words 'state of grace' were worse than grotesque, applied to a man of his condition), but even more from a wish to do nothing to disturb it.

This importunity had hardly arisen before it was gone. A rock-dove, gliding placidly along before him, abruptly swerved, flying very fast northwards; a peregrine, stooping from high above with the sound of a rocket, struck a cloud of feathers from the dove and bore it off to the mainland cliff, beyond the *Surprise*. As he watched the falcon's heavier but still rapid flight he heard eight bells strike aboard, followed by the remote pipe of all hands to breakfast and the much more emphatic roar of the hungry seamen: a moment later he saw Jack Aubrey, mother-naked, plunge from the taffrail and swim out towards Old Scratch, his long yellow hair streaming behind him. When he was half way across two seals joined him, those intensely curious animals, sometimes diving and coming up ahead to gaze into his face almost within hand's reach.

'I give you joy of your seals, brother,' said Stephen, as Jack waded ashore on the little golden strand, where the skiff now lay high, dry and immovable. 'It is the universal opinion of the good and the wise that there is nothing more fortunate than the company of seals.'

'I have always liked them,' said Jack, sitting on the gunwale and dripping all over. 'If they could speak, I am sure they would say something amiable. but Stephen, have you forgot breakfast?'

'I have not. My mind has been toying with thoughts of coffee, stirabout, white pudding, bacon, toast, marmalade and more coffee, for some considerable time.'

'Yet you would never have had it until well after dinner, you know, because your boat is stranded and I doubt you could swim so far.'

'The sea has receded!' cried Stephen. 'I am amazed.'

'They tell me it does so twice a day in these parts,' said Jack. 'It is technically known as the tide.'

'Why, your soul to the Devil, Jack Aubrey,' said Stephen, who had been brought up on the shores of the Mediterranean, that unebbing sea. He struck his hand to his forehead and exclaimed 'There must be some imbecility, some weakness here. But perhaps I shall grow used to the tide in time. Tell me, Jack, did you notice that the boat was as who should say marooned, and did you then leap into the sea?'

'I believe it was pretty generally observed aboard. Come, clap on to the gunwale and we will run her down. I can almost smell the coffee from here.'

Towards the end of their second pot Stephen heard a shrill fiddle no great way forward and after its first squeaks the deep Shelmerstonian voices chanting

Walk her round and walk her round, way oh, walk her round
Walk her round and walk her round, way oh and round she goes.

Somewhere at the edge of remembrance he must have heard and just retained the cry of All hands unmoor ship and the familiar pipe, for now he said 'It is my belief they are pulling up the anchor, the creatures.'

'Oh Stephen,' cried Jack, 'I do beg your pardon. I had meant to speak of it as soon as we were aboard, but greed overcame me. The present idea is to weigh, tow out on the tail of the ebb and stand eastwards on what air there is. What do you think of it?'

'My opinion on the subject would be as valuable as yours on the amputation of young Edwards' leg, which I may say in parenthesis he is likely to keep, with the blessing; but I am aware that you speak only out of complaisance. My sole observation is that since the *Diane* is to sail on the thirteenth, I had expected, and dreaded, at least two more of these infernal nights.'

'Yes,' said Jack. 'She is to sail on the thirteenth. But you know how often we have been windbound on this side of the Channel, particularly at Plymouth, and it would fairly break my heart to be there too late. What is more, it occurred to me in the middle watch that if the *Diane*'s officers and senior midshipmen are anything like ours they will spend the night of the twelfth with their friends ashore, which should make cutting her out, if not easier, then at least somewhat less difficult. And less bloody, perhaps far less bloody.'

'So much the better. Have you considered how you shall set about it?'

'I have done little else since we left Shelmerston. As I believe you know, the squadron stands in by day and off by night. I hope to join them offshore on the night of the eleventh and consult with Babbington. If there is agreement, they will stand in at dawn as usual and we will stand somewhat farther out, spending the day changing long guns for carronades. On the night of the twelfth they retire, all lit up; we join again, receive their volunteers and sail in, all lights dowsed, and drop anchor in twenty fathom water pretty well abreast of the lighthouse, quite close in but just out of direct fire from the fort. But before this the train of boats will have pulled away in the dark, and as soon as we hear from them we start bombarding the east end of the town, as though we were going to land on the isthmus as we did before, and burn the yard. And while we are blazing away as fast as we can load – firing blank, so as not to knock the people's houses about their ears, which I have always thought poor sport – the boats do their business. That is how I see the main lines; but there is no defining the details until Babbington has given his views. Indeed, it is possible that he may not agree with the general plan.'

'You would never doubt William Babbington's good will, for all love?'

'No,' said Jack. And after a pause, 'No. But the position is not what it was when he was my direct subordinate.'

In the silence Stephen heard the cry from the bows 'Up and down, sir,' and the much louder response from the capstan, 'Thick and dry for weighing.'

Shorly after this Tom Pullings appeared with a smiling face and reported that the ship was unmoored, that the launch and both cutters were out ahead with a tow-line, and that there was the appearance of a westerly breeze in the offing.

'Very well,' said Jack. 'Carry on, if you please, Mr Pullings.' And then hesitantly, with a hesitant smile, 'Fair – fair stands the wind for France.'

CHAPTER SIX

On the misty night of Thursday the *Surprise* kept a lookout aloft, and now from the foretopsail yard he called 'On deck, there. I think I see 'em.'

'Where away?' asked Jack.

'One point on the starboard bow. Not above two or three mile.'

The ship was under all plain sail, with what inconstant breeze there was mainly two points on her quarter; there was little to be seen ahead from the tops, therefore, so Jack, slinging his night-glass, climbed the taut, dew-damp shrouds to the main crosstrees. He gazed for some time, but nothing did he see until the haze parted and there, much closer than he had expected, lay a line of four ships, exactly spaced, close-hauled on the larboard tack: quite certainly the St Martin's squadron. On this warm night and in this calm sea most of their gun-ports were open and the light streamed out: he counted the ports, and he had time to see that the third ship in the line was the eighteen-gun *Tartarus* before the mist so blurred them that they were four yellow bars, dwindling until they vanished altogether. When they reappeared all the foremost ports were dark, eight bells having sounded, and aboard the *Tartarus* nothing was to be seen but a bright scuttle or two, a cabin port and the stern lantern. Eight bells struck on the *Surprise*'s battered old bell; he heard the bosun's mate piping lights out down the hatchway; and he reached the deck as the watch was being mustered.

'Someone has been flogging the glass in *Tartarus*,' he said to Pullings, having given the course. 'They are a good two or three minutes before us.' And as he walked into the cabin,

'Lord, Stephen, I am so very deeply relieved. The squadron is hull-up in the north-east, and we shall speak them within the hour.'

'I am so glad that your uneasiness is removed,' said Stephen, looking up from the score he was correcting. 'Now perhaps you will sit down and eat your supper in peace: unless indeed you choose to wait and invite William Babbington and Fanny Wray. Adi has a superb bouillabaisse prepared, and there will be enough for four, or even six.'

'No. The council of war must certainly take place aboard the *Tartarus*.'

'Very true. And in any case some food now would help to calm your spirits. You were in a sad taking, brother; I have rarely known you so impatient.'

'Why,' said Jack smiling as he let himself down in his chair, 'I believe any commander would have found today quite trying.' He thought of attempting to make Stephen understand some of the difficulties the *Surprise* had had to contend with – lack of wind for much of the day and strong contrary currents. The spring-tides were near at hand, and in these waters the floods set strongly against her, so that although she seemed to be towing at a fair rate, with all the boats out ahead and the men pulling like heroes, her movement was forward only in relation to the surface, while the whole body of the sea, with the ship and the boats upon it, was in fact gliding backwards in relation to the unseen land for hours on end; while beneath all, like a ground-swell in Jack's mind, was the dread that the *Diane*, aware of the blockading squadron's true weakness, might have sailed some days ago. Then there was the descending cloud and drizzle – no noon observation, no sight of the coast to check a position that must be exact for the night-meeting, nothing but a dead-reckoning horribly complicated by currents and very frequent changes of course to take advantage of the light and variable airs. In addition to this there was no real certainty about Babbington's course that night: if the *Surprise* missed the squadron she would have to look for them inshore the next morning, off St Martin's, in sight of every

French sailor, soldier or civilian possessed of a telescope, thus losing what seemed to him the very great and even perhaps decisive element of surprise. But these were regions into which Stephen could not follow him: no one without a nautical education could understand the refinements of frustration he had had to strive against; no one without an intimate knowledge of the sea could understand the infinity of things that could go wrong in so simple a voyage as this or the infinite importance of getting them all right – not that in the present case getting them right and joining the squadron offshore was in itself success, but it was a necessary condition for success; and the relief of having reached at least that stage was something that only another man with so much at stake could fully comprehend.

But he was sorry he had let his impatience – his almost choking fury on occasion – be seen, and now, reaching for the decanter of madeira, he said, 'I tell you what, Stephen: let us eat up our bouillabaisse when we have had a whet, and then, until we hail the *Tartarus*, we might play your piece.'

'Very well,' said Maturin, a simple pleasure showing on his usually by no means simple face. 'Killick, ahoy. Aho. Let the feast appear as soon as Adi can fry his croûtons.'

The piece, Stephen's own variations on a theme by Haydn, was correct and fluent but it was not particularly interesting until the last sheet, where Stephen and Haydn came together in a curious hesitant phrase whose two beats of silence were singularly moving. The violin played it first, and while the 'cello was answering they heard the hail from no great way off: 'The ship, ahoy. What ship is that?' and the full-voiced reply just overhead '*Surprise*'.

The 'cello made its pause, completed the phrase, and the two combined to work it towards the full close. The door opened and Pullings stood there with the news: Jack nodded, and they played on to the deeply satisfying end.

'*Tartarus* is just to windward, sir,' said Pullings, when they put down their bows.

'I am most uncommon glad to hear it,' said Jack. 'Pray let

the Doctor's skiff be lowered down – Stephen, you will lend me your skiff? – and Bonden will pull me over. Killick, my good blue coat.' He took his chart of St Martin's from the locker and said in an undertone, 'Stephen, should not you come too?'

'I believe not,' said Stephen. 'I must not advertise the tenuous connection I have with intelligence; whatever details there may be to be settled in that line, we can arrange between ourselves. But I should like to accompany the attack on this occasion, if it is agreed to be made.'

'Welcome aboard again, sir!' cried Babbington. 'Doubly welcome, since I did not look to see you this tide.'

'You very nearly did not, neither,' said Jack Aubrey. 'A needle in a haystack would not bear the comparison, on such a thick night; but a stitch in time saves nine, as you know very well, and we set out betimes. Shall we go below?'

In Babbington's little cabin he looked quickly round for signs of Fanny Wray but saw nothing except a piece of sailcloth with the words Heaven Preserve our Tars in rather shaky cross-stitch. 'So you were expecting me?' he said.

'Yes, sir. A cutter brought me word from the Admiral that it was possible, wind and weather permitting, that you might appear on the thirteenth and I was to cooperate with you in any operation you might contemplate against the *Diane*, at present lying in St Martin's.'

'She is still lying there, ain't she? She has not sailed?'

'Oh no, sir. She is lying there against the quay, moored to bollards head and stern. She does not mean to sail till the dark of the moon, the thirteenth.'

'You are sure of that, William? Of her lying there, I mean.'

'Oh yes, sir. When we stand inshore of a morning I often go aloft and look at her. She has had her yards crossed this week and more. And as for the thirteenth – why, we never interfere with the fishing-boats, and there are some that bring us crabs and lobsters and capital soles, coming to the blind side at dusk, before we stand off for the night. They know very well what the poor old *Dolphin* is worth, for all her fresh putty and paint and gingerbread-work, and just how the *Camel* transport and the *Vulture* slop-ship are armed, and they beg us to keep well out in the offing on the thirteenth, and to take no notice, because the *Diane* is new and fast and has scantlings like a forty-gun ship – carries heavy metal – would sink any one of us with a single broadside – crew admirably well trained with both great guns and small-arms – her tops full of riflemen like those in the *Redoutable* who killed Lord Nelson. And in any event a heavy corvette is going to wait for her off the cape and see her well clear of soundings in case she should run into *Euryalus*, due to come up from Gib about the middle of the month. They may exaggerate our fate a little, but I think they speak in real kindness. They were very fond of Fanny, who did most of the talking in French – a splendid accent, very like that of Paris, I am told.'

'Shall I have the pleasure of seeing her this evening?'

'Oh no, sir. I packed her off by the cutter. I really could not in conscience carry her into action, could I, sir? I remember clearly, though it was at least an age ago, when we were in the *Sophie*, that the Doctor told me there was nothing worse for the female frame than gunfire. I am so sorry he did not come across.'

'He thought he might be out of place in a council of war.'

'I should have liked to tell you both my good news. But perhaps you would be so kind as to tell him from me.'

'I should be very happy to do so, if you will let me know what it is.'

'Well, sir – I am ashamed to mention it before far more important things, but the fact of the matter is, I am to be made post.' He laughed from pure happiness, adding 'With seniority from the first of next month.'

Jack sprang to his feet – a lifetime at sea shielded his head even now from the low beams above it – and grasped Babbington's hand. 'Give you joy with all my heart, William,' he cried. 'I have heard nothing that has given me so much pleasure this many and many a day. May we not drink a glass to your coming flag?'

As they drank it Babbington said 'I know very well it is mostly parliamentary interest – did you see they made my uncle Gardner a peer last week? Lord, the Ministry must be hard up – yet even so it makes me wonderfully happy. It makes dear Fanny very happy too.'

'I am sure it does. But do not carry on at that rate about interest. You are a far better seaman and a far better officer than at least half the men on the list.'

'You are too kind, sir, too kind altogether. But I am not to be prating of my own affairs for ever. May I ask you, sir, whether you do contemplate any action against the *Diane*, and if so how I may best cooperate with you?'

'Yes, I certainly do contemplate an action – have been contemplating it pretty hard for some time. I will tell you the main lines of my plan: and I can speak without any kind of reserve, now you are to be made post. Yet even so, I will say this, William: you are the senior King's officer in this squadron, and if there is anything in my scheme you do not like for your ships or your men, tell me plain. We can settle it between us before the full council.'

'Very well, sir. But it would be strange indeed if we did not agree.'

Jack looked at him affectionately. What Babbington said was true: but it was even more wholly true now that he was sure of promotion. 'Well now,' he began, 'my idea is to cut her out: all the more so now that you have told me about the corvette that is to meet her off the cape.' He spread out his chart. 'If you have an intelligent master in the squadron, William, get him to check these soundings: they are the only things likely to have changed. Now we anchor the *Surprise* here' – pointing to the south side of Cape Bowhead – 'with a spring on her cable; and if we can place her just right – when we come to details, you must tell me the exact set of the tides inshore on the twelfth –'

'The twelfth, sir?'

'Yes. I hope that the night before they sail most of the officers will be bowsing up their jibs ashore, which will prevent their being knocked on the head or encouraging their men to any wild extreme.'

'Brilliant,' said Babbington, who could conceive of no man spending the night before sailing as far as Margate in any other manner.

'If we can place her just right, then, this rise in the land protects her from the fort covering the isthmus. We drop anchor at say three-quarters flood. The boats pull off round the cape. They may be challenged at the breakwater. They will probably pass, but if they do not and we hear a musket, we start bombarding the isthmus: or rather Tom Pullings does, since I mean to lead the boarding-party myself. He does so in any case if I and the boats send up a blue light, meaning we are about to board. He blazes away like smoke and oakum, which will divert the enemy's attention – it was the isthmus that we invaded before – and give the boats time to cut the *Diane* out, sail her clear of the batteries at the bottom of the bay if the breeze is fair or tow her if it is not. Indeed, tow her in any event, for this sort of thing must be done quick. By that time the tide should be just on the ebb, which will be a great help. What I should like your squadron to do is to bring the ships in close in case of an emergency and to provide four boats to help in the towing.'

'Mayn't we board too?'

'No, William; at least not in the first assault. The Surprises have been going through all the motions of boarding a frigate twice a night since what seems the beginning of time; they know exactly what to do – each man has his own task – and the presence of other people would only distract them. But of course if the Dianes prove uncommon awkward, we can always sing out for help.'

Babbington considered for some moments, looking at his former captain now and then. 'Well, sir,' he said, 'it seems a capital plan to me, and I certainly cannot suggest any improvements. Should you like me to signal for all captains now?'

'If you please, William. And there is a point I had almost forgot: when you stand in tomorrow, I shall stand farther out. Then tomorrow evening you make a particular point of moving out into the offing very well lit up: when you are far out I shall slip past you without a glim, taking your boats in tow as I pass. I need hardly say that if any of your lobster-boats hears of *Surprise* being here, we might as well go home, rather than creep in under courses with the hope of finding the *Diane* unprepared.'

'I shall look after that, sir.'

'But discreetly, William, discreetly. Do not treat them un-friendly or wave them away, or they will smoke there is something amiss.'

'I shall chatter with them myself, and allow no one else to speak.' He went on deck to give orders for the signal and when he came back Jack said 'I remember the Doctor talking about women and gunfire: it was off Cape Creus in the last war, when we took a French sloop loaded with powder. The master had taken his wife with him and she was having a baby – the Doctor delivered it. Dear me, those were happy days. The Admiral gave us cruise after cruise.'

'And we took prize after prize. Oh, it was glorious. And then there was the *Cacafuego*! Do you remember how we starbowlins blacked our faces in the galley and boarded her screeching like boiled cats? Mowett wrote a poem about it.'

They were still talking eagerly about the last war when the first of the boats came alongside, followed almost immediately by the others.

'Sir,' said Babbington, after the sounds of proper reception, the midshipman's announcement, and the procession on the ladder, 'Sir, allow me to name Captain Griffiths of the *Dolphin*, Mr Leigh, captain of the *Camel*, and Mr Strype of the *Vulture*.'

'Good evening, gentlemen,' said Jack, looking at them attent-ively: Griffiths was a small, bright-eyed, round-headed very young commander newly appointed to a very old sloop that should not have been at sea at all; Leigh, a tall, elderly, one-armed lieutenant without the least hope of promotion who was happier in the command of a transport than living ashore with a large family on less than a hundred pounds a year; Strype, of the *Vulture* slop-ship, was so silent and pale as to be almost non-existent – it was strange to see him wearing the King's uniform.

'Now, gentlemen,' said Babbington, and Jack was astonished at the unassuming natural authority with which he spoke – astonished, because their conversation had so vividly brought back the little boy of the midshipmen's berth in the *Sophie*, who still had to be told to blow his nose – 'I have orders to cooperate with Mr Aubrey of the *Surprise* in an operation he intends to carry out against the *Diane*. I will beg him to give an outline of his plan for your information, but first I must observe, that he and I are in entire agreement as to the general strategy. You will therefore be so good as to listen without comment until he asks for your observations, which will bear only upon such points as currents, soundings or the enemy's dispositions on which you may have particular information. Mr Aubrey, sir, allow me to bring the lamp a little nearer.'

Jack described his plan once more, pointing to the various positions on the chart as he did so and ending 'If any officer has questions to ask or observations to make, I should be glad to hear them.'

There was a long silence, broken only by the lapping of the sea against the *Tartarus*'s side, until the grizzled lieutenant stood up and placing his hook on the breakwater said 'The only observation I have to make is that at flood and slack water there is a current that sets up against the rampart here. Time and again I have seen smallcraft fend off from the wall or absolutely graze it as they turn into the harbour. You might think that worth bearing in mind for the boats, sir, if they wish to pass unseen.'

'Thank you, sir,' said Jack. 'That is a most valuable point. Captain Griffiths, did you wish to speak?'

'Only to say that with Captain Babbington's permission I should be happy to lead the squadron's boats, sir.'

Babbington instantly said 'Mr Aubrey and I are agreed

that the captains should remain with their commands. The squadron will stand in shortly after the operation begins, and there may be important decisions to make in the event of – if all don't go well.'

'Bless you, William,' said Jack inwardly. 'I never knew you were so quick.' And aloud, in answer to the unspoken question that hung there in the cabin, 'Captain Pullings, who accompanies me as a volunteer and who is the most senior King's officer in these waters, will be taking command of the *Surprise* in my absence. Mr Strype, have you a remark?'

'Yes,' said Strype, and for the first time it became apparent that he was drunk, pale drunk with solitary gin, 'how do we stand for prize-money?'

This was said with a particularly knowing, cynical leer, and the others reddened with shame. Jack looked at him coldly and said 'That is surely selling the bear . . . that is surely counting your bears . . .' he hesitated. 'In any case the question is premature and likely to bring misfortune,' he went on. 'It will of course be dealt with according to the custom of the sea. Those that tow share equally with those that take.'

'Fair enough,' said Leigh. 'It was like that in the last war, and in the American war before that.'

'And now that we have returned to the subject of boats,' Jack continued, 'I will be more exact. Captain Babbington and I are agreed that the largest belonging to each ship, launch, longboat or pinnace, would be best. They should be fully manned, with spare rowers for a long pull, and the men should be well armed for boarding, though I hope they will not be called upon to do so. They should be equipped with hook-ropes and all the necessary tackle and they would be best commanded by the bosun or a senior master's mate. Yet even more important, they must be made to understand that silence is absolutely essential – matting on the thole-pins or rowlocks, naturally, but above all no talking: not a word. The boats lie on their oars when I cast them off and neither move nor speak till they are called in by name, either to tow or help in overcoming resistance. Since they may have to board they should have white armbands, to be put on at the last moment, like the Surprises: the password is Merry Christmas and the answer Happy New Year. I think that is all, gentlemen.' He stood up: he had seen far too many meetings of this kind rendered vague and obscure by an interminable discussion of points that had little or nothing to do with the main issue, and it seemed to him better to leave his plan in its simplest form. Yet when the captains were gone he sat down with Babbington and the master of the *Tartarus*, checking soundings and bearings and the order of the French ships along the quay: a worthless brig, two gunboats mounting thirty-two pounders, the *Diane*, and two fair-sized merchantmen that had recently moved from the bottom of the basin, presumably with the intention of slipping out in her wake. These, together with the shoals to be avoided on leaving the port, they traced in three copies, together with a statement of the successive stages of the operation in the simplest, most unambiguous language they could work out; and when the three were finished Jack Aubrey said 'There. I believe we have done all we can. If you will issue these as part of an order, William, and let your captains mull over them all tomorrow, getting them by rote themselves and teaching the boat-crews until they are word-perfect, you will do me a great service. I shall leave you now and take the ship some way out into the offing. I shall pick up the boats tomorrow on my way in, and if all goes well I hope to see you about midnight or a little after. But if it don't, William, if I make a cock of it, you must not – I repeat *must not* – follow me in or let any of your ships do so. If this business drags out long enough for the French to recover their wits and find that the isthmus is not being invaded after all, they will keep up such a fire on the narrow pass that no ship will get out alive. I have told Tom Pullings the same, and he has agreed.'

'Well, sir,' said Babbington unwillingly, 'I shall do what you say; but I wish to God I were going with you.'

During the short pull back to his ship Jack studied the sky with the closest attention: its veils of mist were still just to be made out, but they were dissipating fast and the high sky was almost clear, with a few streaks of lofty cirrus moving gently across the stars from the west-south-west.

'I wish it may not turn dirty before morning,' he said to Bonden, by way of averting ill-fortune.

'Not on your life, sir,' said Bonden. 'I never seen a prettier night.'

Having given the orders that would take the *Surprise* north-west for a couple of hours, there to stand off and on for the rest of the night, Jack went below. The cabin was lit but empty; Stephen had already gone to bed, leaving some medical notes, three books with their places marked, a half-written score, and, lying next to a magnifying glass, three Naples biscuits, already attacked by rats. Jack tossed the biscuits out of the scuttle, took the glass and studied his hanging barometer: it had risen a tenth of an inch and the quicksilver showed a marked convexity, confirming his already set opinion. He opened his desk, where his serial letter to Sophie was still spread out from the day before, and sitting down he wrote 'My dear, I am just returned from *Tartarus* – William is made post! – He is so happy about it, and so am I – it is as pretty a night as ever I have seen, with the wind at WSW or a trifle S of it, and a gently rising glass. God bless you, my dear: I am just about to turn in – It was quite a busy day today and I hope it will be far busier tomorrow.' With this he lit his hand-lantern and went to bed. The lantern hooked into a slot within hand's reach of his cot and with its slide almost entirely closed it sent out no more than a very soft narrow beam that lit two feet of deckhead. He contemplated this beam for perhaps two minutes with an easy mind: it appeared to him that he had done everything that he ought to have done and that if the weather was kind he had a fair chance of success tomorrow – the enterprise was perfectly justifiable even if very much less depended on it; he would have undertaken it in any circumstances. He knew that his colleagues were fallible, that the simplest order could be misunderstood or disobeyed, and that grotesque ill-luck could always intervene; but now the dice were thrown, and he must abide by the result. Gazing at the beam he was dimly aware of the ship's living sound as she moved north-east with a slight following sea, the contented hum of the well-set-up rigging (taut, but not too taut), the occasional creak of the wheel, and of the complex aroma, made up of scrubbed plank, fresh sea-breeze, stale bilge-water, tarred cordage, paint and damp sailcloth.

By the later part of the forenoon on the twelfth, a grey peaceful day with the small breeze steady in the west-south-west, the only comfortable place in the *Surprise* was the mizentop. The decks were entirely filled with parties engaged in hoisting up the remaining carronades from the hold and striking down the long guns and with making all fast in preparation for the night's bombardment; for not only could carronades be fired much faster than long guns, thus making an even greater noise in the aggregate, but only a couple of hands were required to work them as opposed to the great gun's team of six or eight. The cabin was taken up by the captain, his officers and the boats' coxswains, settling a host of details. The medical men had therefore gone aloft quite early, with books, telescopes and chessmen. There was a draught-board neatly carved in the floor of the top and on this they had played a not very aggressive game, ending in a draw, and now they were reclining on the folded studdingsails.

From a scattered body of gulls, working slowly against the wind with angled wings, Stephen had picked out what was almost certainly *Larus canus*, usual enough in the Irish parts of his youth, some of which had been spent in the west, where they nested in quantities on the cliffs and the more lonely strands, but quite rare in these waters, and he was just about to say 'I believe I see a common gull' when Martin asked 'How would you render *peripateia*?'

'Why surely a reverse. But no doubt you mean it in the dramatical sense: can you not say peripety in English? The French certainly have *péripétie*; though to be sure they use it loosely, in the sense of ordinary vicissitudes.'

'I believe I have seen peripety. But it is scarcely current

English, and I do not think it would leave Mowett much the wiser.' He passed Stephen a little slim book, Aristotle's *Poetica*, and said 'I promised to translate this for him.'

'That was benevolent in you.'

'It would have been more truly benevolent if I had realized the difficulty; but I did not. I had read it at the university with my tutor, an excellent man, bless him, a scholar with a great gift for making duller minds understand and even love a text. With his help I did grasp the essence and I have retained it; but now turning it into an English that is both accurate and tolerably fluent, an English that might be spoken by a Christian, is I am afraid a task beyond my powers.'

'From what I remember of the book's strange flitting nature and its many technicalities it would be beyond mine too.'

'Pride and precipitancy were my undoing. When Mowett told me he meant to write a very ambitious piece called *The Sea-Officer's Tragedy*, based on Captain Aubrey's career, his victories and his misfortunes, I told him I hoped he would make it end happy. "I cannot possibly do that," says he. "Since it is a tragedy, it must end in disaster." I begged his pardon for disagreeing, but I had the support of the greatest authority in the learned world, Aristotle himself, in saying that although tragedy necessarily dealt with the doings of great-minded men or women, in a high and serious manner, it by no means necessarily ended unhappy: and I quoted the lines I have ventured to render thus: *The nature of the tragedy's action has always required that the scope should be as full as can be without obscuring the plot, and that the number of events making a probable or necessary sequence that will change a man's state from unhappiness to happiness or from happiness to unhappiness should be the smallest possible*, and desired him to observe that not only was the change from evil to good eminently possible in tragedy, but that Aristotle put it first.'

Two bells. The *Surprise* had softened many of the rigours of naval life: no officers or bosun's mates started the hands into brisker motion with plaited canes or blows from a rope's end; the stowing of hammocks in the nettings each fine morning was not a breakneck race; no one was flogged for being last off the yard; and people walked about in a free and easy fashion, talking or chewing tobacco as they saw fit. But brahminical cleanliness remained; the watches and their exact relief were still holy; and so was the ceremony of meals. During the later part of the game of chess, quite destroying their concentration, the pandemonium of all hands being piped to dinner had broken out below them, with the banging of mess-kids and plates as the salt beef came aft from the galley and the muffled thunder of blackjacks as the beer came forward from the hatchway butt – for the ship was not yet in grog waters and the people had to be content with their traditional gallon a day at twice, which the tradition-loving *Surprise* still served out in leather jugs. And now the drummer at the capstan – no longer a Marine, but a moderately gifted foremast jack – gave a preliminary thump and then launched upon his version of *Roast Beef of Old England*, the equivalent of the officers' dinner-bell, the warning that dinner would very soon be on the table.

They leapt to their feet, and as they gathered books, papers, chessmen, Stephen said, 'I am so glad to hear what you tell me, about Aristotle. I had forgotten those words or had skipped them – the whole book I read with a cross, superficial mind, having taken against him in those far-off days because of his weak remarks about birds and for his having brought up that showy brute-beast Alexander, as great a public nuisance as our Buonaparte – but of course he was the great learned man of the world.' He lowered himself through the lubber's hole, and as he hung there by his elbows with his feet searching for the shrouds below he said to himself, 'Tonight is perhaps Jack's true peripety. Dear Lord, how I pray that his tragedy may end happy and that . . .' Here kindly hands seized his ankles, guiding them to a firm foothold.

In the cabin he was shocked to find Jack Aubrey standing waiting for him, unusually tall, grave and stern, dressed in a fine bottle-green coat and a gleaming newly-tied neckcloth. 'Really, Stephen, what a fellow you are,' he said. 'We are invited to dine in the gunroom and here you are like something sent aboard from the receiving-ship. Padeen, there. Pass the word for Padeen.' And to Padeen, 'Shave and brush your master directly: put out his best coat, black satin breeches, silk stockings, silver-buckled shoes. He will be here in five minutes.'

In five minutes he was there, bleeding from three small cuts and looking somewhat confused. Jack dabbed at the blood with his handkerchief, twitched Stephen's wig and waistcoat straight and walked him quickly to the gunroom, where they were welcomed by their hosts as three bells struck in the afternoon watch.

It so happened that this was the first time the captain of the *Surprise* had dined as a guest in the gunroom since she became a private man-of-war. Before the taking of the *Spartan* and her prizes the officers had been too poor to invite him and during the strenuous days in Polcombe cove there had been no entertainment possible. It was therefore an unusually splendid meal, all the more so since the gunroom cook was determined to outdo Adi; yet though the table was loaded with such things as lobsters, crayfish, crabs, soles, and mussels in three separate ways – all corruptly obtained from the *Tartarus* – there were desperately wide spaces between the diners. Jack had known this table for a great many years, always pretty full and some-times packed with guests elbow to elbow; but now there were no Marine officers, no master, no purser, no chaplain, no guests from the midshipmen's berth or from other ships, and he occupied one whole side to himself, on Pullings' right. On the opposite side sat Stephen and Davidge, while Martin had the foot of the table; and heavy work they made of it, at least to begin with. Jack Aubrey, though acquainted with West and Davidge and aware of their professional competence, had never known them outside the service and he was not on easy terms with them – nor with any other stranger for that matter, since his trial. For their part they found him intimidating; and they too had been strangely damaged by losing their commissions and with them their livelihood, their future and much of their identity. Then again those who were not going on the cutting-out expedition were strongly aware that in a few hours time the others would be setting off – even more strongly aware than those directly concerned – and they felt that gaiety was out of place. There was tension among those who were going, too, and in Jack Aubrey's case it was a tension he had never known before, although he had seen more action than most sailors of his age. He observed, to his astonishment, that the piece of lobster that he held poised on his fork while he waited for Davidge to finish his period was trembling. He ate it rapidly and continued listening, with inclined head and civil smile, to the wandering tale that was very slowly drawing to its disastrous want of an end: Davidge had travelled in France during the peace; he had wished to dine at a famous eating-house between Lyons and Avignon, but the place was full and he had been told of another just as good, by the cathedral. There he was the only guest, and he entered into conversation with the master of the house; they spoke of this cathedral and other cathedrals and Davidge observed that at Bourges he had been much struck by the extraordinary beauty of one of the choir-boys. The inn-keeper, a paederast, had misunderstood him and had made a scarcely veiled proposal; Davidge however had managed to decline without offence and the man had taken it so well that they parted on the best of terms, all payment for the splendid meal being resolutely declined. But Davidge, having at last reached the Rhône by way of innumerable parentheses, suddenly felt that sodomy, as a thing amusing in itself and the justification for any anecdote however long, would not do for his grave, attentive captain, and he tried to give his tale some other turn that would not sound too foolish – a vain attempt from which he was only rescued by the next course, which consisted of soused pig's face (one of Jack's favourite dishes) and a saddle of mutton, the joint being put down for Martin to carve. Martin, a chop-house bachelor until his recent marriage, had never carved a saddle of mutton. He did not carve one now, but with a powerful thrust of his fork flung it straight into Davidge's lap. It saved Davidge from his predicament at the cost of his breeches – cheap at the price, he thought – and it was silently passed on to Stephen, who cut it up in the approved surgical manner.

It was good mutton, well hung and roasted to a turn, and with it came a truly beautiful claret, a Fombrauges which so pleased Jack Aubrey that after the first glass he produced one of the very few remnants of his brief education on dry land. '*Nunc est bibendum*,' he said with a rather triumphant look at Stephen and Martin, 'and upon my honour, you could not ask a pleasanter vino to bib.'

After this the dinner-party grew easier, though the tension could not be entirely set aside, since two grindstones had been brought up on deck and their high-pitched scream as the armourer and his mate put a fine edge upon cutlasses and boarding-axes necessarily kept the immediate future in mind. Yet even so, the party was not exactly convivial, since it split into two groups: Aubrey and Pullings talking quietly of former shipmates and former voyages, while Stephen and Davidge spoke of the difficulties of remaining alive as an undergraduate at Trinity College in Dublin: Davidge had a cousin there who had been pierced three times, twice by a sword, once by a pistol-bullet.

'I am not a quarrelsome man nor inclined to take offence,' said Stephen, 'yet I must have been out a score of times in my first year. It is better now, I believe, but it was a desperate place in those days.'

'So my cousin said. And when he came to see us in England my father and I gave him some lessons: it was riposte, counter-riposte, parry or tierce all through that summer; but at least he survived.'

'You are an eminent swordsman, I find.'

'Not I. But my father was, and he did make me at least competent. It was useful to me later on, when I was in a sad way, having left the service, because Angelo employed me for a while in his *salle d'armes*.'

'Indeed? It would oblige me extremely if you would exchange a few passes with me after dinner. I am somewhat out of practice, and it would grieve me to be cut down like a simpleton tonight.'

Stephen was not the only man in the *Surprise* with the same notion, and as the dinner-party came up to take the air on the quarterdeck they heard the steady pop-popping of hands right forward shooting bottles at close range with their pistols, for by now the carronades were all in position, the boats were towing two-abreast astern, and arms had been served out. The sea, the breeze and the sky were much as they had been, gentle, grey and steady: a timeless kind of day.

Jack studied the log-boards, whistling quietly to himself, and then he said to the officer of the watch, 'Mr West, at eight bells we will wear and stand south-east a half east under easy sail.' After a turn or two he fetched his fighting-sword, a heavy cavalry sabre, from the cabin, stood swishing it for a while, and carried it forward to the armourer for a shaving edge.

'Now, Doctor,' said Davidge, 'do you choose to have a bout?'

'I should be very happy,' said Stephen, throwing his cigar-butt into the sea, where it gave a momentary hiss.

'These are Angelo's particular patented pride,' said Davidge, when they were ready, with their coats folded on the capstan and their neckerchiefs loosed. 'They fasten over the point, doing it no harm, so that you can use your real sword. Far, far better than any form of button.'

'Glory be,' said Stephen.

They saluted and stood poised for a moment, with minute, scarcely perceptible threatening movements of point or wrist; then Stephen, tapping twice with his foot like a torero, flew straight at Davidge with inconceivable ferocity. Davidge parried and they whirled about one another, their swords clashing now high, now low, their bodies now almost touching, now at double arm's length.

'Hold hard,' cried Stephen, leaping back and raising his hand. 'My breeches band is destroyed. Martin, pray do up the buckle, will you, now?'

The buckle made fast, they saluted again, and again after the reptilian stillness Stephen leapt in, crying 'Ha! Ha!' It was the same parry, the same whirling and clashing with swords darting so fast that only the swordsmen could follow them – the same stamping feet and heavy gasping breath as they lunged, the same extraordinary agility – but then came a check in the rhythm, a subtle flaw, and there was Davidge's sword in the hammock-netting.

He stared at his empty hand for a moment, deeply shocked, but quickly, in the general cheering, he put what face he could upon it and cried 'Well done, well done! I am a dead man – one more of your corpses, no doubt.'

Then, having recovered his sword and found that it was unhurt he said 'May I look at yours?' Stephen passed it; Davidge turned it about and weighed it and looked closely at its guard and grip. 'A spring quillon?' he asked.

'Just so. I catch my opponent's blade here; the whole thing is a matter of timing and leverage.'

'It is a murderous weapon.'

'After all, swords are for killing. But I thank you very heartily, sir, for this exercise; you are complaisance in person.'

Eight bells struck: at once there was the cry 'All hands wear ship', and the *Surprise* began the long smooth turn that brought her head to south-east a half east, and she travelling smoothly towards the point where her course would intersect that of Babbington's squadron standing out to sea. The sun would set in the last dog-watch, and everyone knew that this was the last leg before they stepped into the boats for the long pull round Cape Bowhead. Although some of the younger topmen, little more than boys, skylarked in the upper rigging, following-my-leader from truck to truck and back by the crosstrees to the jib-boom strap, the atmosphere aboard was grave. Jack and Stephen both made the arrangements usual before action and gave the documents to Pullings; all the officers in the ship had done this quite often – it was a matter of course before battle – and yet today it seemed something more than a conscientious precaution, more than a formal bow towards fate.

The bells followed one another; the sun sank until it was below the foreyard; hands were piped to supper.

'At least everything does not have to be struck down into the hold,' said Stephen to himself, fixing a score in Diana's music-stand-writing-desk. He swept some deep harsh chords that made the stern-windows rattle and then began feeling his way through a piece new to him, a Duport sonata. He was still in the andante, his nose almost touching the score, when Jack came in and said 'Why, Stephen, you are sitting in the dark. You will ruin your eyes if you go on like that. Killick. Killick, there. Bear a hand and strike a light.'

'The sun has set, I do suppose.'

'It will do so, from time to time, they tell me. The breeze has freshened and we are under staysails alone.'

'Is that a good thing?'

'It means that if any busy fellow wandering about on Cape Bowhead in the middle of the night should chance to see us looming faintly in the darkness, he will take us for some little fore-and-aft affair of no consequence. I am going to shift my clothes.'

'Perhaps I should do the same. I must certainly attend to the revolving pistol Duhamel gave me, a most deadly weapon too. I grieve for poor Duhamel still, a man of such amiable parts. By God, I had almost forgotten this,' he cried, clapping his hand to his breeches pocket. He hurried down to Pullings' cabin and said 'Tom, pray attach this to the little packet I gave you, if God forbid you have to deliver it. And pray take great care of it for the now – never out of your pocket at all – it is a prodigious great jewel of a thing.'

'I will keep it here in my fob,' said Pullings. 'But I am sure you will have it back before morning.'

'I hope so, honey, I hope so indeed. Tell me, now, what would it be proper to wear on such an occasion?'

'Hessian boots, loose pantaloons, a stout frieze jacket, sword-belt, and a line round your middle for pistols. Oh Lord, Doctor, how I wish I were going with you.'

Back in his own cabin, Stephen turned over his meagre wardrobe for the nearest equivalents that he could find, with only moderate success; he also, but in this case with greater success, turned over the question of whether the present conjuncture allowed him to depart from his rule and take an extra dose, not indeed as a soporific – very far from it – but as a means of doing away with illogical purely instinctive uneasiness and thus of enabling his mind to deal more freely with any contingencies that might arise in the new situation. If instead of his tincture he had those blessed coca leaves he had encountered in South America, there would have been no possible doubt: they unquestionably stimulated the entire system, bracing the sinews and tautening the nerves; whereas it had to be admitted that the tincture had a tendency, a very slight tendency, to induce a more contemplative frame of mind. But he had eaten or rather chewed all his coca leaves long since, and there remained the fact that in emergencies the tincture had always answered – its virtues far outweighed its slight disadvantages – and in any event the external stimulation that this kind of encounter must necessarily produce would more than counteract any very trifling degree of narcosis. The *Diane*'s destination made it certain that she would have an important agent aboard; it was of the first consequence that he should be taken; to omit any step that might increase the chances of doing so would be wrong indeed; nothing was weaker than supposing a necessary contradiction between duty and inclination.

He finished his glass of laudanum with pleasure though without the fullest satisfaction, and sat down to the exact, methodical loading of his revolving pistol, while Killick and his mates fussed about the great cabin shipping deadlights. By the time he came on deck it was quite dark. To the south-east the squadron could be seen standing out to sea, stern-lanterns and gunports brilliant, in line ahead on the starboard tack: and beyond the ships, well beyond them, the steadily repeated flash of the Bowhead light.

All the officers were on the quarterdeck, silently gazing at the ships: Jack stood by the windward rail, alone, with his hands behind his back, swaying to counteract the pitch and roll. There was no gleam aboard, apart from the binnacle-glow, and there was not much from the sky, the old moon in her last day having set and the haze obscuring all but the brightest stars, and they a mere blur: an uncommonly dark night. Although the shore was still a great way off it seemed natural for those few who spoke to do so in undertones. Killick's disagreeable nasal voice could be heard wrangling with the captain's cook far down in the bowels of the ship: 'Just you make your fucking patty now, like I said, mate, and I will make my toasted cheese last minute, while you beat up a egg in marsala. The Doctor said he was to be preserved from what we call the falling damps; but he won't come down before we've picked up the boats.'

Killick was right. Nothing but the Day of Judgment would have moved Jack Aubrey from the rail before he had the squadron's boats in tow. From time to time he called 'Look out afore, there' to the man in the crosstrees, and once the man hailed the deck 'I think I seen a light go down the side of *Tartarus*.'

Half an hour passed, the line of ships coming closer, closer, until Jack, filling his lungs, called '*Tartarus* ahoy.'

'*Surprise*?' came the answer. 'Boats will cast off directly and pull south-west. Will you show a glim? Jack opened his dark-lantern for a moment and he heard the order 'Boats away'. And then, as they passed on opposite tacks another voice, Babbington's, 'God bless you, sir.'

The squadron carried straight on, and presently lanterns, shaded from the still-distant coast, could be seen in the boats. Low, urgent cries as the boat-keepers in the *Surprise*'s train of six made the newcomers fast, and Jack called over the taffrail 'Boat commanders come aboard.' With his eyes so accustomed to the dark he could see them quite well by the reflected light from the compass: a brawny master's mate of about thirty from the *Tartarus* and the bosuns of the other three, thoroughly experienced seamen of the kind he knew and esteemed. They named their ships and the number of men embarked; from their answers to his questions it was clear that they understood what they were there to do and from the look of them there was a fairly strong probability that they would do it.

'Did all hands have a good supper before leaving the ship?' he asked. 'If not, they can be fed here. In such a business a full belly is half the battle.'

'Oh yes, sir,' they said. Fresh pork had been served out, and in the *Tartarus*, figgy-dowdy.

'Now, sir, if you please,' said Killick's querulous, hard-used voice just behind him, 'your patty is ready, and the toasted cheese will go to ruin if not ate up hot.'

Jack considered the distant shore, nodded, and walked below. Stephen was already there, sitting by the light of a single candle. 'This is not unlike being on a stage and waiting for the curtain to go up,' he observed. 'I wonder whether actors have the same sense of distorted time, a present that advances, to be sure, but only like the shadow on a dial, imperceptibly: and even then it may go back.'

'Perhaps they do,' said Jack. 'They tell me that stage feasts are all made of cardboard – cardboard sausages, cardboard legs of mutton, cardboard ham, cardboard goblets they make believe to drink in. By God, Stephen, this is the most famous Strasburg pie. Have you had any?'

'I have not.'

'Let me give you a piece.'

Ordinarily opium so cut Stephen's appetite that after a considerable dose he took little pleasure in meals, but this time he said 'It is uncommonly good,' and passed his plate for more. Then came the toasted cheese, and with it they shared a bottle of Hermitage; they were both very fond of wine and they both knew that this might be the last bottle they would drink. If that should prove the case, then at least it would be a noble close, for it was a fine great generous wine in the prime of life, one that could stand being tossed about at sea: they drank it slowly, not saying much but sitting there in a companionable silence in the candle-light while the ship moved steadily inshore.

Bells had not been struck this last hour and more, but Jack heard the wheel being relieved at the end of the spell. He finished his glass, and with the wine still savouring in his gullet brought out an azimuth compass of his own design: he said to Stephen, 'I am going to take our bearings.'

Far astern the squadron could still be seen, though by now it was much more subdued, lights out having sounded very soon after their meeting: and right ahead the tall Cape Bowhead loomed up, a blacker blackness some three miles away. Every two minutes the headland vanished as the beam from the lighthouse came to the full, blinding the observer; but when it had passed away there was time for night-vision to return and for the speckling of lights on shore to be made out, together with something of the shape of the coast north-north-east of Cape Bowhead. Presently the white line of surf would show all along, especially at the foot of the headland, for there was a considerable swell, and now the tide was on the make. He knew the lie of the land very well, having an excellent visual memory and having gone over and over his chart, and he knew that in half an hour he would be able to shape his course for the anchorage he had in mind, the good holding ground quite close in where the frigate would be sheltered from the fire of the guns that protected the vulnerable isthmus.

'Mr Pullings,' he asked in the silence, 'is the anchor a-cock-bill?'

'Yes, sir: with a spring from right aft.'

'Then let it be lowered inch by inch to the hawsehole: then we can let it go without a splash. I am going to look at the boats.'

He gave the quartermaster his compass and walked aft. He was as much at home in the *Surprise* as he was at Ashgrove – perhaps more so – and he went over the taffrail and down the stern ladder without a thought. He made his way along the train of boats to the *Tartarus*'s launch: 'What cheer, Tartaruses,' he said in a low voice. 'What cheer, sir,' they all replied, quite as softly. He felt their muffled thole-pins and said 'Good, very good. Now we shall be putting off presently, so remember, not a word, not a word, and pull soft. When you are cast off, lie on your oars, put on your armbands and be ready to stretch out like heroes when I hail, but not a moment before.'

'Ready, aye ready, sir,' they murmured.

The Dolphins, the Camels and the Vultures had the same greeting, the same message, and they too seemed deeply impressed with the need for silence. When he was aboard again he began to take his bearings: he could see the surf now, and with the flap of his hat shielding his eyes the travelling beam of the light was a great help. He stood at the con, giving quiet directions to the helmsman, and as the lines of bearing came true he reduced her spread of canvas, so that she ghosted in on the tide of flood with no more than foretopmast and main staysails, the gentle wind abaft her starboard beam. In dead silence they passed under the tall lighthouse cliff so close inshore that they were on the very edge of the breakers, so close that men held their breath; and even when they were past the bulge of the headland they had the steady beat of surf within pistol-shot to larboard. Now they were under the shadow of the cliff and even the dispersed light of the beam did not reach them; but it did light the hill, the vital shielding hill this side of the fort. He started the sheets and murmured 'Stand by to let go.' The *Surprise* drifted on with the tide; again the beam swept round and lit the hill; she was exactly where he wanted her and he said, 'Let go, there,' quite loud. The anchor plunged silently into eighteen fathom water; they veered away in a fair scope of cable with half-words and gestures, and then, the anchor having gripped, they heaved upon the spring until her broadside bore on the isthmus, where several lights were to be seen, the most southerly parts of the town.

Jack looked at his watch by the light of the binnacle and said 'Blue cutter's crew away.' They had been gathered on the starboard gangway this half hour and they filed by him with the bosun; then the red cutter from the larboard gangway with the gunner; after them, from alternate gangways, the pinnace, with Davidge, the gig, with West, the jolly-boat, with Beattey the carpenter, and lastly his own launch's men. As Bonden passed, Jack took him by the arm and said in a low voice,

'Keep very close to the Doctor when we board.' Then he went below, where Stephen was playing chess with Martin by the glittering candle with his sword on the table in front of him. 'Will you come with me?' said Jack. 'We are on our way.'

Stephen stood up, smiling, and put his sword-belt over his shoulder; Martin fastened it behind, an expression of very great concern upon his face. Jack led the way up to the quarterdeck, aft to the taffrail, where Pullings and Martin followed to wish them God-speed, and over on to the stern-ladder. The boats had already formed in the long linked line that the captain's launch was to lead; and as Jack reached it, the last of the cutting-out party, Bonden shoved off and Jack murmured 'Give way.'

At first they had to row against the tide, the swell and the moderate breeze, but zeal made nothing of it for the first three quarters of an hour; by this time they were off the point of Bowhead, well clear of the breakers, pulling strongly with an even stroke, never a creak from rowlock or pin, never a sound but a strangled cough. From Bowhead, Jack looked out to sea: no squadron. Babbington would be moving quietly in.

Along the face of the cape and even more when they bore eastwards the tide was with them: Jack checked their speed which was growing impetuous, and passed the word back down the line to change rowers.

Another twenty minutes and the far side of the port was beginning to open, with a fair glow of light over it. It increased quite fast and now the whole northern side, the well-lit bottom of the bay, and, of infinitely greater consequence, the break-water, could be seen. Nearer, nearer, rowing soft; and round the breakwater a small light, bobbing about and closing with them fast. Perhaps it was only a fishing-boat going out for the night. Jack opened his dark-lantern.

'Ohé, du bateau,' called the boat.

'Ohé,' replied Stephen, Jack's hand on his shoulder. 'La Diane, où ce qu'elle se trouve à présent?'

'Au quai toujours, nom de Dieu. T'es Guillaume?'

'Non. Etienne.'

'Ben. Je m'en vais. Qu'est-ce que tu as là?'
'Des galériens.'
'Ah, les bougres. Bon. Au plaisir, eh?'
'Au plaisir, et je te souhaite merde, eh?'

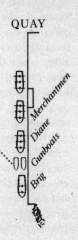

QUAY

Merchantmen

Diane

Gunboats

Brig

They pulled on, their stroke a little less steady; and now the breakwater, with lights shining from the embrasures of its rampart at the landward end, was full in view. And there was clearly a party going on in the rampart – singing, laughter, music of a sort. Jack took the tiller from Bonden's hand: he felt the current – the ebb had just begun – and he bore over, giving the breakwater as wide a berth as he dared for the sandbank on the other side. No challenge for the launch. No challenge for the next boat, no challenge for the third: no challenge at all. They were through, into the port: perhaps into the trap. And speaking quite distinctly over the laughter from the rampart Jack said to Bonden, 'Stand by with the blue light.' He was himself standing up and in the suffused glow he could make out something of the quay, with the shipping moored along it: quietly they moved a little closer and it was almost clear – a brig, some other craft, the *Diane*, and two merchantmen. Still closer, just paddling now, and the object ahead of the *Diane* could be seen to be two gunboats, now moored abreast.

'Very well,' said Jack. '*Tartarus*, *Dolphin*, *Camel*, *Vulture*, lay on your oars. Bonden, the blue light.'

Bonden clapped his glowing tinder to the fuse, and with a wavering flight at first but then a determined soar the rocket climbed, climbed, and burst with a great blue star that floated to leeward together with its own white smoke. Within a second of the burst the whole southern sky flashed as the *Surprise*'s broadside answered.

'Cast off and stretch out,' cried Jack, and as the boats leapt into motion the deep thunder of the carronades reached them, echoing from one side of the port to the other and back again.

The boats raced to their posts. As the launch bumped heavily alongside the mainchains an indignant voice called out '*Mais qu'est-ce qui se passe?*' and a man peered over. But he was instantly overwhelmed by the boarding party that leapt up the side, while the rest of the meagre harbour-watch, chatting over the rail with friends on the quay, were swept down the hatchways by parties coming from head and stern. Stephen, followed by Bonden, darted not into the great cabin but into that where he would have been himself in similar conditions: and here, writing at a table, he found a middle-aged man, who looked up with angry astonishment. 'Pin him, Bonden,' said Stephen, his pistol levelled at the man's head. 'Tie his hands and toss him into a boat. He must not call out and he must not escape.' Meanwhile Padeen and Darkie Johnson, racing over the brows fore and aft, the gangways to the quay, cut the cables; the topmen laid aloft and loosed the foretopsail, cutting the buntlines and clewlines as they did so; three boatloads of boarders were sweeping the lower deck clear of the watch below, turning them out of their hammocks and driving them and their girls down into the hold and clapping the hatches shut. And all this while the *Surprise* bellowed and thundered like a ship of the line, while in St Martin's the church bells rang madly, drums beat from a dozen points, trumpets sounded, and lines of torches could be seen hurrying towards the isthmus.

The boarders on deck and between decks rounded up the stray Dianes – there were a few scuffles, a pistol shot or so – and herded them too down into the hold, where the afterhatch was raised to let them pass. 'Mr Bulkeley,' said Jack, standing by the men appointed to steer, 'and Master Gunner, take the cutters and tow her head clear.'

The cutters' crews were over the side in a moment, and they carried out a line, pulling splendidly; but their zeal and an unhappy gust in the loosed topsail ran the *Diane*'s stem tight between the two gunboats moored close ahead. Jack raced forward and peered down into the black water. 'Mr West,' he said, 'jump down with a party and carry the off gunboat out into the stream.'

'Sir,' cried West, coming back soaked, gasping, black in the face, 'she's moored with a chain fore and aft.'

'Very well,' said Jack, and he saw that Davidge was next to him, and men all along both gangways. 'You two take your boats' crews and shift those two merchantmen astern. I do not think they will give you much trouble.'

Nor did they. But as the ships moved out into the stream so the scene changed entirely. From a street leading from the hill into the middle of the quay a group of sailors on horseback, the *Diane*'s officers, followed by her liberty-men and a body of soldiers came pelting along over the cobbles.

Jack leaned over the starboard rail and hailed loud and clear, 'Davidge, West, heave her stern clear, and bear a hand, bear a hand, d'ye hear me?' There was no time for more. The *Diane* still had her brows across, and though she was free aft her larboard bow was wedged between the gunboats, fast against the quay forward; and the ebb was now wedging her tighter still.

The foremost officer leapt his horse clean on to the frigate's quarterdeck, his pistol aimed at the helmsman; but his horse missed its footing and came down. Jack plucked the man clear and hurled him across the deck into the sea. But others followed him – five horses at least – and men on foot were swarming aboard over the brows fore and aft, some hauling on the buntlines and clewlines to take their power from the sails, only to find them cut, while others tore along the gangway to join the very violent confused struggle on the quarterdeck: there were fallen horses kicking madly and forming a barrier, but as two of them got to their feet they left room for a singularly furious attack led by the *Diane*'s captain. Jack, wedged against the capstan by the surging crowd, saw Stephen shoot him coolly in the shoulder and pass his sword through his body. Then came a heaving struggle, even closer-packed than before, with blows felt but unseen, Surprises from below and from the boats roaring Merry Christmas and flying into the thick of it with cutlasses and boarding-axes. But now there were far more people on the quay. The Surprises were outnumbered and the tide was setting against them; they were being thrust against the wheel and the mizen and the far rail.

Jack had forced his way to the front rank in the centre; here there was no room for fine-work, no room for sword-play; it was all furious short-armed cutting strokes, swords clashing like a smithy, until a maddened horse dashed between the opposing sides. Through the wider gap a French soldier, rising from the deck on which he had tripped, slashed upwards with his sabre, catching Jack's leg above the knee. His friends, pushing forwards, trampled the soldier down again and one of them lunged fast and hard; Jack parried, but a trifle late and the point ploughed up his forearm. The thrust brought the man within reach and Jack caught him with his left hand, stunned him with the pommel of his sword and flung him bodily against his supporters with such force that three of them fell. In the momentary interval he half turned to hail the squadron's boats and as he turned he felt a blow from behind, like a kick. 'Horse,' he thought, and filled his lungs to hail, yet now the savage attacking cry of the Dianes and the soldiers changed to a bellowed warning – run, run while you can. It was almost too late. Davidge and West now had a real purchase on the frigate's stern; they heaved, and first the after and then the forward brow left the quay and fell down the ship's side. Some Dianes leapt back before the gap was too wide, some leapt but fell short, some fought on with their backs to the taffrail until, hopelessly outnumbered, they threw down their arms.

Yet there was still pistol and musket fire from the quay, and Jack, calling out 'Come on Plaice, come on, Killick,' ran forward to the forecastle carronades – flint-lock pieces – heaved the short gun round to bear on the soldiers, and though his arm was streaming with blood he pulled the laniard. It was only loaded with ball, not the much more deadly case-shot, but it shattered the cobbles and the front of a house, scattering the men entirely.

'And now we are here,' said Jack, 'I'll be damned if we don't take the gunboats too.' As he said this the battery at the bottom of the harbour came to life at last, but the gunners' aim was impeded by their own vessels, and their shots only ruined the port-office and part of the quay. Jack's aim on the other hand was perfectly clear. 'Belay, there,' he called to those heaving the stern, as the next carronade aft bore full on the mooring-bollard. Again he pulled the laniard and the gun roared out, its long tongue of fire almost touching the target; when the smoke cleared there was no bollard to be seen, but the gunboats had swung out with the tide, and the chain, a loop-chain, had run clear.

'Mr Bentley,' he said to the carpenter, 'take the jolly-boat and your men and take care of the gunboats.'

The *Diane* now had way on her; the men on the quarterdeck had cleared the wheel; they had hoisted topsails and forestay-sail, and with the tide, the cutters' towing, and the light breeze she was moving slowly away from the quay. Now at last Jack hailed the waiting Tartaruses, Dolphins, Camels and Vultures; there were five prizes and he had to get them clear of the port before the French galloped field-pieces down to the quay.

No field-pieces; and they moved out, a solemn procession, though faster and faster as both ebb and breeze increased upon them: a brisk fire of musketry at the narrow pass, soon discouraged by the *Diane*'s full broadside, and they were out in the open sea, heaving on the familiar swell, with the impass-ive beam of the lighthouse sweeping the air overhead, the *Surprise* and the ships of the squadron standing in, not a mile away, top-lanterns all ablaze.

CHAPTER SEVEN

With Bonden pushing him from behind Jack Aubrey managed to climb up the stern ladder, but the ivory pallor of his face in the lantern-light shocked Tom Pullings extremely. Pullings' look of fierce happiness and triumph vanished; he cried 'Are you all right, sir?' and sprang forward to take his arm.

'A little hacked about, no more,' said Aubrey, and he walked along the quarterdeck, blood squelching from his boots at each step. 'What is this?' he asked, looking at a great gash in the ship's larboard rail and side, right aft.

'A bomb, sir. They got a mortar up on to the hill just as we were winning the anchor; but it was only the quarter-gallery – no harm below.'

'Then we can have –' began Jack, turning to look at the wreckage; but the unfortunate twist sent such a flood of pain through him that he had to cling to a backstay not to fall, and moments went by before he could say '– quarter-davits at last.'

'Come, sir, you must go below at once,' said Pullings, holding him firmly. 'The Doctor has been aboard this half glass, working in the orlop with Mr Martin. Bonden, give me a hand.'

Jack could not resist: he only said 'Close the *Tartarus* under all plain sail' and let them ease him down into the brightly-lit orlop, where Stephen and Martin were each dealing with a wounded man. He sat on a rolled-up hammock, crouching in the only position that gave any relief: at some point his senses must have reeled away from him, for when he was fully aware again he was lying naked on the bloody canvas-covered chests with Stephen and Martin examining the small of his back.

'It is not there that it hurts,' he said in a surprisingly strong voice. 'It is in my goddam leg.'

'Nonsense, my dear,' said Stephen. 'That is only referred pain from the great sciatic. We are on the very spot itself. It is a pistol-ball lodged between two vertebrae.' He tapped the general region.

'There? I thought that was the kick of a horse – nothing much at the time.'

'We are all of us fallible. Now listen, Jack, will you? We must have it out directly, and then with the blessing all will be well, a week's stiffness, no more. But when my probe reaches the ball and shifts it there will be a very great deal of pain, more than your body can bear without moving; so I must fasten you down. Here is a leather pad to hold between your teeth. There, all is fast. Now, Jack, bite hard and let your back lie as easy and uncontracted as ever it can. The strong pain will not last long. Martin, will you pass me the long-nosed crow-bill, now?'

Long or short seemed to bear no relation to the agony that followed these words: it was all-embracing and it distorted his body under the leather-covered chains in spite of his utmost fortitude, and he heard a great hoarse animal noise coming from his own throat, on and on. Yet an end it did have at last, and there was Martin casting off the chains while Stephen took the gag from his mouth and gently mopped away the sweat that ran down his face. The pain was still there; it echoed and re-echoed in great waves through his body; but it was no more than a reminder of what it had been, and each wave was less, an ebbing tide.

'There, my dear,' said Stephen. 'It is all over. The ball came away charmingly: if it had not, I should not have given a great deal for your leg.'

'Thankee, Stephen,' said Jack, still panting like a dog as they wound a cingulum round him and turned him on his side to dress the other wounds: right forearm, superficial but spectacular, and a deep gash in his thigh. He had not taken much count of either when he received them, but they had cost him a great deal of blood. The same insensibility was on him now; he was aware of the probing and pricking and sewing, he could see, hear and feel Stephen at work, but it scarcely affected him at all.

'What was the butcher's bill?' he asked.

'Tolerably severe for so short an action,' said Stephen. 'We have no dead, but there are three abdominal wounds I do not like at all, and Mr Bentley was cruelly bruised when he tripped over a bucket and fell down the main hatchway; while there were many kicked or bitten by the horses, an unreasonable number, for a naval engagement. Take a sup of this.'

'What is it?'

'Physic.'

'It tastes like brandy.'

'So much the better. Padeen, let you and Bonden bear the Captain away on this sheet. He is not to be bent, but to be laid flat in his cot. Next case.'

Stephen had long been familiar with his friend's descent into sadness after the exhilaration of battle, and when, coming round with a lantern in the middle watch to see how he did, he found him awake, he said 'Jack, with your recent anguish and your loss of blood and your present pain – for sutures are always uncomfortable – you may feel low in your spirits; but you are to consider that you have taken a French national frigate of greater force than your own, together with two national gunboats and their valuable cannon, as well as two fully-laden merchantmen belonging to the enemy.'

'Dear Stephen,' said Jack, and his teeth gleamed in the half-darkness, 'I have been considering just that ever since you was kind enough to sew me up; and that is why I have not gone to sleep. But dear Lord, Stephen,' he added after a pause, 'I really thought I had lost the number of my mess that bout. I scarcely noticed it at the time and then all at once there I was a-dying; or so I supposed.'

'The pain must have been very great indeed, I am sure; but with the ball gone you have no more to fear. It came out exactly as it had gone in – no turning, no cloth carried in, no laceration at all – there was a laudable flow of cleansing blood, and the wound is now quite trifling. As for the others, they are ugly gashes, sure, but you have suffered a dozen far worse with no lasting ill effects; and if you will drink this, compose your mind, and go to sleep, you will feel somewhat better even tomorrow morning; while you may be fit for service, gentle service, as soon as the stitches are out. Your wounds nearly always heal by first intention.'

Dr Maturin had rarely made a better forecast. In the forenoon of the thirteenth Jack Aubrey was carried up on to his quarterdeck in an elbow-chair, and there he sat in the mild sunshine, contemplating the string of prizes and receiving congratulations. 'By God, sir,' said Babbington, 'this matches the *Cacafuego*. You could not have succeeded more fully. But I do hope that you have not paid too high.'

'No, no, the Doctor himself says it is quite trifling.'

'Well, if he calls that trifling,' said Babbington, nodding at the slung arm and the heavily bandaged leg and the waxen face, 'God help us if ever he tells us we are seriously hurt.'

'Amen,' said Jack. 'William, have you considered the *Diane*?'

'Yes, sir, and a very pretty ship she is – a fine narrow entry and the most elegant lines, though she is so low in the water she don't appear to advantage.'

'Why, she has twelve or even eighteen months stores aboard: she was going foreign, far foreign. But what I meant was, all those young women walking about her deck. Have you considered them?'

'Oh yes, sir,' said Babbington, a lubricious creature who had been considering them through a telescope at close range ever since they began to appear. 'There is a particularly handsome one in green just abaft the hances.'

'You always was an infernal whoremonger, William,' said Jack, though without any moral superiority: moral superiority he could not afford, since it was pretty well known in the service that in his youth he had been turned before the mast for keeping a black girl in the cable-tiers of HMS *Resolution* off the Cape; while as lieutenant, commander and post-captain he had never really shone as a model of chastity. 'I remember your sailing with a whole harem of Greek wenches in the Ionian, when you had the *Dryad*. But my intention was rather to suggest that you should pack them off home in a flag of truce, together with the wounded.'

'Certainly, sir,' said Babbington, reluctantly taking his eye from the girl in green. 'A brilliant idea. No doubt the Doctor will tell me which of the wounded can be moved; but now I come to think of it, I have not seen him this morning.'

'Nor I don't suppose you shall, not until about noon. Poor soul: he fought like a hero in the cutting-out – pistolled the French captain as neatly as you could wish – and then spent most of the rest of the night sewing up the Frenchmen he had punctured, as well as our own people. It was a French quartermaster he operated on after me – blood bubbling out of his lungs.'

'What did he do to you, sir?'

'Well, I am ashamed to say he took a pistol-ball out of the small of my back. It must have been when I turned to hail for more hands – thank God I did not. At the time I thought it was one of those vile screws that were capering about abaft the wheel.'

'Oh, sir, surely a horse would never have fired off a pistol?'

'Yet fired it was: and the Doctor said it was lodged hard up against the sciatic nerve.'

'What is the sciatic nerve?'

'I have no idea. But once it had recovered from being as I take it stunned, and once I had given the ball an unhandy twist, sending it closer still, the whole thing – I shall not attempt to describe how disagreeable it was, until the Doctor took it out.'

Babbington shook his head, looking very grave; and after a while he said, 'The Americans speak of a sciatic stay, leading from the main to the foremast head.'

'So I recall. No doubt shipping it causes them the utmost

agony. But there is Mr Martin: he will tell you which of the French wounded can be moved.'

Half an hour later the whole force and its prizes, an imposing body of ten sail covering a fine stretch of sea some two miles off Cape Bowhead, was standing south-west on the west-north-west breeze with the larboard tacks aboard, moving just fast enough to have steerage-way. The boats plied to and fro, lowering the wounded with great care into the *Tartarus*'s launch under the care of her surgeon, while the girls, together with a disagreeable old woman, understood to be a procuress, were handed down, with a much greater degree of merriment, into the *Surprise*'s pinnace. The boats stepped their masts, set sail, and bowled away for St Martin's with a flag of truce.

The squadron had worn twice, and it was crossing the harbour mouth again – the returning boats could be seen near the breakwater – when Dr Maturin came on deck, a cup of coffee in his hand. Having bade his shipmates good morning and having asked Jack how he did – 'Amazingly well, I thank you, so long as I sit still; and am infinitely obliged to you for your care of me. Will you just cast a glance at that beautiful *Diane* astern?' – Stephen turned and said 'Captain Pullings, my dear, may I have a boat to go and see my prisoner in the *Diane*? I desired Bonden to put him in the hold with the rest, so that he should not be in the way during the towing.'

'Bonden will pull you across himself, sir. Pass the word for Bonden.'

Once again Stephen Maturin took a chair from the Grapes to Shepherd Market; once again Sir Joseph opened the door to welcome him; but this time they both had to carry the files and bundles of paper into the library.

'Sit down, my dear Maturin, and let us drink a glass of madeira while we recover our breath. But first let me congratulate you and Aubrey on your famous victory. I have seen no more than the very brief report transmitted to the Admiralty, but reading between the lines I see that it must have been one of those brilliant dashing expeditions in which our friend excels; and of course I have heard the roar of public applause. Yet from your reserved and indeed – forgive me – melancholy air, I am afraid that although the affair has certainly answered Aubrey's ends it has not done the same for you. Perhaps the *Diane* was not all I represented her to be?'

'Not at all. She was indeed intended for the very same mission to the Spanish colonies, forestalling us; and these papers show the names of all those with whom the French agents might profitably enter into contact, together with a quantity of other information, such as the sums already disbursed to various officers and so on. There is also a plethora of other folders that I have not decoded, probably appreciations of the local situation by resident correspondents.'

'Well, my angelic Doctor, what more could you ask?' cried Sir Joseph, caressing the files with a voluptuous hand and running quickly through the headings. 'Here is all our work done for us – their agents are all betrayed, their schemes laid open. How can you look so sad?'

'Because I should have brought the Red Admiral too, the author of half these notes.' The Red Admiral was a French sea-officer called Ségura who had distinguished himself in the massacres after the Allied evacuation of Toulon and who had joined one of the intelligence services. He was not in fact an admiral but he was a singularly cruel and bloody-minded man and now he was one of the most important members of his organization. 'I had him, bound hand and foot, in the bottom of the launch in the first few minutes of the attack: then, when the *Diane* had to be towed out, I had him placed in the hold with the other prisoners. There, with criminal levity, I left him until the next day: and by then the wicked dog, wearing a skirt and with a bloody clout round his head, had gone ashore with the women and the lightly wounded. We searched, we searched, and we found his breeches, with the waistband marked Ségura, Paul.'

'How you must have cursed, dear Maturin. It must have vexed you to the very heart. I believe I should have gone near to cutting my throat, or hiring someone to hang me. But when you had time to reflect, you cannot have failed to perceive that apart from the personal satisfaction, his presence was of no real consequence and that his absence in no way diminished your triumph. Even under very great pressure, he could not have told us more than is set out in these papers; for unless I am very much mistaken they lay out the whole of his department's reflexion on the matter, together with the agents' instructions.'

'We could perhaps have induced him to tell us where they had concealed the sums intended to convince the officials in South America, the equivalent of that monstrous amount I recovered last voyage. The whole must certainly represent a first-rate ship of the line at the very lowest estimate; and I should like to think that I had added such a vessel to the service. After all, Jack Aubrey sank one of theirs when he had the horrible old *Leopard*, which is much the same thing in reverse.'

'There you may set your mind at rest. The *Diane* will certainly be bought into the service, and the shipwrights will go through her with a fine tooth comb. We have in fact two men who are particularly skilled in these matters and it will be strange if their minds do not work along the same lines as the Frenchmen's.'

'You are a present comfort, Sir Joseph dear: it was stupid of me not to have thought of that.' He smiled, nodding to himself and sipping his madeira; then he said, 'This tooth-comb, now, this fine tooth-comb that the worthy shipwrights will be using – we often hear of it; it appears in daily speech. And yet who has ever combed his teeth, in this or any other day?'

'May it not be that the *fine* qualifies the tooth rather than the comb? That what is intended is a comb with fine teeth, that is to say with thin teeth set close together?'

'Of course, of course,' said Stephen, clapping his hand to his forehead. 'This is not my most brilliant hour, I find. And I will confess that I am equally stupid about the present situation as far as it affects Aubrey: may I beg you to enlighten me?'

'If he had still been on the list, this would have been a knighthood, even a baronetcy – he would have had one for the *Waakzaamheid* if his lamentable old father had not kept on harrying the Ministry in the Commons – but even so this feat, coming on top of the coup in the Azores, has aroused a fine pitch of enthusiasm in the service and, what is more important for our purposes, in the public. There are ballads in the street already. Here is one I bought yesterday: the poet feels that Aubrey should be made a duke, or do strawberry leaves come down lower than dukes?'

'I fancy they may descend as far as mere earls, but I am not sure of that,' said Stephen, taking the broadsheet, which began

> The ermine robe, the golden crown,
> And the leaves of strawberry oh,
> Who's the Tar we'll see in Town?
> Sure 'tis Captain Aubrey oh.
>
> Who smote 'em low, who smote 'em high?
> Hey the leaves of strawberry oh,
> Who did the Frenchmen in the eye?
> Sure 'twas Captain Aubrey oh.
>
> In Martin's port the other night,
> Hey the leaves of strawberry oh,
> Who woke them with a horrid fright?
> Who but Captain Aubrey oh?

'Well,' said he, 'one cannot but approve the sentiment. But allow me to break off and ask whether there is any news of General Aubrey?'

'There is nothing certain, but that remarkably sharp, pertinacious, intelligent man of yours, Pratt, believes he may be on a true scent at last, in the north country.'

'So much the better. Now may we return to the present situation? I perfectly see that as a mere civilian Jack Aubrey cannot look for a title – which in passing I may say he probably would not desire – but can he look for reinstatement, which he most certainly does desire with all his heart and soul?'

'Maturin,' said Sir Joseph, after a considering pause, 'I wish I could say "Yes, and in the near future rather than at the next coronation". But there is something damned odd about the whole situation.' He drew his chair nearer and went on in a low tone, 'I told you some time ago that I was not satisfied with the way Wray and Ledward were pursued after we had made such a cock of taking them. It should not have been possible for them to leave the country; yet they did leave the country. I suspect they have some very highly-placed ally: this ally would naturally be opposed to Aubrey, and his presence would help to explain the inveteracy against our friend – an inveteracy that goes beyond the Ministry's dislike of him for having used him so ill, beyond their hatred of his father's Radical associates, beyond their extreme reluctance to admit they made a mistake. Yet on the other hand here are people who were ill-disposed and who are now well-disposed, Melville and some of the junior lords, for example, as well as several respectable members: and naturally there is the great force of public opinion. My impression is that at the present moment the balance is tolerably even, and that if we . . .' The little silver bracket-clock struck the hour and Sir Joseph stood up. 'Forgive me, Maturin,' he said, 'but I had no dinner and am perfectly faint with hunger. Besides, I asked Charles to keep us the corner table by the window, and if we are not prompt it will be torn from him.'

They walked down to their club, and once again Stephen observed the discreet nods and becks, the quiet 'Give you joy, sir,' that were directed at him as one connected with a splendid victory. Their corner table in the supper-room, over by the far window and remarkably secluded, was waiting for them, and in the few minutes that elapsed before the appearance of the boiled fowl with oyster sauce, his usual supper dish, Sir Joseph eagerly ate pieces of bread. 'As you are no doubt aware,' he said, 'the official dispatch, or rather report, was extraordinarily laconic: all it said was that the *Surprise*, having been honoured with instructions to intercept the *Diane*, proceeded to St Martin's and removed her from her moorings there on the night of the twelfth instant, together with the ships and vessels named in the margin; they were towed out of the harbour with the assistance of boats from HM ships and so on and delivered to the Port Admiral at Plymouth. Of course there have been unauthorized accounts in all the papers, the one more sensational than the last, together with the factual statement of receipt from Plymouth; but I should be very glad to hear . . .' At this point the fowl was placed on the table, and Blaine, having served Stephen, was about to engulf a leg when the Duke of Clarence came hurrying across the room, larger than life in a bright blue coat with the star of the Garter gleaming on his manly chest. They leapt to their feet as he hailed them in his powerful voice: 'Maturin, there! How d'ye do?' – shaking his hand – 'Sir Joseph, good evening to you. As I was leaving Joe told me the Doctor was here, so I thought I should just run in and ask him how he did, though I have not two minutes to spare.' Blaine looked despairingly at his chicken and wiped away a dribble of saliva. 'Was you there, Maturin? Was you there with Aubrey at St Martin's?'

'I was, sir.'

'Was you, though? Was you? A chair, there. Light along a chair, Arthur. Sit down, gentlemen, and let me hear about it between bites. Lord, I wish I had been with you, Maturin; it was the completest thing, from what I understand. Though I don't suppose you saw much of it, in the orlop.' A man in black walked swiftly over from the door and murmured in the royal ear. The duke stood up. 'They are waiting for me,' he said, 'and I have to go down to Windsor early in the morning. But I tell you what, Doctor: let Aubrey know that when he comes to town I should be very glad to see him. My compliments, and should be very glad to hear it all from his own lips, when next he comes to town.'

'Another five minutes, and I should have grown sullen,' said Sir Joseph, wiping his lips some time later. 'I might indeed have committed lèse majesty. Now, Maturin, if you are a little less sharp-set, you will oblige me with a really full account, bearing in mind that I am no great seaman.'

He listened attentively, watching the explanatory crusts with keen intelligence: at the end he sighed, shook his head and observed, 'As the Duke said, it was the completest thing.'

'It would I believe have been the perfect cutting-out, but for those infernal gun-boats and the ebbing tide. If it had not been for those few minutes, which allowed the Dianes on shore and the soldiers to come down, I think we should have carried her away with no blood shed at all.'

'It must indeed have been a very severe engagement until the gangplanks parted. You did not mention the number of casualties, I think, and I forgot to ask, being carried away with the general triumph.'

'We had no men killed, though we had a power of wounded, some of them gravely.'

'You were not hurt yourself, I trust?'

'Never a scratch, I thank you; but Aubrey had a pistol-ball within an inch of his spinal cord and closer still to his great sciatic.'

'Good God! You never told me he was wounded.'

'Why, it is nothing much of a wound now, though it was near to being his last at the time. We extracted the ball very prettily and the small hole – for it was no more – is healing as I had hoped. But he also had a couple of slashes, thigh and forearm, that cost him half the blood in his body, he being so active at the time.'

'What things you tell me, Maturin! Poor fellow: I am afraid he must have had a great deal of pain.'

'The extraction of the ball and the period just before was cruel indeed. But as for the rest, you know, people feel surprisingly little in the heat of battle. I have seen horrible wounds of which the patient was quite unaware.'

'Well, well,' said Blaine, meditating. 'That is some kind of a comfort, I suppose. But I dare say, having lost so much blood, he is tolerably pale?'

'His face might be made of parchment.'

'So much the better. Do not think me heartless, Maturin, but a pale hero is far more interesting than a red-faced one. Can he be moved?'

'Certainly he can be moved. Did I not carry him back to Ashgrove Cottage, where he is now walking quietly about among his roses, putting soft-soap to the greenfly?'

'Could he be brought as far as London, do you think, in easy stages? I ask, because it seems to me that this is the very moment to produce him to the public gaze and, even more, to the gaze of some of the men who help to make decisions. But you feel the journey would be too much, I collect?'

'Not at all. With well-sprung carriages, and they driven gently on modern turnpike roads, a man might be in his easy chair all the way. No: it is that I have kept him to pap almost entirely and I have cut off all wine, spirits and malt liquors with the exception of a tablespoon of port before retiring; then again he sometimes shows signs of that nervous irritability so usual among the convalescent, and he might not do himself justice in a large gathering.'

'I could limit it to a short dozen.'

'And I could give him a comfortable dose that would ensure a benign tranquillity, if not any very high degree of brilliance in discourse. Yet to what extent is a physician entitled to manipulate his patient in anything but strictly medical matters? Perhaps you will allow me to reflect for a while.'

They took their coffee in the library, and as they sat there Stephen said, 'The invalid's pettishness may set in very early. We had a striking example of that in Shelmerston. The captured ships had gone off to Plymouth to be condemned in the prize-court and the *Surprise* was alone when a Royal Navy sloop stood into the harbour, crammed with men. Her intention was only to escort and even sail the *Surprise* to Dock, where the Port-Admiral wished her to be repaired in the royal yard at the King's expense; but the hands, many of whom were liable to be taken up on a variety of charges, particularly desertion, did not know this, and they were determined to make the sloop stand right out again – there were no quarterdeck officers present, all of them having gone off with the prizes. Captain Aubrey was composing his report at the time, but as soon as he heard their voices raised he came on deck in a very furious rage and reduced them to silence – goddam swabs – lubbers – not fit to man the Margate hoy – never to be sailed with again – a hundred lashes all round – damn their eyes – damn their limbs – sodomites, all of them – they were to let the boat come alongside at once and hand the young gentleman aboard with man-ropes – did they not know what was due to the King's coat? – forward pack of scrovies – they should all be cast on the beach within the hour.'

'Were they very much distressed?'

'They were not. They knew they had to look dumbfounded, amazed, shocked by their dismission, and they did so to the best of their ability. In the event he forgave them, and advised those who thought it better not to be seen in Plymouth to go ashore at once.'

'So she is being repaired at Dock: come, that was handsome in Fanshawe. Was there much damage?'

'A bomb-shell carried away the little privy and washing-place on the larboard side, no more; it does not greatly signify, since there is another to starboard and its absence will allow the erection of a kind of crane, a desirable crane.'

Sir Joseph nodded, and after a while he said 'Yet I cannot but feel that if Aubrey were to go off to South America now – for I take it you will pass him fit for service quite soon?'

'Once the repairs are done and the vast quantities of stores are in, he can sail with a quiet mind, above all with such a second as Tom Pullings.'

'Very good. But if he were to go off to South America now he would sail away far out of public knowledge; he would sail away into oblivion, and even if he were to defeat all the French and American vessels in those parts at the cost of his right arm and an eye he could not reach home in time to profit by his glory – that it to say in terms of public acclaim and its official consequences. In two or three months the glory would be cold.

He would never have the same favourable combination of circumstances again. He would have missed his tide!'

'Indeed,' said Stephen, 'that is a very grave consideration.' All his naval life he had heard these words, both in their literal and their figurative sense and sometimes uttered with such concern that they might have referred to the ultimate, the unforgiveable sin; and they had acquired a great dark significance, like those used in spells or curses. 'If he were to miss his tide, that would be very bad.'

Sir Joseph's rarely-used long dining-room could not be faulted: it was old-fashioned – walnut rather than satinwood or mahogany – but the severest shrew could not have found a speck of dust; the twelve gleaming broad-bottomed chairs were exactly aligned, the cloth was as white as newly-fallen snow and as smooth, for Mrs Barlow would have none of those folds whose rigour so often spoilt the pure flow of linen; and of course the silver blazed again. Yet Sir Joseph fidgeted about, tweaking a fork here, a knife there, and asking Mrs Barlow whether she was sure the removes would be hot and whether there would be plenty of pudding – 'the gentleman is particularly fond of pudding, so is Lord Panmure' – until her answers grew shorter and shorter. And then he said 'But perhaps we should alter the whole arrangement. The gentleman is wounded in the leg, and no doubt he should be able to stretch it out, on the leg-rest in the library. To do so comfortably he would have to be at the end of the table. But which leg, and which end?'

'If this goes on another five minutes,' said Mrs Barlow inwardly, 'I shall throw the whole dinner out into the street, turtle soup, lobsters, side-dishes, pudding and all.'

But before the five minutes had passed, before Blaine had even displaced more than a couple of chairs by way of experiment, the guests began to arrive. They were an interesting body of men: apart from the two colleagues Blaine had invited from Whitehall, four were Fellows of the Royal Society, one was a politically active bishop, others were country gentlemen of considerable estate who either owned their boroughs or represented their counties; and of the two City men one was an eminent astronomer. None of them belonged to the Opposition, but on the other hand none of them held any office or desired any decoration; none was dependent on the Ministry and all of those who had seats in the Commons or the Lords were capable of abstaining or even of voting against the government on an issue where they strongly disagreed with official policy. And those who did not have seats were nevertheless men whose advice carried weight with the administration.

For occasions of this kind Sir Joseph hired men-servants from Gunter's, and the splendid butler had announced nine gentlemen before calling out 'Dr Maturin and Mr Aubrey.' The gathering looked eagerly at the door, and there, next to Maturin's slight form, they saw an exceptionally tall, broad-shouldered man, thin in his black coat, pale and severe. Part of the pallor and severity was caused by extreme hunger – Jack's stomach was used to the naval dinner time, several hours before that of fashionable London – but his wounds had their effect upon his colour too, while almost the whole of his severity was an armour against the least hint of disrespect.

Blaine hurried forward with his congratulations, his thanks for this visit and his anxious hope that Mr Aubrey's wounds did not cause him very great inconvenience – would he like a leg-rest at table? He was followed, sooner than etiquette allowed, by a round pink man in a cherry-coloured coat whose face fairly radiated goodwill and friendliness. 'You will not remember me, sir,' he said with a particularly engaging bow, 'but I had the honour of meeting you once at the bedside of my nephew William – my sister Babbington's boy – when he was hurt during that glorious action of yours in the year four – one of your glorious actions in the year four. My name was Gardner until the other day. Now it is Meyrick.'

'I remember it perfectly, my lord,' said Jack. 'William and I were speaking of you not a fortnight ago. May I offer my best congratulations?'

'Not at all, not at all,' cried Lord Meyrick. 'The boot is on the other foot entirely. Being shifted from one House to another is not to be compared with cutting out a frigate, I believe.' He said several other most obliging things, and although his words were mostly drowned by the greetings of the men Jack already knew and by Sir Joseph's introduction to the rest, their evident sincerity could not but please. None of the other guests quite came up to Lord Meyrick – they lacked his complete simplicity – yet their cordial, unfeigned congratulations would have satisfied a man with a far higher notion of his deserts than Aubrey. His reserve and severity – never natural to him until these last months – quite vanished; and the change was made all the quicker by Sir Joseph's sherry, which spread an amiable glow in his pinched, abstemious belly.

Babbington's uncle absolutely insisted upon giving him precedence, and Jack sat at Blaine's right hand in a pleasant state of mind and a lively anticipation of the turtle soup that his practised nose had long since detected. The Bishop said grace; the promise became reality, green calipash and amber calipee swimming in their juice; and after some moments Jack said to Blaine, 'These classical fellows may prate about ambrosia till they go black in the face, but they did not know what they were talking about. They never ate turtle soup.'

'Are there no turtles in the Mediterranean, sir? You astonish me.'

'Oh yes, there are turtles, but only loggerheads and the sort they make tortoiseshell of. The true turtle, from the ambrosian point of view, is the green one; and to find her, you must go to the West Indies or Ascension Island.'

'Ascension Island!' cried Lord Meyrick. 'What vistoes that calls to mind! What oceans of vast eternity! In my youth I longed to travel, sir; I longed to view the Great Wall of China, the deadly Upas Tree, the flux and reflux of the fabled Nile, the crocodile in tears; but in crossing to Calais I found it would not answer. My frame would not bear the motion. I waited in that vile town until a day of total calm, a true halcyon day, and then I was rowed gently back, still half dead and far gone in melancholy. Since then I have travelled, fought, suffered, survived and conquered solely in the person of William. Such things he tells me, sir! How you and he, in the *Sophie* of fourteen guns, took the *Cacafuego* of thirty-two . . .' And so he went on, with an accurate account of Aubrey's battles – and Aubrey had been unusually favoured in the way of action – until the two country gentlemen on the other side of the table gazed at Jack with renewed respect, even wonder, for it was in fact a most uncommon record, and one told with complete sincerity.

'Mr Aubrey,' murmured Blaine, interrupting the flow just where the *Surprise* was sinking a Turk in the Ionian, 'I believe the Bishop means to drink to you.'

Jack looked down the table and there indeed was the Bishop smiling at him and holding up his glass. 'A glass of wine with you, Mr Aubrey,' he called.

'With the utmost pleasure, my lord,' replied Jack, bowing. 'I drink to your very great happiness.'

This was followed by several more glasses with other gentlemen, and Stephen, half way down the table on the other side, observed that the colour was coming back into Jack's face: perhaps rather more colour than he could have wished. A little later he also observed that his friend had launched into anecdote. Jack Aubrey's anecdotes were rarely successful – his talent did not lie that way – but he knew his role as a guest and now with a candid look of pleasure at his immediate neighbours he began, 'There was a bishop in our part of the country when I was a boy, the bishop before Dr Taylor; and when he was first appointed he made a tour of his command – of his diocese. He went everywhere, and when he came to Trotton he could hardly make out that such a scattered place – just a few fishermen's huts along the shore, you know – could be a parish. He said to Parson West, an excellent fisherman himself, by the way; he taught me to sniggle for eels. He asked Parson West . . .' Jack frowned slightly and Stephen clasped his hands. This was the point where the anecdote might so easily break down again, an unhappy echo of the word *place* appearing as *plaice* in the bishop's question. 'He asked Parson West, "Have you many souls here?"' Stephen relaxed. 'And

Parson West replied, "No, my lord; only flounders, I am afraid."'

Jack Aubrey, pleased at the kind reception of his tale, pleased at having got it all out in one piece, and pleased at having fulfilled his social duties for some time to come, applied himself to his excellent mutton, and the talk flowed round him. Someone at the Bishop's end spoke of the curious French ignorance of English titles and ways, and one of the Whitehall men said 'Yes. When Andréossy was here as Bonaparte's envoy he wrote to my chief as Sir Williamson, Esquire. But he did worse than that; he intrigued with the wife of one of our colleagues, a Frenchwoman. And having heard that the Devonshires were in a very sad way, he sent her to the Duchess with a plain downright barefaced offer of ten thousand pounds for Cabinet secrets. The Duchess told Fox.'

'It is ignorance that will lose the French this war,' said his neighbour. 'They began by cutting off poor Lavoisier's head, observing that the Republic did not need men of science.'

'How can you speak of French ignorance, when you compare their attitude towards balloons with ours?' cried the man opposite him. 'Surely you must recall that from the beginning they had an aerostatic corps and that they won the battle of Fleurus almost entirely because of the accurate information derived from balloons poised at an immense height over the enemy? His numbers, his dispositions, his movements were all open to view. But what do we do about balloons? Nothing.'

'The Royal Society decided against them,' said the Bishop. 'I particularly remember the reply when the King offered to pay for some trials, because I was in the closet when it came: "No good whatsoever can be expected from such experiments" said the Society.'

'A part of the Society,' said one of the Fellows sharply. 'A very small part of the Society, a committee largely made up of mathematicians and antiquaries.'

The other Fellows present disagreed with this and with each other; but Aubrey and Maturin, though much attached to the Society, were often abroad; they had little knowledge of its often passionate internal politics and less interest; neither took any part in the discussion. Stephen devoted his whole attention to his right-hand neighbour, who had made an ascent, and a glorious ascent, at the time of the first enthusiasm before the war. He was too young and foolish, he said, to have recorded any of the technical details, but he did still retain that first vivid sense of astonishment awe wonder and delight when, after a slow, grey and anxious passage through mist, the balloon rose up into the sunlight: all below them and on every hand there were pure white mountains of cloud with billowing crests and pinnacles, and above a vast sky of a darker, far darker, purer blue than he had ever seen on earth. A totally different world, and one without any sound. The balloon rose faster in the sun – they could see their shadow on the sea of cloud – faster and faster. 'Dear Lord,' he said, 'I can see it now; how I wish I could describe it. That whole enormous jewel above, the extraordinary world below, and our fleeting trace upon it – the strangest feeling of intrusion.'

The cloth was drawn: the time for toasts was coming and Jack rather dreaded them. His wounds, his recent milk-and-water diet and the lack of exercise had lowered his resistance and even from the moderate amount he had drunk already his head was not as solid as he could wish. He need not have been afraid. After they had drunk the King, Sir Joseph sat musing for a little while, fitting two walnut-shells together: on his left hand Lord Panmure said 'Not long ago that toast stuck in a quite extraordinary number of throats – quite extraordinary. Only yesterday Princess Augusta told my wife that she never really believed in her rank until the Cardinal of York was dead.'

'Poor lady,' said Blaine. 'Her scruples did her honour, though I fancy they were highly treasonable; but she may be easy in her mind now. It would never have stuck in your throat, I dare say say, sir?' – turning to Jack. But Jack was still following an account of Babbington's description of HMS *Leopard*'s encounter with an iceberg in the Antarctic and her repair on Desolation Island; he had to be disengaged and the question put to him again. 'Oh no,' he said. 'I have always followed Nelson's advice in that as I have in everything else, as far as my powers have allowed me. I drink to the King with total conviction.'

Blaine smiled, nodded, and turned back to Lord Panmure: 'What do you say to taking our coffee in the drawing-room? It is so much easier to circulate, and I know there are many gentlemen who would like to speak to Aubrey.'

Many of them did indeed speak to Aubrey, and as the evening wore on Stephen saw him growing paler and paler. 'Sir Joseph, my dear,' he said at last, 'I must take my patient away and put him to bed. Please may his servant be told to fetch him a chair?'

The servant in question, Preserved Killick, was drunk, drunk even by naval standards, incapable of movement, but Padeen was at hand and sober and in time he brought two chairs carried by Irish chairmen, the only ones who could understand him. During the delay one of the Whitehall men, Mr Soames, drew Jack aside and asked him where he was staying – asked too whether he might have the honour of waiting on him: there were one or two questions he would like to ask.

'By all means: I should be very happy,' said Jack; but he had almost entirely forgotten him the next day, when Mrs Broad of the Grapes announced 'Mr Soames to see you, sir.'

Jack received him with decent urbanity, although yesterday's unaccustomed food and wine were still with him, hanging like a debauch, while his leg wound was itching extremely and his spirits were ruffled by an interview with the sullen, dogged Killick, who among other things had lost, or failed to pack, a book promised to Heneage Dundas and now to be carried out by a friend bound for the North American station.

They exchanged remarks on the previous evening, Sir Joseph's capital wine, the near certainty of rain later in the day, and then 'I find a certain difficulty in opening my errand,' said Mr Soames, eyeing the tall figure opposite him. 'I am most unwilling to seem busy.'

'Not at all,' said Jack in a reserved tone.

'The fact of the matter is that I have been asked to have a few unofficial words with you on the possibility of a favourable outcome, in the event of a proper solicitation for a free pardon.'

'I do not understand you, sir. A pardon for what?'

'Why, sir, for that – for that unfortunate affair at the Guild-hall, to do with the Stock Exchange.'

'But surely, sir, you must be aware that I pleaded not guilty? That I said upon my honour that I was not guilty?'

'Yes, sir, I remember it perfectly.'

'Then how in God's name am I to be forgiven for what I have not done? How can I conceivably solicit a free pardon when I am innocent?' Jack had begun the interview in a state of strong, ill-defined, diffused irritation; he was now white with anger and he went on 'Do not you see that if I ask for a pardon I am giving myself the lie? Proclaiming that there is something to be forgiven?'

'It is no more than a formality – it might almost be called a legal fiction – and it must affect the question of your eventual reinstatement.'

'No, sir,' said Jack, rising. 'I cannot see the matter as a formality at all. I am aware that neither you nor the gentlemen who desired you to speak to me means any offence, but I must beg you to return them my compliments and state that I see the matter in a different light.'

'Sir, will you not consider for a while, and take advice?'

'No, sir; these are things a man must decide for himself.'

'I regret it extremely. Must I then say you will not entertain the suggestion?'

'I am afraid you must, sir.'

CHAPTER EIGHT

'He has missed his tide,' said Sir Joseph. 'I have rarely been more vexed.'

'Soames handled the matter like a fool,' said Stephen. 'If only he had taken it lightly, if only he had started talking about the daily civil lies of "not at home", "humble obedient servant" and so on, had then moved on to the various face-saving formulae of treaties and the like, treating them as the silly unimportant trifles they are, and had then asked Aubrey to put his name to the solicitation, all ready and made out, he might well have signed with a thankful heart, a heart overflowing with happiness.'

'It is the damnedest thing,' said Sir Joseph, following his own line of thought. 'Even with all the susceptibilities that had to be taken into account – Quinborough and his allies, to name only them – for the moment the balance was just leaning in Aubrey's favour, just leaning far enough for the decisive action. Could not you persuade him to tell Soames that on mature consideration et cetera? After all, like every other sailor he has been brought up to think nothing of cheerful corruption. Vast quantities of stores disappear, dead men and non-existent servants continue to draw their wages; and to my certain knowledge he has been guilty of at least three false musters, entering his friends' sons on the ship's books in order to gain them sea-time when in fact they are at school on dry land. Why, in a ghostly form his own half-brother was aboard, last time you were in the Pacific.'

'Cheerful corruption, yes; and if that had been the approach, he might possibly have *worn it*, as sailors say. But now that it is a high moral issue, with all cheerfulness flown out of the window, I could not possibly shift him; nor should I attempt it.'

'Well, as I say, it is the damnedest thing. To be so near success and then to . . .'

After a pause Stephen said hesitantly, 'I suppose there is no possibility of an act of grace, without any formal solicitation?'

'No. At the moment Aubrey has a good many allies and therefore a great deal of interest, but he has not enough for that. Considerably more would be needed.'

'This makes no difference?' Stephen pointed to the carefully-written pages in which Pratt reported his discovery of General Aubrey, dead in a ditch near the alehouse in which he had been living under the name of Captain Woolcombe.

Blaine shook his head. 'No,' he said. 'As far as the Ministry is concerned the General and his Radical friends were quite exploded when they failed to answer their bail – they ceased to exist politically – even the most disreputable opposition newspapers could have nothing to do with them – and the General might just as well have died then as now. And it makes no difference from our point of view either, since Pratt and his colleagues have been through and through the General's papers without finding the least hint of any contact with Wray and Ledward.'

'Of course not. There can have been no possible connection.'

'On the other hand,' observed Blaine, 'it might be said that this death does do Aubrey's cause some little good, in that the involuntary Radical link is done away with; but the good is nothing remotely like enough, alas and alas. What do you propose to do now, Maturin?'

'I shall send Pratt the necessary instructions to deal with the body and post down to Aubrey tomorrow. Then, since the *Surprise* is yet to be prepared and provided with the vast quantity of stores required for the South American voyage, I believe I shall go to Sweden and wait for him there. I shall take the packet from Leith.'

'You do not suppose that this death will change Aubrey's plans?'

'It would surprise me if he were much affected. The General was not a man to inspire any great liking or esteem.'

'No. But there is a not inconsiderable estate, I am told.'

'Little do I know of it, except that it is sadly encumbered; but even if it were half the county I do not believe it would keep Jack Aubrey from the sea. He has engaged for this voyage; and in any case it is said that the Americans have sent one or perhaps two frigates of our own class round the Horn.'

The Aubreys had been buried at Woolhampton for many generations, and the church was filled with people. Jack was surprised and touched to find that such numbers had come to honour the funeral, since for a great while now Woolcombe House had seen none of the solid, long-established families who had dined there so regularly in former times, when Jack's mother was alive. There were some missing faces, of course, but many, many fewer than Jack had expected; then again the congregation was made up not only of old friends and connexions of the Aubreys but also of tenants, villagers, and men and women from the outlying cottages, who seemed to have forgotten ill-treatment, rack-rent, and the oppressive enclosure of Woolhampton Common. Another thing that particularly moved him was the way women from the village, many of whom had been his mother's and even his grandmother's servants, had hurried up to Woolcombe to make the house fit to receive so many guests. It had been allowed to run down sadly, even before the long period when the General was flitting about in the north country, afraid of arrest; but now the drive was as trim as ever it had been, and the public rooms at least were scrubbed, swept and beeswaxed, while tables had been set out to feed those who had come from a distance. One table, with all its leaves spread, was in the dining-parlour, and another, to be presided over by Harry Charnock of Tarrant Gussage, Jack's nearest cousin, stood on trestles in the library.

The General's widow played no part in any of this. As soon as the hearse was known to have reached Shaftesbury she had taken to her bed and she had not moved from it since. Various reasons for her behaviour were put forward, but no one ever mentioned extreme grief: whatever the cause, Jack was heartily glad of the fact. She had been a dairymaid at Woolcombe, a fine snapping black-eyed girl, apt to come home late from fairs and dances and pretty well known to the local young men, including Jack. Although he felt a certain moral indignation when his father married her it had soon worn off; he did not think her a bad woman at all – for example he did not believe the present rumour that she was keeping her bed because the family silver was hidden under it – but he had not forgotten their nights in the hay-loft either, and this made their meetings awkward; and he had to admit that on those rare occasions when he came down, it could not but wound him to see her sitting where his mother had sat.

So Mrs Aubrey stayed in bed, and Sophie, being most reluctant to obtrude on her sorrow or to appear in the house as its present mistress so soon, had stayed in Hampshire; but the second Mrs Aubrey's son Philip had been brought back from school. He was too young – a very little boy – to have much piety, and at first he had not been sure whether this was meant to be a celebration or not; he soon caught Jack's tone however, and now, in his new black clothes, he walked about with his tall half-brother as they acknowledged their guests' kindness in coming and echoed his 'I thank you, sir, for the honour you do us.'

He spoke up well, with neither too much confidence nor too much timidity, and Jack was pleased with him. They had not met half a dozen times since Philip was breeched, but Jack felt a certain responsibility for him, and in case he should wish to make the Navy his career rather than the army he had had his name entered on the books of various ships for the last few years, while Heneage Dundas (soon to be home from North America) had provisionally agreed to take him to sea as soon as he was old enough. Jack thought it probable that the boy would do him credit.

But he had little time to reflect on Philip's future, because as he was trying to induce his guests to sit down he saw an elderly man, indeed an old man, thin and very tall in spite of his stoop, walk slowly into the dining-parlour and peer about the crowded room. This was one of the missing – the understandably missing – faces he had regretted in the church, Mr Norton, a very considerable landowner on the other side of the Stour. Although his connexion with the Aubreys was fairly remote, its existence and the close friendship between the families meant that Jack had been brought up calling him Cousin Edward. It was Cousin Edward who had nominated Jack's father for the pocket-borough of Milport, which lay on one of his estates and which the General had represented in parliament first as a Tory and then as an extreme Radical, according to what he considered his interest. Echoes of the furious quarrel that resulted from this change and indeed from the member's general course of conduct had reached Jack on the other side of the world, distressing him very much; on coming home he found that the echoes fell far short of the truth, and he had never supposed he should see Mr Norton at Woolcombe again.

'Cousin Edward,' he cried, hurrying forward. 'How very good of you to come.'

'I am so sorry to be late, Jack,' said Mr Norton, shaking his hand and looking into his face with grave concern, 'but my fool of a coachman overturned me the other side of Barton and it was a great while before I could get along.'

'I am afraid you were much shaken, sir,' said Jack. He called out 'Ladies, pray be seated without ceremony. Gentlemen, I beg you will sit down.' He led Mr Norton to a chair, poured him a glass of wine, and the meal began at last.

A long meal, and tedious, with all the awkwardness inherent in such occasions; but it did have an end in time, and upon the whole it went off very much better than Jack had feared. When he had seen the last of his guests into their carriages he returned to the small drawing-room, where he found Cousin Edward dozing in his wing-chair, one of the few old pieces of furniture that had escaped the modernization of Woolcombe

House. He tiptoed out, and in the passage he came upon Philip, who asked 'Should I not say good-bye to Cousin Edward?'

'No. He will be staying the night: his coach was overset the other side of Barton and broke a wheel. Besides, he was much shaken. He is very old.'

'Older than my father – our father – was, I dare say, sir?'

'Oh, much older. He and my grandfather were contemporaries.'

'What are contemporaries?'

'People of the same age: but it usually means people you knew when you were young together – school friends and so on. At least that is what I mean. Cousin Edward and my grandfather were contemporaries, and they were great friends. They had a pack of hounds together when they were young fellows. They hunted the hare.'

'Have you many contemporaries, sir?'

'No. Not by land. There was almost no one here of my age whom I knew well apart from Harry Charnock. I went away to sea so early, hardly much older than you.'

'But you do feel at home here, sir, do you not?' asked the boy with a curious anxiety and even distress. 'You do feel that this is a place you cannot be turned out of?'

'Yes,' said Jack, not only to please him. 'And now I am going to look at the vine-house and the walled garden. I used to play fives, left hand against right, on the back of it when I was a boy. Yet now I come to reflect, since we are brothers, you should probably call me Jack, although I am so much older.'

Philip said 'Yes,' and blushed, but spoke no more until they came to the vine-house, disused now as it had been in Jack's day, where he showed him a frog, said to be tame, in the stone bath that perpetually overflowed, still with the same musical drip. The walled kitchen-garden was even more unchanged, if possible; the same exact rows of vegetables, bean-poles, gooseberry-bushes, currants, the same cucumber and melon frames, so vulnerable to a flying ball, and the same smelly box-hedges, while on the red-brick walls themselves apricots and peaches were changing colour. Indeed the whole back of the house, stable-yard, laundry, coach-house, all the unimproved part was infinitely familiar, reaching back to the first things Jack had ever known, as familiar as cock-crow, so that at moments he might have been far younger than the little boy running about in his incongruous black suit.

By the time they went in bats were mixing with the swallows that skimmed over the horse-pond, and Mr Norton had already gone to bed. Jack did not see him again until well on in the next morning.

The Dorchester attorney had just taken his leave, carrying off his bag of legal papers, when Cousin Edward appeared. 'Good morning to you, Jack,' he said. 'You have had a long session of it, I fear. I saw Withers arrive as I was shaving. I hope that does not mean disputes or wrangling?'

'No, sir, it all ended happy,' said Jack, 'though there were many details to be sorted out.' Most of the delay had in fact been caused by his step-mother's extreme unwillingness to reveal the fact that she could not sign her name, but that was not a point Jack chose to raise. He said 'Shall we have a pot of coffee in the morning-room?'

'I can no longer find my way about this house,' said Mr Norton as they walked in. 'Apart from my bedroom and the library, everything has been changed since I was here last: even the staircase.'

'Yes. But I intend to put at least the hall back as it was,' said Jack, 'and my mother's rooms. I found nearly all the old panelling heaped up in the barn behind the rick-yard.'

'Do you mean to live here?'

'I don't know. That depends on Sophie. Our place in Hampshire is mighty inconvenient, but she has known it all her married life, and she has many friends there. But in any case I should like Woolcombe to look more or less as it did when I was a boy. My step-mother does not wish to stay here: it is much too big for her and she would be lonely. She thinks of settling in Bath, where she has relatives.'

'Well, I am glad you are going to keep at least one foot in the county,' said Cousin Edward with a significant look; and when the coffee came he said, 'Jack, I am happy to have you alone like this.' There was a pause, and when he went on his tone was quite different, as though he were reciting words he had composed earlier with some care, perhaps changing them from time to time; it was also evident that he was nervous. 'I dare say you was surprised to see me yesterday,' he said. 'I know Caroline was, and Harry Charnock, as well as some others; and ordinarily speaking I should not have come.' Another pause. 'I do not mean to blackguard your father, Jack, though you know very well how he treated me.' Jack inclined his head in a gesture that might have meant anything. 'But my reason for coming was partly to do what was right by the family – after all, your grandfather and I were the closest of friends, and I loved your mother dearly – yet even more to mark my sense of what was due to you for your splendid feat at St Martin's and even more for the damnable injustice you met with in London.'

The door opened and Philip burst in. On seeing Cousin Edward he stopped, then came forward with a hesitant step. 'Good morning, sir,' he said, reddening; and then, 'Brother Jack, the chaise is come for me. I have said goodbye to Mama.'

'I will come and see you off,' said Jack. And in the hall he said 'Here's a guinea for thee.'

'Oh thank you very much, sir. But would it be very rude were I to say I had rather have something of yours – a pencil-end or an old handkerchief or a piece of paper with your name wrote on it – to show the fellows at school?'

Jack felt in his waistcoat-pocket. 'I tell you what,' he said, 'you can show them this. It is the pistol-ball Dr Maturin took out of my back at St Martin's.' He lifted the boy into the post-chaise and said 'Next holidays, if your Mama can spare you, you must come to Hampshire and meet your nephew and nieces. Some of them are older than you, ha, ha, ha!'

They waved until the chaise turned the corner, and then

Jack walked back into the morning-room. The embarrassment had dissipated, and Cousin Edward asked quite easily, 'Shall you be staying some time? I hope so, if only for the sake of your wounds.'

'Oh, as for them, they were troublesome for a while, but I heal as quick as a young dog and now the stitches are out I scarcely think of them. No: as soon as I have made my round of thanks in the village and at the cottages, I am away. *Surprise* is fitting foreign, and there are a thousand things to attend to, as well as the repairs. My surgeon is quite satisfied, so long as I travel by chaise, not on horseback.'

'Could you not spend an afternoon at Milport, to meet the electors? There are not many of them, and those few are all my tenants, so it is no more than a formality; but there is a certain decency to be kept up. The writ will be issued very soon.' Then, seeing Jack's look of astonishment, he went on, 'I mean to offer you the seat.'

'Do you, by God?' cried Jack; and realizing the extent, the importance, the consequence of what his cousin had just said he went on, 'I think that amazingly handsome in you, sir; I take it more kindly than I can say.' He shook Mr Norton's thin old hand and sat staring for a while: possibilities that he hardly dared name flashed and glowed in his mind like a fleet in action.

Cousin Edward said 'I thought it might strengthen your hand in any dealings with government. There is not much merit in being a member of parliament, unless perhaps you represent your county; but at least a member with merit of his own is in a position to have it recognized. He can bite as well as bark.'

'Exactly so. He carries guns. The other day there was a man connected with the Ministry who came to see me unofficially and said that if I crawled flat on my face and begged for a free pardon it might perhaps be granted. And he either said or implied – I forget which – that if it were granted I might be put back on the list: reinstated. But I told him that asking forgiveness for a crime necessarily meant that the crime had

228

been committed, and as far as I was concerned no crime had been committed. In effect I said dirty dogs ate hungry puddings – that is to say, hungry dogs ate dirty puddings; but in this case either I was not hungry enough or the pudding was too dirty, and I begged to be excused. So we left it; and I thought I had destroyed my chances for ever. But had I been a member, I do not think he would ever have broached the matter like that; nor, if he had done so, would he have left it there.'

'I am certain he would not, particularly if you were a steady, middle-of-the-road, Church-and-State kind of member, with no rant of any kind, as I am sure you will be. Not that I make any conditions, Jack: you shall vote as you please, so long as you do not vote to do away with the Crown.'

'God forbid, sir! God forbid!'

'Yet even as things stood, that was scarcely the way to speak to a man of your reputation.'

'I do not think he meant it ill. But he is one of those people in Whitehall, and I have always noticed that they really do believe they belong to a much higher order, as though they had been born on the flag-officers' list.'

The butler came in, and addressing Mr Norton he said, 'Sir, Andrew desires me to say, with his duty, that the wheel is repaired; he has the coach in the yard at this moment, and do you please to have it round now or shall he put the horses up?'

'Let him bring it round now,' said Mr Norton, and as soon as the door was closed, 'Come, Jack, indulge me in a day's canvassing, will you? The Stag at Milport will give us quite a decent dinner and then we can have a bowl of punch with the burgesses afterwards. It is no more than a form, of course, but they will take it kindly. No doubt they will prate about the political situation rather more than is agreeable, but it is right to pay them this attention, and you can still be home on Wednesday. Or is it too great a sacrifice? Country politics can be a sad bore, I know.'

'Sacrifice, Cousin Edward?' cried Jack, springing up. 'You

could ask a very, very great deal more than that, upon my word and honour. I should give my right arm to be back on the Navy List, or even half way there.'

In Dr Maturin's already comfortable, lived-in, book-lined room at the Grapes he and Padeen contemplated their baggage with satisfaction. One item was a trifling affair, as tight as a Leadenhall sausage, holding what was needed for Stephen's journey to Edinburgh – Stephen's alone, for Padeen was to sail north in the *Surprise*. But their real triumph was the Doctor's sea-trunk: Padeen had profited much from his friendship with Bonden, a prodigy with cordage, and the trunk now stood there in the middle of the floor, fastened with an intricacy of diagonal lines, a sort of network that would have filled any seaman with admiration: the laniards at each end were finished with a handsome Matthew Walker and the whole was topped with a double-crowned wall-knot.

'You have never forgotten my draught, Padeen, I am sure,' said Stephen. He did not choose to be more specific, but by *draught* he meant his nightly comfort of laudanum, as Padeen knew very well, it having, by this stage, become so much his own that he would as soon have forgotten his shirt (though indeed Padeen's steady dilution with brandy, even greater now, because of their temporary separation, had reduced the taking to little more than an act of faith). 'I have not, gentleman,' he replied. 'Is it not under the lid itself? And padded like a relic at that?'

A heavy step on the stairs, and Mrs Broad, pushing the door open with a crooked elbow, came in with two piles of fresh laundry between her outstretched arms and her chin. 'There, now,' she cried. 'All your frilled shirts got up prime, with the finest goffering-iron you ever seen. Mrs Maturin always liked them got up in Cecil Court,' she added in an aside to Stephen, and then loud and clear to Padeen, as though he were at the mast-head, 'In the wery middle, Padeen, between the spare sheets and the lamb's wool drawers.'

Padeen repeatedly touched his forehead in submission, and

as soon as she had gone he and Stephen, having looked quickly round the room, moved chairs to the foot of a tall wardrobe. Even with a chair, however, Stephen was unable to reach the top and he was obliged to stand there, giving Padeen pages of *The Times*, then shirts, then more pages, and advice on just how they were to be laid; and he was in this posture, uttering the words 'Never mind the frill, so the collar do not show', when the slim, light-footed Lucy darted in, crying 'An express for the Doctor – oh, sir!' She understood the position in the first second; she gazed with horror and then with extreme disapprobation. They looked wretchedly confused, guilty, lumpish; they found nothing to say until Stephen muttered 'We were just laying them there for the now.'

Lucy pursed her lips and said 'Here is your letter, sir,' putting it down on the table.

Stephen said, 'You need not mention it to Mrs Broad, Lucy.'

Lucy said, 'I never was a tell-tale yet; but oh Padeen, and your hands all covered with the dust up there, for shame.'

Stephen took the letter, and his look of nervous guilt vanished as he recognized Jack Aubrey's hand. 'Padeen,' he said, 'wash your hands, will you now, and leap down to the bar and ask them to let me have a jug of lemon barley-water.' He pulled his elbow chair to the window and broke the familiar seal:

Ashgrove Cottage

My dear Stephen,

Give me joy! In his very great goodness my Cousin Edward has offered me the seat for the borough of Milport, which he owns: we went and passed a day or so among the burgesses, an affable set of men who were kind enough to say that because of St Martin's and the Azores affair they would have voted for me in any case, even if Cousin Edward had not advised them to do so.

While we were there a messenger came posting down from the Ministry with proposals for my cousin; but, said he, they could not be attempted to be entertained, since he was already committed to me: the messenger looked blank, and posted off again.

So I went home, after another day at Cousin Edward's place – he particularly wished me to see his roses at their height and I absolutely could not do less – and I was telling Sophie the news, with all that I hoped might follow from it, for perhaps the twentieth time, when Heneage Dundas walked in.

I knew *Eurydice* was come back, but I had not had time to go down to Pompey to welcome him home, and when I sent to ask him to dinner they said he had gone up to town, so we were not astonished to see him; we supposed he was returning to his ship and had turned off the road at the Jericho to look in upon us.

But we were surprised when, after having spoken very handsomely indeed about the *Diane* and having begged me to describe the cutting-out in the greatest detail, he grew rather strange, shy and reserved, and after a while said he was come not only as a friend but also as an emissary. The Ministry (said he) had heard that I was to be member for Milport; his brother rejoiced at the news because this additional influence in my favour would allow him to urge his colleagues even more strongly that I should be reinstated by mere motion – that is to say, without having to sue out any pardon. But in order to do so with full effect Melville would have to be able to assure them of my attitude in the House. It was not required that I should engage to support the Ministry through thick and thin, but Melville hoped he could say that at least I should not violently and systematically oppose it – that I should not be a vehement or enthusiastic member. I looked at Sophie, who knew perfectly well what I meant; she nodded, and I said to Heneage that it was excessively unlikely I should ever address the House on anything but a naval question, for I had seen too many sea-officers brought by the lee, meddling with politics; that in general I should be happy to vote for almost any measure proposed by Ld Melville, whom I esteemed so highly and whose father I owed such a debt of gratitude to. While as for enthusiasm or ranting, even my worst enemies could not accuse me of either. Heneage agreed and said nothing could possibly make him happier than carrying back such a message; that Melville had told him that in the event of a favourable answer the papers would be put in hand directly, and that although they would take some months to pass through all the proper channels, while the official announcement would not be made until it could coincide with some victory in the Peninsula or even better at sea, he undertook that my name and present command should be placed on a special list, and that I should not suffer in seniority.

Lord, Stephen, we are so happy! Sophie goes singing about the house. She says she would give anything for you to share our joy, so here I am scribbling this in the greatest haste, hoping it may catch you before you set out for Leith. But if it don't, then I shall have the delight of telling you when we meet in Sweden. There is only one change in our arrangements I wish to suggest, and that is that since we shall already be in the Baltic I should run across to Riga for cordage, spars and especially poldavy for our voyage: the finest poldavy I ever saw in my life came from Riga. God bless you, Stephen. Sophie bids me send her dear love.

Yours ever

Jno Aubrey

'What now?' cried Stephen, quickly sliding the letter under a book.

'If you please, sir,' said Mrs Broad, whose mild face was perfectly unconscious of the wardrobe, 'Sir Joseph is below, and asks if you are at leisure.'

'Certainly I am at leisure. Pray beg him to walk up.'

'Heavens, Maturin, how glad I am to find you,' said Blaine. 'I was so afraid you might have set off already.'

'The mail does not leave until half-past six.'

'The mail? I had imagined you would take a chaise.'

'At fourteenpence a mile?' said Stephen, with a knowing, worldly look. 'No, sir.'

'Well,' said Sir Joseph, smiling, 'I can save you not only the monstrous expense of the mail, but also the dismal jerking and trundling crammed night and day into an airless box with a parcel of strangers, more or less clean as the case may be, the hurried meals, the incessant don't forget the coachman, sir, and even the cruel bore of running down from Edinburgh to Leith and then going aboard the packet at even greater cost to both purse and spirit, they being quite fagged out by then.'

'How do you propose to do this beautiful thing, my valued friend?'

'By putting you aboard the *Netley* cutter early tomorrow morning. She is carrying messages and messengers to a number of ships at the Nore; and among them, Maturin, among them, as I learnt by telegraph only an hour or so ago, is the *Leopard*, bound for Gefle.'

'Not the horrible old *Leopard* that took us to New Holland, drowning, wrecking and starving us on the way?' cried Stephen.

'The same: but she is now shorn of most of her guns and she sails under the colours of the Transport Board. Indeed, her present humble task is to fetch marine stores from Gefle, taking the place of another transport seized by a couple of Americans in the Skager Rack. I heard of it only this afternoon, when the commissioner's report came in, stating that with diligence the *Leopard* could be made ready for sea tomorrow. I happened to be in the way, and as soon as I heard she was to sail for Gefle I said I shall tell Maturin at once; they can drop him off at Stockholm without the loss of a minute and it will save him all this wearisome toiling and moiling, bad company and worse food, as well as a mint of money. I hurried out, searched for you at Black's, searched for you in the British Museum, searched for you in Somerset House, and ran you to earth here, where I should have begun in the first place. I would have spared me a world of heat and passion, thrusting my way through slow-moving hordes of bumpkins. London is filled with bumpkins at this time of the year; they stare about them like oxen.'

'It was benevolent in you to grow so hot, Sir Joseph, and I am infinitely obliged to you for your care. Will you take a glass of lemon barley-water, or do you prefer a draught of moist and corny ale?'

'The ale, if you please; and it cannot be too moist for me. I must have lost a stone in my striving course. But it was worth it. Dear me, Maturin, how happy I was to find you! It would really have put me out of temper for a month to have lost my message.' He drank half his ale, gasped, and went on, 'Besides, it would have prevented me from inviting you to hear a very charming *Figaro* with me tonight. The young person that sings Cherubino has an androgynous perfection in breeches; and such a voice!' He went on to speak of the rest of the cast, particularly a glorious Contessa; yet Stephen, watching him, perceived that he was cherishing the secret of some other piece of news, and presently it came out. 'But although listening to the music and telling you about your passage in the *Leopard* was a great point,' said Blaine, 'sending you off with an easy mind was a greater one by far.'

Blaine was an unmarried man with no near family; and though he had a very wide acquaintance he had almost no close friends; while his profession was one in which the kindlier virtues had little play. But this was one of the rare occasions on which friendship and indeed the interest of the service came together, and he gazed affectionately at Stephen for quite a time before saying, 'Jack Aubrey is to be returned for Milport, ha, ha, ha!' He stood up, clapped Stephen on the shoulder and walked about the room. 'For Milport! Ain't you amazed? I was, I can tell you. His father's constituency! Such a degree, such a pitch of magnanimity in the owner of a borough I have never seen nor heard of – above all *that* borough. A remote connexion, I believe? Have you met Mr Norton, Maturin?'

'I just saw him at Jack Aubrey's wedding, a tall, thin gentleman.'

'It makes all the difference,' said Blaine, carrying straight on. 'It comes exactly at the right time. I had of course thought of a pocket-borough to give just that weight needed to bring the balance right down on his side. They tend to be costly, boroughs, but in the circumstances I should have suggested it, if only there had been an uncommitted seat on the market, which there is not – never for a moment did it occur to me that the only vacancy should be as it were poured into his lap.'

'That is scarcely a correct expression, Blaine.'

'No, to be sure. But how beautifully it suits the occasion. Melville has sent his brother Heneage down, and I am sure he will handle the matter far better than Soames. They are old friends, and apart from anything else this is to be one of your discreet mere motion affairs with no explicit conditions of any sort; though I dare say Heneage Dundas, speaking as one sailor to another, may persuade him not to be too hard on Melville and his colleagues.'

'How I rejoice at what you tell me, Blaine,' said Stephen. 'I have no doubt that Heneage Dundas is the perfect negotiator. From what I know of Jack Aubrey's mind he cannot fail to be successful. Yet you might still think it worth pointing out to your political friends that the only absolutely certain way of making sure that a sailor does not address the House at interminable length either on naval abuses or on some subject of which he is deeply ignorant, is to send him on a very long voyage. There is the South American situation to be looked into, sure; but then there are also the complex rivalries between the Malay sultans, which worry the East India Company so; there is all that poor dear Captain Cook and the less satisfactory Vancouver had to leave undone; and think of the untouched entomology of the Celebes! Let us drink a bottle of champagne.'

The champagne and its charming stir of spirits had long, long since faded by the time the *Leopard* was creeping past the

Swin in the graveyard watch on Friday: every minute she fired a windward gun into the fog; her drum beat continually on the forecastle, though the wet took away most of its resonance; and the man in the chains cast his lead without a pause, his hoarse voice chanting 'By the mark seven: by the mark seven: by the deep six: and a half six,' sometimes rising in urgency to 'By the mark five, and a half five' as the leeward bank came closer. The ship was barely making two knots in the murk, but the soundings changed fast; and all around, in directions and at distances hard to estimate, came answering gun-shots, cries and drums from the merchantmen or warships making their way to or from the London river, while dim lights appeared and then vanished in deeper fog when they were even closer.

It was an unpleasant time to be navigating busy shoal water, and the captain, his pilot and the more responsible men were still on deck, as they had been, with rare intervals, ever since Stephen came aboard in the last hour of clear weather. The *Leopard* had been hurried to sea, under-manned and ill-prepared; her decks were all ahoo and his reception did no one any credit, though to be sure he could hardly have chosen a worse moment, with the ship winning her anchor. Yet his heart had sunk long before this, long before the testy 'Go below, sir, go below. Get his goddam chest out of the way.' From half a mile he had not recognized the ship, and had supposed the cutter's midshipman was making game of him; but then, piecing together curves, masses and proportions, all lodged somewhere in the uncatalogued library of his mind, he had seen that this old transport was indeed the *Leopard*. She had hogged, which gave her a droop-eared look of extreme shabbiness; and she had been given a thirty-two gun frigate's masts to lighten her burden, which had deformed her entire outline, rendering it mean; and her paintwork was a disgrace.

That was sad enough, and coming aboard was sad enough, but it was not until he went below to the absurdly familiar wardroom – familiar even in the trick of its door catching on the sill and the tilting scuttle of the quarter-gallery with its worn brass lock – that he realized what kind, affectionate, even loving memories he had preserved and how he resented the old ship's degradation. Dirt and carelessness everywhere; everywhere a change for the worse. Of course she could not be judged by her standards as a man-of-war, when a taut captain and a zealous first lieutenant had three hundred and forty men to keep her just so; yet even by the very much less ambitious notions of the common coasting trade she was a dirty ship. A dirty ship and an unhappy one.

Long before he went up the side, helped by the cheerful cutter's midshipman, Stephen had had a premonition of disaster; and although the happiness or unhappiness of the ship was wholly irrelevant to his sense of personal catastrophe, the feeling was strengthened by his first sight of the *Leopard*'s captain and pilot wrangling, while three of the officers steadily lashed the men heaving at the capstan-bars, swearing as loud as ever they could bawl.

Supper was no very cheerful ceremony either. The drizzling fog, the slight and shifting wind, the dangerous currents and shoals and the risk of collision would have made it an anxious meal even in the old *Leopard*; now it was barbarous as well. The wardroom was divided into two hostile groups, the master's friends and the purser's; and as far as Stephen could see they were equally determined to show their lack of respect for the captain, a tall, thin, elderly, weak, ill-tempered clerk-like man who looked in from time to time. There were also some other passengers for Sweden, marine-store merchants; and each of these three groups kept up its own whispered conversation. The passengers – and Stephen belonged more among them than elsewhere, since the *Leopard*'s surgeon was dead drunk in his cabin – were of no interest whatsoever to the sailors. They were mere landsmen, often a nuisance, often sick, always in the way, come today and gone tomorrow; but they did serve as a means of communication between the hostile camps. Words ostensibly addressed to a hemp-buyer from Austin Friars bounced off him to reach the far end of the table; and in this way Stephen learnt that still another collier had hailed to say that Americans had been sighted off the Overfalls, heading south; so the Old Man was going inside the Ower and the Haddock bank.

Shortly after this all hands were called to fend off a Dutch buss that had fallen aboard the *Leopard*'s quarter in spite of all the yelling and gunfire. Stephen followed the merchants on to the wet, dark, slippery deck, found that he could neither see anything nor do anything, and so retired, the cries of 'Butter-boxes, bugger off' growing fainter as he went down to his cabin and closed the door.

Since then he had lain on his back with his hands behind his head in what had been Babbington's cot during the *Leopard*'s voyage to the Spice Islands by way of the Antarctic – had lain swinging with the easy motion of the ship. In the course of what now amounted to many years he had imperceptibly become so much of a seaman that he found this posture and this living heave the most comfortable attitude and motion known to man, the best for either sleep or reflection, in spite of the sound of the ship's working, the shouts and foot-steps, overhead, and on this occasion the thump of the signal-gun.

For the first part of the night, while he was waiting for his draught to have its effect, he deliberately composed his mind to help sleep come. There was a a vast expanse in which his thoughts could take their pleasure: Jack Aubrey's affairs could hardly be more prosperous, and short of a very hideous mis-chance (Stephen unhooked his hand to cross himself) it was scarcely possible that he should not be fully, publicly reinstated within the next few months. He would most probably be given a command after the South American voyage: and perhaps it would be another independent commission – his genius lay that way. Conceivably they might explore the high northern latitudes together: extremely interesting, no doubt; though they could scarcely hope for the fantastic wealth of the south again. Stephen's mind returned to Desolation Island, where this very ship had taken him – physically these very same timbers, battered and uncared-for though they were now – Desolation, with its sea-elephants and countless penguins, petrels of every kind and the glorious albatrosses that would let him pick them up, warm and if not companionable then at least in no way hostile. Whale-birds, blue-eyed shags! The crab-seals, the leopard-seals, the otaries!

His mind, perhaps a little too conscientious in its pursuit of happiness, turned back to his evening with Blaine. He dwelt for a while on their excellent meal, their bottle of Latour so smooth and round and long, and reviewed Sir Joseph's confidential words as they finished their wine: 'Retirement to the country, to gardening and etymology, did not answer – attempted once: never again – night-thoughts in an unoccupied mind at his age, with his experience, and with his trade behind him, were too disagreeable – pervading sense of guilt, though each separate case could be satisfactorily answered – present activity and the busy persecution of the enemy was the only answer.' And from this he moved to the opera, where they had heard a truly brilliant performance of Le Nozze di Figaro, brilliant from the first notes of the overture to what Stephen always looked upon as the true end, before the hurlyburly of jovial peasants – the part where from a dead silence the dumbfounded Conte sings *Contessa perdono, perdono, perdono* with such an infinite subtlety of intonation. He repeated it inwardly several times, together with the Contessa's exquisite reply and the crowd's words to the effect that now they would all live happily ever after – *Ah tutti contenti saremo cosí* – but never quite to his satisfaction.

At some point he must have dozed off, for as he woke he was conscious that the watch had changed and that the ship's speed had increased by perhaps a knot. The drum had stopped beating on the forecastle, but the gun still uttered its gruff bark every minute or so. And his inner voice was still singing *Ah tutti contenti saremo cosí*: it had the cadences more nearly in their true line, but oh how much less conviction there was in those words at present. They were now purely mechanical, a mindless repetition, because in his sleep that earlier premonition of extreme unhappiness had risen up and now it occupied him entirely.

It now appeared evident to him that his visit to Sweden must be seen as an odious importunity. It was true that he was carrying back her blue diamond, which she valued extremely. But it could have been sent by a messenger; it could have been sent through the legation; and this bringing it in person might be looked upon as a singularly ungenerous demand for gratitude, necessarily self-defeating as far as the essence was concerned. Blaine was probably right in saying that Diana was not or was no longer attached to Jagiello: Stephen hoped so, because he liked the beautiful young man and he did not look forward to the conventional bloody meeting with any pleasure. Yet that did not mean that she was not attached to some other man, perhaps much poorer, more discreet, less in the public eye. Diana was a passionate creature and when she was attached she was usually attached passionately. Stephen knew very well that in their relations the very strong feeling was all on his side: she had a certain liking, friendship and affection for him, but certainly no passion of any kind. Passionate resentment of his supposed infidelity, perhaps, but no other.

There were large and important areas of Diana's mind that were as strange to him as his was to her, but he was quite sure of one thing: her love of high, expensive living was far more theoretical than real. Certainly she hated being pinched and confined; but she hated being commanded even more. She might love careless extravagance, but she would do little or nothing to come by the means of it: certainly nothing against her inclination. She valued nothing so much as independence. Nothing was more valuable to her than her independence.

What had he to offer in exchange for even a very little part of it, for the appearance of even a very little part of it? Money, of course; but of course in this context money was neither here nor there. If kissing did not go by favour it was not kissing at all. What else had he to offer? He might have ten thousand a year and a deer-park, at least a potential deer-park, but by no stretch of the imagination could he be called a handsome husband. Nor even a tolerable husband. He had little conversation and no charm. He had offended her very publicly and very deeply: or so she and her friends believed, which came to the same thing.

The more he reflected on it, lying there in the heave of the sea as the *Leopard* carried him towards Sweden, the more it seemed to him that his premonition was well founded, that his journey could not be anything but an exquisitely painful failure. At the same time he found the unreasoning part of his mind so longing for its success that he became physically distressed, seized with a kind of rigour that made him gasp. Presently he sat up, clasping his hands and rocking to and fro; and in time, against all good sense, all resolution and fortitude, he opened his chest, groped for the bottle, and repeated his night-draught.

He woke not so much from a laudanum sleep, for by now his tincture would have had little effect on a well-grown child, as from an unusual degree of mental exhaustion; yet in spite of that he was still so stupid that he might have been stuffed with poppy, mandrake and nepenthe, and it took him some moments to understand the steward's cry 'Come on, sir. We'm sunk.'

The man repeated his words, shaking the cot's hangings as he did so, and Stephen recognized the steady grinding thump below: the ship was aground, beating not on rock but on sand. 'Sunk?' he said, sitting up.

'Well, no, sir,' said the steward. 'That was just my jovial way of putting it, to rouse you, like; but that wicked little old bugger has run us on to the tail of the Grab, and Mr Roke is going ashore for help. Captain thinks the passengers should run in with him, in case the ship goes to pieces.'

'Thankee, steward,' said Stephen, getting up, tying his neck-cloth (which was all he had taken off) and locking his chest. 'Pray give a seaman this' – handing him a crown-piece – 'to see my dunnage into the boat; and if you could bring me a cup of coffee on deck you would oblige me.'

On the deck itself he found a thin grey daylight – drizzle, but no wind, and the ship beating less as she settled with the falling tide. The bosun had the pilot wedged against the rail and between insults the captain hit him with a rope's end. The other members of the crew were methodically getting a boat over the side, taking little notice of the pilot's cries. No land was in sight, nothing but yellowish-grey drizzle over yellowish-grey sea, but the people seemed confident of their whereabouts and there was no feeling of particular emergency.

Yet once over the side and manned the boat proved leaky, and they had not shoved off five minutes before water was washing about their feet. 'Jog the loo,' cried Mr Roke, addressing Stephen. And then louder, 'Jog the loo, I say.'

A friendly young mate, unseen before this moment, leant over Stephen and briskly worked the pump-handle up and down. They would be in Manton before the turn of the tide, he said, and if Stephen wished to put up at a comfortable inn, he could recommend the Feathers, kept by his auntie. It would not be a long stay, in all likelihood. They had just beat off the rudder and lost some of the false keel, but Joe Harris of Manton would tow them in and put them to rights as soon as she floated. The passengers were only put ashore because of the insurance. Stephen need not be afraid.

'Jog the loo,' cried Mr Roke.

'There's Manton, right ahead,' observed the young man, when Stephen had more or less cleared the boat. It was a promising East Anglian landscape, a flat, flat mingling of the elements, with decayed sea-walls, saltings, reed-beds in the half-light, and the smell of marsh-gas and seaweed mixed.

'Do you know the Reverend Mr Heath, of Manton?' asked Stephen.

'Parson Heath? Why, everyone knows Parson Heath. We always carry him anything rare, like a sea-baby or a king of the herrings.'

Mr Roke started up, balancing in the boat. 'Now, sir,' he

said very loud, 'if you will not jog that bloody loo, change places with me, and I will jog it myself.'

In the front room on the first floor of the William's Head at Shelmerston Sophie read out 'Bread in bags, 21,226 pounds: the same in butts, 13,440 pounds. Flour for bread in barrels, 9000 pounds. Beer, in puncheons, 1,200 gallons. Spirits, 1,600 gallons. Beef, 4000 pieces. Flour in lieu of beef in half-barrels, 1,400 pounds. Suet, 800 pounds. Raisins, 2,500 pounds. Peas in butts, 187 bushels. Oatmeal, 10 bushels. Wheat, 120 bushels. Oil, 120 gallons. Sugar, 1,500 pounds. Vinegar, 500 gallons. Šauerkraut, 7860 pounds. Malt in hogsheads, 40 bushels. Salt, 20 bushels. Pork, 6000 pieces. Mustard seed, 160 pounds. Inspissated lime-juice, 10 kegs. Lemon rob, 15 kegs. The prices are on the list by the ink-well: I have worked out all the sums except the last two, which Dr Maturin has already paid; perhaps we could compare our answers.'

While Mr Standish, the *Surprise*'s new and inexperienced purser, was multiplying and dividing, Sophie looked out of the window at the sunlit bay. The *Surprise* was lying against Boulter's wharf, taking in the vast quantities of stores recorded on the papers lying there on the table: the frigate was not looking her best, with her hatchways agape and derricks peering into her depths, while it would have been folly to lay on her last coat of paint before the lading was complete; but a seaman's eye would have observed the new suit of Manilla rigging, which any King's ship might have envied, to say nothing of the blaze of gold-leaf on her figurehead and the scrolls behind it. In the course of her long career she had been called *L'Unité*, the *Retaliation* and the *Retribution*, and the rather cross-looking image in front had answered, more or less, for any of these names; but now some natural genius had arched her eyebrows and pursed her mouth, so that she really was the personification of surprise – pleased surprise, with a great wealth of golden locks and an undeniable bosom.

As Sophie gazed she saw her children rush by below: saw and above all heard them. They could never at any time have been called genteel children, having been brought up mainly by strong-voiced, plain-speaking, over-fond seamen; but now that they had been let loose for some time among a whole community of adoring privateersmen, stuffed with sweetmeats and nips of sugared gin, loaded with knives, poll-parrots and shrunken heads from foreign parts, they were in a fair way to being ruined. At present Bonden and Killick were nominally in charge of them, but both were encumbered by Jack Aubrey's evening finery – the Aubreys were to dine with Admiral Russell – and they had been left far behind. In answer to their increasingly threatening cries the two girls stopped, poised on the low wall overlooking the hard; with admirable timing their little brother gave them each a shove, so that they fell a good four feet on to the shore. He pelted off for the ship as fast as his short legs could carry him and they were picked out of the low-tide shingle by three women of the town, dusted, comforted and mended in the kindest way – Charlotte's pinafore was torn. They were also told very firmly that they must not call out after their brother with such words as sod, swab and whoreson beast, because their mama would not like it.

Their mama did not like it, and she would have liked it even less if she had not known that they could switch from one kind of language to another without the slightest difficulty; yet even so she turned to Mrs Martin, who was darning her husband's stockings, and said 'My dear Mrs Martin, I shall be heartbroken when the ship sails, but if those children stay here much longer, I am afraid they will grow into perfect little savages.'

'Two more days will do them no harm,' said Mrs Martin comfortably. 'And it is only two more days, I believe.'

'I am afraid it is,' said Sophie. 'The sauerkraut is promised for tomorrow, Mr Standish?'

'Yes, ma'am; and I am confident it will come,' said the purser, adding still.

She sighed. Of course she was sorry, very deeply sorry, to be losing her husband, and the prospect, though foreseen, though inevitable and though prayed for with all her heart and soul at one time, made her desperately low in her spirits; yet some exceedingly small part of this lowness was also connected with her leaving Shelmerston. She had lived a very quiet, retired life, and although she had been twice to Bath, twice to London and several times to Brighton, Shelmerston was unlike anything she had seen or imagined; indeed it was the nearest thing to a Caribbean pirates' base that any English country gentlewoman was likely to see, particularly as the sun had shone brilliantly from the day of her arrival. Yet it was a base inhabited by the civillest of pirates, where she could walk anywhere, smiled upon and saluted, wandering and exploring the narrow sanded streets without the least apprehension, she being the wife of the most deeply admired, most deeply respected man in the port, the commander of that fabulous gold-mine the *Surprise*.

The whores and demi-whores had startled her at first, for although she had noticed the odd trollop in Portsmouth, she had never seen anything like this number – a considerable part of the population, calmly accepted. There were some wicked old screws among them, but upon the whole they were young, pretty, brightly dressed and cheerful. They sang and laughed and had a great deal of fun, especially in the evening, when they danced.

They fascinated Sophie, and as she had several times thanked them openly and sincerely for their kindness to her children, they bore her no ill-will for her virtue. Indeed, the whole town fascinated her; there was always something going on, and if she had not engaged to help young Mr Standish with his accounts she would rarely have left the broad bow-window that commanded the entire sea-front, the wharves, the shipping and the bay itself, a royal box in a never-ending theatre.

The chief event of this afternoon was the appearance of the William's carriage, a vehicle originally intended for the Spanish Captain-General of Guatemala and very highly decorated to impress the natives of those parts; however, it had been taken by a Shelmerston privateer during the Seven Years War and resigned to the William in settlement of a debt some fifty years ago. The builders had had a team of six or eight mules in mind, but now, on the rare occasions the machine came out, it was drawn by four wondering farm-horses from Old Shelmerston. And at this moment, having cleared the arch from the stable-yard, they trotted soberly off towards Boulter's Wharf, accompanied by the children of the town, running on either side and cheering; and Sophie hurried upstairs to put on her sprigged muslin.

For some time it had been an open secret in the Navy that Jack Aubrey was to be restored to the post-captains' list; he no longer declined invitations – indeed, he entertained large parties of his old friends, straining the William's resources to the utmost – and he thoroughly looked forward to dining with Admiral Russell. 'The only thing I regret,' he said, as the carriage bowled along the turnpike road behind Allacombe, 'is that Stephen is not here. The Admiral has invited the new Physician of the Fleet, and they would have got along together famously.'

'Poor dear Stephen,' said Sophie, shaking her head. 'I suppose he will be in Sweden by now.'

'I suppose he will, if he has made a good passage,' said Jack.

They looked at one another gravely and said no more until the carriage turned in at the Admiral's gates.

Stephen had not made a good passage. In fact at this point he had not advanced much above thirty miles towards Stockholm, and even by the time the *Surprise* put to sea two days later, the *Leopard*, with her new rudder and false keel at last, had only just lost sight of Manton church. After the first few days' wait there was little point in Stephen's travelling north by land, because he would never have caught the packet; he therefore stayed where he was, settling at the Feathers and spending much of the day with his friend Parson Heath. As Stephen admitted to himself, he was not unwilling to have his journey delayed by shipwreck, act of God or anything truly out of his control; and then on quite another plane he was happy to become familiar with ruffs and reeves. He had seen them often enough passing through the Mediterranean lagoons on migration – rather dull birds – but now, leading him to a wildfowler's hide day after day, Heath showed him scores and even hundreds of ruffs in the full glory of their mating plumage, dancing, quivering, and sparring with one another, showing the extraordinary variety of their frills in ritual battle, all apparently in a state of unquenchable sexual excitement.

'A powerful instinct, Maturin, I believe,' said Mr Heath.

'Powerful indeed, sir. Powerful indeed.'

The reeves' instinct, though certainly less spectacular, was perhaps stronger still. In spite of total neglect from their mates, the eagerness of predators whose living depended on their efficiency, and some exceptionally bitter weather, Stephen and Heath saw three of the brave birds bring off their entire clutch, while a fourth began hatching just as a choir-boy messenger came to say that the *Leopard* was moving out of the yard.

The Leopards themselves improved slightly on acquaintance. This was partly because as soon as she was towed out of Manton harbour a fine topgallant breeze filled her sails and carried her along at six and even seven knots, a splendid pace for her in her present state and one that put even the sullen Mr Roke in a good humour: it was also because a disabled seaman, once a foremast hand in the *Boadicea* and now employed in the Manton yard, recognized Dr Maturin, while at the same time the broad sheet of sailcloth nailed to his sea-chest, a temporary direction with the words *S. Maturin, passenger to Stockholm*, was torn off as the chest came aboard again, revealing the names of the ships he had served in, painted on the front according to the custom of the service and crossed through with a fine red line at the end of each commission.

Stephen had noticed that seafaring men, though upon the whole somewhat credulous and ignorant of the world, were often knowing, suspicious, and wary at the wrong time; but this independent double testimony was irresistible, and at dinner on the first day out Mr Roke, after a general silence, said 'So it seems you was a Leopard, sir?'

'Just so,' said Stephen.

'Why did you never tell us, when you came aboard?'

'You never asked.'

'He did not like to show away,' said the purser.

They pondered on this, and then the surgeon said 'You must be the Dr Maturin of *The Diseases of Seamen*.'

Stephen bowed. The purser sighed and shook his head and observed that that was the Board all over: they just gave you a chitty saying 'Receive So-and-So aboard, to be borne for victuals only, as far as Stockholm', without a word of his quality: he might be Agamemnon or Nebuchadnezzar and you would be none the wiser. 'We thought you was just an ordinary commercial, going to the Baltic on business, like these gents,' – pointing at the merchants, who looked down at the spotted tablecloth.

'She was still a man-of-war when you was in her, I dare say?' said Roke.

'It was her last voyage as a fifty-gun ship, the voyage in which she sank the *Waakzaamheid*, a Dutch seventy-four, in the high southern latitudes. It was not a well known action, because in those waters there could be no remains, no prisoners; and I believe it was never gazetted.'

'Oh tell us about it, Doctor, if you please,' cried Roke, his face shining with sudden reflected glory, and the other sailors drew their chairs nearer. 'A fifty-gun ship to sink a seventy-four!'

'You must understand that I was below, and that although I heard the gunfire I saw nothing of it: all I can tell you is what I was told by those that took part.' They did not mind at all; they listened greedily, pressing him for exact details, requiring him to repeat various episodes so that they should get it just so; for the *Leopard*, though now at some removes from her state of grace, was still their ship. That was the great point. They were polite about Jack Aubrey's recent feats – indignant at his ill-usage too – but all that was on a different plane and quite remote: it was the *Leopard*, the tangible *Leopard*, that really mattered.

In the next few days he told the tale, or particular actions in it, again and again; sometimes in the captain's cabin, where he was invited to dine and where he pointed out the exact places where the stern-chasers had been made fast and where traces could still be seen, sometimes on the quarterdeck, where his hearers put him right if he made the slightest change of epithet or order; and all this while the breeze held true, running them north-north-east as fast as they could wish. Faster than ever Stephen wished. He saw his first northern birds - eider in the Skager Rack – with a sinking heart. A kindly western shift wafted them down the Cattegat and right through the Belt. Never a pause until a broken foretopmast checked them a little north of Öland; from then on their progress was slow and they lost all hope of an excellent run, which caused a great deal of cursing and irritation; yet their progress could not be too slow for him, and these hours of dawdling were a relief from his continually mounting tension.

But for all that on Thursday morning, when the *Surprise* heaved in sight, he went aboard her directly.

He had come on deck unusually early, having had a poor night and having been unable to bear another comic sneeze in the wardroom. His colleague, the present surgeon of the *Leopard*, was not a bad young man, but he had come by the notion that it was droll to exaggerate the sound of a sneeze; by now it had grown perfectly habitual, and every time he made this din, which was quite often, he would gaze round the table to share the fun.

Stephen was early on deck, therefore, and he found the captain and most of his officers peering anxiously at a vessel to windward, hull up on the starboard quarter.

'She has no pennant,' said the captain. 'She cannot be a man-of-war.'

'No. She is a privateer for sure, an American privateer,' said the master.

'If only you had got the topmast up last night we might have run in to Vestervik. There is no hope now: look at her feather.'

A very fine feather it was: with topgallants and weather

studdingsails abroad she was making better than ten knots, and her bows threw the white water wide on either side.

During their mutual reproaches – for the master naturally returned the captain's blame – the pleasant young mate, whose name was Francis, borrowed Roke's telescope. He stared long and hard, and then with a worried face he passed the glass to Stephen.

'Comfort yourself, Mr Francis,' said Stephen when he had made triply sure. 'That is the *Surprise*, commanded by Mr Aubrey. He was to meet me in Stockholm. Captain Worlidge, may I beg you to lie to and hang out a flag to show that we should like to communicate with her? She will take me in to Stockholm, and that will be a great saving of time.'

He had acquired great authority as the oldest Leopard of them all; he now spoke with staggering assurance; and the alternative was so worthless that Worlidge said he was always ready to oblige a King's officer, and the *Leopard* laid her main topsail to the mast.

No one could have looked at the new Member for Milport's face without his heart lifting: it was not that Jack Aubrey's was exultant or filled with obvious pleasure – indeed for some time after they had lain close to the *Leopard* it was clouded – but it possessed a shining inner life, a harmony of its own, and the strange almost paralytic deadness that had hung over it in repose these last months was now quite gone. His had been a naturally cheerful countenance until all joy was driven out of it, a fine ruddy face whose lines and creases had been formed by laughter and smiling; now it was essentially the same again, ruddier if anything, and lit by eyes that seemed an even brighter blue.

Stephen felt his sadness and near-desperation recede, almost vanish, as they talked and talked about Cousin Edward Norton's extraordinarily handsome conduct, and about the House of Commons, where they agreed that Jack's wisest course would be silence except in the case of overwhelming conviction on a naval point, and a general but by no means unconditional support of the Ministry: or at least of Lord Melville. Then, having heard a fairly detailed account of the *Leopard*'s grounding, Jack, together with Pullings and Martin, showed Stephen the new Manilla rigging and the slightly greater rake they had given the foremast. 'I believe she gains an extra fathom of line,' said Jack.

'Sure, she is going as fast as a horse at a good round trot,' said Stephen, looking over the side at the swift smooth run of the sea, dipping to show the ship's copper amidships; and as he spoke he realized that each hour was bringing him some ten miles nearer Stockholm and that tomorrow would probably see him ashore.

'I should not trust this wind, though,' said Pullings. 'It has been veering all this watch, and I doubt the studdingsails stand until eight bells.'

This view of the present racing along to become the future grew in Stephen's mind as they ate their dinner, and by the time they had said everything that could be said about parliament, Ashgrove, Woolcombe, the children, Philip Aubrey and the *Surprise*'s new iron water-tanks, his mind tended to stray away. In spite of the very profound satisfaction of seeing the old Jack Aubrey on the other side of the table, his anxiety was welling up again.

Jack knew why Stephen had come into the Baltic, of course, and towards the end of the meal he saw that his friend was looking both wretchedly ill and ten years older; but this was ground he could not possibly venture upon unasked, and after a long, awkward silence – most unusual with them – it occurred to him that he must not return to his own affairs, that he had already been far too self-centred and unfeeling. He therefore called for another pot of coffee and spoke about Standish and music. 'Since we met,' he said, 'I am glad to say the ship has acquired a purser. He is not at all experienced – has never been to sea, and Sophie helps him with his sums – but he is a gentlemanlike fellow, a friend of Martin's, and he plays an amazingly fine fiddle.'

Standish was of a naval family, though not an eminent one

– his father had died a lieutenant – and he had always wanted to go to sea; but his friends were very much against it and in deference to their wishes he had studied 'for the Church, in which a cousin could provide for him. His studies however were more in the boating and classical line than the theological and it never occurred to him to read the Thirty-Nine Articles with close attention before he was required to subscribe to them. He then found with great concern that he could not conscientiously do so; and that without doing so he could not become a parson. In these circumstances he was at liberty to go to sea, the only thing he really wanted to do; but of course he was now far too old to make his first appearance on the quarterdeck of any man-of-war. The only way into the Navy was as a purser, and in spite of his inexperience – most pursers started quite young as captain's clerks – an old shipmate of his father's would have used his influence with the Navy Board to have him appointed: but a purser of even a sixth rate had to put up a verifiable bond for four hundred pounds, and Standish, having disobliged his family, did not possess four hundred pence.

'I thought we might waive the bond in view of the fiddle,' said Jack. 'I do assure you he has a wonderfully true ear and the most delicate touch, neither sweet nor yet dry, if you understand me; and since Martin can scrape away pretty well on his viola, it occurred to me that we might try a quartet. What do you say to our having a bowl of punch, and asking him to share it? We will ask Tom and Martin too.'

'I should be very happy to meet the gentleman,' said Stephen. 'But it is long, long since I touched my 'cello, and I must have a word with it first.'

He went into his cabin, and after the squeaks and grunts of tuning he played a few bars very softly and called to Jack 'Do you recognize that?'

'Of course,' said Jack. 'It comes at the end of Figaro, the loveliest thing.'

'I could not sing it quite right,' said Stephen, 'but it comes out better with a bow.' Then he closed the door, and some moments later the after part of the ship, usually quiet with a following wind and a moderate sea, was filled with a great deep roaring Dies Irae that went on and on, quite startling the quarterdeck.

Later, much later, after the punch, the introductions and a good deal of talk, the cabin sang again, but this time with none of the same terrible conviction, more quietly, more gently altogether, as the four of them made their tentative way through Mozart in D major.

Stephen went to bed very late that night, his eyes red and watering with the effort of following a little-known score by lamplight, but his mind was wonderfully refreshed, so much so that once he reached the blessed point of sleep he plunged down and down, reaching a world of extraordinarily vivid dream and never rising up until Jack said 'Forgive me for waking you, Stephen, but the wind has veered nine points and I cannot get into Stockholm. There is a pilot-galley alongside that will take you, or you could run across to Riga with me and put in on our return. Which had you rather?'

'The galley, if you please.'

'Very well,' said Jack. 'I will tell Padeen to bring the hot water.'

While he was waiting for it to come Stephen stropped his razor; but when all was ready he found his hand shake too much to attempt shaving. 'I am in a sad foolish way, so I am,' he said, and to pull himself together he reached for his draught. He dropped it before he had poured a single drop into his glass. The cabin was filled with the smell more of brandy than of laudanum, and for a moment he stared at the broken pieces, perceiving the contradiction but lacking the time and mental energy to resolve it. By going below and rousing out a great carboy and a small bottle he could replace what he had lost. 'The hell with it,' he said. 'I shall get some more in Stockholm; and I shall be shaved at a barber's, too.'

'There you are, Stephen,' said Jack, looking at him anxiously. 'You will have a long pull of it, I am afraid. Are you not taking Padeen?' Stephen shook his head. 'I just wanted to say, before you come on deck – I just wanted to ask you to give Cousin Diana our love.'

'Thank you, Jack,' said Stephen. 'I shall not forget.'

They walked up the ladder. 'This wind never lasts,' said Jack, handing him over the side, where Bonden and Plaice eased him down into the boat. 'We shall be back from Riga in no time at all.'

CHAPTER NINE

Although the *Surprise* had stood in as far as ever she could, far in among the countless islands, the pilot-galley still had a long pull before it set Stephen down on the broad quay in the heart of the town.

Once the sun had risen the day was fresh and brilliant, the breeze, though contrary, was full of life; and by the time Stephen reached dry land he had almost entirely detached himself from that other world, the world of his dream with its extraordinary beauty and its potential danger, its half-understood threat of extreme danger to come.

The pilot, a grave, respectable man, fluent in English, took him to a grave, respectable hotel, equally fluent. Here Stephen called for coffee and buns, and much refreshed he went to see his banker's correspondent, who, having received him with the deference that he was now beginning to think his due (or at least that he no longer found particularly amusing), provided him with Swedish money and the address of the best apothecary in the capital, 'a learned man, a man of encyclopaedic knowledge, a pupil of the great Linnaeus himself', whose shop was not a hundred yards away. Dr Maturin had but to turn twice to the right, and he was there.

Dr Maturin turned twice to the right and there indeed he was: the window was quite unmistakable, being filled not only with the usual great jars of green, red and blue liquid, clear and jewel-like, and with bunches of dried herbs, but also with a large variety of monsters and uncommon animals in spirits, together with skeletons, one being that of an aardvaark. Stephen walked in. There appeared to be nobody in the shop, and he was looking attentively at the foetus of a kangaroo – he had in fact reached out his hand to turn the jar – when a very small man stepped from behind the counter and asked him his business in a sharp, troll-like voice.

Stephen felt certain that the encyclopaedia's knowledge embraced neither English nor French, so he said 'I should like some laudanum, if you please: a bottle of moderate, portable size,' in Latin, to which the apothecary replied 'Certainly,' in a more benevolent tone. While the tincture was preparing Stephen said 'Pray, is the aardvaark in the window for sale?'

'No, sir,' said the apothecary. 'He belongs to my own collection.' And after a pause, 'You recognized the animal, I perceive.'

'At one time I was well acquainted with an aardvaark,' said Stephen. 'A most affectionate creature, though timid. That was at the Cape. And I saw a skeleton belonging to Monsieur Cuvier, in Paris.'

'Ah, sir, you are a great traveller, I find,' said the apothecary, clasping the bottle with both hands and raising it to head-height.

'I am a naval surgeon, and my profession has carried me to many parts of the world.'

'It was always my dream to travel,' said the apothecary, 'but I am tied to my shop. However, I encourage the sailors to bring me what falls in their way, and I commission the more intelligent surgeon's mates to find me botanical specimens and foreign drugs, curious teas, infusions and the like; so I travel vicariously.'

'It may well be that you travel better than I. Until you have experienced it, you cannot conceive the frustrations that attend the naturalist in a ship. He has no sooner started to get some order among, let us say, the termites, than he is told that the wind has changed, or that the tide serves, and he must repair aboard, or he will infallibly be left behind. I was in New Holland once, and I saw these creatures' – pointing to the kangaroo – 'sporting on a grassy plain: but was I indulged in a horse to approach them, or even the loan of a perspective-glass? No, sir, I was not: I was told that if I was not on the strand in ten minutes a file of Marines should be sent to fetch me. Whereas you, sir, have a hundred eyes and only the single inconvenience of remaining physically in the same place while your mind roams abroad. You have some remarkable collections,' looking at the walls.

'Here is the true balm of Gilead,' said the apothecary. 'And here salamander's wool: here the black mandrake of Kamschatka.' He showed many more rarities, chiefly of a medical nature, and after a while Stephen asked, 'Have any of your young men ever brought you back the coca or cuca leaf from Peru?'

'Oh yes,' said the apothecary. 'There is a small sack behind the camomile. It is said to dissolve the gross humours and do away with appetite.'

'Be so good as to put me up a pound,' said Stephen. 'And lastly, can you tell me where the district of Christenberg lies? I should like to walk there, if it is not too far.'

'It will not take you above an hour. I will draw you a map. This is a meadow filled with iris pseudocorus, and on the shore just beyond it, near the bridge, you may see a nest of the tuberculated swan.'

'The name of the house that I wish to find is Koningsby.'

'It is here, where I put the cross.'

Stephen's intention was to determine the place where Diana lived, and to get some feeling of the country around her: he then meant to come back to his hotel, summon a barber, change his shirt (he had put up three, a spare neckcloth and a waistcoat), dine, and send a message asking if he might call. He had no notion of making his appearance at her door without a word of warning.

He crossed the necessary bridges and passed the Serafimer Hospital, looking attentively at it as he went by; the houses soon thinned out and presently he was walking along a wide road between fields, in gently rolling country, mostly pasture, with woods on either hand – a pleasant impression of prevailing green. Moderate farms, some cottages, and here and there a large house among its trees. He noticed with satisfaction that the crows were all of the grey-backed Irish kind.

There was not much traffic on the road, broad and well-kept though it was; two coaches, the occasional gig and farm cart, and perhaps half a dozen horsemen: a few people on foot. They all called out a greeting as they passed, and Stephen, influenced by the greenness and the crows, replied in Irish: God and Mary and Patrick be with you.

Not much traffic on the high road and even less when Stephen, having looked at the apothecary's map again, turned off right-handed on what was no more than a narrow country lane leading through meadows, all fenced with shabby post and rail, as though they belonged to one large but somewhat neglected estate, an impression strengthened by occasional glimpses of a long park wall to the south.

He had found the marshy fields of irises and he had seen the swan upon her nest when he heard the sound of horses' hooves ahead; an alder-grove hid them, but they were certainly near and they were certainly drawing a vehicle at a fine clipping pace. He looked about for somewhere to get off the lane, even more constricted here because of the ditches on either hand, broad ditches with a bank on the far side and the fence on top of it. He chose the least broad part of the right-hand ditch, took the string of his parcel in his teeth, sprang across, caught the rail, and stood there poised on the bank. As the carriage came into sight he saw that it was a phaeton with a pair of chestnuts; and a moment later his heart stood still – Diana was driving.

'Oh Maturin, God love you!' she cried, reining in hard. 'Oh how happy I am to see you, my dear.' The groom ran to take the horses' heads and she sprang down on to the green verge. 'Give a good leap,' she called, holding out her hand, 'and you will clear the ditch for sure.' She caught him as he landed, took his parcel, and kissed him on both cheeks. 'How happy I am to see you,' she said again. 'Get in, and I will drive you home.'

'You have not changed at all,' she went on, setting the horses in motion.

'You have, my dear,' he said in a fairly level voice. 'Your complexion is infinitely improved: you are a *jeune fille en fleur.*' It was true; the cooler, damper northern climate and the Swedish diet had done wonders for her skin. Her particular black-haired, dark-blue-eyed kind of beauty required an excellence of complexion to set it off at its best and she was now in a finer bloom than he had ever seen her.

They reached a gate into a field and here she turned the phaeton with her usual skill, driving back along the lane at an exhilarating speed, the more so since in some place the wheels were not six inches from the edge and since the near horse showed a tendency to toss his head and play the fool, calling for a very firm hand and great watchfulness – too much for sustained conversation. They repassed the alder-grove, struck into a broader road – 'That is the way to Stadhagen,' she said – and reached a pair of open iron gates where the horses turned in of their own accord.

The weed-grown drive made a couple of winds among the trees and then forked, one branch leading across the park to a large house, rather fine but blind and lifeless, being almost entirely shut up. 'That is Countess Tessin's place,' said Diana. 'Jagiello's grandmama. I live over there.' She pointed with her whip, and at the far end of the park Stephen saw a smaller, much older building with a tower: he took it to be a dower-house, but made no observation.

The phaeton drew up; the groom leapt down and led it away. 'Would that man be a Finn, at all?' asked Stephen.

'Oh no,' said Diana, amused. 'He is a Lapp, one of Jagiello's Lapps; he owns a dozen or so.'

'Slaves, are they?'

'No, not really, I think; more in the way of serfs. Stephen, do come in.'

The door had opened and a tall, bent, elderly maidservant stood there, curtseying and smiling. Diana shouted something in Swedish very close to her ear and led Stephen into the hall.

She opened one door, shut it again with the words 'Too squalid' and opened another, which led into a pleasant little square room with a piano, bookshelves, a great china stove, two or three elbow chairs and a sofa; the window looked out on to a lime-tree. Diana took one of the chairs, said 'Sit where I can see you, Stephen. Sit on the sofa.' She gazed at him affectionately and said 'Lord, it is so long since I saw you and there are so many things to talk about I do not know where to begin.' A pause. 'Oh, I will just say something about Jagiello. It is not that I owe you any explanation, Maturin, you know,' – quite kindly – 'but he will be here presently and I do not wish you to think yourself obliged to cut his throat. Poor lamb, that would be too hard! When I told him that I should be happy to put myself under his protection to go to Sweden I meant just that – protection against insult or persecution or ill-treatment – and no more, as I said quite clearly. And I said I should of course pay my own way. Protection in the plain sense was what I wanted, not a bed-fellow. He did not believe it – indeed, even while he was protesting all possible respect, brotherly sentiments and so on, he smirked, as men will smirk, I am afraid. For a great while he would not be persuaded that I meant what I said. But in the end he was obliged to; I told him it was no use – I had sworn I should never put it in any man's power to hurt me again. Do not look so *catastrophié*, Stephen: it is all over now – I am heart-whole – and I hope to God we are not such simpletons as to let it prevent us from being very, very fond of one another. But as I was saying, he had to believe it, and now we are friends again, though he does keep trying to prevent me from going up in balloons. He is to be married to a sweetly pretty young woman that dotes upon him – not very clever but good family and a splendid portion. I helped to arrange it, and his grandmother is so pleased with me – that is to say, when she remembers, which is not always the case.'

'I am glad to hear what you tell me, Villiers dear,' began Stephen, but he was interrupted by the coming of the maid-servant, to whom Diana roared as loud as she was able and then, rather hoarse, said 'Ulrika tells me there are only eggs in the house and smoked trout – I was going shopping when we met – and she asks whether the gentleman would like some of the Lapp's dried reindeer.'

Ulrika watched Stephen's face, and seeing its look of pleased acquiescence, walked off chuckling.

'Well, that deals with Gedymin Jagiello,' said Diana. 'Though by the way, when they come we shall have to speak French: her English is even worse. Now let us begin at the beginning: where have you come from?'

'From England, in the *Surprise*, with Jack Aubrey.'

'Is he in Stockholm?'

'He has run across to Riga, but he will be back in a day or two. He sends his love – their love. He particularly said "Give Cousin Diana our love."'

'Dear Jack. Lord, we were in such a rage about that monstrous trial, Jagiello and I. He is constantly at the legation and has all the English papers. Did Jack take it very hard?'

'Terribly hard, indeed. During the voyage before last, running down to the Azores, you would hardly have known he was the same man: cold, unsmiling: no human contact with the new officers or men, little even with the old. He put the fear of God into them. I have noticed that in a ship you cannot act a part successfully for long; the people very soon detect any falsity, but they recognize true feelings, and in this case they were quite terrified of him.'

'Yet it was in the Azores that he made all those prizes. Surely that put him in a better humour?'

'Oh, he was relieved for Sophie and the children – things were in a sad way at Ashgrove, I believe – but the prize-money, even though it came in such floods, did not touch the heart of the matter. It was the St Martin's affair which did that.'

'Oh yes, yes! How we cheered! There was Captain Fanshawe at the legation who said it was the completest thing of its kind ever seen this war. Surely he will be reinstated now?'

'I believe he may: the more so as his cousin Norton has given him the seat for Milport, a pocket borough in the west.'

'That makes it a certainty, with divisions so close. I am so glad for them both; I am very fond of Sophie. Stephen, forgive me for a moment: I must see about that reindeer. The Lapp may be difficult with Ulrika. He does not belong to this house, you know – Jagiello just lends him to me, together with the phaeton and the horses, to take his grandmother to church and sometimes to town – but he is quite all right with me.'

Left alone, Stephen reflected. At one time it had occurred to him that Diana might possibly make her balloon ascents by way of amusement; now it seemed far more probable that his first idea, and Blaine's, was right. Her present life might not be grinding poverty, but it was certainly very far from wealth. His mind ran on, trying to compose his extreme hurry and agitation of spirits so that he might work out a persuasive, coherent way of expressing himself. He took the apothecary's bottle from his pocket and he was breaking the sealing-wax on the wrapping when she came back, carrying his parcel. 'Stephen,' she said, 'you left this in the carriage. Pishan brought it to the kitchen.'

'Oh thank you,' he cried, thrusting the bottle back. 'It is the coca-leaves I bought in Stockholm.'

'What are they for?'

'They relieve fatigue, and properly administered they make you feel clever and even witty. I sent you some from South America.'

'Alas, they never came. I should have liked to feel clever, or even witty.'

'I am so sorry. Things miscarry. Tell me, did you ever receive a letter I sent from Gibraltar, just before sailing on the South American voyage? I gave it to Andrew Wray, who was travelling home overland.'

'Surely to God, Maturin, you did not trust that infernal scrub Wray, did you? I saw him once or twice after he came back – said he had seen you in Malta and that you had listened to music together – you seemed to be amusing yourself prodigiously with a diving-bell and the other delights of

Valletta. He never spoke of any letter or message. I hope it was nothing confidential.'

'There was nothing in it that a stranger would have understood,' said Stephen standing up, for at this point an old lady opened the door. She was Countess Tessin. Diana made the introductions, speaking French and adding that Stephen was a friend of Gedymin's; she presented him as Monsieur Maturin y Domanova, which was perfectly correct, though disingenuous. She need not have troubled: the old lady was somewhat confused, and on learning that Jagiello was not expected until after dinner she set off again, though pressed to stay.

'May I give you my arm, ma'am?' asked Stephen.

'You are very kind, sir, most amiable; but I have Axel waiting for me, and he is so used to my pace.'

'If ever I become old,' said Diana at dinner, 'I do hope I shall manage to keep up with the changing ideas of money.'

'Not many people do so.'

'No. Countess Tessin has not; and the change has frightened her into – well, I do not like to say avarice, because she is really very kind. But she says she has to watch every penny, and she has turned almost all her servants away. She charges me a shocking great rent and she has let out practically the whole park for grazing, so that I have only one poor little paddock. I had so hoped to breed Arabians, but there is no room. Stephen, you are not eating. I have a couple – one an enchanting little mare that I must show you after dinner – but if only I had anything like that fine sweep of short grass at Jack Aubrey's place, up on the down, I should have a score.'

'I am afraid my agitation is affecting her,' thought Stephen. 'This is not her manner at all.' He applied himself to eating with all the appearance of appetite he could manage, and listened to her remarks about English lessons: little scope for her endeavours, since so many Swedes spoke English anyhow – and about this absurd showman who gave her quite large sums for going up in balloons. 'He wants me to wear spangles next time,' she said.

Stephen had rarely been less master of his emotions, less capable of small talk; he felt this increasing upon him and he positively blessed the false movement on Diana's part that sent the decanter crashing to the ground.

'That was the last of the wine,' she said with a smile, 'But at least I can make you a decent cup of coffee. That is one thing I *can* do in the domestic line.'

The coffee was indeed excellent. They drank it sitting on a terrace to the south of the house, and the Arabian mare came to see them, walking with polite diffident steps until she was sure of her welcome. She stood with her head over Diana's shoulder, looking into her face with great lustrous eyes, and Diana said 'She follows me about like a dog, when she can get indoors, upstairs and down. She is the only horse I have ever known I should dare to get into the car of a balloon with.'

'I doubt I have ever seen such a beautiful and sympathetic creature before,' said Stephen. The mare's beauty heightened Diana's and the pair they made filled him with a troubled joy.

When they had seen the stables, the other Arabian – 'only a gelding', Diana observed – and when they had thoroughly condemned the paddock they walked back to the house. The tension had fallen and they talked easily: Diana's cousins, Sophie's children, the rebuilding of the Grapes, Mrs Broad's prosperity. In the hall Stephen said 'My dear, may I retire? and may I also have a glass? I must take a dose.'

Sitting there he measured out the laudanum, his practised thumb over the bottle's mouth: a dose suited to the occasion. The first sip startled him extremely. 'Jesus, Mary and Joseph,' he said, 'the troll must use akvavit.' He soon grew used to the different taste, however – a difference that he attributed entirely to the different spirit used in the tincture. When he had finished his glass he took off his breeches and not without pain he disengaged the blue diamond, strapped to his person with court-plaster. He wiped the warm stone, looked at it with renewed admiration, and put it into his waistcoat pocket.

Even as he went down the stairs he felt that his dose was already working, and he walked into the little square room in a reasonably collected state of mind, determined to stake his happiness on the one throw.

Diana looked round with a smile. 'I must get this piano tuned,' she said, playing a little ripple of notes with her right hand as she stood there. 'Do you remember that piece of Hummel's that Sophie used to work at so hard, long, long ago? It came into my head, but there is a false note here' – playing it – 'that throws everything out.'

'A Judas of a note,' said Stephen. His hands wandered over the keys, taking pieces from the Hummel, working out variations on them, improvising, and then he played the air of Almaviva's *Contessa perdono*. He could not trust himself to sing with it; his voice would be ludicrous or false or both; but closing the piano he said 'Diana, I have come to be forgiven.'

'But my dear you *are* forgiven. You have been this great while. I am very fond of you. There is not a scrap of rancour or resentment or ill-will in my heart, I swear.'

'That is not quite what I meant, honey.'

'Oh, as for the rest, Stephen, our marriage was absurd in the first place. I should never make any kind of a wife for you. I love you dearly, but we could only wound one another – completely unsuited – each as independent as a cat.'

'I should ask nothing but your company. I have made a great deal of prize-money; I have inherited more. I say this only because it means you could have room for your Arabians – you could have half the Curragh of Kildare – you could have a great stretch of English downland.'

'Stephen, you know what I said to Jagiello: I will not put myself in any man's power. But if ever I were to live with a man as his wife, it would be with you: there is no one else at all. I beg you to take that for my answer.'

'I will not be importunate, my dear,' said Stephen. He stood at the window, looking out on to the lime-tree's perfect green. After some moments he turned with a somewhat artificial smile and said, 'Will I tell you an extraordinarily vivid dream I had this morning, Villiers? It had to do with a balloon.'

'A fire-balloon or an air-balloon?'

'I think it must have been an air-balloon: I should have remembered the fire. In any event, there I was in its car and I was above the clouds, a vast stratum of white clouds, rolling and immensely domed in themselves, but all in a united plane below me. And above there was the unbelievably pure and very dark blue sky.'

'Oh yes, yes!' cried Diana.

'All this I had from a man who had been up, for myself I have never left the ground at all. But what I had not derived from his account was the extraordinary intensification of living, the palpable depth of the universal silence, and the very great awareness of the light and colour of this other world – an otherness that was made all the stronger because through an occasional gap in the clouds our ordinary world could be seen, with silver rivers very, very far below and the roads distinct. Yet in time that changed to rock and ice, even farther below; and in my keen delight there was mingled an undefined sense of a dread as huge as the sky itself; it was not merely a fear of being destroyed, but worse; perhaps that of being wholly and entirely lost, body and soul.'

'How did it end?'

'It did not end at all. There was Jack roaring out that the boat was alongside.'

'Jagiello used to tell me dismal stories of people being carried higher and higher and farther and farther – swept quite away – perished with cold – starved – never seen again. But I only go up in an air-balloon, one with a valve so that you can let the stuff out and come down; and we have an anchor on a long rope. I always have Gustav with me; he is thoroughly experienced and very strong, and we never go far.'

'Dear Villiers, I am not trying to frighten you or put you off, God forbid. This was my dream, not a lecture or a parable. I found it deeply impressive, particularly the enhanced sense of colour – the balloon itself was a noble red – and I told it to you partly for that reason, though the Dear knows my account was most pitifully bald, never touching the essence at all, and partly to set a space between what we were talking about before and what I am going to say next. A space by way of symbolizing the total independence of the two conversations. Do you remember d'Anglars, in Paris, La Mothe's friend?'

'Yes,' she said, her somewhat remote, defiant expression changing to one of enquiry.

'He promised that you should have your great diamond back, the Blue Peter: that eventually he would send it after us. He kept his word, and a messenger brought it just after Jack's trial. Here it is.'

He had never seen her lose her composure to such a degree. As he passed the stone naked in the blaze of the sun her face showed doubt, amazement, delight and even a kind of fear before dissolving entirely as she burst into tears.

Stephen returned to the window and stood there until he heard her blow her nose and sniff. She sat there with the diamond cupped in her hands; he observed that her pupils were dilated, so much so that her blue eyes looked black. 'I never thought I should see it again,' she said in a tremulous voice. 'And I loved it so; oh I loved it sinfully. I still love it sinfully,' she said, turning it this way and that in the shaft of sunlight. 'I cannot tell you how grateful I am. And I was so odiously unkind to you, Stephen. Forgive me.' A voice outside called 'Diana!' She said 'Oh God, there are the Jagiellos' and looked quickly round; but there was no escape and a moment later the door was pushed open. It was the little Arabian mare that walked in, however, followed some moments later by the Jagiellos.

Although Stephen was standing with his back to the strong light Jagiello recognized him at once; for a moment his first look of astonished delight changed to one of extreme reserve, but then his potential adversary came forward, took him affectionately by the hand, thanked him for his kindness to Diana and congratulated him on his coming marriage and his promotion; for Jagiello's beautiful mauve coat now had a colonel's marks of rank, and he wore golden spurs.

Diana had a great sense of social duty and having led the

horse away and done what she could to a face much altered by tears – *blubbered* was hardly too strong a word, for she was not a woman who cried easily or without trace – she did her best to entertain her guests. But Lovisa, Jagiello's fiancée, was exceedingly young; she had always been in awe of Diana, held up by Jagiello as a paragon; and now her youth, her respect, and her sterling native stupidity combined with her ignorance of French and her suspicion that the atmosphere was uneasy to make her a very heavy burden. Jagiello was a little better, but he did see that his usual gay prattle would be out of place in the present context, and being so taken aback by the whole situation he could not readily hit upon an alternative. Stephen, whose social sense could never have recommended him anywhere, said a few civil things to Lovisa, who was indeed absurdly pretty, and then, perceiving that Diana was telling Jagiello the latest news of Jack Aubrey, he too lapsed into silence. He had been feeling very strange for some time, and this he attributed to intensity of emotion: just what the nature of the emotion was, apart from the obvious desolation of failure, he could not yet tell – there was the analogy of wounds in battle: you knew you had been hit and roughly where, but whether by blade, point, ball or splinter you could not tell, nor how gravely, until you had time to examine the wounds and name them. Yet he did long for these people to go away so that he might take a second dose, a dose that would quieten his heart and enable him to walk back to Stockholm with at least the appearance of equanimity.

At last Diana was inspired to tell Jagiello that his grandmother had called before dinner and to suggest that he should hurry to the big house to prevent her setting out again. Countess Tessin would surely have seen them go by, and the double walk would be too much for her.

Jagiello thankfully agreed; he had felt in the way from the first few minutes without being able to contrive any plausible reason for taking his leave. But after the first farewells, and at the open hall door itself, Lovisa began to tell Diana about her wedding clothes. She went on and on and on, in Swedish most

269

of the time, and Stephen backed and backed until with a final bow he could disappear upstairs.

Once again he was astonished at the strength of his draught, and this time it occurred to him that the difference might lie in the opium rather than the menstruum. 'And yet,' he reflected as he walked downstairs, 'I have never heard of any marked variation between the pharmacopoeias of different countries in that respect. Within the range of a few scruples to the ounce, the tincture is the same at a respectable apothecary's in Paris or Dublin, Boston or Barcelona.'

'Lord, Maturin,' said Diana, 'I thought they would never go. That silly pretty goose was still talking about the embroidery on her gown when Countess Tessin came in sight. But then I did give Jagiello a shove at last and he took her away.'

'There is much to be said for Jagiello.'

'Yes. And this time he did not utter a single word against balloons, though he knows very well I mean to go up on Saturday.'

'This coming Saturday?'

'Yes. They have begun filling it already.'

'May I come too?'

'Of course you may. It is the red balloon this time, so there will be plenty of room in the car. Would you like to see it?' Stephen did not answer until she said 'Would you like to see it?' again. Then he looked up, a little dazed, and replied 'That would be delightful. Do you keep it here?'

'Oh no, no. It is a vast great thing. But they are filling it at the foundry – they use iron filings and vitriol to make the inflammable air, you know – and you can see it from the tower. Stephen, are you feeling quite well?'

'A trifle odd, my dear, I must confess; but then I was roused before dawn. I am perfectly capable of running up the tower.'

'We will take it gently. There is a spy-glass on top of the cupboard behind you.'

She led the way to a vaulted corridor at the back of the hall and so to the dark tower beyond, far older than the present

270

house. 'Take great care, Stephen,' she called back as she climbed the spiral staircase. 'Keep to the wall side, there is no rail in the middle after half way.'

Winding and winding in the dim shadows they came to a dwarvish door at the top and crept out into the brilliant light. They were surprisingly high and the whole island lay spread out below them. 'This way,' said Diana, leading him to the eastern parapet: there was the old city of Stockholm about an hour's walk away and rather to one side of it the tall chimneys of industry. Diana had been carrying the Blue Peter; she now wrapped it in a handkerchief, put it in her pocket, and levelled the telescope at the chimneys. 'There,' she said, 'Get the one that is smoking so, move to the left, and there in the yard you see the upper half of a great round red thing. That is my balloon!'

'God bless it,' said Stephen, handing back the glass.

'I think we should go down and have a cup of tea,' said Diana, studying his face. 'You look like whitey-brown paper. You go first and I will follow; I know just where to find the bolts.'

Stephen opened the door, said something indistinct about Saturday and pitched headlong into the void.

It seemed that in spite of obscure delays and disturbances the ascent had been postponed rather than cancelled; at least if it had been a public performance at all it must have been on a very modest scale, since he could remember no crowd, no noise. He did have confused memories of a tumble, of indeterminate injuries and fuss, which muffled the immediate past, and now they had risen above the clouds – a fairly apt parallel for his passing fogginess of mind – and now they were in the pure upper air with that strangely familiar dark blue above and on either hand unless he looked over the edge of the car and down to the fantastic convolutions and the slowly changing geography of the cloud-world below: all much purer and more intense even than his dream, which he remembered perfectly. And although his dream had heightened colour it had not done so to this miraculous degree; the wickerwork of the car had an infinity of very beautiful shades from dark brown to something lighter than straw, while the ropes that led from the network enveloping the balloon itself had a subtlety all their own. It was as though he had never seen rope before, or as though he had recovered his sight after many years of blindness, and when he looked across at Diana, the perfection of her cheek fairly caught his breath. She was sitting there in a green riding-habit with her hands folded in her lap; she was looking down at her diamond and her eyes were almost closed, the long lashes hiding them.

They were both of them silent – this was a world of silence – yet he was conscious that they were perfectly in tune and that no amount of talking would make them more so. He reflected upon height, the effect of height: how much was it height alone that gave this much keener sense of life? He retraced his very long climb up the flank of the Maladetta to the highest point he had ever reached on land. A mule in the morning darkness from Benasque, up and up through the forenoon to the highest cow-pasture, wth streams as thick as a barrel gushing straight from the bare rock-face by the path, a pause at the hut and then on by foot, up through vast sweeps of low rhododendron until they gave way to gentians, countless gentians in the short turf, up to the rocky edge of the glacier where a host of tall primulas stood in their perfection, exactly disposed, as though all the king's gardeners had been at work; all these things, together with the troop of fleeing chamois below him and the pair of eagles turning and turning above, had been very clearly perceived in that thin keen air. But not with anything like an equal clarity; and here there was also a difference in kind. During that long day he had been strongly aware of time, if only because he had to avoid being benighted on the mountainside: now there was no time. That is to say, there was succession, in that a gesture or a thought followed its predecessor, but there was no sense of duration. He and Diana might have been floating there for hours or even for days. And then again although the Maladetta was physically dangerous it had nothing of the indefinable threat present in this immensity.

Diana had almost certainly dozed off, and he said nothing; nor did he speak of the high mist that veiled the sky, giving the sun a double halo and producing two fine prismatic sun-dogs. He was in fact surprisingly sleepy himself, and presently he too closed his eyes.

At the very beginning of his dream he could say 'I am dreaming' but his perception of it faded almost at once and he was filled with as much anxiety as he would have been if he had never had a hint of this being only the disturbance of a sleeping mind. It was clear to him now that they had set off, the wind being favourable, for Spitzbergen, where they would surely fall in with the whalers who congregated there at this time of the year, and where they would view the wonders of the Arctic so well described by Mulgrave, and the northern wall of ice that had barred his way to the Pole. But there had been some disagreement and although at one time a rocky landscape had been seen below they had not made any attempt to descend and now there was nothing in sight but grey ocean stretching from sky to sky.

Dream within dream; and this dissolved to an unknown room. Diana was there, no longer wearing her riding-habit but a plain grey dress, and Jagiello, together with two men in black coats and bob wigs who were obviously physicians, the one a fool and the other exceptionally intelligent. They spoke to Diana in Swedish, which Jagiello usually translated, her acquaintance with the language being barely enough for ordinary housekeeping; and they discussed the case between themselves in Latin. Soon they were joined by a third, whom they treated with marked deference – he wore the star of an order – and who recommended cupping: the leg, he said, presented no particular problem; he had seen many fractures of this kind and they had always yielded to Andersen's Basra method, so long as the patient was in a reasonable state of health. Here, to be sure, there was a vicious habit of body, some degree of under-nourishment, and what he would scarcely hesitate to call incipient melancholia; yet they were to observe that the frame, though spare, was well-knit; and there were still some lingering traces of youth to be made out.

Stephen watched them for a while as they went through the grave gestures of consultation, part of the gravity being directed at the audience, part at one another; but he was too familiar with this kind of meeting for it to have much interest and presently his attention shifted to his surroundings, and to Diana and Jagiello. The intuition peculiar to dreams told him that this was Diana's room, that this was her bed itself, and that she spent her time on the chaise-longue beside it, looking after him with the utmost tenderness. He also knew that Jagiello had called in the king's physician, the person with the star, who was now saying that when he came to the point of eating solids, the patient should be allowed no beef or mutton, still less any swine's flesh, but rather a hazel-hen, seethed with a very little barley.

'Hazel-hen,' he thought. 'Never have I seen a hazel-hen; yet if this good man's advice is followed I shall soon incorporate one. I shall be in part a hazel-hen with whatever virtues a hazel-hen may possess.' He reflected upon Finn Mac Coul and his salmon and while he was reflecting there in the twilight, lamps were lit; he was reflecting still when they were put out, all but a single one turned low; and now the chief light in the room came from a fire away on his right hand, a live flickering glow on the ceiling. There had no doubt been discreet farewells, and someone had surely prescribed; but now Diana was alone, sitting on the chaise-longue beside the bed. She laid her hand on the back of his and said very quietly 'Oh Stephen, Stephen, how I wish you could hear me, my dear.'

But now there was this evil balloon again, and now he was living with time in the sense of duration once more, for he knew with dreadful certainty that they had been rising for hours on end, that they were now rising faster still. And as they soared towards this absolute purity of sky so its imminent threat, half-perceived at first, filled him with a horror beyond anything he had known. Diana was wearing her green coat again and at some point she must have turned up the collar, for now its red underneath made a shocking contrast with the extreme pallor of her face, the pinched white of her nose and the frosted blue of her lips. Her face showed no expression – she was, as it were, completely alone – and as she had done before she held her head down, bowed over her lap, where her hands, now more loosely clasped, held the diamond, very like a sliver of this brilliant sky itself.

She was breathing still, but only just, as they floated away, always higher and into even more rarefied air; breathing, but only just – a very slight movement indeed. Then even that stopped; her senses were going, going; her head drooped forward, the diamond fell; and he started up, crying 'No, no, no,' in the extremity of passionate refusal.

'Quiet, Stephen,' she said, taking him in her arms and easing him back in bed. 'Easy, there,' as though she were talking to a horse; and then, as though she were talking to a man, 'You must take care of your poor leg, my dear.'

He leant on her warmth, slipping back through several realities to this, though without much certainty of its existence. Yet his certainty grew stronger as he lay there through the night, watching the glow of the fire and hearing a clock strike the hours; and sometimes she moved about, putting on more wood, or attending to his squalid needs, and doing so with an efficiency and a tenderness that moved him very deeply: and in these short exchanges his words were relevant and intelligible.

They had known one another these many years, but their relations had never called for tenderness on her side and he would have said that it formed no part of her character: courage, spirit and determination, yes, but nothing nearer tenderness than generosity and good nature. He was weak, having been much battered in his physical and metaphysical fall and having eaten nothing since, weak and somewhat maudlin, and reflecting upon this new dimension he wept silently in the darkness.

In the morning he heard her stir and said 'Diana, joy, are you awake?'

She came over, looked into his face, kissed him and said 'You are in your right wits still, sweetheart, thanks be. I was so afraid you would slip back into your nightmares about the balloon.'

'Did I talk a great deal?'

'Yes you did, my poor lamb – there was no comforting you – it was oh so distressing. And oh so long.'

'Hours, was it?'

'Days, Stephen.'

He considered this, and the violent stabs of pain in his leg. 'Listen,' he said, 'would there be any coffee in the house? And a piece of biscuit, maybe? I raven. And tell, did the bottle in my pocket survive?'

'No. It broke. It nearly killed you – a most frightful gash in your side.'

When she had gone he looked at his leg, deep in plaster according to the Basra method, and under the bandage round his belly. The broken glass must have gone very near the peritoneum. 'Were I in a still weaker state I should look upon that as an omen, an awful warning,' he said.

They had finished their breakfast and they were talking companionably when Dr Mersennius, the most intelligent of the medical men, came to ask how the patient did and to dress his wound. Stephen mentioned the pain in his leg.

'I trust you will not ask me to prescribe laudanum, colleague,' said Mersennius, looking him in the eye. 'I have known cases where a few minims, taken after a very massive dose, accidental or otherwise, have caused extreme and lasting mental distress, allied to that which you have just suffered but more durable, leading on occasion to lunacy and death.'

'Have you any reason to suppose that I had taken laudanum?'

'Your pupils, of course; and the apothecary's label was still on the broken glass. A wise physician would no more add a drop of laudanum to an already overcharged body than a gunner would take a naked light into a powder-magazine.'

'Many medical men use the tincture against pain and emotional disturbance.'

'Certainly. But in this case I am persuaded that we should be well advised to bear the pain and deal with the agitation by exhibiting a moderate dose of hellebore.'

Stephen felt inclined to congratulate Mersennius on his fortitude, but he did not and they parted on civil terms. Within the limits of his information Mersennius was right; he obviously thought that his patient was addicted to laudanum, and he had no means of knowing, as Stephen knew, that this frequent and indeed habitual use was not true addiction, but just the right side of it. The boundary was difficult to define and he did not blame Mersennius for his mistake, the less so as his body was at this moment feeling more than a hint of that craving which was the mark of a man who had gone too far. Yet the present unsteady emotional state must be taken in hand. The pain he could bear, but he would never forgive himself if he were to weep at Diana or behave weakly.

Diana came back. 'He is so pleased with you, and with your wound,' she said. 'But he says I am not to give you any laudanum.'

'I know. He thinks it might do harm in this case: he may be right.'

'And Jagiello asks whether you would like his man to come and shave you, and then whether you would feel strong enough to see him.'

'Should be very happy; how kind in Jagiello. Diana, my dear, please may I have that little parcel I brought with me?'

'The leaves that make you feel clever and witty? Stephen, are you quite sure they will not do you any harm?'

'Never in life, my dearest soul. The Peruvians and their neighbours chew coca day and night; it is as usual as tobacco.'

By the time Jagiello's valet had shaved him, Stephen's mouth was already tingling pleasantly from his quid of coca; by the time Jagiello had paid him a short but most cordial visit, the leaves had entirely taken away his sense of taste – a small price to pay for the calming and strengthening of his mind. The loss of taste could hardly have come at a better moment, for after

Stephen had been contemplating the coca's undoubted action on his leg for some time, Diana brought a bottle of physic, sent by Mersennius – a spectacularly disagreeable emulsion.

Nor could the consolidation of his mind, now firmly seated on its base, because three days later, three days of an unabated tenderness that had bound him to her more than ever before, Diana came in at the stroke of ten with bottle and spoon, and having dosed him she fidgeted strangely about the room before settling at last on the chaise-longue. 'Maturin,' she said in an embarrassed voice, 'what happened to my wits the day we met I cannot tell. I have never been clever at remembering years or history or the order things happened in, but really this goes beyond all . . . It was only as I was running downstairs just now that a flash of common sense burst upon me and said "Why, Diana, you damned fool, it might have been his answer."'

Stephen did not like to seem to understand at once; he shifted the ball of coca-leaves into his cheek, considered for a moment, and said 'The letter I gave Wray was an answer to one of yours in which you were not quite pleased – in which you desired me to explain rumours that I was flaunting up and down the Mediterranean with a red-haired Italian mistress.'

'So it *was* your answer. You *did* answer. Stephen, I should never worry you about ancient history at a time like this, but you look so well, you eat so well, and Dr Mersennius is so pleased with his hellebore, that I thought I might just mention it, to show that I was neither unfeeling nor altogether stupid.'

'I never thought you were either, soul,' said Stephen, 'though I did know that your sense of chronology was little better than mine; and I cannot remember my age without I do a subtraction with pen and ink. The letter was indeed my answer, and a mighty difficult answer it was to write. For one thing it had to be written quick, because we were under sailing orders, because I wanted you to have it as soon as possible, and because I had an overland messenger waiting. For another thing I *had* been flaunting a red-haired lady up and down the Mediter- ranean – or at least down it, from Valletta to Gibraltar by way of the African coast – and it certainly looked as though she were my mistress. But, however, she was not. The fact of the matter is – but this must not go beyond the two of us, Diana – the fact of the matter is that she was concerned with naval intelligence; the French at that time had some very dangerous secret agents in Malta and there was a nest of traitors in the city itself; at a given crisis it was thought necessary to remove her at once. The removal certainly preserved her life, but it damaged her reputation among those who were not connected with intelligence. Even Jack was deceived, which surprised me; I had thought he knew me better.'

'So was Wray. So were a great many other people. I heard it on all hands. Oh, it was so galling to be treated tactfully. And never a word from you. *Theseus*, *Andromache* and *Naiad* all came in, all of them with letters or messages for Sophie, and not a word for me. I was furious.'

'I am sure you were. Yet the letter was written: and as I say, it was difficult to write, because there would have been criminal imprudence in speaking of any matters to do with intelligence in a letter that might fall into the wrong hands; and without doing so I could hardly exculpate myself, for to my astonishment I found that my bare assertion carried no weight. People smiled and looked knowing: perhaps it was because her hair was red – there are all sorts of lubricious ideas abroad about red-haired women. Though I may add that her husband, an officer as far removed from the *mari complaisant* as you can possibly imagine, was not deceived: he knew that red hair and chastity were perfectly compatible.'

'Stephen, you did say that she was *not* your mistress?'

'I did. And I will say it again on the holy Cross if you wish.'

'Oh don't do that. But then why did you say you had come to be forgiven?'

'Because I had so mismanaged things that you thought I needed forgiveness – because I caused you distress – because I was too stupid to send a copy of my letter by *Theseus* – because I was fool enough not to suspect that traitor Wray.'

'Oh Stephen, I have used you barbarously, barbarously,'

she said: and after a pause, 'But I will make it up to you if ever I can. I will make it up to you in any way you like.' They both raised their heads at the sound of a carriage. 'That will be Mersennius,' she said. 'I must let him in. Ulrika will never hear and the Lapp is cutting wood.'

Mersennius it was. He was particularly well-disposed towards Stephen as a grateful, responsive patient and a perfect example of what hellebore could do. He pointed out its virtues again, and Stephen said, 'Certainly: I shall prescribe it myself. Tell me, dear colleague, you would have no objection to my leaving your care in a day or so? There is a ship coming for me – indeed she may even be in Stockholm at this moment – and I should not like to keep her waiting.'

'Objection? No,' tapping Stephen's leg – 'none, with my Basra dressing, so long as you can travel by coach and be conveyed directly to your cot. I will put up hellebore for your voyage. Is the ship coming from England?'

'No. From Riga.'

'Then you may set your mind at rest. The wind turned fair today, but for a great while it was foul, and no ship could have got out of the Gulf of Riga except by venturing upon the Suur Sound. I have a small pleasure-boat, and I watch the weather most attentively.'

'At least I shall have time to pack,' said Diana, and then in a very much happier tone, 'Stephen, what am I to do while you are in South America?'

'Stay with Sophie while you look about for a place with good pasture for your Arabians, and a house in London town. I think I heard that the one in Half Moon Street was for sale.'

'Shall you be long, do you suppose?'

'I hope not. But I tell you, my dear, that until the war is properly over and that Buonaparte put down, I must stay afloat, at least most of the time.'

'Of course,' said Diana, who was of a service family. 'I believe I should best like to stay with Sophie until then, if she will have me: and perhaps I could use Jack's stables, they being empty. Stephen, did you mean we could *buy* a house in town? They are terribly expensive.'

'So I understand. But my godfather, God rest his dear soul, left me a terrible lot of money. I forget what it comes to in English pounds, but the part that is already invested brings in far more than the pay of an admiral of the fleet. When peace comes we can have a house in Paris too.'

'Oh what joy! Stephen, could we really? I should love that. What a sad mercenary creature I am – I find my heart is quite thumping with happiness. I was quite pleased to have my husband back, but to find him covered with gold from head to foot as well fairly throws me into transports. How vulgar.' She sprang up from her seat, walked up and down the room with an elastic step, looked out of the window and said, 'There is Jagiello in his coach. And Lord,' she cried, 'he has Jack Aubrey beside him on the box!'

Jack came into the room on tiptoe, with an anxious, apprehensive face, followed by Martin and Jagiello. He kissed Diana in an absent, cousinly way, and took Stephen's hand in a warm, dry, gentle grasp. 'My poor old fellow,' he said, 'how do you do?'

'Very well, I thank you, Jack. How is the ship, and has she her poldavy?'

'She is in fine form – brought us out of the Suur Sound under topgallantsails, going like a racehorse, starboard tacks aboard, studdingsails aloft and alow, nip and tuck in that damned narrow Wormsi channel – you could have tossed a biscuit on to the lee shore – and she has a dozen bolts of the kind of poldavy they serve out in Heaven.'

Stephen gave his creaking laugh of satisfaction and said 'Diana, allow me to present my particular friend the Reverend Mr Martin, of whom you have heard so much. Mr Martin: my wife.'

Diana gave him her hand with a welcoming smile and said 'I believe, sir, you are the only gentleman among our friends that has been bitten by a night-ape.'

They spoke at some length about the night-ape, the capy-
bara, the bearded marmoset; Ulrika and the Lapp brought
coffee; and in a pause Stephen said, 'Jack, are you alongside
that elegant quay in the old town?'

'Yes, moored head and stern to bollards; and she is already
turned round.'

'Would it be convenient if we came aboard tonight?'

'I should like it of all things,' said Jack. 'I do not trust this
breeze to hold for another twenty-four hours.'

'Can you indeed travel with a broken leg?' asked Jagiello.

'Mersennius said I certainly might, if I went to the ship in
a coach. Jagiello, would you be so kind?'

'Of course, of course. We will carry you downstairs on a
door taken off its hinges, and prop you up inside, with Mr
Martin to hold you. I shall drive at a very gentle trot, and you
shall have a colonel's escort from my regiment.'

'Diana, my dear, does that suit you at all? Or would you
sooner have another day or two to pack?'

'Give me a couple of hours,' said Diana with shining eyes,
'and I am your man. Gentlemen, do not stir, I beg, but finish
your coffee. I will send Pishan up with some sandwiches.'

Presently the gentlemen did stir, however; or at least Aubrey
and Jagiello went off to see whether a door Jagiello remembered
in his grandmother's barn would answer, and whether one of
her remaining maids might not bear a hand in the packing.

'Surely I hear Bonden below,' said Stephen when he and
Martin were alone. 'Is Padeen here?'

'To tell you the truth,' said Martin, 'he is not. Unhappily
we had a disagreement this morning, and Captain Pullings put
him in irons. I do hate informing,' he went on, 'but without
the least intention of catching him out I came upon him
siphoning laudanum from one of the carboys and replacing the
tincture with brandy . . .'

'Of course, of course, of course,' murmured Stephen. 'What
a heavy simpleton I was never to have struck upon that.' And
when Martin had finished his sad tale of Padeen's violence on
having his bottle taken away from him he said 'I was very

much to blame for leaving such things in his reach. We shall have to take the whole matter seriously in hand – we cannot turn him into the world a mere opium-eater.'

They mused for a while and Martin gave Stephen an account, a very long and detailed account, of their doings in Riga and of the manners of the Letts and their Russian masters. He had gone on to speak of the presumably Sclavonian grebes far out on the broad Dvina when Diana came in. She gave Stephen an extraordinarily violent shock, one that needed all his recovered strength and the leaves he was chewing to withstand, for she was wearing the green riding-habit of his dream. 'Stephen,' she said, her eyes brighter still, 'I have packed all I need for the time – a couple of trunks – the rest can follow by sea. The coach will be round in five minutes, with Countess Tessin's door. But I am not coming in it with you. You need a man to hold you, and with him and the door there is no room for me, so I am going to ride' – laughing with pure joy – 'I am going to fetch your things from the hotel and put flowers in our cabin.'

'My dear,' said Stephen, 'do you know an apothecary's shop near the hotel, with monsters in the window and a stuffed armadillo?'

'And the apothecary very small?'

'That is the place. Pray step in – have you someone to hold your horse?'

'The Lapp will go with me.'

'And buy all the coca leaves he has left; it is only the tail of a sack.'

'Stephen, you will have to give me some money.' And when he waved to his coat, 'You see, Mr Martin, what horse-leeches we wives do become.'

The *Surprise* lay, as Jack had said, moored head and stern against the quay. Her deck had a somewhat deserted look, for Tom Pullings and the purser were below, trying to disentangle the Riga merchants' accounts, and a fair number of men were on shore-leave until six.

West was the only officer on the quarterdeck, and it so happened that the party of hands making dolphins and paunch-mats on the forecastle were all Shelmerstonians. West was gaping rather vacantly over the taffrail when he saw an extraordinarily handsome woman ride along the quay, followed by a groom. She dismounted at the height of the ship, gave the groom her reins, and darted straight across the brow and so below.

'Hey there,' he cried, hurrying after her, 'this is Dr Maturin's cabin. Who are you, ma'am?'

'I am his wife, sir,' she said, 'and I beg you will desire the carpenter to sling a cot for me here.' She pointed, and then bending and peering out of the scuttle she cried 'Here they are. Pray let people stand by to help him aboard: he will be lying on a door.' She urged West out of the cabin and on deck, and there he and the amazed foremast hands saw a blue and gold coach and four, escorted by a troop of cavalry in mauve coats with silver facings, driving slowly along the quay with their captain and a Swedish officer on the box, their surgeon and his mate leaning out of the windows, and all of them, now joined by the lady on deck, singing *Ah tutti contenti saremo cosí, ah tutti contenti saremo, saremo cosí* with surprisingly melodious full-throated happiness.

Patrick O'Brian

'At least as great a talent as J.G. Farrell.'
John Bayley, *London Review of Books*

'Pope, Kent and Parkinson were all first-class naval constructors, plot-smiths to a man, adept at buckling every swash in sight. But none holed Forester below the water-line. Then, suddenly, Patrick O'Brian's Jack Aubrey appeared and all was changed.'   Frank Peters, *The Times*

'Patrick O'Brian is one author who can put a spark of character into the sawdust of time. Aubrey and Maturin may yet rank with Athos/d'Artagnan or Holmes/Watson as part of the permanent literature of adventure.'
Stephen Vaughan, *Observer*

Patrick O'Brian is now acknowledged to be the greatest writer alive or dead of tales of the Navy of Nelson's age. Read all his novels in Fontana Paperbacks:

MASTER AND COMMANDER
POST CAPTAIN
HMS *SURPRISE*
THE MAURITIUS COMMAND
THE FORTUNE OF WAR
THE SURGEON'S MATE
THE IONIAN MISSION
TREASON'S HARBOUR
DESOLATION ISLAND
THE FAR SIDE OF THE WORLD
THE REVERSE OF THE MEDAL
THE LETTER OF MARQUE
THE THIRTEEN-GUN SALUTE
THE NUTMEG OF CONSOLATION

FONTANA